RIVER OF TEARS

RIVER OF TEARS

ROCK NEELLY

ISBN: 978-1-948374-66-8

Enigma House Press

Goshen, Kentucky 40026

www.enigmahousepress.com

To the memory of Jack Olsen

Your kind words of inspiration lit the fuse all those years ago.

*"Lyin' here at night alone, I keep on wonderin' Just what went wrong.
River of tears, oceans of heartbreak..."*
— Bonnie Raitt

Prologue

Day one:

The black girl went missing three days before the letter arrived. And the letter changed everything.

Cincinnati police were doing what they could, but there wasn't much to go on. No one knew what happened to the ten-year-old girl, not her brother, her mother, nor her aunt, and the community search for her didn't begin until well after dark. By then, she'd been gone for six hours. Paisley Park Jefferson, age ten, gone. Gone like smoke the day after a fire.

Police were notified four hours after locals came up empty in their search. Detectives were assigned from the First District, Violent Crimes Squad out of Cincinnati's downtown precinct. An AMBER Alert hit the airwaves mid-morning the day after her disappearance. Cell phones and electronic billboards throughout the region received notifications of the alert.

The media immediately picked up the story and gave expansive coverage to the girl's disappearance on local radio and television that afternoon. Tips poured into the city's 9-1-1 system. A BoLo, a "Be on the Lookout" for was sent out to city, county, and state officers. Every police unit on the road had flyers to distribute. For uniformed officers on their beat, the girl's disappearance was the highest priority. Cincinnati was on high alert for little Paisley.

The publicity did lead to a major discovery nineteen hours after she'd last been seen. A machinist taking out some trash noticed a bicycle matching the PD's description. It was tossed in a Colby Alley dumpster near Findlay Market, two blocks from where Paisley had last been seen riding her bike. This piece of evidence changed the police protocols from searching for a missing child to investigating a probable kidnapping.

Within the hour, the two detectives first assigned to the case, Madison Jane Monroe, M.J. to her friends, and Rosie Coleman, together with six uniformed officers, began a canvas of the neighborhood. The surrounding area was a particularly impoverished section of town, with Race Street as its eastern border to W. McMicken to the north, Central Parkway to the west and W. Liberty to the south. This grid search included the entirety of Findlay Market. The search lasted all Tuesday afternoon but yielded no leads.

The two policewomen first interviewed the mother, who'd been at work when the child went missing. The two detectives learned nothing helpful, as Paisley's mother was nearly disabled with grief. The detectives compiled a list of Paisley's friends, all of whom would be contacted by uniformed officers. The mother told them that the father of the girl, Nathan "Nat" Lee, was not involved in his daughter's life, had not seen her in more than two years, and paid no child support. His address and whereabouts were unknown.

Detectives Monroe and Coleman also interviewed the missing girl's aunt, who felt painfully guilty for being asleep on the couch when Paisley went missing. The aunt had worked a double shift at an all-night diner and was asleep on the couch after sixteen hours of slinging hash and coffee. She added nothing helpful to the investigation.

After the bike's discovery, the two policewomen talked again to the two boys who'd last seen Paisley, the girl's brother, Princeton, and his friend, Travon. The boys told the same story as before; they had stopped to watch an old man named Grandy Wilson argue with a street thug during a car-to-street drug deal. Most people in the hood knew better than to "throw shade" on a deal going down. The boys, young though they were, knew dealers found ways to exact retribution on anyone who interfered with their business.

Old Grandy Wilson's interfering with the drug purchase stopped the boys in their tracks, or rather on their spokes. They paused to watch the show, but Paisley, one year older and certainly the wiser for it, wanted none of Grandy's trouble. Her mother had warned her to stay away from the gang bangers selling crack or small baggies of heroin for cash.

Paisley kept right on pedaling past the spectacle, heading two blocks south, and the boys, their attention elsewhere, never saw her turn on Elon. Both were too engrossed with Grandy Wilson's harsh words directed at the gang member. They were no help, even with a time line. Neither had a watch or a phone.

However, the old man, Grandy Wilson, was more than ready to tell his story to the two detectives, and he knew exactly when he dressed down the drug dealer. It was 6:05, Monday night. That was when Paisley disappeared.

After determining that the missing girl was most likely the victim of an abduction, each district, number one thought seven, assigned two of their detectives to assist, Detectives Monroe and Coleman.

Interviews with neighbors were expanded. The mother and the aunt had their lives examined up one side and down the other. All men in their lives were checked for pedophile arrests. Their past lovers interviewed. Their current lovers interviewed. Tenants in their building were interviewed. The landlord and the owner of the apartment building were interviewed. Any contractor who'd been to the building in the last year was tracked down and their whereabouts on the day of the abduction assessed. Each person in the contact lists of their phones was checked for police records. The women's employers and co-workers were interviewed.

No one who might have had contact with Paisley had a past record which would have made him a person of interest. All were determined to have reliable alibis for the time of the abduction. Most verified where they were at the time because they were at home in front of the TV having dinner before the big Monday night football game.

Detectives also interviewed the girl's teachers at school. School counselors were asked to give input on Paisley's mental state. Students known to be Paisley's friends met with police, and those interviews were conducted only with parents present. The Criminal Investigation Section examined the family's apartment, eliminating the family's fingerprints and attempting to track down any prints not from the four primaries. No latent prints found led to anyone who might be considered suspicious or a person of interest.

The work of the additional detectives revealed less, that is, nothing. The contingent of detectives also followed standard operating procedure for day one of a child's abduction investigation, visiting each and every registered sex offender in the immediate vicinity of the child's residence and/or location of abduction. The detectives received the verified list of R.S.O.s four hours after the discovery of the bicycle. By then, the girl had been gone for twenty-three hours. None of the offenders on the list were known for having molested a girl of similar age. The detectives saw no one on the list who popped as a pedophile upon first examination.

The team split up the list, and despite having two people who no longer lived at their registered address, they did verify the alibis of the first four. Detectives Monroe and Coleman reported the remaining two names to the city's parole supervisory board for violations.

At that point, the officers had been on the streets for seventeen hours. They returned to District One, filed reports, and went home for five or six hours of sleep. The first forty-eight hours were vital in kidnappings; half of that time had now passed.

Both Paisley's mom's and aunt's faces showed the worry that Paisley was already dead, though neither voiced it.

Detectives on the second shift followed up on uniformed officers' canvassing. In the graveyard hours, they ran background checks on neighbors and reviewed all 9-1-1 calls during the previous week to perhaps find a clue to the girl's abduction.

———

Day Two began with a review of the forensics report on the bicycle, which yielded very little of note. No fingerprints other than Paisley's were found on the bike, but two smears on the cross bar of the aluminum frame's underside showed someone had lifted the bike using only the notches between the index fingers and thumbs of each hand. This maneuver and the relative location of the bike on the trash heap inside the dumpster showed a high level of strength, leaving the lab report speculating that the perpetrator was male.

They were looking for a relatively strong male over six feet tall; the list of potential perpetrators thereby winnowed to somewhere around a half million candidates in the Cincinnati metro area. The proverbial needle in the haystack. But the detectives kept at their task.

Also, that morning, the local FBI office announced it would investigate the kidnapping as a federal crime. Two feds interviewed the mother, aunt, and two boys again. They elicited no new information on the abduction. The FBI only assigning two agents to the case showed a minimal interest in the missing girl. Over eighty percent of kidnappings were by family members. The FBI's initial assessment was that with the girl and her father both missing, it was likely the two were together. An all-points bulletin, APB, for the father, Nat Lee, was issued by the feds.

Late in the morning of day two, Monroe and Coleman ran down one of the young offenders guilty of sex with a minor, Dewade Jenkins, except his alibi was airtight. He'd been in jail for violating his curfew three nights prior. His ankle bracelet had alerted his parole officer of the curfew violation. He was still in jail awaiting his hearing when Paisley disappeared. Having been locked up during the commission of the crime, Jenkins was no longer a suspect.

That left one young man, DeAndre Marquis, age twenty-one, who was on probation for having sex with a minor. He seemed an unlikely perpetrator, as his crime was that his girlfriend was underage, and the girl's mom turned him in.

The two policewomen were more interested in the last

name on the list, Willie Grips, age thirty-seven, guilty of two counts of rape, having served ten years. The whereabouts of both Marquis and Grips were unknown and APBs were issued to find them.

The rest of day two was spent in running down leads from the tip line, but none proved fruitful. The two women went home well after dark without a lead. With forty-eight hours gone, the odds were no longer in law enforcement's favor. Statistics told Monroe and Coleman that after two days the chances of the child returning home safely were greatly reduced. Little Paisley was in big trouble.

———

Day three provided slim progress. A uniformed police officer, Mateo Ramirez, returned to canvassing apartments where no one had been home on earlier visits. One proved interesting; an old woman, who'd been out of town the past two days, thereby missing the first canvas, answered the door. The old woman reported seeing a white van parked under the largest tree on Elon, a block from her second-story window. That intersection of Elon was but a block from where Paisley's bike had been found.

The old woman was a shut-in and spent hours by that second-story window. She knew all the comings and goings of Elon Street. She had noticed the van parked there and could see someone at the wheel. But the woman eventually went to put on some dinner, and when she returned, the van was gone. There was no certainty that the van's driver was involved in the kidnapping, but after officer Ramirez's report, the two detectives considered the possibility they were looking for a white van driven by a six-foot tall male.

It was a mere thread of a lead, but the detectives went with it. They worked with the precinct captain and asked for street camera footage for the streets of W. McMicken, Central Parkway, Race, and Liberty, along the stretches significant to their canvas, and six blocks beyond those confines in each direction. It would take some time for technicians in the forensics lab to run down those stop camera videos.

While they waited, Monroe and Coleman assembled a list of known associates of Willie Grips, who at this stage was their best target. Grips was the one known sex offender, and his whereabouts remained unknown.

A contingent of more than a dozen detectives tracked down three of Grips's running buddies within hours. However, none of them offered up anything that helped to locate the convicted rapist. The detectives waited for a plate report on white vans in the grid area after the abduction. But before the report came back, everything changed because of the letter.

———

The case changed completely during the afternoon of day three. Along Erie Avenue in a posh area of town, three miles east from where Paisley Park Jefferson had disappeared, a second girl was taken.

This time, the abduction was not in a slum and not a black girl. Hyde Park Square was perhaps the oldest, most established, and most moneyed shopping district in the city. The Square was a favorite dining spot for well-to-do Cincinnatians with restaurants like Tellers, The Echo, or Arthur's Café filled morning, noon, and night. The well-heeled shopped along Erie Ave. and Edwards Road. The surrounding blocks had nice homes and great apartments. Along that stretch of Erie

Ave., the city seemed safe, exclusive, and most importantly, immune to serious crime. Those who called this neighborhood home were not used to children being abducted from their streets or parking lots. And yet it happened.

A white girl had disappeared from a parking lot. Her mother and younger sister were just around the corner, mere yards away. Again, no one saw a thing. It was deeply unsettling to the entire city. Cincinnatians knew their city had crime, but not in Hyde Park Square.

The girl had walked ahead of her mother and three-year-old sister to the parking lot behind the deli where they'd dined. When Mom arrived with the toddler in tow, the older daughter was nowhere to be found. Klaire Keller, a blonde eleven-year-old, was gone. For city leaders, it was time to pull out all the stops. Two detectives from Violent Crimes and two local FBI agents leading the investigation would not do.

Police arrived at the scene within minutes of the mother's 9-1-1 call. Cameras from the surrounding businesses were examined in the first hour to no avail. A team of uniformed officers and detectives from around the district arrived to interview everyone on the street. AMBER Alerts hit cell phones, radio, and TV within two hours. The city experienced a wave of hysteria, connecting the two disappearances as the acts of a serial rapist or killer of young girls. However, police knew there was no evidence to connect the two disappearances.

Before any serious police coordination could be mounted in Klaire Keller's apparent abduction, the letter arrived, one copy to the mayor's office and one to *The Cincinnati Enquirer*, the city's major newspaper. Both envelopes were postmarked from the West Price Hill Post office on the previous day. The premeditation inherent in the message made the second abduction even more shocking. The letters had been mailed prior to the kidnapping. The message, however, was such that it could not have been more frightening. The letter itself was a single page, size 72 font. It read,

Find the black girl and we'll return the white girl.

Chapter One

"Why do they always take the black kid first?"

Detective M.J. Monroe looked away from the sidewalk alongside The Taste of Belgium, a restaurant at the corner of Vine and 12th St. in OTR, where the two policewomen had just eaten waffles. Daylight brightened the eastern sky. Monroe's eyes moved from the two homeless men panhandling on the corner and focused on her partner. Instead of directly addressing her partner's words, M.J. offered a question. "Do you want the lid off your coffee?"

Partners know these things, and M.J. knew that Rosie did not like drinking through a plastic lid. "Yeah."

M.J. took off the lid and handed the go cup to her partner. Only then did she circle back to the comment. "Are you saying race is a predominant factor in street crime, in particular crimes against children? Or are you agreeing with the FBI's initial assessment of a single assailant in the two kidnappings?"

Rosie took a sip of coffee, so M.J. added, "I mean, we both know that sexual deviants assault both white and black children. Are you speaking metaphorically; do you believe these two kidnappings are perhaps political? Or do you believe we have one perp, like the FBI says, and the perp took the black girl first? Your comment reminds me of the famous line from Toni Morrison's *Paradise*, " 'They shot the white girl first.' "

Stopping for a light, Rosie looked over her coffee cup's lip. Smiling, she said, "Don't think I need any of your entitled white girl educated talk at this time, detective."

M.J. glanced back, and they both laughed. "I hardly think quoting the late, great Toni Morrison is white girl talk. And by the way, you graduated with honors from Ohio State with a degree in African American Studies."

Rosie snorted. "Girl, I graduated from *The* Ohio State University because I anchored the four times four hundred relay team and ran the hundred meters. Won two Big Ten Track and Field Championship medals. Went to Nationals."

It was M.J.'s turn to snort. "This is where you are supposed to say 'twice.' "

Rosie laughed. "Well, I did win them two years in a row."
"Which is the definition of twice," M.J. said.

Rosie laughed. It was normal banter between them. Had someone else heard their words, it might have seemed combative. But it was just loose talk to cover the tension they both felt for the missing girls.

The light turned green, and with her eyes back on the road, Rosie was suddenly serious. "I *was* speaking metaphorically. How about you? Do you believe the FBI's initial assessment? That having two kidnappers snatch two young girls separately in three days' time in a city the size of Cincinnati is statistically improbable?"

"We'll officially see what the bureau has to say in about fifteen minutes, but I agree that it's improbable."

"You think it's one person?"

M.J. paused for one beat. "I didn't say that."

Rosie gave her that look, and they were both quiet until the traffic light turned green again. "And I didn't go to a university so insecure it needed a capital letter on 'The,' " M.J. teased.

"Yeah, yeah," Rosie retorted with a wide grin. "University of Miami in Oxford. Did they even have sports when you were there?"

"Love and honor, baby, love and honor," said M.J., reciting the university creed.

They drank their coffee in silence the rest of the way to the mayor's office. Both detectives knew that now, more than seventy-two hours out from the first abduction, the chance to find the ten-year-old alive, or even at all, was shrinking. It was a sobering topic for breakfast.

———

District Two, the locale of the second kidnapping and the initial site of the FBI assessment, is the largest geographical area for any precinct in Cincinnati. District Two patrols the eastern part of Cincinnati proper, including the neighborhoods of Evanston, East Walnut Hills, O'Bryonville, Hyde Park, Mt. Lookout, Oakley, Madisonville, Kennedy Heights, Pleasant Ridge, East End, Columbia-Tusculum, Linwood, Mt. Washington, and California.

Klaire Keller, the white girl, had been taken from Hyde Park, very near the precinct building, which is located on Erie not a half mile east of Hyde Park Square. Over a hundred sworn officers were assigned to District Two. At any one time, roughly ten percent of District Two's officers are out for vacation, medical, or other leave, but still, given the time of day of the white girl's abduction, over fifty uniformed officers were on duty. M.J. knew the district well, having spent her time in uniform working Oakley and later the meaner streets of Mount Washington.

District Two had an Investigative Unit, which was commanded by Captain Delores Knowles. Her reputation was solid, her personality flat and businesslike. M.J. had reported to her briefly and knew she ran a tight ship. The Investigative Unit was responsible for processing crime scenes for evidence and the investigation of criminal offenses in the district. Therefore, Capt. Knowles worked with Forensics every day, as did all investigative supervisors.

District Two also had a sergeant and five detectives assigned to the Violent Crimes Squad. Those officers are responsible for addressing violent crimes and drug investigations in District Two. Two detectives were assigned to find Klaire Keller. Their names were David Meagers and Rob Staples. Both were detective first class and good cops. Their arrest-to-conviction ratio was good, and they closed a high number of cases. M.J. was sure both would be at the meeting.

M.J. wasn't sure of the full complement of those who would be attending the kidnappings' coordination meeting. The mayor, Lyle Lark, of course, would be there since it was now his party and at City Hall. Police Chief Moss Jenkins would certainly be there, as would their supervisor from District One, Lt. Tobias Meyer. Definitely Capt. Knowles, along with Detectives Meagers and Staples. The lead agent from the FBI and the statistical profiler with the bureau's initial crime assessment would also be in attendance. There would probably be even more feds as about thirty agents lived in the greater Cincinnati area.

Rosie parked the unmarked Dodge in front of the gothic-looking red brick building at 801 Plum. She placed the red and blue light from the floor onto the dash to show "Police Business" to anyone seeing the car parked illegally.

Exiting the vehicle, she stood, adjusted her sidearm on her belt, and buttoned her suit coat.

M.J. did the same.

Their gold shields glistened in the morning light on leather fobs fastened to their left chest pockets.

They walked up the steps, pausing for a moment on the landing, gilded letters above announcing *City Hall* to the citizens it served.

Rosie Coleman was a tall woman with broad shoulders, narrow hips, and a chiseled face with cheekbones New York models would die for. She was 5'10", thin, but busty. Most of her height was legs. Her skin tone was chestnut, burnished and blemish free. She wore her hair in a tight, close-clipped afro with a razor part on the right side. Minimal lipstick and makeup.

Her eyes, however, after six years as a detective in violent crimes, showed some weariness. Sometimes on tough cases with long hours, she showed purple fatigue half-moons under her eyes. But not today. Rosie had been off last week. Her smile was broad and her teeth perfect and brilliant white as her partner turned to face her.

"You ready for this?"

M.J. shrugged. "I do not suffer fools gladly."

Rosie gave a short laugh. "Oh, you don't, Lady M.J.? I take it you're speaking of the mayor?"

"Goes without saying. You see him on TV at the ten thousand over the weekend, campaigning?"

Rosie nodded. "Chris Farley, but without the sophistication."

M.J. smiled at the apt comparison.

The two women walked down the marble-floored hallway, their heels clicking. M.J.'s look was yin to Rosie's yang. She was petite at 5'4" with a slimmer build than her athletic compatriot. Her hair was sandy brown with gold highlights, cut very short and spiked in front.

M.J. had green eyes, severe eyebrows, and a small, puckish mouth. Her face was plain, with a slender nose that upturned slightly. She was small-boned, flat-chested, and didn't tan except to freckle. Like her partner, the detective did have some muscle in her biceps. M.J. worked out at her gym and sported a pretty good set of guns. Her hips were slim, her legs toned from running through the streets of Newtown where she lived, or when the weather was intolerable, putting miles on the treadmill.

M.J. had smaller hands than her partner, so she carried a smaller firearm. For that reason, Rosie carried the Glock 22, a bigger firearm by a couple of inches than standard uniform issue, and one with a wallop.

While the detectives wore plain clothes, they were not really concerned about concealment of their weapons. Although the 22 showed as a large bulge on the hip, Rosie carried the gun because it had the capability to shoot both 9mm and .40 caliber ammunition. Before the Glock 22, there was no Glock in between .45 caliber and 9mm. Rosie contended she carried the bigger gun because if she did have to shoot someone, then she wanted him to go down with the first shot and stay down.

M.J. carried the Glock 19 and fired 9mm shells exclusively. M.J. countered when Rosie expounded on her Glock 22's attributes that hitting the target precisely worked just as well as a bigger bullet. Both women were excellent shots, but neither had ever fired a weapon in the line of duty. However, not a week went by that they were not forced to draw their weapons out as precaution. Being a detective in violent crimes meant the detectives dealt with violent criminals; firearms went with the territory.

Looking at her watch and seeing it was 7:55, M.J. pulled the front door open, allowing her partner to enter. "It's time. We want to get a good seat."

Rosie smiled going through. "You know," she said, "they shot the white girl first in *Paradise* because she had committed the crime of hanging out with the black folk."

M.J. responded wryly, "Doesn't say much for my chances."

Chapter Two

M.J. had always heard that celebrities and politicians had bigger heads than most people, which somehow makes them seem bigger than life on camera. That was certainly the case with the mayor, who sat behind his enormous mahogany desk, his head attached to his neck and shoulders like a pumpkin stuck atop a suited mannequin's body.

He stood, rising from behind the desk to totter forward toward the Persian rug in the center of the room. He was so short and the chair he'd left so elevated; he was not much taller standing than seated. The mayor read the photocopied note in his hand again as he positioned himself in the middle of the room. "Find the black girl back and we'll return the white girl," he read, then looking up, said, "Does anyone want to interpret that?"

The police chief, Moss Jenkins, was a tall, thin man, pale and bald, whose face revealed his thirty years as a cop and all the suffering he'd seen. Standing before them, his hangdog eyes surveyed the group as if looking for dissent. "It seems to be an extortion solicitation. We solve the black girl's abduction; they return the white girl."

The mayor nodded dully. "Yeah, I think we got that part. I meant what was the motivation for sending it?"

No one took the bait.

The mayor paused and then shrugged. "I guess I'll bring it up if nobody else is going to. Do we think the black girl's family took the white girl to increase attention to Paisley's disappearance?"

M.J. glanced across the room at her partner.

Rosie drew in a breath like she was about to explode, but she didn't speak.

Chief Jenkins worked his long chin back and forth. "Of course, we've considered that. But the two women, the mother and aunt, they don't even own a car."

"Then boyfriends? Other family members?" The mayor threw his hands in the air. "That possibility seems the most likely to me."

Rosie seemed to be grinding her teeth now.

"We'll check it out," the chief said, trying to change the subject.

"Think about it," the mayor snapped. "Why would someone kidnap a black girl and a white girl and then send a note like that to me and the newspaper?" He turned as though the question was now rhetorical. "Perhaps the FBI has some thoughts." His eyes panned the room. "Folks, this is Senior Special Agent Neal Saunders. He's taken point in the FBI's investigation of these two kidnappings."

A tall black man with a receding hairline, intense eyes, and with the bureau's ubiquitous navy-blue suit and red tie, stood beside the mayor.

"Thank you, Your Honor. Ladies and gentlemen, I'm

Senior Special Agent Neal Saunders, out of the Nashville office. Seated in the armchair over there is Special Agent Rudolph Messerschmitt, also from Nashville." He nodded to the other FBI agent with his chin. "We are a small contingent of a rather large FBI task force arriving in Cincinnati today. The mayor called and requested our involvement, based upon the possibility of a hate crime having been committed in the second kidnapping. While kidnapping is a federal crime and the FBI will investigate both cases, my team concentrates on hate crimes. And it would seem by the note, the Keller girl's abduction is racially motivated. Perhaps both cases are. This is why we are here. We do intend on taking the lead in, at the very least, the Keller investigation. It is not because of any transgression you might have committed or lack of progress in the case.

"Our review of your work so far reveals much dedication and hard work. We received the case files from Police Chief Jenkins last night, and as you know, there is very little to go on regarding physical evidence at this time. Therefore, I asked Agent Messerschmitt to join me at this meeting." Saunders motioned again with his chin for the other agent, dressed nearly identically as his boss, to address the group.

Messerschmitt stood up shorter than his boss, the senior officer, by maybe three inches. His face was tan with a flat ledge across his nose. His eyes too were dark and serious.

"Hello, I'm Special Agent Rudolph Messerschmitt. I am a statistical profiler for the FBI. We have profilers, of course, who use psychiatric tendencies to predict possible motives and future behaviors of the perpetrators of crimes, but we now also use super computers and the new science of predictive policing to gauge criminals' next steps. In many ways, I'm a programmer and a systems analyst. I do my work based upon the bureau's now nearly one hundred years of cases logged in what we call The Vault. Using these records, we can fairly accurately predict motives and sometimes future actions, especially in conjunction with a psychiatric profiler's additional input."

Saunders interrupted at this point. "We have not, at this point, included a second profiler into this case, as our Nashville supervisory teamed determined there was not enough hard evidence at this early juncture to warrant a psychiatric profiler's time." He looked back to Messerschmitt, "Go ahead, Rudy."

Messerschmitt nodded, wormed a finger around the collar of his shirt, and then spoke again. "As you may know, two hundred and three children are abducted by their parents each year in this country. An additional fifty-eight thousand are taken by non-parents, primarily with deviant sexual motivation. The United States only averages one hundred and fifteen kidnappings of children each year that end in murders. These numbers remain stable as a percentage of population and grow as our population grows. Things such as recessions and seasonal bad weather can increase or decrease these totals, but they are relatively stable statistics.

"Only about seven thousand of those fifty-eight thousand non-parental abductions are not resolved in a single day. Over fifty thousand of the kidnappings are resolved on the same day. Therefore, the two girls taken here in the last week would already constitute being in the great minority of outcomes, as at this stage we don't find any parental involvement. The fact we haven't found the girls yet also makes these cases unusual."

Messerschmitt looked around the room. "I want to preface what I've said with two disclaimers. One, I only received the case files at roughly midnight last night, and therefore, my findings are, at best, preliminary. And two, these statistical analyses are based upon mathematical probabilities. We must remember that sometimes criminals act erratically."

M.J. looked across the room at Rosie.

Rosie mouthed the word "*Sometimes?*"

M.J. nodded and then trained her eyes back on the profiler.

Messerschmitt continued. "So here are our preliminary findings. One, looking at the top seventy cities and then the top three hundred cities in population over the last fifty years, there have never been two separate, what I'll call 'longitudinal kidnappings by strangers,' at the same time in the same city in the same week. Not even in a copycat sense. Never.

"That encompasses the examination of twelve and a half million cases. It's never happened before. Based on that, and on the lack of any evidence to the contrary at this time, the FBI's current theory of the crimes is that they have been committed by a single individual. That is not to say evidence later discovered might not change our preliminary determination." Messerschmitt lowered his head to indicate he had finished speaking.

Saunders took control again. "To reiterate, the bureau sees these two kidnappings as hate crimes perpetrated by one person or persons. We will start our investigation based upon those suppositions, though they may prove to be wrong. As our team arrives from around the country today, we will be including you in the formation of our task force. Does anyone have any questions?"

The mayor said, "And what about the Jefferson family? What about their possible involvement?"

"Two of our agents interviewed the two women. They are extremely distraught. To the point, our assessment was their emotional tumult would be difficult to feign. Our current evaluation, based only upon our initial interview, is the women are not involved in either kidnapping."

The mayor felt the need to reassert himself once again. "How about from my people? What do we have so far?"

Chief Jenkins angled his long face around the room and said, "The FBI is already analyzing all the video from street cameras around the Hyde Park abduction site; from Madison to the north, Marburg and Linwood to the east and south, then along observatory and back I-71. They're cross-referencing it with cameras from the Findlay Market grid search and from I-75 north and south of downtown. We will also check cameras from I-71 north and south of downtown in the hour immediately after the first girl's disappearance. We sent the techs in Washington the electronic files sometime after midnight. Maybe we'll get a hit on a white van in both spots."

"How soon will we have info?" asked the mayor.

"There are five bridges. The Brent Spence, alone, gets one hundred sixth thousand cars per day," Jenkins replied. "The first snatch happened at rush hour or just after. We're probably talking with northbound included on both highways at three hundred thousand vehicles a day. Narrow it to one hour both directions at that time, and we're talking thirty thousand vehicles. FBI says nine percent of the vehicles on the roads are vans. That's two thousand seven hundred vans. Then, they'll have to cross reference with the cameras in the Hyde Park search. It's a needle in a haystack thing."

"I asked how soon." The mayor looked agitated.

"Maybe late tomorrow." The chief looked to Saunders for affirmation.

The senior special agent bobbed his head in agreement.

"And let's hear from District One," the mayor motioned to Lieutenant Tobias Meyer, Rosie, and M.J.'s supervisor. Meyer was a severe-looking man in a black suit, the shoulders of which were covered in dandruff. He was short, curly haired, and intense. He was also brilliant. M.J. counted her lucky stars that she'd met him and learned so much about smart detection from him. "It appears we have a person of interest, an ex-con named Willie Grips."

"Tell me about him." Mayor Lyle Lark pivoted to peer at the two women detectives.

M.J. blinked at the attention but didn't pause as she stepped into the circle. "Person of interest might be a little over-stated, but as you said, we're trying to find Willie Grips, age thirty-seven, a convicted felon. We want to speak to him regarding his whereabouts during the commission of the crime on Elon three days ago when Paisley Park Jefferson, age ten, was taken.

"We have no specific information about Grips's involvement, but because he has committed violent rapes on underage girls in the past, we're looking for him. He is a registered sex offender with an address in the immediate vicinity of the crime.

Grips was convicted of rape, served eleven years in Youngstown, and was paroled two years ago. His parole officer says Grips has reported in as required during the last twenty-four months. However, the address we had for him is no good. Grips hasn't resided there in at least a month. He was employed with a road construction company, rehabbing orange barrels, loading trucks and such, but he hasn't shown up since just after his last meeting with his P.O. last Wednesday."

The mayor nodded, grimly. "So he's missing. Why isn't his name and photo on every news broadcast in this city?"

"We really have no reason to think—" M.J. began, but the City Attorney Mel Graves cut her off.

Mel Graves was a tall and graceful man. His gray hair was longer than most in his line of work. He combed it straight back and it fell in loose swirls at his collar. His nose was aquiline, his height maybe 6'4", his cheekbones high, and his eyes blue-gray and intelligent. He seemed to be everything in a politician that the mayor was not. He wore a gray suit the same color as his hair and a black silk tie. He smiled perfunctorily as he took the stage from M.J.

"Which direction do we want to take this, Lyle?" asked the attorney.

"What do you mean?" the mayor replied.

Graves moved to the bookcase and leaned his hip against it, glad to have the room's attention. He waited for all eyes to be upon him. "Are we offering these abductions to the media as two related hate crimes with a racial component as the FBI says, or are we presenting them as two abductions committed by separate person or persons, the latter of which using race to justify his crime? Just a confluence of timing? A city's bad luck? Two separate nut jobs? Because if we go with a serial kidnapper taking kids, the city is going to panic."

The mayor seemed to ponder this question for a while. It seemed beyond him to carry both ideas in his mind at the same time, so he turned to the only two men in the room who had not spoken, the detectives from the Second District. They were assigned to the Klaire Keller abduction in Hyde Park. "And what do you two have?"

"Not much," admitted the first, Detective First Class David Meagers. Meagers was a good cop. M.J. had partnered with him for a short time while still in uniform. All four detectives in the room worked in the Violent Crimes Squad of their respective districts.

Meagers stepped toward the center of the circle. "Klaire Keller was taken less than twenty-four hours ago. She dined with her mother and little sister at noon yesterday at Quiffen's Deli. They left the restaurant together. The parking off observatory Ave. is behind the restaurant. There is a cut-through between two buildings to the parking lot.

"When the younger daughter took a spill, the mother stopped to brush her off. Klaire Keller, age eleven, proceeded out back ahead of the other two. Her mom followed a minute or two later. Klaire was gone. Nobody saw anything, and there are no cameras in that lot to assist us at all. Poof, she'd gone. Just like the Jefferson girl three days prior."

"And the letter addressed to the mayor was mailed the day before the second kidnapping?" City Attorney Graves knew the answer, but asked it, nonetheless.

"Yes," Meagers said. "That makes us suspect an inside job, although we have no proof of the parents being involved in the abduction. The father, the mother, or another family member, who knows at this stage? Otherwise, how would the kidnappers have known they would get the girl a day before they took her?"

"What about the father?" the mayor asked.

"Joel Keller?" Graves asked. "He owns a garage door company, third generation Republican. Fat cat. Big contributor. He gave to your campaign. He didn't kidnap his own daughter for political purposes."

"What about a racial motivation? A hate crime like Agent Messerschmitt said."

Meagers interjected. "We've examined the father and mother. No known affiliations with any white supremacist organizations, nothing on their social media sites. Both have squeaky clean records. Parking tickets, that's it."

"Maybe the second kidnapper just wanted to take any white girl." Detective Rosie Coleman spoke for the first time. "As the only woman of color in the room, I have to tell you I'm interpreting the note and the white girl's abduction in a whole different manner than the rest of you. At least I think so."

"Elaborate," said the mayor.

Both Police Chief Jenkins and Lt. Meyer looked nervously at her. The two FBI agents were silent and respectful of her words.

"I see the note as coming from a different perpetrator than the Jefferson abduction of three days prior. I think the note's author is someone of color who is tired of a different level of police, shall we say, involvement when the victim is black. Thus they, hypothetically, took the white girl to raise the stakes. The City of Cincinnati finds the black girl, it gets the white girl, too. Justice for all. I see us as having two different perps, which means looking for a white van at both scenes makes no sense to me."

The mayor's face suddenly became very red. He waved his hands in a dismissive way and returned to sit on his throne. He looked to Meagers and his partner. "Detectives, if you'll give us the room." Then, he turned to Rosie and M. J. "Ladies..." and he motioned with his hand toward the door.

As the two females cleared the foyer from the mayor's sanctum, Rosie smiled and said, "I'm sure he meant to refer to us as detectives, too, don't you think?"

M.J. grinned at her partner. "After what you said, I'm surprised he didn't bust us down to meter maids."

Rosie smiled, "Maids? I'm sure you meant monitors."

Both laughed.

Detective Meagers met them in the lobby.

He and his partner, Rob Staples, said hello.

Meagers rolled his eyes at the door of the mayor's office. "We're out of here. Still doing some canvassing. Checking on the whereabouts of some registered S.O.s." He looked to Rosie. "You really think these are two unrelated crimes?"

Rosie shook her head. "Not unrelated. Just not committed by the same perp."

Meagers raised an eyebrow but said nothing.

M.J. nodded. "Stay in touch. We didn't know the van video had been fast-tracked over to the FBI. We could use the report on the vans in our case. It seems that City Attorney Graves is working the FBI side against the middle."

Staples agreed. "It's always politics down here."

"Even when it's about two scared little girls," said Rosie.

M.J. said, "Yeah, I didn't notice a lot of empathy in there."

Meagers and Staples nodded, agreeing.

Then, without speaking, the men walked down the marble-floor hallway and out the doors.

The two females moved back to the entryway of the mayor's office. The double doors were still ajar by a couple of inches. M.J. and Rosie stood close by and listened.

Inside, the politicos talked freely.

M.J. maneuvered until she could see most of the room through the crack.

"Should we move a couple of homicide detectives over to the Keller case?" The mayor's question sounded a bit desperate.

"Her father, what did you say his name is? Joel Keller? You say he's influential in the local GOP."

Graves replied. "Donates big. Has a golf tournament for local candidates. We need to stay on the right side of this."

"Should we stack some homicide guys on top? Who's our best?"

City Attorney Graves replied with more volume. "You'd be giving the Dem city commissioners the ammo they're looking for. You double the detective load for the white girl and the black community screams discrimination. You will have proved the note writer's point. If you add detectives to the case, you have to do it for both investigations."

Mayor Lark's voice almost squeaked. "Politically, this couldn't be worse. An election in two months, a girl from Indian Hill taken in Hyde Park. Enough to rile up our best contributing donors, a kidnapping happening in our suburban bastion. Highest concentration of millionaires in southwest Ohio. Surprised we haven't found something in this case to anger the folks in Amberley Village."

Graves ducked his head away from Lt. Tobias Meyer's face and said, "We don't get the Jewish vote, anyway."

The mayor said, "Money protects money. We get our share of the Jews." He looked around the room, and his eyes rested on the FBI agents. "You have any suggestions on how we should proceed locally?"

Saunders shrugged. "As I said, we'll be releasing information on the formation of a task force later in the day. Maybe you could assign a couple of homicide detectives to the task force once we've got our feet on the ground?"

Nobody spoke for a long minute.

The city attorney finally filled the silence. "What do we do, Lyle?"

"I don't know. It looks like we've assigned the B-Team, especially having two women on the black girl's case."

Lt. Meyer objected. "You know the two women clear more cases than the men, both in violent crimes and homicide?"

"What have they been working?" Mayor Lark barked, "Meth heads robbing convenience stores, some loser stealing women's purses out of their car at gas pumps, domestic disputes?"

"We move homicide detectives over, we're sending a bad message to the evening news," said Chief Jenkins. "The media will suggest, without us saying it outright, that we think the little girls are dead."

"And we don't know that they are," said Meyer.

The mayor slammed his hand down on his desk. "Maybe we should just sit on our hands until the girls' bodies show up and then have the FBI clean up after us."

"Nobody is suggesting we do nothing," Capt. Knowles added, speaking for the first time.

"So how are we handling things, mayor?" asked the chief. "We have a press conference at 10:00 a.m. Do you want us to announce changes in detective assignments today, Your Honor?" asked the captain.

The mayor threw up both hands in frustration.

City Attorney Graves bowed his head.

"Do nothing for now," said the city's leader. "We'll assign more detectives to the case tomorrow. Today, just announce the task force."

Chief Jenkins strode out of the office with Cap. Knowles and Lt. Meyer in tow.

The two female detectives fell into line with their boss, Lt. Meyer.

Lt. Tobias Meyer looked forlornly across his shoulder to his subordinates. "How much of that did you hear?" he asked M.J.

"Every word of it," she replied, "every word."

Rosie looked at them. "You know something? Every case I ever caught was the first time someone had been victim of that particular crime. Agent Rudy in there saying these kidnappings never happened before like they did so they can't have happened that way! Posh! Ain't no crime ever happened before, but then it did." Rosie looked at her partner. "What do you think?"

"Posh!" replied M.J., and even Lt. Meyer laughed.

Untitled

RADIO WHTY, ClnClnnATI

"If you're sitting in a car listening to me, then you're probably stuck in traffic caused by the tractor trailer jackknife at the Cut in the Hill. I-75 is backed up for miles, past two 275 into Florence, Kentucky this morning. But hey, it's Ray Sunstone, here for you from six to nine Monday through Friday mornings on WHTY, Cincinnati's leader in news, talk and profes-sional baseball. We've got traffic, weather and news on the eights, plus breaking news as it happens. Radio WHTY when you need sunshine in your day.

We'll have more talk about our Bengals' flop in their opener at Balti-more, but first we've got the latest for you on the kidnapping of two little girls, including full coverage of the press conference with Police Chief Moss Jenkins. That's coming up at 10:00 a.m. I've got sources in the police department, and let me tell you, they are pulling out all the stops to find these girls. The police here are working hard to protect us. Yes, sir, the thin blue line here in this city is dedicated to our safety. But this case is a tough one. Or two, as it turns out. I know all of us out there are praying for those little girls to come home safely.

Right now, we've got Jeanette Willoughby on the phone. Jeanette has invented a new way to keep fruits and vegetables fresher in the fridge. Jeanette, I've been looking forward to hearing from you all week."

Chapter Three

Rosie and M.J. got back on the clock.

Rosie pushed the police strobe from the dash back under the passenger side seat.

M.J. made the call to dispatch.

While it was possible to log in via the car computer, most detectives took the time to call in to put themselves "on the board." That way, calls for backup or info to dispatch for a potentially dangerous stop were not a surprise to those usually civilian operators who worked the radio.

No surprises of who was on the clock left less to chance. Less chance for errors meant better policing. Routine stops at the courthouse, jail, Hall of Records, and City Hall could be logged by computer entry. First call in the morning and last call at night before and after being on the street were by radio.

M.J. made the call and put the detectives on the clock. While they weren't on the board to catch incoming active calls, all police were required to respond to calls for backup, suspects attempting to elude police, and, of course, officer down and shots fired calls. This time, when M.J. made the call, dispatch had a message for the two detectives.

"Detective Monroe, here's the message," said dispatch. "Monica Jefferson, the mother of your kidnap victim, wants you to come by. She said you had her address and phone."

"Did she say why?"

"Only that her son, Princeton, had something to tell you, but he wouldn't tell his mom what it was. He insisted he tell you and Detective Coleman."

They arrived at the apartment in over-the-Rhine in less than ten minutes. There, they informed dispatch by computer log they were going inside. The street was abandoned, the sky overcast. M.J. and Rosie headed up the stairs of the third-floor walk-up.

Monica Jefferson answered as soon as they began to knock, looking even worse than when they'd last seen her. Paisley's mom moved to the side then motioned them into the room, only after she locked, dead-bolted, and chained the door. The deadbolt looked new.

"Ms. Jefferson," said Rosie, taking her hand in more sympathy than handshake.

"Do come in. Sit down."

"Is your sister here?"

"Waitressing now," she replied with a bit of aggression in her voice. "Is there any news?" Paisley's mother asked, her voice wavering.

M.J nodded. "The full FBI team has arrived in town. They will be investigating both abductions. They are running down a list of all the white vans that passed by a street camera on both days. We have a massive team running down each vehicle. There are lots more resources being added to assist in the search."

"Lots more FBI added after they took a white girl," said

the mother. "Two agents came by and interviewed me two days ago. They asked the same questions you did."

"That's not surprising. The feds work differently than us, but we're all looking for the same information. It's a matter of statutes," replied Rosie. "Sometimes a crime, even a really horrible crime, isn't necessarily a hate crime. Your daughter's abduction, for instance, did not immediately bring about a federal hate crime investigation."

M.J. added, "The note sent to the mayor and to the newspaper gave a racial component to the second abduction that made it appear that hate was part of the crime. Hate crimes are investigated by the FBI. There are special funds available for those kinds of crimes. Thus, the note precipitated federal response. More than normal."

"The additional notoriety will hopefully help find Paisley sooner. More FBI is a good thing," Rosie added.

The mother nodded, numb after eighty-four hours of crying.

"Why did you need us to come by, Ms. Jefferson?" Rosie asked. "Is there something wrong with Princeton? Did he remember a detail or something?"

"I don't know. He won't tell me anything. He just insisted I call and leave a message for you."

M.J. looked around the shabby room, nodding at the posters of the music star Prince, the only décor on the dingy beige walls. "I take it you're a fan."

Monica Jefferson nodded, her face still grim. Smiling seemed beyond her capacity now. "Yeah, I saw him, you know. He came here for a secret show at Bogarts in 1984 before the *Purple Rain* movie and tour.

"I fell in love with him, me and my sister. Then, when I named my babies after him, first my baby girl, Paisley Park, for his studio in Minnesota, and then a year later my little man Princeton." Her eyes began to rim with tears.

Rosie patted her hand.

M.J. stood. "Is Princeton in there?" She pointed to the bedroom off the living room.

Monica nodded.

M.J. knocked lightly on the half-closed door and then stuck her head in. The boy was lying on the top mattress of a bunkbed and was watching a cartoon show with a bunch of dogs solving crimes.

"Hey, Princeton," said M.J. "I heard you had something to tell us. Can we talk?"

The boy glumly nodded.

Rosie entered behind her partner.

M.J. moved to the TV and asked if it was okay to turn it off.

The boy nodded.

She clicked the power button.

Rosie took the lead in situations like this, this being talking to black children. The race factor tended be minimized with a black woman doing the interrogation. "What did you want to talk about?"

Princeton looked out into the hallway.

M.J. followed his thoughts. "You want me to close the door?"

He nodded again, still not speaking.

The boy's bike was leaned against the door. M.J. had to move it to close the door.

When she did, Princeton sat up.

M.J. gave Rosie a quick glance.

Rosie revealed a secret smile.

Princeton was attempting to control things as best he could, being nine. He had maneuvered himself to a height slightly above the two detectives by sitting up and against the wall as they faced him on the bunkbed.

Princeton nodded at the bike. "Mom won't let me ride it now unless she's outside."

Rosie nodded, sympathetically. "Understandable, given the situation right now. She just wants to make sure you're safe."

"Yeah, but she's *never* outside, so I *never* ride."

"It'll probably be just for a little while," said M.J.

What did you want to talk to us about, Prince?" asked Rosie, subtly switching to the more familiar name.

"It's about Travon," he said.

"Yes, we met your friend Travon," she said. "What about him?"

"He told me something. He saw something out riding yesterday."

"And you want to tell us about it?"

The boy fidgeted a bit before responding. Finally, he allowed his gaze to meet Rosie's eyes. "Yeah, 'cause like you're supposed to report a crime when you see one, right?"

Rosie nodded. "Yes, you are. Did Travon witness a crime?"

Prince nodded. "Yes, but he made me promise not to tell anyone, especially not my mom."

"What did he see? Did he see your sister get taken?"

Prince looked shocked. His mouth fell open. "No, nothing like that. He saw old man Wilson. The old guy who yelled at the gang."

"Yes, we talked to him, too. What did he see Grandy Wilson do?"

"He didn't do anything. The gang caught him in Colby Alley last night and beat him down bad. Afterwards, Travon thought Mr. Wilson might be dead, but then after a while, he tried to get up. He called for help and the man who found

Paisley's bike came out of his shop, but not until after them that beat Mr. Wilson left.

"The white guy wanted to call an ambulance, but old man Wilson said he couldn't afford any ambulance ride, so the man loaded him into his car and took him to the emergency room. At least that's what Travon thought happened. The white guy and Mr. Wilson didn't see Travon because he was up the alley, hiding behind some old barrels. Travon thinks the old man died on the way there. He was in bad shape. The white guy came back without him. Is old man Wilson dead?"

———

It turned out that Grandy Wilson was not dead, but he was, indeed, in bad shape. He was convalescing in Good Samaritan Hospital on Dixmyth, down the hill from the UC campus in Clifton. His current condition was listed as stable. He had a broken nose, three broken ribs, several lacerations, and some internal bleeding that doctors were still watching, hoping to avoid surgery. Wilson was sedated, but conscious. The doctor on duty allowed the detectives in the room for three minutes.

This time, M.J. took lead. "Hello, Mr. Wilson, you are not looking so good. Are you in a lot of pain?"

Grandy Wilson looked up out of his bandages at the police officers and forced a grin. A tooth was missing. "Ain't felt like this since I got clean. Good horse used to give me this kind of ride. Ain't taken that stuff in thirty years. Guess they gave me morphine. Been having some crazy, crazy dreams."

"Who did this to you?"

"Hooper's hoodlums. Same ones been vexing our neighborhood for some years now."

"Geroy Hooper. Is that who you're referring to? The banger?" Rosie asked.

"Well, it wasn't him did the beat down, one of his boys. The one they call Catfish. He's a big one. Stupid, too, but mainly just mean as an old junkyard dog."

"We'll talk to them. You want to file charges on this Catfish creep? We'll arrest him. Get him off the streets," M.J. said, anger rising in her like mercury in a thermometer.

"Won't do no good if I filed charges. Hooper would just sic another of his kind on me, only worse. I'm too old to take a beating like this again. Lucky to live through this one. Docs say I'm still bleedin' inside some."

"You get well, Mr. Wilson," said Rosie. "You don't need to worry. We won't arrest Catfish, and we won't cause you any more trouble. You just get well."

Grandy Wilson forced a pained smile at the two women again. He closed his eyes for a moment. "You know, I didn't tell you something I should of the other day when you first came to speak with me."

Rosie and M.J. formed a semi-circle at his bedside.

Grandy looked up at them through the gauze on his eyebrows and the stitches that held them together. "I seen the girl with her daddy a few times."

"You saw Paisley Park Jefferson with her father? Nat Lee?"

"Yeah, maybe three times. Paisley didn't want her momma to know she was meeting him, so them two met at that bench at the end of my lot. It's kind of off by itself. He'd drive up. She'd get rid of her brother and that tagalong, Travon."

"How many times exactly did you see her with her father?"

"Like I said, three over the last couple of months. This summer, you know. No special time that I noticed. Just once in a while."

"When was the last time?'"

"Maybe two weeks ago. I could have told her momma, but

I didn't. Figured it was good they saw each other, you know? Girl should have a daddy."

"Did you speak to either of them about it?"

"Did her. Said it was nice she was seeing her father."

"What did Paisley say back?" M.J. asked.

"Said he gave her money, like for clothes. Girls like clothes. And her mom and her aunt, they just barely making ends meet. Lots of poor people in our neighborhood. Them two's trying, but they ain't got two nickels to rub together as hard as they work. So I kept my mouth shut. Figured it was the least her father could do was give her a little pocket change. The word on the street round here is that he's not paying his child support."

At that moment, the doctor entered and addressed the detectives. "You'll have to leave now. Mr. Wilson needs his rest. If you need to speak to him further, perhaps you'll call tomorrow, in advance..." The doctor's words trailed off, an order issued in the nicest way.

The two detectives nodded and wished Grandy Wilson a speedy recovery.

Leaving the room, walking down the hospital hallway, Rosie looked over at her partner. "What you thinking?"

"I'm thinking we finally do have a person of interest in this abduction. Ninety percent of missing children are taken by a family member, more than seventy percent by a parent. We got a missing parent and a missing kid, I figure they're together," M.J. said the words, her heels clicking on the marble hallway.

The sound of an oxygen machine hissed in rhythm with her steps. "I'm also breathing a little easier. Paisley gone off with her dad is a lot better than what we thought yesterday. Her future was looking pretty sketchy. Some perv locking her in a dungeon or something." M.J. looked to her partner. "What are you thinking?"

Rosie gritted her teeth. "I figure we need to pay a visit to Geroy Hooper. Talk to him about his employee's manners. We can't let a banger beat up one of our witnesses and not respond, not even one named Catfish."

"So first we better let Lt. Meyer know we're looking at Nat Lee as the prime on this case now."

Rosie nodded. "Yeah, he can let the FBI know. Get a BoLo out there on Nat Lee. If Paisley is with her dad, it sure makes the FBI profiler, that Rudy guy, look like an idiot."

"He's just an accountant with a badge, Rosie," replied M.J. "I'll call Lt. Meyer. You want to request backup for a meet-and-greet at Geroy's playhouse? Ziegler Park, right?"

Rosie nodded. "Yeah, 13th and Yukon. But how 'bout we keep this one off the radar? No reason that Lt. Meyer or anyone should know we stopped by to see Geroy. Might complicate things."

"Okay, but we should have backup going into a known drug dealer's house, Rosie."

"Yeah, how about Mateo Ramirez, the kid who found the old woman for us? Him and his partner, what's her name? Ah, Geri Jackson?"

"She a redhead? Lots of freckles?"

"Yeah, that's her. She and Ramirez are both okay. Call him. See when the two of them can meet us to roust Geroy. It'll have to be when they're off the clock. Uniforms would have to clock out otherwise. We don't want to put him in a spot to lie or go off the grid while on duty."

"Girl, you think I'm straight out of boot?"

"No," said M.J., smiling. "I think you're salty as they come. Very, very salty."

Rosie laughed and said, "I am salty. Like dry roasted peanuts, like the Great Salt Lake, like," she paused for effect, "like LeBron."

M.J. laughed. "Let's not get carried away. You make your call. I'll make mine."

They both drew to their holsters and grabbed their smartphones, laughing at the fake gun battle they had played out many times.

M.J. noted internally that she was maybe a smidgen faster.

Rosie read her thoughts and shook a finger at her, already speaking to Ramirez. The visit to Geroy Hooper was on for 1:00 p.m.

Chapter Four

When the two detectives arrived back at the car, they had a message to contact dispatch. A quick call got M.J. transferred to the tip line operators. Someone had called in with an address for the last of the four young men who'd been charged with statutory rape, DeAndre Marquis. He was one of the remaining two unfound registered sex offenders on their list.

According to the tipster, DeAndre Marquis was only about four blocks away from the Jefferson's apartment. It was a quick roll to the Vermillion Apartments, second floor, #214. The two officers took the appropriate procedure for knocking on the door of a suspect, hands on weapons in holsters on hips, knock twice, stand to the side in case someone should decide to shoot through the door.

M.J. wondered vaguely after knocking if the door wasn't thicker than the flimsy walls of this complex.

A weathered black woman of about forty years of age answered the door. The look on her face was that of fatigue and consternation at the two policewomen who addressed her.

"Good morning, ma'am," said Rosie, brightly, with a smile

to disarm. She pointed to the shield on her jacket pocket. "Cincinnati Police, I'm Detective Coleman. This is Detective Monroe. What is your name if I might ask?"

"Dorita Anderson. No one in this house done nothing for the police to come."

"Perhaps not," answered Rosie. "We're here to speak with DeAndre Marquis. We've reason to believe he's here. Is he inside, Ms. Anderson?"

The woman narrowed her eyes and then looked away as if to think of a lie, but the two detectives could see inside the tiny apartment's front room.

A young man lay in a tangle of blankets on the sofa. His one eye was open just enough to let the detectives know he was awake and paying attention to the activity at the door.

Rosie leaned her shoulder over the woman's blocking stance and said, "Sir, are you DeAndre Marquis? We're going to need to see some identification."

The woman shrugged as if the cards had been dealt and stepped away, allowing the two detectives into the room.

Rosie stepped in, cautiously, as the man's hands were still under the blanket, "You DeAndre?"

The young man, perhaps twenty-two or twenty-three years of age, tugged the blankets off his shoulders and sat up, yawning. He nodded, sleep still on his face. "Yeah, my name's DeAndre. But I ain't done nothing wrong."

Rosie shrugged. "You're on probation, Mr. Marquis. Your address is on file with your P.O. You're not living there. That's technically a violation."

Dorita Anderson, dressed in the uniform of the local grocery chain, moved beside the young man on the couch. "That's my fault. I invited DeAndre to live here. Figured since the lease is in my name, I got the right. even though it was me who originally filed the charges…"

M.J. stepped up. "Wait a second. Mr. Marquis here got popped on a statutory rape charge. Are you saying you're the girl's mother? You're the complainant?"

"She was only fifteen when that happened, but hell, they's in love. I wasn't going to keep them apart with a crowbar. Seemed crazy him maintaining his own apartment when he started spending all his time over here after she turned sixteen, anyway."

DeAndre didn't speak but did shrug.

About this time, a young woman in a cotton robe came in from the bedroom holding a bottle of Coke. "Oh," she said, "I didn't know anyone was here."

M.J. looked at the girl. "Have a seat, Ms.?"

"Kennedy. Kennedy Jones," said Dorita. "I'm her mother."

"And to clarify things, Ms. Anderson, you're the one who filed charges against DeAndre? Got him arrested, jailed, and have an existing restraining order against him, but now he's sleeping on your couch? That about the size of it?"

"Yep, you got it. Kennedy's legal now. She wants him here, and I was okay with it since he pays half the rent. No worries here."

Rosie smiled and nodded. "Well, technically there are problems here. DeAndre, you need to get your address changed, and you, Ms. Anderson, need to get the judge in the case to remove the restraining order. Otherwise, Mr. Marquis here will be in violation of the law and we'll have to come back and arrest him. Seems silly to do it, but we'd have to."

DeAndre Marquis stood. He wore sweatpants and no shoes. His tank top showed off his great upper body and biceps. He was a handsome man. "You two plainclothes came over here to check me out on a parole violation? I never heard of detectives doing that."

M.J. shook her head. "We actually have some questions to ask you. Would you be willing to step outside with us?"

DeAndre was quite surprised to hear he was on the preliminary list of suspects for Paisley Park Jefferson's abduction. "You mean because me and Kennedy fell in love and all before her sixteenth birthday that I'm a suspect for kidnapping a kid?"

"You're a registered sexual offender, DeAndre," replied Rosie. "We're required to check in with you if a sex crime occurs close to your place of residence. As you're in violation of your registered address, we're supposed to take you in. Now, where were you on Monday night at 6:05 p.m.? I hope you can clear that up because you haven't handled this situation very deftly so far."

"Kennedy and me were in Chicago. She won a free hotel room and two tickets to the Lil Wayne and Crew tour over the weekend. We had to check out of the hotel on Monday, but we stayed until pretty late in the day. Went to the Navy Pier, saw the Bean, took the Mega Bus back that night for nineteen bucks apiece. Got home around ten Monday night."

"Your parole officer know you went to Chicago?"

DeAndre shrugged.

"You got your ticket stubs or receipts? We'll have to verify," Rosie replied to his nonverbal reply.

"I don't, but Kennedy keep a scrapbook. She's got all that stuff, I'm sure."

After a quick look through Kennedy's scrapbook at the concert ticket stubs, the comped hotel room receipt with a zero-sum owed, and the letter of congratulations from the local hip-hop radio station, the two detectives could scratch one more potential suspect off the list of suspects for the disappearance.

The detectives didn't mind, though, because both now

believed in their hearts Paisley was with her father. And both women's hearts were a little lighter with that prospect. It was much better than thinking a stranger with sexual motivations had nabbed her.

Back in the car, M.J. laughed. "That's a new one, statutory rape, S.O. missing and found sleeping on the couch of his victim's mom's apartment."

Rosie shrugged. "Love happens, even on these mean streets."

M.J. smiled back. "Yeah, and he pays half the rent."

"Don't be so jaded," Rosie said, wrinkling her nose. "It was pretty romantic. The mother couldn't keep 'em apart with a crowbar. Nothing says love like a crowbar resistant embrace."

M.J. nodded. "Where to now? We got an hour before we're meeting Ramirez over at Geroy's."

"How about some fries and a cold Coke over at Arnold's?"

M.J. looked at her with fake surprise. "Holy cow, woman. We just ate. You sure you're not eating for two?"

Rosie smiled. "Sure, I'm not that, but it ain't because I'm not getting any."

"Oh," said M.J., "do tell."

Rosie shook her head, laughing. "I don't kiss and tell."

M.J. laughed. "I might. But I haven't been kissed in a while."

"No law against sex, Mads."

"I'll check the statutes on my own. Thank you very much. Now, about this mystery man."

Rosie laughed. "I said I ain't talking about it."

"I'll get it out of you over fries."

"Your interrogation skills aren't that good."

"Then, I'll buy."

Rosie thought for a second. "That might work."

And they both laughed.

Rosie did spill the beans over lunch at Arnold's Bar and Grill on 8th Street. The oldest bar in Cincinnati, Arnold's, was founded in 1861, originally a place for just men to get whiskey cheap. The owners who lived upstairs added a kitchen during prohibition, now its food is probably more famous than its alcohol.

Three nights a week, jazz or blues filled the air in the back-room, which had one time been the carriage house. During the day, the room was used for overflow from the main dining hall, and it was full of business people talking and checking cell phones.

The front room, where the two detectives sat housed a single line of tables and a walnut-and-whisky stained bar the same length as the thin room. The owner, Ronda Androski, stopped by with their chili fries and said hello. Cops were always taken care of at Arnold's. Not that they didn't have to pay, but the staff there learned the police officer's name and always had a smile. It made a difference when the shift was a tough one.

"I'm seeing David again," Rosie said, conspiratorially as she sipped on a cherry Coke from the bar.

David was Rosie's ex and the father of her teenage daughter, Marie. David was a handsome man, big, virile, and sometimes a little too angry for M.J.'s tastes. She shook her head at the news. "Seems like a bad idea. How many times you two tried and went bust?"

"I know, I know," said Rosie, "but we can't seem to stay away from each other. Marie was gone on Friday for the Winton Woods football game. David came by. I was making some spaghetti. Things led to things."

"Yeah," M.J. said, "spaghetti does that. I think it's the red sauce."

They both laughed.

"Are you sure it's what you want?" asked M.J. "You two's things usually lead to physical altercation."

"He completed his anger management class."

"As stipulated by the court."

Rosie nodded. "He can't change what happened."

"And you divorced him the first time. Filed and dropped charges the next time."

"I know, but we just can't keep our hands off each other if we're alone together."

"You know what I'd say to that," M.J. replied.

"Don't be alone with him," Rosie said. Her face showed a little chagrin.

"I guess you know what you're doing," M.J. said. "Actually, I don't think that, but I love you, anyway."

"I know. But how about you? You ever going to see someone?"

M.J.'s situation was complicated. She was married, but her husband, Greg, had been in a coma for two years. A truck driver, head full of hydrocodone, ran a red light and t-boned her husband's car.

Greg had been on staff at UC's research hospital in Clifton. Coming home from work, he pulled away from the traffic light at Martin Luther King and Reading Road. The truck, a full tanker of milk, ran the light and hit Greg broadside. Despite airbags deploying, the vehicle did little to stop a semi going nearly fifty miles per hour. Along with breaking eleven major bones, Greg sustained a skull fracture and major brain hemorrhaging. He never regained consciousness, but instead survived in a vegetative state. He was now in a convalescent home.

The accident occurred when M.J. was still a rookie detective. She took six weeks leave, but after doctor after doctor assured her the man she'd known was no longer inside that broken shell, she'd gone back to work. She still wore a gold band, and in her mind was still married; for better and for worse had been the pledge, but M.J. was now long past the grieving.

M.J. tried to visit her husband twice a week. Each visit was difficult. Each time, she saw just a tiny bit less of the man she loved. Every four days, he became just a little less Greg. His face thinned, his hair receded and turned gray. His body atrophied. Yet his heart, still the same one she used to press her hand to as they slept, beat strong.

Doctors had no timetable for his demise. He was not on any kind of respirator, and although Greg was fed intravenously, he seemed in many regards healthy. Several of the physicians at UC said they could assist her in seeking a legal path to withholding nourishment, but it wasn't in her to do so. She could not herself be responsible for his death. Her Catholicism would not allow it; Greg's co-workers at the hospital said they understood and went away. His parents had long ago passed, and as an only child, he no longer had any visitors but her.

M.J. didn't answer Rosie's question. The words, "You ever going to see someone?" hung in the air. M.J. stared off into space for a moment. Rosie let her go and then reeled her back by addressing her another way. "Did you reconsider signing up for that dating site? I sent you the link."

"I saw. I went in and looked at the profile page. You have to certify that you are single. I'm not. I'm still married. Greg is still living. He's still my husband."

Rosie nodded. "He wouldn't mind. He wouldn't want you to be alone."

M.J. shook her head, rejecting the argument. "It just doesn't feel right. Can we drop it? Only one of us can have relationship trouble at one time, and since you're seeing David again, we're already at capacity."

Rosie laughed. "I think you said something about paying for lunch."

––––––––

Geroy Hooper was not your stereotypical TV show drug dealer, far from it. He was a light-skinned African American with his head shaved bald. His clothes appeared to be from Abercrombie's. He wore a baggy pair of khaki pants, Timberland boots, laces tucked in. His shirt was a buttoned lapis blue flannel, sleeves rolled up. A gold chain with a shark's tooth hung around his neck like a choker. His eyes were emerald green. He looked every bit the model on the cover of a fashion magazine, but both detectives knew by his reputation that Geroy was not just a pretty face.

Geroy's location was known to all Cincinnati cops. His "office" was the first floor of the Yukon Community Apartments. The entire ground floor of this three-story apartment building across from Zeigler Park had once encompassed a rental office, some maintenance closets, and a two-bedroom apartment for the building manager.

All that had been swept away by time and the gutting of the neighborhood by crime, but Geroy Hooper knew good space when he saw it. He rented, painted, carpeted, and later filled the ground floor with furniture from IKEA. It was neat and kept. The old office area now held sentries overlooking the park. They also barred entry to the apartment behind. Who knew what was in those maintenance storage closets?

Rosie, M.J., and officers Mateo Ramirez and Geri Jackson

saw the two sentries examine their approach as they walked to the front door. They heard a voice beyond call out from behind the glass door, "Five-O. Hey; head's up, Five-O comin' in."

In the lobby, Rosie and M.J. showed their shields.

Ramirez and Jackson, in uniform, flanked each side of the room.

"Like to talk to Geroy, if he's in."

One sentry nodded and disappeared through the door behind them, closing it as he went. He returned and nodded without speaking. Technically, if he had refused to allow them passage, they could not have entered. This was an unofficial visit to a residence without a warrant. Word on the street was Geroy, while notoriously violent, could be civil to cops when he encountered them. The two detectives opened the door and entered.

Ramirez, as previously agreed upon, came with the two detectives.

Jackson stayed in the lobby.

Geroy, looking more like a college student than the city's largest dealer of heroin, glanced up from a notebook on the kitchen table. He nodded a greeting but didn't rise.

Two more men sat on the couch. A very large TV mounted on the wall was fixed on CNBC. A face on TV spoke of a rally on the Nasdaq. Numbers and percentages scrolled across the screen.

"Officers," Geroy Hooper said with a nod. "We weren't expecting company. I'm drinking a chai tea from Starbucks. We do have bottled water in the fridge. Maybe could scrape up a can of Coke. What's your pleasure?" He smiled; one tooth showed gold in his grin. It was jarring given the rest of his preppy college boy hype.

M.J. took the lead. "I'm Detective Madison Monroe. This

is officer Ramirez and Detective Coleman. Just needed to speak with you a minute or two. That okay?"

Geroy nodded and closed his notebook. "Before we go any further, I should inform you that the two men in my lobby are armed. They have conceal-and-carry permits and are carrying nine-millimeter Berettas. The rest of us are unarmed. I do have security cameras, which we turned on as you started up the walk, you know, for future litigation should there be a need. Oh, and by the by, my work space is always clean. No drugs, no money, nothing illegal. My rules for my employees. And those rules are followed. The punishment for violation is, shall we say, extreme, and no one has ever violated it twice."

Ramirez positioned himself with his back against the fridge.

Rosie backed his play and gave herself a clear line of sight down the hallway to the bedrooms beyond.

M.J. sat at the table next to Geroy.

He noted each police officer's position with a bob of his chin and smiled. "Make yourself at home."

"This won't take long, Geroy." M.J. placed her card on the table in front of him.

He looked at it casually without picking it up. "My calendar is light today, detective, take your time."

M.J. had to smile. This punk had brass ones, that was for sure.

"We're investigating the abduction of Paisley Park Jefferson, the ten-year-old girl taken from over-the-Rhine four days ago."

"Terrible thing. I've seen the news. Any progress?"

"We're doing our best."

Geroy narrowed his eyes. "You don't think I had anything to do with it? Because that's just ridiculous."

M.J. shook her head. "No, but an old man named Grandy

Wilson is a witness in the case. He was the last adult we know of who saw the girl on her bike before her disappearance. One of your soldiers nearly beat him to death last night. He's at Good Samaritan. Not doing too well."

Geroy raised an eyebrow. "I've not heard anything about any beating, and I stay pretty much on top of things. I'd have to say you were misinformed. I don't think we were involved."

M.J. shook her head. "We have witnesses. And old man Grandy's word, as well. It was one of yours. Big one, name of Catfish. You got someone like that on the payroll?"

"I do. Catfish works for me. Spends most of his time near Findlay Market. Does my fresh market shopping for me. He's one of those likes to eat. Lucky for me, he likes to cook, too."

"Well, he nearly killed one of our witnesses. Anybody messes with us finding the little girl, well, we got a problem with that."

Geroy nodded, acknowledging the threat, but he was not worried by it. He pushed back on his chair, lifting it to sit on the back two legs. "I'll talk to Catfish. See if there was an alter-cation." He took a drink of chai tea. "Are you sure I can't make you a cup of coffee?"

"No," said M.J., "there's something distasteful in the water down here."

Geroy smiled, wistfully. "Now, you're just being mean. I'll tell you what. I have a lot of connections with folks around here. Folks who'd never talk to the police. How 'bout I do you a solid?"

M.J. didn't speak, so Geroy continued. "How about I put out the word on the two men the TV says you're looking for? Willie Grips and Nat Lee? Nat Lee, huh? Just saw that come across my news feed. He's new, isn't he? Hadn't heard his name. He take the girl?"

"He's the father."

Geroy nodded. "Yeah, I already knew that. He's not a customer, but I keep tabs on the people about. Got more ties to the community 'round here than you think. I think I might have a better chance of finding two black men who don't want the cops to find them than you do. There's people out there who curry my favor. People owe me money or want my services. I can do that. Maybe help out." Geroy stood to show the meeting was over.

M.J. stood. "Tell Catfish we want to talk to him."

"I will definitely let Catfish know you came to visit me. That is, if I verify what you say happened happened. Generally, we try to fly under the radar. I'm not much on publicity. Catfish knows that. I'll talk to him."

Rosie stepped up to Geroy, her face close to his. "That old man dies, we'll make your life hell. We know you deal in death. Heroin has ruined thousands of lives, and you're getting rich off of all that suffering."

Geroy raised the left side of his lip in disgust. "Detective, you're targeting me unfairly. I'm just a symptom. I provide a service for a community that is in pain. The poverty, the lack of a future, the lack of hope. Those thousands want something to cope with that pain. Something to take it away, if only for a little while. If it wasn't me, it would be someone else. Some use alcohol, some use drugs. Some use the wrong end of a 'niner. I'm just filling a niche in the sociological construct. Just part of the food chain. Just a lion on the Serengeti instead of a gazelle."

"More of a hyena," Rosie growled.

"Thanks for coming," said Geroy, gaily. "Next time, let me know if advance, and I'll get some pastries or even cater in some lunch. Bye, now." He strode from the room down the hall with his back to them, his shoe laces dragging the carpet as he went.

Chapter Five

The four police officers exited Geroy Hooper's compound.

Rosie and M.J. stopped at the curb to thank Ramirez and Jackson for backing their play.

"You get anything? Any info?" asked Geri Jackson. She had remained in the lobby and had not heard the conversation.

M.J. looked at her. "Wasn't trying to get info. Just sending a message. I think Geroy will make sure his boys don't bother Prince Jefferson or Grandy Wilson going forward."

In the car, Rosie drove and looked over at her partner. "Do you really think Geroy will put the word on the street he wants Nat Lee and Willie Grips found?"

"Maybe," M.J. replied. "But not to help us. He just doesn't like the extra heat in his turf right now. We solve it, get little Paisley home, and then we go away. At least he figures it that way."

"But now he's on your list?"

"Our list, Rosie, our list. Geroy is a parasite. He needs out of District One."

"And in prison."

"That, too."

Just then, M.J.'s cell phone rang. She answered. "Detective Monroe."

It was Detective David Meagers out of District Two. "Jesus, been trying to get you two for about a half hour. Called, texted, and then left a message with dispatch. Where you been?"

"Talking with Geroy Hooper. Had my ringer off."

"Jesus once again. Hooper a suspect?"

"No, but we wanted him to know the neighborhood is going to stay hot until we find Paisley. He might oblige us, get us some help. At least not impede." She smiled to herself. "What you got?"

"FBI task force has the van plate number report done. There's a meeting in twenty-five minutes at their Blue Ash offices. You're supposed to be there. And on time. That's directly from Chief Jenkins."

"You already there?"

"In the parking lot, which is filled with a lot of dark SUVs. The FBI sure spends a lot of money on tinted windows. I'd guess there are fifty-odd vehicles here. Gonna be a big shindig. Better hurry."

"See you there," M.J. replied, ending the call. "Hit it to FBI HQ in Blue Ash. Meeting at 2:00."

Rosie made a quick turn into a drug store parking lot. "We're not going to get there on time unless we run hot."

M.J. nodded, turning on the siren. She pulled the flashing light out from under the seat and placed it on the dash. "Then, we run hot."

The FBI Regional office in Cincinnati is a four-story building of white stone and mirrored glass just south of Montgomery Road, east of I-71. Close to the Kenwood Mall, Cincinnati's premier shopping center, the building houses about thirty agents, but was built to handle many more in emergency situations, like the task force which was there now. Southwest Ohio also has five small offices called resident agencies. These were sometimes actually home offices for agents who travelled the region and didn't need to commute each day across the metro to Blue Ash. It was M.J.'s understanding most of those agents would continue their local case load. The FBI handled a lot of kidnapping cases, and expert field agents from around the country were primarily handling these two abductions.

Expressway traffic was light at mid-day, so Rosie rolled at eighty-five miles an hour the twelve miles to Blue Ash. She parked the car in the nearly full FBI lot at 1:58.

Both detectives made a quick walk across the tarmac, hot in the September sun, conscious not to overtly hurry as they knew eyes would be on them from the mirrored glass above. Never look hurried, especially in front of the feds, who treated local police as second-class citizens most of the time. After a quick elevator ride to the fourth floor, the two detectives entered just as the meeting began. The room was full and somewhat warm with all the bodies, even given the size of the open space.

Neal Saunders, the supervisory administrator for the task force, stood at the front of the room and looked much the same as the previous day. His dark eyes looked just a little more tired. Today's tie was deep navy blue. The rest of his attire was identical to when they'd first met.

"Thank you all for being here promptly. As we know, in abduction cases, time is of the essence. We are nearly forty-eight hours in on the Keller girl and nearing five days on the Jefferson girl. That long missing should be of great concern to all of us. Time is not on our side."

M.J. looked around the room. There were perhaps seventy people present. Nearly all wore what she identified as FBI unis, dark blue suits. Also present were their boss, Lt. Tobias Meyer, Detective David Meagers, and his partner, Rob Staples. Chief Jenkins was also there, dressed in a dark suit to compete with his newfound associates.

She was surprised to see two homicide detectives from District Two standing near the Chief, Detective Dave Decker and his partner, Marion Simmons. Both were nearing fifty years of age and were most senior of Cincinnati's homicide investigators. They were Cincinnati's best.

Decker was red-headed, his stringy hair receding, his skin very freckled on white, white skin. He was a stocky six feet tall. His partner, Marion Simmons, held a porkpie hat in his long slender hands. M.J. always thought Simmons looked like a jazz trumpet player. He dressed in what she considered a hip fashion. His tie matched the lavender color of his shirt. His skin was inky black, lustrous in its almost blue glow.

They were good cops, excellent investigators, known for their professionalism. They had some notoriety for solving high-profile murders around the city. It was only natural that locals called them Black and Decker, given their looks. It was a funny name, but it was never said with disrespect. Black and Decker were the cream of the Cincinnati Police Department.

M.J. caught Simmons's eye and nodded.

His eyes coolly narrowed recognition and a greeting back.

M.J. nudged Rosie and she likewise acknowledged the two homicide detectives' presence.

Decker gave them a blink but then focused on Saunders as he began to speak again.

"Before we begin, I'd like to introduce you to Special

Agent Lisa Agate. Agent Agate is in charge of the Cincinnati office. I want to thank her for having this staging area for the task force ready as soon as we arrived. Without her and the rest of the local team, we could not have hit the ground running like we did. Thank you, Lisa."

The woman he addressed nodded. She wore a female version of Saunders' outfit; her white shirt buttoned to the top collar with no tie was the only variation. Their faces also were similar, like priests having heard one too many sad confessions. And both probably had. That world weariness showed in both agents' tired expressions.

Saunders turned and addressed the room. "Due to some good policing out of District One, we now have identified a primary suspect for the Jefferson abduction." He nodded in appreciation to Rosie and M.J. "Nat Lee, the father of Paisley Park Jefferson, is now our prime for her disappearance. Most kidnappings, as we know, are by a parent. However, we didn't initially list Nat Lee as a possibility since we had been informed by the victim's mother that the father was not a part of the girl's life. We now know, thanks to Detectives Coleman and Monroe, that the father was, indeed, seeing his daughter. With both missing, statistics would tell us he is the most likely culprit."

Saunders looked to Chief Jenkins after he had given the Cincinnati Police a shout-out.

The chief nodded, his jaw set.

Saunders spoke again. "The bureau is now utilizing a facial recognition detection operation on all city-wide cameras. It is likely if Nat Lee enters a store, stops at a traffic light, rides an elevator, or eats at a restaurant, we will get his face on screen. Our plan is to have coverage of FBI or local law enforcement within five minutes of any location in the city if his face is recognized.

"If he is in Southwest Ohio, we'll find him soon enough. That also goes for Willie Grips. Grips is also a suspect. He is a convicted rapist, now out on parole. He has fled his current residence and has not been seen since the first abduction. He has also not reported to his employment at Tucker Road Supply. We are cross-referencing his features in the facial recognition sweep, as well. We'll find them soon enough if either is in town."

Saunders turned to Agent Agate. "Lisa, can you fill the room in on other aspects of local investigation?"

"Sure, Neal," said Agate. She stepped to the center, taking the stage. Her voice was steady and reassuring. M.J.'s first impression was to be impressed.

"Normally, when we issue APBs on potential suspects, we get a friendly judge to issue a warrant to track cell phones. We also examine the perp's call history, all local calls, and then we extrapolate those calls into known associates which we also interview. We haven't been able to do that with either of the men we currently seek, as neither has a cell phone registered to him. That is, as far as we know.

"We really believe that both have burner phones with paid-in-cash access. However, thus far, none of the known associates of Willie Grips has been able to provide a cell phone number. We will continue to provide pressure to get that number. As regards to Nat Lee, we only received the tip on him this morning, so our work is ongoing.

"Neither man has a credit card in his name, so we're basically adrift on that standard tracking procedure, as well. Lee does have a car, a 1996 Chevy Impala SS, maroon with substantial damage to the rear passenger side quarter panel. He was involved in an accident in Harrison three weeks ago. We have photos from the officer at the crash site of the vehicle. Cincinnati PD has provided that photo and plate number.

Uniformed officers have been issued this lead and are on the lookout for Lee's vehicle while on patrol at present. We will also issue an AMBER Alert for that car and plate."

She turned to a table in the rear of the room. "There are white sheets on the vehicle and photos of both men there. Please, be sure to take multiple copies on your way out today."

"Thanks, Lisa," said Saunders. "Now, Rudy, can you get us up to speed on the profile and the van search?"

"I will, indeed," said Agent Messerschmitt, moving from the second row of agents to Saunders's side. He wore a yellow tie in stark contrast to Saunders' blue.

Rebel, thought M.J. with mock consideration.

"We finished the camera search of white vans in the proximity of both abductions. In the hour before and after the Keller snatch, we found three thousand one hundred and twenty-two white or nearly white vans in the Hyde Park area or in adjacent neighborhood cameras.

"That image sweep also included I-71 and I-75 directly north and directly south of Hyde Park. of those, three hundred seventy-nine are only partial or non-recognizable plates. That leaves us with two thousand seven hundred forty-three known plates. We cross-referenced those with the camera search of the Findlay Market area of over-the-Rhine. There are fewer cameras there, and we have ascertained there are paths out of the neighborhood where the crime occurred where cameras would not record a van leaving the scene. That is concerning."

Agent Messerschmitt paused to let that sink in. "However, we did get four hundred twelve vehicles meeting our van profile near where the Jefferson girl was taken. That is more than we anticipated, but being the kidnapping occurred close to a major market, it is a high traffic area for vans. Numerous produce vans deliver into Findlay.

"At the time of the girl's disappearance, many of the shops just closed and were in the process of restocking. Traffic volume at that time is heavy with vans. Of those four hundred twelve vans, we did not determine fully recognized license numbers for thirty plates.

"That leaves us with three hundred eighty-two fully recognized plates. We turned the remaining thirty compromised images over to FBI D.C. for computer reconstructive recognition work. We also turned over the additional three hundred seventy-nine not fully recognized plate images from Hyde Park. The process tends to render a fifty percent success rate of plate recognition, so in a day or so, we may be able to identify about two hundred more plates from the two sites."

Messerschmitt raised his head from his data sheet. "And this is the big news. We have one hundred ninety-six vans that were in both vicinities within an hour of the abductions. Those vehicles and their owners are our first priority."

M.J. looked to Rosie and raised an eyebrow. Hadn't Saunders just acknowledged that Nat Lee was the prime here? Why were the vans first priority?

Saunders again stood to the fore. "Rudy's right here. Being as we do not currently have many leads on either Lee or Grips, we will begin to process the one hundred ninety-six vans with a connection to both kidnappings. But before we do that, I would also like to share some information from our Atlanta office psychological profiler, Kim Rodden. She is our very best and while she's working with our Terrorism Task Force right now, I called her in Atlanta and asked her to give us a quick profile to assist us as we begin our van clear."

Saunders drew several pages of a printed report from his suit pocket. "Ms. Rodden gives us these insights. Most sexual abductions are by white males, but we cannot rule out other races. The typical age of these men is between twenty-four and fifty-six. And age fifty-six is not a cut-off for this sort of behavior she reminds us; it's just that by fifty-six, most of these type perps have been caught and are in the system. Most have some record of violence when captured.

"Usually, this violence has been directed at women. Battery or assault. There may only be a uniformed call to a house for domestic violence and no charges filed, but still some record of violence toward females will most likely exist. As you begin to clear vans this afternoon, we will expand our search of males from age twenty to age sixty.

"We also see these men as being primarily undereducated. High school graduates or lower. Often, we have a DUI on file. We think that correlation has to do with the fact that these men cruise looking for girls and they drink in their vehicles while doing so. To reiterate, males, age twenty to sixty, with a history of violence against women, however minor. Look for assaults and look for DUIs."

Saunders gazed at the group. "We are probably thinking about a lone wolf. But we cannot entirely rule out a team of perhaps two perpetrators. It is rare, but not entirely unheard of. Women have been accomplices, as well. A couple with a history of battery would be of interest, but a woman on her own is almost certainly not our suspect here. One, we have almost no cases of that kind of occurrence. Two, we believe our perp threw Ms. Jefferson's bike into a dumpster.

"It is unlikely a person less than six-foot-tall and with only moderate strength would be our target as the lip of that dumpster was over five feet high. If we are looking at a team of two males, Ms. Rodden says we should look for an older, more experienced molester, perhaps with a record as an S.O., and a younger, shall we say, apprentice. The apprentice may very well have been molested by the older man, then brought in as an accomplice to assist in finding fresher, younger prey.

64

"In any case, it is unlikely that the younger male will have a record, but it is quite likely that the older will. He will rely on the younger to engage in the riskier parts of the abduction, to lessen his danger of capture and arrest."

Saunders folded his papers and replaced them into his pocket. He then scanned the room with those dark eyes. "Any questions?"

No one spoke.

"Okay, then. The FBI has ten field teams of three agents each to begin clearing the vans off our list, and hopefully, we'll find our perps quickly. We have others attempting to acquire leads for both Lee and Grips. Each of our ten field teams will have five vans to investigate this afternoon and evening. We will all meet back here at 10:00 p.m. Hopefully by then, we'll be able to ascertain further interest in a suspect connected to one of those fifty vehicles or eliminate them as potentials by then. We will continue to look for Nat Lee and Willie Grips, as well."

Saunders looked to Chief Jenkins. "Chief, the floor is yours."

"Thank you, Agent Saunders, Agent Agate. As some of you will have noticed, we have added two new members to the task force, two of our best. From Homicide Investigations, Detective Dave Decker and Detective Marion Simmons will be working the case now, as well. They will report directly to me, not to either District One or District Two's investigative heads."

He glanced at M.J., Rosie, Meagers, and Staples to see their reaction.

M.J. made sure not to have any.

Rosie also kept her face blank.

The Chief continued, "Each of our three detective teams will also take five vans to clear this afternoon and evening.

Together, we'll get through sixty-five vans today. After our debrief at 10:00 this evening, we'll assign each team another ten for the next day. That will get us all two hundred looked at in the next thirty hours."

Rudy Messerschmitt said, "And by the morning, D.C will probably have identified another one hundred to two hundred plates. Some of those will likely appear on both lists. I'll update you as soon as we have something."

With that, the meeting came to an end.

In the first-floor lobby, Detective Meagers asked Rosie and M.J. to follow him down Montgomery Road to the McDonald's across from Kenwood Town Center.

Five minutes later, the four detectives stood in the parking lot by their cars.

"What did you think of all that?" Staples asked as soon as Rosie and M.J. exited their vehicle.

"Pretty much baloney," said Rosie. "If we have Lee as the primary, then why are the cross-referenced vans any more significant the other two thousand seven hundred?"

M.J. pointed out. "If Lee is the perp, then why are we using thirty-six investigators to look at vans at all? We have no evidence Klaire Keller was taken by van. Not one shred. District One should be rattling the cages of anyone who has ever had contact with Nat Lee. District Two should be rousting all the sexual offenders on file in the city."

Rosie said, "You should get a print out on all the S.O.s in the region. Run them for vehicle registration. Then, the FBI should run a camera plate analysis of all those vehicles. See if any S.O. was in Hyde Park Square." The black woman shook her head, mournfully. "Three thousand white vans. If the task force clears a hundred a day, we're talking a month. Those poor babies be dead by then, for sure."

Meagers said, "That's a good idea on the cross reference

with the S.O.'s. I'll run it through Capt. Knowles. Have her give it to the chief."

M.J. nodded. "Knowles will get it done. And let's face it, if any of us suggested it at the briefing just now, the bureau would deem it unimportant and not do it or slow walk it because they didn't think of it themselves."

Meagers laughed. "Yeah, that's true enough. Us detectives don't do much thinkin', right?"

Staples nodded in agreement as Rosie and M.J. laughed, knowing it was not at all funny.

The two men got into their car and drove away.

While Rosie went inside to buy two iced teas, M.J. called dispatch to get back on the clock.

The dispatcher had news. "M.J., you're to head to Clifton Heights, border of Corryville, alley off Euclid Ave. behind the Kroger there."

"What we got?"

"Body."

M.J.'s heart sank. "Young girl?"

The dispatcher threw her a curveball. "Nope. Male, don't have anything else."

Rosie was walking back.

M.J. motioned to her to throw the drinks into the trashcan.

Rosie frowned but did so.

For the second time that day, they rolled hot.

They pulled into the alley within ten minutes. Black and whites blocked the scene. Uniformed officers kept the public back.

M.J. and Rosie got out, flashed their badges, and bypassed the security line. As they walked halfway down the alleyway, the women could see Black and Decker were already there.

M.J. and Rosie slowed, taking everything in. Blind alley, no houses immediately adjacent to the actual crime scene. A good out-of-the-way place to dump a body.

"What we got?" M.J. asked for second time in the last fifteen minutes.

Dave Decker rose from his crouching position over the body, but his face and concentration stayed on the prone form before him.

A medical examiner dressed in khakis and white lab coat was beginning to process the scene. She hovered over the body with caution and a deliberative process that might be mistaken as tenderness. M.J. knew it was not. She was simply making sure not to contaminate the scene. Her assistant was filming the me's every move, catching the monotone report issued for posterity.

Simmons and an uniformed were stretching yellow crime scene tape around the perimeter.

Simmons nodded at the two women as they ducked under his tape.

Rosie moved toward Simmons to indicate she wanted to talk.

He nodded but raised a finger for her to let him finish with the tape.

M.J. repeated herself. "Hey, Decker, what we got?"

Decker did not answer or even acknowledge her presence. With her words repeated, Decker rotated his body to look at her. It was an odd motion, like someone who had a stiff neck would do. It was like the dead body held him in sway.

Finally, Decker turned his face to M.J. His voice was official by the book. "Deceased black male, in his twenties. Looks like he was beaten to death with a two-by-four. Apparent weapon was in the trash can there. The lumber is blood-spattered. Not much attempt to hide it. It was a vicious killing.

Personal. Violent and excessive. A number of the blows appear to be post-mortem after the victim was down."

Decker looked at her, strangely, to make sure M.J. was following him. "Driver's license gives his name as Warren Jacoby. That name mean anything to you?"

M.J. shook her head. "Nope. Why?"

"He's got your business card shoved in his mouth."

Untitled

RADIO WHTY, CInCInnATI

"Woody Long here for your afternoon drive on WHTY, home of Cincinnati's news and weather, whether you like it or not. Here's what Cincinnati is talking about. We've got another killing in the Clifton/Fairmount area.

"Police coroners have been summoned to a Corryville address, but a little birdie is telling our newsroom police believe the body was killed elsewhere and left in that alley. Maybe the killer or killers were just trying to make it handy for our city's crime lab to get to the scene. You know the CSI lab is just down the street from that Corryville address. Let's talk to our reporter on the scene, Frieda Nutt. What can you tell us, Frieda?

"Woody, we have a deceased, young, black man. Police have not yet released his name. They've blocked off the alley, and we aren't close enough to report. I don't know much right now."

"That's amazing, Frieda. What have police said?"

"Woody, police have been pretty closed-lipped, but an EMT I spoke to says the death is what police are describing as a gang-related homicide, but that, of course, is unofficial. I don't have any facts at this time."

"*So once again, Frieda, it's these drug dealers who sell poison to our kids. Gangbangers wreaking havoc on our streets. It was those people, huh, Frieda?*"

"*Yes, Woodman, you speak the truth. Druggies killed someone again, or so it appears for now. Of course, I am only speculating.*"

"*It's always from these same neighborhoods. You'd think the police would just assign patrol cars to just circle the block.*

If it's not Price Hill, Roselawn or Over-the-Rhine, it's Clifton/ Fairmount these days. Now for closing stock prices."

Chapter Six

Geroy Hooper looked up from his peach-flavored iced tea and nodded his head slightly toward the four detectives walking at him.

M.J. noticed his acknowledgement but did not reciprocate. Truth was, she was angry. A man was dead. He was someone she had never met, but his death was on her. M.J. mentioned the man's name to this psychopath, and Geroy either killed him or had him killed; of that she was sure. She felt her cheeks flush and her eyes dart out as they approached the booth where Geroy sat.

After leaving the body of Warren "Catfish" Jacoby in the capable hands of the medical examiner and her assistants, M.J. and Rosie led Black and Decker, the two homicide detectives, back to Geroy's pad by Ziegler Park.

But the gang leader wasn't home, nor were the two sentries whom Geroy earlier described as armed. The two oversized men on the couch were still watching CNBC, stonily staring at the scroll of stock prices on the screen. One of them, letting the detectives in from the lobby, said Geroy was at the Panera near the university.

Once again, Black and Decker followed the two women to Calhoun Street, just off from UC's campus.

Inside, Geroy was holding court with two very attractive women, probably not quite twenty. Both wore short shorts and midriff tops, gold metal studs in their bellybuttons. They wore stacked, open-toed shoes. Each displayed tattoos on bare arms.

The detectives decided, outside, that Simmons and M.J. would take lead.

Rosie pointed out for Decker the two sentries, who now flanked their boss. The two thin-faced men were sitting on opposite sides of the restaurant, each casually guarding a door. Rosie sat by the first, and Decker crossed the room and flopped into a chair opposite the second. Rosie caught Decker's eye. She patted her left hip at the beltline, indicating the sentry was most certainly heeled with a firearm.

Decker leaned toward his adversary, pointed to the "no guns" sticker on the window. Then, he raised his shield, nodding toward the door. Decker then said something under his breath.

The young black man shrugged, stood, and shoved the door open. He left without looking back.

The one across from Rosie gave her a sneer but did the same.

Rosie nodded to M.J. that it was her turn.

M.J. and Simmons approached the corner booth, the drug dealer and his two gal-pals.

The girls giggled as M.J. stopped at the table.

M.J. didn't speak but simply held her shield up in her left hand. She kept her right free and near her weapon. That was now practiced and unconscious behavior.

Geroy smiled in a placated way. He shooed the two girls away like scared ravens.

They gave M.J. the evil eye as they strutted to a table on the far end of the room.

Geroy smiled. "Nice to see you again so soon, Detective Monroe." He patted the seat beside him.

M.J. stood as if in stone.

The gangster looked up with one eye closed at Simmons. "You got you a dark one with you this time, Detective Monroe. Puts a shame to my heritage. Got me a white daddy, don't you know." He addressed Simmons. "You gotta be right off the boat with that skin color. Where you from? Ghana? Liberia?"

Simmons shrugged, smiling. "Toledo."

M.J. interrupted the fun and games. "Did you kill Catfish Jacoby after I spoke to you?"

Geroy feigned shock. He didn't try very hard and failed. His lips trailed away to a sickly smear of a grin. "I assure you, detective, I've been right here since about fifteen minutes after you left my business establishment, as security footage will, no doubt, verify. Been here, what, about three hours now? Girls met me here. They'll be glad to give witness statements I've been here the whole time."

"Then, you had someone do your dirty work."

"It is true I delegate," Geroy said in a deadpan manner.

"And you made it personal. Had my business card put in his mouth," M.J. spat back, her anger bleeding through. Her eyes were dark and gleaming with emotion.

Geroy turned from her glare to Simmons. "You just muscle?"

The tall detective narrowed his eyes at the disrespect. "Here's my card. Detective Marion Simmons, homicide. Open wide. I'll put it in your mouth. Save me some time when I punch your clock."

Geroy leaned back, startled for just a moment. Then, he roared with laughter. "That was good. Very, very good. I recognize your name. You've been on the news; on the street you're called Black." Geroy pointed at the red-headed detective near the far door. "That must be Decker. I am honored."

Decker, upon hearing his name, reacted only by pursing his lips into dissatisfaction.

Simmons snorted. "That's my partner, all right. He don't talk to your kind much. More particular than me, I guess."

Geroy, tired of Simmons, turned back to M.J. "To answer your accusation, Detective Monroe, here's the business card you gave me. I still have it." He reached into the left chest pocket on the preppy shirt he still wore.

He took M.J.'s card from it and held it for her to see. "You see, I had nothing to do with Catfish's death, but I must say, you can't be too displeased. At one this afternoon, you told me dear departed Cat harmed a witness in your abduction case. I hadn't even had time to address the issue with him yet, and you burst into my, ah, my talent search here, I guess I'll call it, to let me know one of my employees has been killed. It's rather insensitive how you handled it all, don't you think?"

"I'm sure you know what I think of you." M.J. wanted to leave.

Simmons took his business card and slid it with his slender blue-black fingers until the edge of the card was under Geroy's glass. "You can bet we'll be viewing that security footage. Taking statements from those girls, too."

"Good," Geroy said, "best to eliminate suspects as soon as possible."

Simmons backed away, his eyes impossibly narrow.

M.J. raised an eyebrow to Geroy. "I think you made an enemy of Detective Simmons this afternoon. He's a bad enemy to have. I feel sorry for you."

Geroy smiled, wolfishly. "Yeah, well, I'll just have to take those two girls back to my place and allow their nubile flesh to ease my psychic pain."

M.J. shrugged. "Nah, that's not going to happen. Detective Coleman is already calling dispatch to get some black and whites out here to take those young ladies in to get statements. Probably take two or three hours at least. Guess you'll have to go solo. You right or left-handed?" She left him there stewing.

Outside, Simmons braced her. "M.J.," he said, "you think you got it all wrong with this Catfish? Geroy still has the card you gave him this morning. How'd Catfish end up with one in his mouth if Geroy still has his?"

Decker sidled up beside his partner. "We've caught this murder, by the way, so it's important for you to think about this answer and get it right. Did you give Catfish your card?"

M.J. shook her head. "I never met or even saw Warren Jacoby when he was alive. I gave out lots of my cards during the canvass of the neighborhood on Tuesday morning. I gave Grandy Wilson my card when I spoke to him that day. I'm guessing Catfish found the card on the old man after he beat him."

"Probably be a good idea you stay clear of Grandy Wilson here on out," said Decker.

"Yeah," said Simmons. "We'll ask Grandy over at the hospital if he still has your card."

"Besides," M.J. added, "I was with fifty feds, you two, Tobias Meyer, my partner, the chief of police, and Mayor Lark when the murder took place, so giving me the third degree is a little much, don't you think?"

Simmons snorted. "Inquests are funny things, M.J. Time of death is based on science, but it can find some wiggle room over in Internal Affairs. Best watch your P's and Q's."

"You think I beat somebody to death with a two-by-four?"

Decker shook his head. "But I've seen your partner playing softball. She's the best with a Louisville Slugger of any woman I ever saw."

"Best woman? I don't think so," said M.J. "Best anyone."

Simmons smiled. "True dat."

———

By the time Rosie and M.J. got back on the clock investigating the five vans on their list, it was 4:00 that Friday afternoon. Traffic was stalled everywhere; construction projects slowed progress everywhere. There seemed to be more orange barrels lining the lanes of the interstates than cars.

The two women made poor progress for two hours, only managing one vehicle verification, a tan van used for pharmaceutical deliveries by a Springdale-based, privately owned drug store. The owner was still in at 6:00, filling prescriptions for those who lived paycheck to paycheck and had cash to pay for pills on payday.

The van, he verified, was always in use in the afternoons. The driver, licensed to carry a firearm, and the pharm tech, licensed to dispense, were both clean. The driver was an ex-sheriff's deputy and functioned as an armed guard for a van because it always carried thousands of painkillers. In this opioid-crazed region, just having those drugs on board made them a target.

The tech was a twenty-four-year-old Xavier student working her way through grad school. The owner verified both employees. M.J. and Rosie spoke with both. Their timelines and stories checked out. Neither fit the profile offered by the FBI. M.J. crossed the first van off the list.

It wasn't until after 6:00 when, finally, the owner of the second van called back. M. Marsdale turned out to be Marsha

Marsdale. Ms. Marsdale was a licensed veterinarian. She ran an X-ray, MRI, and chemo treatment service for large animals out of a paneled van.

Yes, she'd been in both areas, one for an ongoing chemo treatment on a Great Dane in Hyde Park when Klaire Keller was taken, and for the first she'd been to the zoo to assist in the treatment of several geriatric animals. Yes, she could provide times, documentation, and witnesses. No, no one else had access to the vehicle. And with verification, M.J. scratched Marsdale from the list.

After a quick taco out of a truck on Fountain Square just after 8:00 p.m., Rosie and M.J. worked the phones on the remaining three vans on their list. Although they'd earlier left messages with those owners, it wasn't until after nine that the three did finally return calls.

The two detectives visited all three owners' homes. Two used GPS tracking for mileage tax deductions on their vans. One was a plumber. He provided the GPS link and password for the detectives, showing he had been working downtown, fixing a leaking toilet at the Taft Theater before Monday night's Ziggy Marley show. The plumber finished shortly before the doors opened at 7:00, clearing him of Paisley's abduction. He had no alibi for the time of the Keller abduction, but both detectives were sure he was not their guy. Rosie crossed his name off their list.

The fourth van was owned by a contractor. That van had been in use by two male employees during both critical times. The two employees were Hispanic, and M.J. had the feeling from the contractor's nervous demeanor that they were probably illegals, but a green card violation was not the crime of the hour. Once Rosie and M.J. verified the two men were on-site at a new restaurant across from Washington Park next to Zola's during both abductions, M.J. crossed them off the list.

The final van was even easier to clear once the owner returned the detectives' call at 8:45. Rosie and M.J. were just leaving the Colerain home of the contractor when they got the last call back. Van number five turned out to be owned by a vending machine operator named Wilforce. He and his wife stocked soft drinks and snacks in vending machines around the city, picking up change and cash from the machines. He was in his mid-sixties; his wife ten years younger. The van was equipped with Lo-Jac security because of the amount of cash they sometimes carried.

A quick ride to the couple's Norwood residence told the detectives all they needed to know. The van, none too new, was parked in the driveway, its bumper against the rear-retaining wall on the property, their version of security for the crackers and soda pop stacked inside. The Lo-Jac report, already printed before the detectives arrived, revealed the vending machine operators' multiple stops during the hours of the two abductions. Plus, the gray-haired couple were too old, too beaten down, and too passionless. They did not fit the profile. M.J. crossed the last van off their list.

Chapter Seven

The 10:00 p.m. debrief at FBI Blue Ash was at least brief. A scan of the room told M.J. what she already knew; everyone was exhausted. of the sixty-five vans investigated, only five had not been verified. Of the sixty that checked out, only seven had been deemed by the investigators to need follow-up.

Three of the vans were owned by men who could not, or would not, reveal their whereabouts during one or both time periods in question. The other four were being driven by men with past run-ins with the law involving abuse. The FBI would work up data on the seven individuals in question overnight.

Special Agent Messerschmitt revealed that computer analysis in D.C. had given them twenty-two more vans and plates. Those would be added to the remaining list of 140 vans. With the five remaining on today's list, the additional twenty-two meant that each of the eleven teams investigating vans tomorrow (two teams were being pulled to interview the seven potential suspects from today's search) would now get twelve vans to clear.

A large number of those remaining vans were in Kentucky

or Indiana, bordering Cincinnati to the south and west. The Cincinnati PD could not cross the state lines for those investigations, so Kentucky and Indiana vans were FBI turf.

Rosie dropped off M.J. at her Jeep Wrangler in the District One parking lot. It seemed like a million years since she'd parked there this morning.

M.J. drove east on Ezzard Charles across Fourth and took US 50 east toward her home, a small house in Newtown, a block away from the banks of the Little Miami River. It was now 11:00 p.m., and traffic was light heading out of downtown.

She drove east on Columbia Parkway away from downtown, south along the base of Mount Adams, past Jeff Ruby's famed restaurant, The Precinct, and to Newtown. Below the blacktop down on the black water of the river, she could see tugs pushing barges, long and dark, marked only with navigation lights. Those barges carried coal from West Virginia down to power plants belching smoke, converting the black nuggets to make the electricity for Midwestern towns.

M.J. saw flashing lights ahead and groaned. An accident was something she didn't need. Traffic started to back up, and all too quickly, she was stopped. Not liking herself for doing it, M.J. placed her flashing red and blue light on her dash and lit up the night.

She veered to the right as she rose up the hill. The Columbia-Tusculum neighborhood rose steeply on her left. House lights glittered in their exclusive climes, families in for the night. Those doctors and lawyers took no notice of the snarl of traffic below them.

M.J. rolled slowly until she reached the first black and white, light flashing red/blue to purple in the night. The cruiser was parked sideways to the lanes of traffic. The detective peered briefly down, and perhaps a half mile below this vantage, she could see the reflection of the rotating lights, blue, white, purple, upon the mighty river's dark progression.

With one wheel in the ditch, M.J. closed the half-mile distance until she saw a cop holding back traffic on this side of the four-lane.

The big man stared sullenly at the Jeep with cop lights, giving it permission to break formation, complicating his job. His face showed displeasure.

She understood she was pulling rank by bypassing all the cars with her lights on. She recognized the cop holding back the traffic.

Officer James Riggio narrowed his eyes but then grinned as he recognized M.J. getting out of her Jeep.

"If it ain't the city's most underrated detective herself," he said.

"How you been, Riggs?" M.J. said, moving slowly to where he stood on the backside of his patrol car. Looking back over her shoulder, she could see aggravation in the faces of the passengers in the cars blocked by Riggs's patrol car.

M.J. studied those scowls for a few seconds. She understood their frustration and figured more than one of them needed to piss after too many beers downtown. *Serves them right*, she thought, *drinking and driving.* Beyond Riggs to her left, three younger policemen in uniform were slowly getting the cars in the line turned around at a cut-through to head back toward the city. One at a time, they directed the vehicles across the median and back along Columbia Parkway west.

"Good to see you, M.J. How am I doin', you ask? Without. Wife left me." The man's face betrayed a brief instant of sorrow. His hulking frame and puffy face showed, if only for a moment, his twenty-plus years on the street in full detail.

M.J. was surprised at the personal revelation. "I'm sorry, Jim. Truly sorry."

Riggs noted her switch to his proper name. It moved him. M.J. detected a flicker in his eyes. Moving past it, he smiled, saying, "Aw, hell, it's better for both of us. The kid is gone, anyway."

M.J. nodded. Cops and divorces went together like peanut butter and jelly, like turkey and dressing, like corned beef and rye bread. M.J. realized with a start that she was starving.

"What are you doing out here?" Riggs asked. "They haven't busted you down to filling out reports on roadkill, have they?"

"Might like it better." She smiled. "No, I live in Newtown. Never sold the house after my husband's accident."

Riggs's eyes turned soft again for a moment. He nodded, not saying anything, but knowing the story. His eyes showed the touch of pity that M.J. didn't like, but she was used to it.

"What we got? A wreck?" She looked down the hill toward the dark river below. Before it, there were lights, but no vehicle could have driven the slope. Anybody down there was in deep trouble.

"Yeah, cement truck driver headed east hit the dividing wall in the left lane, came hard right, and got a wheel up on the guard rail somehow. We're guessing his load shifted and he went over. Maybe he was drunk, maybe he fell asleep. Don't know. Know we won't get to ask him. Dead as a doornail. Came out the windshield when he first hit. Body stayed up here. Truck went down there."

M.J. looked over the rail. She couldn't even see the truck in the gloom.

Riggs moved beside her with a big flashlight. "See that big pylon, that concrete column about three feet thick, right there." The cylinder of concrete was butted into the bridge, part of a second set of them, the first set shorter and closer to the bedrock before the bridge itself. It was too dark to see how many of the concrete pylons, big as Roman columns, supported the bridge.

"Yeah," said M.J. "I see it."

Riggs moved the flashlight's beam. "Look, there used to be two of them up front here, too. See that broken stub? That cement truck must have been real heavy 'cause it sheared that second pylon, metal rebar and all, right off. Now, this side of the bridge is going to have to be evaluated for structural integrity. Might not be open for a long, long time." He laughed.

"Might not get that heavy, ole truck out of there, either. There's a big retaining pond below those trees. Like three hundred feet across, nine feet deep. Truck and the pylon went into that pond. Guess the pond is supposed to hold the run on off from the California Nature Preserve, to keep it from eroding the cliffs here. All those river rats' homes down below would be long gone if that water was free to just flow down the hill when we get to rainy season every fall."

River rats, M.J. knew, were Cincinnatians and northern Kentuckians who lived a hardscrabble life along the Ohio. Every ten years or so, they'd lose their homes, built at water level or just above, to flooding, but some families had ties to the Ohio River going back a century. They would never be convinced to leave. So they rebuilt. They were a hardy, if impoverished, breed. But M.J.'d seen enough. She was hungry and tired.

"Riggs, I hate to ask you, but could you get me across to the other side? I need to get home, and I don't want to head back downtown and start over all the way around on 275."

"Can't let you use this side of the bridge, but we'll block off the other side and let you pass if you can get your Jeep across the ditch back there." He pointed back down the hill before the bridge's buttresses began.

M.J. smiled. "Owe you one, Riggio." And with that, she returned to her Jeep. Once one of the junior officers blocked oncoming traffic for her, she navigated across the grassy slope and onto the westbound lanes. She was home in ten minutes.

———

It was nearly midnight when M.J. pulled into the garage, which now only held one vehicle, a reminder of her husband's accident M.J. never failed to notice.

Inside, the home was clean and simple. Her TV was a quarter of the size of Geroy's, but she didn't turn it on. Instead, she bent to pick up the jumble of envelopes and catalogs on the floor. Her mailman, an old friend at this stage, was still kind enough to drop mail through the slot in her door. M.J. examined it, absentmindedly, as she put some John Klemmer on the stereo. His sax moaned throughout the house, but her stomach growled in competition.

She made a sandwich with some ham salad and lettuce, a bit of mayo, and slices of banana pepper on top. She opened a bag of Salt and Vinegar Mike's Chips, then drank two fingers of vodka with orange juice.

After placing the dishes in the washer, she showered. By the time she finished letting the hot water work the kinks from her neck, the music ended.

M.J. dried herself and entered her bedroom without turning on the lights. She pulled back the sheets after plugging in her cell phone on the bedside stand. She lay back, nearly asleep already. Looking at the clock, she groaned. Only five hours until the alarm would go off.

She felt the quiver of her muscles as she nodded off, but just as her conscious thoughts turned to dream, her cell phone rang. With another groan, she sat up and opened her sandpaper eyelids. M.J. examined the number. She didn't know it. With some trepidation, she answered. "Detective Monroe."

"This too late to call?" M.J. recognized Geroy's voice. She wondered for a moment if this was a nightmare. Nope, the phone was real as was the call.

"Yeah, pretty much too late," M.J. said, her anger returning instantaneously. Twice today now she wished she had not given that gangster her card, especially one with her private number on it.

"Sorry about today," he said, his voice softer than both times she's seen him earlier. "Words were said and deeds were done…" his voice trailed off.

"You just call to apologize or you gonna confess to something?"

"No, it ain't that. I got something for you. You know your missing girl? Purple or whatever her name is?

"Paisley Park Jefferson."

"Yeah, her. Well, her baby daddy, I put out the word. Just got some news. Said I would, and I did."

"Nat Lee? What about him?"

Geroy's voice was calm, thick like syrup, and M.J. realized for the first time that he was really high. Perhaps almost to unconsciousness. He didn't slur, but he didn't speak normally. His words were echoing over the phone line, like he was speaking from inside the barrel of his own intoxication. "Nat Lee, yeah, that him. A little bird told me where he works. You like the horses? I go sometimes. Put down some bets."

"Get to the point, Geroy," said M.J., "before you pass out."

"Yeah, like I said, Nat Lee, he like the horses, too. Workin' out there near Belterra Race Track. Think they call it a racino these days. Maybe he could get us some inside dope."

"I think you've had plenty of dope for one night. Now, out with it. Where's Nat Lee work?"

Geroy laughed. "Don't got no name exactly. I think it's Feather Bed Downs. You know, like a play on words."

"Anything more?"

"Jeez, seems like that's a lot. We square?"

"Oh, Geroy," M.J. said, her voice as full of fact as his was full of fancy, "we're not even close to even. Not even close."

Chapter Eight

M.J. answered her cell phone at 5:20 am. She noticed her alarm clock radio was off. She'd hit the button and gone back to sleep.

"You awake?" It was Rosie's voice on the other end.

"Barely." M.J.'s voice was scratchy like she'd smoked a pack of cigarettes the night before.

Rosie laughed, briefly. "You even remember calling me last night? There was a day when you would have rousted me out of bed to track down the little girl's daddy, not turn it over to the FBI task force."

M.J. nodded, not agreeing, but not disagreeing. "It was a bad day yesterday. Geroy killing that Catfish guy just to get a rise out of me. Working like twenty hours, and then I worried all through the night about little Paisley. Not resting."

"Yeah, me, too."

The two women were silent for a moment, almost like they shared an unspoken prayer.

M.J. broke the reverie first. "FBI get Nat Lee?"

"No, that's why I called you. I called Special Agent Lisa

Agate, the woman who heads up the Blue Ash FBI office. The task force is going to hit Feather Bed Downs at 6:00 am. Since we came up with the lead, she invited us to join them. Figure we should show up. Get the department a slice of the arrest if Nat Lee did take his little girl."

M.J. groaned. "Okay, give me fifteen minutes. Can you pick me up? Belterra is only about three miles from here. Feather Bed Downs is right down the road from it, right?"

Hanging up the phone, M.J. rolled out of bed. Her floors were not even cool to the soles of her feet. It was going to be a hot day. Then, M.J. remembered about the highway. She called Rosie right back.

"Rosie?"

"Yeah?"

"50 east is closed. Cement truck took out part of the bridge there at the retaining pool below the California neighborhood."

Rosie took that in for a moment. She was tired, too. "So how do I get there?"

"West is open. I'll drive in to Jack Casino, meet you on level three of the parking garage in twenty minutes or so. We can run hot down 471 and up 275 the back way and still get there before 6:00."

M.J. was thankful she'd made coffee the night before. It had been set on automatic. She threw on a pair of black slacks, a white cotton blouse, and after putting her weapon on her hip, she covered it with a black denim jacket. Once the sun came up, she'd ditch the jacket, but she wanted it for the task force takedown on Nat Lee if there was to be one.

Sliding into her Jeep, she put her go cup of coffee in the holder between the seats, raised the garage door, and started her vehicle. Then realizing Riggs would still be on duty, his last hour in a twelve-hour shift, M.J. went back into the house and poured a second cup.

————

M.J. pulled off to the side at the accident site. Riggs was still there, alone now, his squad car blocking the roadway. A false dawn was bleeding light on the eastern horizon. M.J. pulled the Jeep off the blacktop into the grass median. The line of traffic from the night before was gone. Detours, rerouting, and the early hour had reduced traffic flow to nearly nothing since she'd gone home.

M.J. assessed the policeman as he stood where she'd left him the night before. James Riggio was a big man, barrel-chested, with large shoulders and arms. His waist was narrow, his legs maybe even a little birdlike, like all his weight was stacked above his ribcage. M.J. could see the fatigue on his face as he talked on his car radio. She guessed it would be dispatch organizing his replacement, due in just more than an hour.

M.J. stepped from the jeep, and Riggs looked past his vehicle's lights to her.

He grinned, seeing the coffee in her hands.

She smiled back, and he nodded appreciation at the steam rolling out the lip of the tall ceramic cup.

"You still here?"

"You know the drill," Riggs replied.

M.J. nodded, handing him the cup. "You go back on at 7:00 tonight?"

Riggs shook his head. "No, got a reprieve. Go back on Sunday morning. Brad Bennett, you know him? He's got season tickets to the football games. Wants to see the home-town team lose in person, you know, so we traded."

M.J. whistled. "He's taking twenty-four straight and then going to a football game?"

"Yeah, but the Bengals don't play until 4:00, so it's cool." Riggs smiled again. "Coffee's good. Thanks." He paused. "You ever go to the games?"

M.J. shook her head, suddenly a touch uncomfortable, like the coffee had signaled something to him she hadn't intended. "No, not a football fan, really. Usually go to Rosie's. She gets her father out of the rest home on Sunday, so she puts on a spread. I go over to eat."

Riggs smiled. "Sounds good. I haven't had a good, home-cooked meal in a while. Cooking for one is such a pain." Then, he faded off.

M.J. turned her head slightly in agreement and discomfort. Yes, she had, indeed, learned how cooking for one was difficult.

Riggs seemed to read her face. "Oh, hey," he said, still squinting and showing concern that he had offended her.

M.J. didn't have time to reassure him, as she had moved on to thinking that, just maybe, they'd find Paisley Park Jefferson in the next hour.

M.J. shushed him with a wave of her hand. "No offense taken, but I gotta go. I have to meet Rosie at the Jack, and I'm going to be late. I gotta run."

Riggs frowned. "Hate to ask you since you say you're behind schedule, but can you run me down the hill? I really want to keep my vehicle blocking access to this bridge until they get the barricades up later today, and I need to talk to the river rats down there. All three kids I got with me are manning access points down from Mount Adams until the barricade trucks from the city get here."

M.J. internally moaned. *No good deed goes unpunished*, she thought. "Sure, I can take you. How do we get there?"

"Just on down the hill to the first exit. First left down the hill. I can walk from there."

"Why do you need to talk to the river rats?"

Riggs sat down in her passenger seat and nodded toward the darkness below the bridge. "The retaining pond is losing all its water. Engineers out here last night think the truck or the concrete pylon might have just punctured its base and is letting all three million gallons head down the hill. Could take those rickety old houses right off the foundations and out into the river. Gonna have to evacuate those five families."

"Oh, you're going to be Mr. Popular, aren't you?"

Riggs nodded, ruefully, as M.J. reached the bottom of the hill. By now, she was running very late. Riggs tipped the coffee cup at her as he got out.

M.J., in a total rush, yelled a goodbye as he slammed the door. She even spun a little gravel, much to Riggs's delight, as she did a 180 and returned toward the highway.

———

Feather Bed Downs was a facsimile of a southern plantation, complete with horse barn, pitch-black railed fencing, and a six-columned manor house seated among several magnolia trees. The main house was surrounded by five outbuildings. The grass was green and lush. The fence blocked the horses' access to the river, which was beyond the property line by no more than 300 yards. Inside the fenced area, adjacent to the stable, a half-mile track of well-kept tilled dirt was opposite the house. Just across the river, Kentucky was dappled in light. The dawn now in a full attempt to warm the day lit each bank, and every blade of grass glistened in the new day's sunlight.

As Rosie rolled down the chert-rock drive, they could see the FBI had arrived before them. Rosie was a bit dismayed.

She did not like being late anywhere, and M.J. had made them late. Perhaps fifteen agents and another dozen techs milled in the yard. Special Agent Lisa Agate, wearing her navy-blue windbreaker jacket emblazoned with *FBI* on the back, was at the front door, serving the warrant.

Rosie said, "Missed cocktail hour, but still in time for the appetizer."

M.J. smiled. All was forgiven.

Agent Messerschmitt met the two detectives, saying out loud as they approached. "The principal owner of Feather Bed Downs is one Christopher Cottonton. Business is an LLC registered to him and his wife. We pulled social security and withholding records, and no Nat Lee is on the books, but that doesn't mean he isn't working here. Lots of day laborers in horse operations."

The search and interview took about two hours. Feather Bed Downs ran a dozen thoroughbreds owned by the Cottontons. They also leased space for another seven horses. The day starts early at a horse farm. Perhaps fifteen employees were at work. Several jockeys took the horses onto the track. Others, whom M.J. later learned were stable boys, moved the animals from the stable to the fenced enclosure.

A white man with an eyepatch seemed to be in charge. Danny Elliott, head trainer, was his name and title. He was about forty, wearing a white snap-front shirt, Levi's, and boots.

Another man, swarthy and dark-haired, stayed with him. The assistant trainer was Felipe Lopez, and it seemed to be his job to translate for Elliott to his jockeys and stable boys. It seemed all of them were Hispanic. M.J. was surprised they hadn't all started to run when the FBI showed up, figuring all of the workers were illegals who would think the feds must be ICE on an immigration raid.

M.J. and Rosie soon learned, despite the invite to attend

the raid that they weren't participants, only spectators. No one introduced them to any of the principals here, and none of the principals spoke to either Cincinnati cop.

Rosie shrugged after a while. "Should have let you get another hour of sleep."

M.J. nodded. "Yeah, looks like a bad lead. Geroy was pretty high."

They watched Agents Messerschmitt and Agate conduct the interviews. M.J. was impressed the techs with the agents all had translators. Evidently, Special Agent Agate had her act together.

But even after interviewing all the jockeys, stable boys, the assistant trainer, the trainer, the owner and his wife, they had no additional information on Nat Lee. None knew him, and he didn't work there.

Disappointment welled up in M.J. She thought Rosie was close to tears. They so hoped to bring Paisley home this morning.

Agent Messerschmitt strode up to them. "Might as well mount up. False lead, I guess. We'll continue to check the paper trail here, but the witnesses are all pretty convincing." He turned his back and returned to his vehicle.

M.J. nodded the agent's direction, but Rosie veered off to some picnic benches under the largest of the magnolia trees. There, a Hispanic woman worked over a butane camper grill. She toasted tortillas while the men finished their morning's chores. The tortillas were served with coffee and egg burritos. Rosie smiled and asked the Latina for a cup.

Agent Agate approached M.J., her red hair in a tight bun. She watched Rosie over M.J.'s shoulder. "What's your partner up to? We interviewed that woman. She is just a weekend cook. Didn't even know the trainer or assistant trainer's names."

M.J. shrugged. "I guess Rosie just wants a cup of coffee."

Agent Agate shrugged, dismissing the two cops, and turned to her vehicle.

M.J. saw her partner smiling as she strolled back. "Hey, Cheshire Cat, what's the grin for?"

"Well, just as the FBI was finishing up, I noticed there were no black folk working here." She paused. "And I noticed several of those horses were taking rather large craps."

M.J. laughed. "Yes, Miss Marple, I don't see a connection."

"I prefer Veronica Mars," Rosie laughed then continued. "No one there was mucking out any of those stalls in the stable. Not even the Latin stable boys; even *they* seemed above it."

The light went on for M.J. "*You thought What downtrodden race might be in a position to take that kind of job, mucking out horse manure?*"

"Exactly."

"Therefore, you decided to speak with the person who had the least visibility here, at least to the FBI. You spoke to the woman cooking the food."

"Yep."

"And what did the cook say?"

"She said a company comes in at 4:00 p.m. every day and cleans out the stalls."

"She know Nat Lee?"

"No, but she said there are several black men on the crew."

"Guess we're coming back at 4:00."

"Yep. Guess so."

Chapter Nine

At 4:00 p.m., M.J. and Rosie pulled back in the long drive at Feather Bed Downs. They parked and entered the barns. Sure enough, three men, all black, were busy mucking out the stalls. One was leading a horse to a clean, spare stall; a second, using a grain shovel, lifted piles of manure out into a large, deep-sided wheelbarrow. The third man scattered fresh straw into the stall.

The two detectives watched the scene for five minutes through the dust motes, which danced in the light from the open loft door above. It was quiet in the barn. The only sound was the men's breathing punctuated every minute or so with a horse's whinny. Both M.J. and Rosie had looked at Nat Lee's photo many times. He was not one of the men here.

Rosie approached the men, who paused in their efforts as she addressed them.

"Hi, guys, I'm looking for Nat Lee. I thought he was going to be working this afternoon. You know him?" She held his photo up for them to see.

Nobody volunteered anything.

"Yeah, I know," Rosie added, "I'm a cop, but Nat's not in trouble. It's about his daughter. Her mom reported her missing. We're just following up. Nat's not wanted or anything."

With that reassurance, at least one of the men's memory was restored. He nodded quietly. "He's hurt. Can't stand very well right now. He's out in the vehicle, driving the manure wagon today."

"Thanks."

Outside, M.J. and Rosie turned the corner of the barn and both pulled up short. The manure wagon was a large wooden flatbed trailer with rails around it. Inside the rails, several tall dumpsters stood in a row. Flies buzzed and the stench was dense and oppressive. But it was not the stench which stopped the detectives. It was what was pulling the manure wagon, a dirty white van.

M.J. looked to Rosie, "Ready? I'll take passenger side."

Rosie smiled without humor. "Only fitting I take lead with one of *my people*."

Rosie moved to the driver's side door. The window was halfway down., but she still placed her gold shield against the glass.

The man at the wheel raised his hands from the wheel very carefully. It was Nat Lee.

"Mr. Lee, I'm Detective Coleman with the Cincinnati Police Department. On the other side is my partner, Detective Monroe. We need to speak to you a moment. Would you mind stepping from the vehicle?"

Lee's eyes showed his surprise at the policewomen's presence, but he opened the door. Below the door frame on the passenger side, M.J. had her hands on her service weapon, but there was no need. Lee stepped gingerly from the van. His left foot was heavily bandaged.

"You mind if I reach in and get my crutches? Got an

infected foot. Stepped on a pitchfork in the barn last week, and with all the manure around, it got infected. Can't put any weight down."

Rosie nodded, and the man reached across the cab. He pulled two aluminum crutches with white towels taped on the supports to provide more cushion under his armpits. Now positioned on the crutches, he looked Rosie straight in the eye. "That's better. Now, what can I do you for?" He smiled, nervously.

M.J. crossed to the driver's side from the front of the van. She assessed Nat Lee as she cleared the door. He was perhaps thirty, of medium build. He had lean arms and wore jeans too big for his small waist, so a cinched belt kept them up. Lee was unshaven, and his shiny dome showed just a bit of stubble, as well. He was a decent looking man, but his eyes were a bit narrow and showed poverty as a form of defeat, like he was embarrassed to be caught in the act of driving a manure truck.

"Mr. Lee, were you aware that your daughter is missing?"

Again, shock showed on his face. "What? Paisley? What do you mean missing?"

"Your ex-wife filed a report on Monday evening. No one's seen her in six days. We've been trying to find you. There's been an AMBER Alert citywide for a number of days. It's been on TV and radio continually. Where have you been?"

Lee's face still registered shock and now fear. "Wait a second, Paisley's gone? Like lost? or like kidnapped or what?"

"We suspect foul play at this point, but we don't really know. We wanted to talk to you. Have you been in contact with her?"

Lee hedged for a heartbeat. Then, he spoke carefully. "I seen her a few times this summer. I live out here along the river now. Don't have no car. But the boss lets me borrow the van sometimes. I did go see Paisley once a couple weeks ago. Gave her a little bit of money."

"You don't know where she is right now?"

"No, no. I didn't know…" his voice trailed off. "What day did you say she went missing?"

"Monday. Six days ago. Where were you that day?"

Lee's spine jolted, like he just realized the detectives thought he was responsible for his daughter's disappearance. "I stepped on that pitchfork last Sunday. We work seven days. Horses don't take no weekend breaks from poopin'. Anyway, after I stepped on that fork, I was bleedin' pretty bad, so the guys helped me over to the main house. Mr. Cottonton owns the manure company, too, besides Feather Bed Downs. He got his doctor to look me over. Cleaned up my cut and gave me some antibiotics."

"Chris Cottonton, the owner here, owns the manure removal company?"

"Oh, it ain't just a manure company. He has crews picking up all the manure from all the horse farms, here and in Kentucky. Brings it up to Brown County and then dries it, breaks it up, and bags it for gardeners." Lee smiled. "I shovel the stuff. It pays the bills, and he don't ask too many questions, you know?"

M.J. spoke for the first time. "Cottonton has a doctor on staff?"

Lee ducked his head a touch. "For the horses, yeah, he do. But when I got hurt, he went over to the infirmary at the track and got some antibiotics to take care of me. It ain't like I got a healthcare plan."

Rosie tried to get back to the topic at hand, Paisley's disappearance. "You're saying you don't know anything about your daughter's disappearance?"

"No, none. I just now heard it from you. I don't have TV

or nothing in my cabin. And to be honest to you, I was in a lot of pain right after getting hurt, so I was pretty medicated." He laughed. "Truth was I was drunk as a skunk for about three days. Then, I came back and started driving the van here on Thursday. You can see, it don't have no radio. I just don't have no contact with the outside world."

"Unless you borrow the van to go into town?" Rosie asked.

"Yeah, unless that."

M.J. nodded. "And did you see anybody during your three-day binge down at the cabin?"

Lee narrowed his eyes. "You know, I don't think so. The fellas would have been out working for the most part, and I couldn't get around. I just stayed in the cabin with a couple a bottles. Didn't see a soul."

It was Rosie's turn to nod. "Mr. Lee, we'd like to have you come into town and get all the relevant information from the FBI about your daughter's disappearance. It's important to us to keep you in the loop about Paisley."

"Well, of course," Lee said, bobbing his head. "Maybe after my shift?"

"No, we'll get a squad car to come out and take you in. Probably need to take you to the emergency room and make sure your foot is okay, too. On the way, I mean."

Lee shook his head. "That ain't necessary. I'll be fine."

"It's a requirement, Mr. Lee. Regulations, you know."

Lee slowly agreed, his face showing acceptance.

"Can we get the address of your cabin, Mr. Lee? We want to run by and make sure everything is secure since we're taking you in town for a while. I'm not sure how long the FBI briefing will take. Is it okay if we bring you some things? Clean clothes? You're all right with us entering your home, right? Is there anything you want?"

"Nah, there's nothing there worth bringing in town." He

paused. "I can't even believe the FBI is looking for my little girl."

"I can't, either," Rosie said. M.J. agreed.

"One more thing, Mr. Lee. Can you tell us where Mr. Cottonton would be this time of day? Is he up at the house?"

"Oh, heck no," said Lee. "There's racing today. He'll be at his box. Private box, number two one six. Second level, great viewing from there. I went into it one time when there was no races. We clean the stalls at the track, too, you know."

———————

Chris Cottonton was, indeed, in private box 216 at the horse track. The two detectives sent a steward from the track into the suite to inform Cottonton they needed to see him. No sense going in them waving badges if they didn't have to.

Cottonton wore a white three-piece suit and with a grizzled goatee, he looked the part of a southern plantation owner from 150 years ago. He stepped outside his private box, closing the door with click.

M.J. showed her badge. "Need to ask you a few questions about Nat Lee."

The man wrinkled his nose. "The FBI was already at my farm this morning. Check with them." With a motion of his head, Cottonton dismissed them, his hand already reaching for the doorknob.

"Oh, that was before we found him working for your fertilizer company. You're spreading a lot of that around, it seems," said M.J.

That got Cottonton's attention. "Special Agent Agate never asked me if Lee worked for Perfect Food Fertilizer. She asked if he worked for Feather Bed Farms. He doesn't."

"I'll bet she asked if you knew a Nat Lee."

"I couldn't possibly know every single employee who works for me."

"Yeah, but I'll bet you remember the guy who stepped onto a pitchfork and needed medical attention, so you called your vet to come over and look at him," M.J. said back. She smiled, benignly.

Cottonton's shoulder sagged a bit. "Look, sure I know Nat Lee. He works as a day laborer for the fertilizer company. He wanted to be a cash employee, didn't want his ex to take all his money in child support. Lee himself suggested no doctor. He didn't want a worker's comp file on him. Thought it might get back to his ex-wife. I insisted he get care, regardless."

Rosie stepped forward. "Well, we sent him to the ER after we took him in. Seems Lee has blood poisoning. Red streaks running up his leg. Got him some proper attention to save his leg. We authorized the ER to send you the bill. I suggest you pay cash."

Cottonton threw up his hands, grudgingly. He smiled to disarm the two women. "Sure, I'll cover it. Is that all?"

Rosie leaned into him. It wasn't often she allowed herself the luxury of anger on the job, but M.J. could see it welling up in her now. "No, that's not all. His daughter's been kidnapped. We think she might have been taken by someone in a white van. Lee has access to your white van. He didn't work on Monday. Could he have taken his daughter? Where was the van on that day?"

Cottonton narrowed his eyes.

Rosie's face was close to his. Her nostrils flared as the two stared at each other for a long moment.

"Look," he finally said, "I have no idea if Lee took her or if he used the van. See, there was a big horse sale here at the track on Monday. I had all my horses brought over that day. The stalls were mucked out early on Monday, before noon. The van wouldn't have been in use after like one in the afternoon. Lee does have a set of keys. But you saw him. He wasn't up to walking much that day."

"But he was off work. No one saw him all day and he had access to the van which was not in use? Maybe he decided he needed his daughter to look after him, with him being injured and all?" Rosie wasn't backing off an inch.

Cottonton just shrugged. "I just don't know." His hand went back to the doorknob.

M.J. handed him her card. "We'll be in touch. And we will be reporting all of this to the FBI task force. As a matter of fact, our next stop after checking Mr. Lee's cabin is to see the feds. We'll let them know you may have not provided all the information you had at your disposal earlier today."

Rosie raised an eyebrow. "You better hope Lee doesn't lose that foot. He'll own your horse farm if he does. I know some attorneys in town who work on commission."

On the way to the car, M.J. laughed at Rosie. "You know some attorneys in town? Did you just threaten Cottonton with threat of suit from a potential perp?"

"I didn't much care for Snidely Whiplash back there. I expect he is not kind to the black folk."

————

Lee's cabin was unlocked, and he had been honest about having nothing worth stealing. The one-room shack did not contain a missing little girl. In fact, it was a complete waste of time. The drive back into the city was solemn.

"Do you think he took her? Has her stashed someplace else? He seemed genuinely surprised when we braced him,"

M.J. posited the question in the car, knowing Rosie was as stumped as she was.

"Statistics would say he does."

"I didn't ask that."

"I know. I don't think he took her, and that scares me a lot, especially when Paisley's disappearance is complicated by the white girl gone missing, too. I got a bad feeling about all of it. We're getting close to a week and we got just short of nothing. FBI is twiddling their thumbs on this white van theory. They got no solid leads. None whatsoever."

"I know."

"I've been praying hard for God to lend us a hand."

"Keep the faith."

"And work our butts off."

"Amen, sister."

———

M.J. and Rosie spent the rest of the day clearing the remaining white vans on their list.

Late after dark, they spoke to Special Agent Agate, who was furious that Cottonton earlier lied to her by omission. But the truth was Lee hadn't really provided anything new to the FBI in four hours of grilling while in custody.

And to top it off, the vet on Cottonton's payroll backed up Lee's description of events of the previous Sunday. While Lee had no alibi for the time during the abduction of his daughter or that of Klaire Keller's disappearance either, no one could connect him to either crime. The truth is that after finding the father, they were back to square one.

Both Rosie and M.J. headed home that night, depressed and defeated. They agreed to sleep in a bit, then work from eight until noon, when Rosie's father would be delivered from the church to Rosie's home by his rest home's transportation service. Rosie needed to be home by the time he arrived.

"See you tomorrow, Rosie. Maybe something will turn up in the morning. Remember, keep the faith," M.J. said.

Rosie nodded, sadly, and drove away.

M.J. understood. All she wanted right now was sleep.

Chapter Ten

"Hullo," M.J. said, sleep still in her voice.

"M.J., it's Riggs."

"Huh?"

"I woke you, huh? Sorry, but if you could, I need you to come down here to the retaining pond. Hey, are you with me?"

M.J. sat up in bed, her consciousness rising in her like water in a kettle put on to boil. "Who is this again?"

"It's Riggs. You know, officer James Riggio. Jeez, you're really out of it."

M.J. shook her head. "Sorry, still asleep. Okay, yeah, Riggs. Hey, I don't deliver coffee every morning, man."

Riggs laughed. "No, it ain't that. This is serious. You need to get down here. The water's drained out of the retaining pond. And we got a body. In a trunk."

"A car trunk?"

"No, like a wooden trunk."

M.J. stretched. "Hey, I appreciate the call, but that's

District Two. I'm District One. Just call it in. dispatch will get a weekend crew out."

Riggs stammered for a second. "Mads," he said, "it's a young black girl."

Suddenly, everything came into focus. "I'll be right there."

———

M.J. drove back down 50 so fast, she was stopped at the one light in Newtown before she realized she'd left the garage door open to the house. At the red light, she texted her neighbor,

Ted, when you are up and around, check my garage door. I left in a hurry. —M.J.

He replied as she was arriving at the flashing lights on the bridge.

Garage door up, door to garage open, go cup filled on counter, coffee pot on and every light in the house shining bright. WTH? I got it covered! —T.

M.J. smiled in spite of her anxiety, turned off the Jeep, and strode across the ditch to the eastbound lanes where Riggs stood waiting for her.

"Hey, you got here fast," he said.

"You think it's her?" M.J. asked, a tremolo in her voice.

"Don't know. The two engineers from the city's water department found the trunk about an hour ago. They opened it and found the body right as I got here, I called it in and then called you. Homicide will be here in a few minutes and the M.E. too, but I thought you should have the first look."

She nodded.

Riggs reached into a pick-up bed behind him. "Had my brother drive my truck over. I wanted us to have these." Riggs lifted a man's and woman's set of waders from the truck bed.

M.J. looked at the waders. "You had him bring a set of waders that would fit me?"

Riggs looked chagrined. "Ex left them behind. We once thought trout fishing might aid our marital discord."

"And?"

Riggs laughed. "Not so much. Go put them on behind your Jeep. They might fit better without your pants on."

She did as Riggs instructed, placing her slacks on the seat, folded. She shimmied into the green waders with built-in boots. Afterwards, she tugged them up until they came to her bustline and then she struggled to get the overall straps into place. She finally gave up on them. She rejoined Riggs, carrying her Glock-9 in one hand.

Riggs was wearing his waders, looked at her and again laughed, his eyes crinkling. "Let me help you adjust those things." As he did, he said, "What do you think you're going to do with that weapon?"

"Jeep's a ragtop. Doesn't lock. Can't leave my weapon." With those words, she slid the pancake holster into her cleavage, minimal though it was.

Riggs led her down the slope from the roadbed. It was light now, but barely. The sun peeked over their left shoulders as they cautiously navigated the hillside which was covered with scrub willows of various heights.

When they reached the rim of the retaining tank, the concrete side was as tall as M.J.'s head.

Riggs looked her in the eye and said, "May I?"

M.J. nodded, and he grasped her around the waist and lifted her butt to a sitting position on the wall. Then, he pulled himself up.

Slowly, they rotated their bodies to the riverside view of the tank.

The retaining pond was massive. Three hundred feet long

and probably eighty feet wide, the bowl was fifteen feet deep at its center. Inside the rim, M.J. could see miner's lights on the foreheads of the two engineers, but it was light enough she could also see their silhouettes in the morning sun.

They were only fifty feet from her, but it would not be an easy fifty feet to traverse. The rim of the bowl was filled with willows, again at various heights, but some as tall as fifteen feet. Mud also was packed in below them and across the vast pond, which now only had puddles of water in its lower recesses. The mud must have been the result of many years of sediment from erosion from the hillside above.

The retaining pool was doing its job very well, or had been, until the cement truck and the jagged pylon had punctured its base. M.J. could see the cement truck on its side, a third of it buried in mud and the concrete column sticking into the muck like a broken chopstick into chicken chow mein.

Riggs gave her a moment to orient. Then, he dropped from the concrete lip into the mud. His boots, even at the edge, sunk as much as a foot. The big man lifted her down, hands under her armpits. Then, hand-in-hand, they walked to the engineers, using their spare hands to grab the willow saplings, which ended as the bowl flattened out to what would have been the pool of water.

Riggs said, "When I got here right after the accident the other night, the water was all the way up to where those biggest of the willows are growing. Now, it's just mud. We got all the folks out down below, except for one old crazy bat, Mrs. Hondros, who refused to leave. Her house is probably off the foundation with the all the water running down the slope. I'll check on her later today. Betty Hondros, what a pain in the ass that lady is."

"How 'bout this lady?" asked M.J., pointing at herself as she said it.

"A welcome respite," Riggs said, their eyes connecting for just a moment, but then they were forced to concentrate to walk in the eighteen inches of mud pulling at their boots.

Finally, they reached the two men and the trunk.

Riggs introduced M.J. to each.

"This is Fares Merchin, lead engineer here and his assistant, Bill Zook. They found the trunk this morning when the last of the water drained out of the basin."

M.J. the investigator began to interview. "What time was that?"

"Around 6:00, just when there was enough false dawn for us to see the trunk sticking out of the mud." Merchin did the talking. He had a soft Spanish accent to his speech. His accent was pleasing.

"And you opened the case?"

"Yes. I guess we shouldn't have, given what we found inside." He paused at the gravity of his comment. "But to be honest, we were like a couple of kids. It was like we just found pirate treasure. Are you going to want to look inside? It isn't pretty, not by a long shot."

"In a few moments. What else can you tell me about the trunk and its location on the scene here?"

Merchin tipped his head to his partner, "You tell them your thoughts."

Bill Zook was a stocky blond man, maybe in his early thirties. He stroked his chin, briefly, choosing his words carefully. "We're thinking it's been here a really long time. A *really* long time.

"We dug around the trunk's base a bit, and it's sitting on concrete for the most part. This retaining pond structure was built back in the '30s, but it was drained and scraped clean in 1973. According to our estimation, the pond gets about a third inch of sedimentation a year. That gives us an average of fifteen inches' sediment, mud, if you will, since it was last drained and cleaned out."

M.J. was following it. "And the trunk did not have a mud base under it, so your estimation is it came to rest on concrete and not sediment? You think the body was left here around 1973?" Saying the words made M.J. relax a bit. This corpse could not be Paisley Park Jefferson.

"Well," said Merchin, "closer to 1973 than to now."

"And how did the trunk get here? Boat?"

"No," Zook responded, "it was thrown over the edge of the bridge up above. See how the oval of the retaining pond extends to the widening of the bridge in that one spot. Someone would have pulled up. Probably in a pick-up truck and pushed it over."

M.J. looked at the edge of the bridge far behind her. "No one could have thrown this trunk with a body in it all that way."

The trunk, perhaps three feet long and almost that high, was of black wood, thick planking, perhaps more than an inch thick. M.J. assumed the deep coloration was from being submerged in water. It might have been lighter originally, but she thought by looking at the lines it was mahogany or something similar.

The edges of the lid and sides appeared to be decorated with brass fittings. Tiny nails, now brown with age and rust, were tacked into the edges of the fittings. Metal plates, likewise tacked into place, wrapped the lid, which was curved like a loaf of bread. The overall effect was that of a keepsake, even after decades under water. The trunk was substantial. It would have been heavy, really heavy with a child inside.

"Oh, no, you're right, nobody could have thrown it here, and I don't know that there's ever been a boat on these waters," agreed Merchin. "But currents and gravity are funny things. The trunk probably drifted down to the deepest part of the bowl over time, especially if the concrete was comparatively free of mud. And we've had earthquakes occasionally, though no one thinks of Cincinnati as having them, which would have moved the trunk more than likely, as well."

"Anything else?"

"There was about a foot of mud on the trunk's top when we found it, consistent with our assessment that it's been here since at least the early '80s."

"And how'd you get inside it?"

"Broke the lock off with my shovel," said Zook, sheepishly. "I dug it out of the mud when it came loose." He pointed to his wader's hip. The lock hung there by its hasp, a big key lock rusted and brown with mud.

M.J. nodded. "Anything else before we open it up?"

Merchin grimaced. "The interior appears to have been airtight. The trunk's construction was so tight, the joints swelled after it was submerged. Sealed it perfectly. There's no water inside or water damage to the inside of the trunk or to the...body. The body's in a bad way, like a mummy almost. A lot of decomposition, but I'm no expert in those kinds of things.

"But I *am* an expert in water damage. I can tell you there has not been water inside this trunk for forty plus years. Nothing made of leather would have survived. This trunk is a very fine piece of workmanship in my estimation. Not something somebody bought at Walmart."

"Probably would have been Sears, not Walmart back in 1980," Riggs said, trying to lighten the mood.

Then, M.J. nodded at Zook, and he understood her import.

With Merchin on the opposite side, they carefully lifted the lid.

M.J. held her breath and as she did, she felt Riggs by her side.

He squeezed her arm as the lid revealed the trunk's contents.

It was a child, a young black girl; her afro gave that away. The skin, however, was gray and patchy. Her body was bent forward, her face away from M.J. Her arms were bound with a coat hanger behind her back, her knees drawn to her chest. She appeared to wear the remains of a T-shirt and shorts.

M.J. could see the body was barefoot as her feet extended beyond her torso. The rest was decay and the result of something evil. Cause of death was not immediately evident.

RADIO WHTY, CInCInnATI

"Hello, Cincinnati, it's Ron Chee, your host while the rest of the gang takes the evening off. The story tonight is traffic and yet another body after the discovery yesterday in Clifton.

"This one found in a retaining pond over off Columbia Parkway. No news on whether it's being ruled a homicide, but word on the street is that famed detective duo, Black and Decker, have been assigned to the case and are on scene. Let's take a caller. Hello, caller number one!"

"Hey, Ron Chee! All these deaths these days, you think it's minorities causing them? Not that all minorities are bad, I don't mean that. Your last name is Chee, isn't it? Is that like Oriental?"

"Asian. Yeah, moving on. What you got, caller number two?"

"I listen to the police scanner all the time, and I heard the body out there was found in the trunk of a car."

"Yes, we've heard that, as well, but it hasn't yet been confirmed by police."

"Ron, I have this friend, Heddy. She married a black guy, and he treated her like gold. I don't care what your other callers say. It ain't because of race, all this violence."

"Thanks for that. I think we have time for one more. Hello, Caller number three!"

"Yeah, here's my take on it, Chee. The problem's our schools. Coddlin' these kids. Need to use a belt on them. Smack 'em around a bit. My father beat the hell out of me as a kid, and I never killed no one and put them in a car trunk."

"We're all glad for that. And now a word from Cincinnati's best cosmetic surgeon, Wilma Wacker."

Chapter Eleven

The first vehicle to come in with lights carried the two homicide detectives from the Two, Black and Decker. As they exited the car, M.J. called out, "You two the only ones working in homicide these days?"

Simmons smiled, coolly, in the early morning light. "When dispatch got the call and heard it was a young black girl, we caught it, being we're on the task force. Guess they assumed it was Paisley."

"Nope," M.J. said.

"We're glad it's not," Decker said as he stepped from the driver's side and saw Riggs against the rail of the bridge.

"What's up, big man? Got you working homicide now?"

"Was working the traffic cluster from the bridge accident, came on at 7:00 just as the water dept. engineers found the body. Called Det. Monroe, as she lives just up the road. Knew she was working the Jefferson kidnapping."

Decker raised an eyebrow at the connection.

Simmons gave a secretive smile, and M.J. knew she'd get

some ribbing later. She'd shut it down quickly. She was married and wanted nothing out there in the rumor mill.

Simmons sidled up to M.J., who had previously wiggled out of the muddy waders and was again in detective attire. "What we got?"

M.J. shook her head. "Not Paisley Park Jefferson, that's for sure. Cold case. Preliminary puts it at maybe forty years old. The trunk is old and water-logged. Air tight inside, though. Body's mummified. It'll take some logistics to even get the trunk out of there back to the morgue."

Technicians began to rope off the area to start the grim task of recovering the body, collecting evidence, and recording all that took place.

Decker and Simmons interviewed Merchin and Zook.

Riggs took M.J. over to his car by the side of the road, as the two were now nonessential to the investigation: M.J. was out of district; Riggs was out of rank.

"You okay?" he asked her. Riggs fished into his glove compartment and came up with a pack of cigarettes. He lit one and handed it to M.J.

She took it and leaned against the concrete abutment of the bridge. It had been ten years since she'd had a cigarette, but she drew on it and felt the smoke in her lungs. Somehow, it felt right after seeing the death and the evil before her just a half hour before.

"I'm okay. Think I'll go back up to the house and shower. Get it off of me."

Riggs nodded. "Yeah, the mud stinks. And probably the waders are smelly, too. Fishing and such."

M.J. shook her head. "No, that's not what I want to shower away."

"Oh," he said, having lit a second match for his own spike.

"I'm slow on the uptake with women sometimes." He paused. "All the time."

M.J. felt like the day was forty hours long already. She looked at her watch. "I need to let Rosie know I'm going to be late. No football game for me today, not if I'm going to clear my list of white vans for today."

"How 'bout you tell Rosie to go ahead and get her father and watch the game? I'll call the desk sgt. and get a replacement to cover me here. I'll sick out. Then, I can go around with you and clear those vans on today's list. That way, Rosie can have the time with her family." He paused. "I mean if you don't mind riding with somebody in unis."

M.J. dropped her cigarette and rubbed it out with the toe of her shoe. "Of course, I don't mind. And I don't think you're particularly slow on the uptake with women, either."

Riggs laughed and went to use the phone.

———

It was an uneventful day. M.J. and Riggs were able to clear all twelve white vans and their owners off the list of suspected vehicles. All those vehicles were business-owned, and all the owners could verify their vans' use and driver at the time of the two kidnappings. Clearing them took all afternoon, but it was good, honest police work, and the two enjoyed each other's company as they made their rounds.

Halfway through the day, M.J. asked, "Don't take this the wrong way, Riggs, but why haven't you ever taken the sergeant's exam? You got twenty years in, right?"

He smiled. "Let me answer it this way, M.J., if I asked you who you were, what would you say? Probably a detective, right?"

M.J. nodded. "Maybe wife at one time, but maybe not so

much now. That's kind of faded into, well, I'm not sure what it's faded into really."

"So detective?"

"Yes," answered M.J. "And you? Policeman?"

Riggs laughed. "No, that's just a paycheck and an interesting job of sorts. I could never hack all the time riding a desk if I got the stripes. Too boring. Life's too short."

"Then what?"

"It might have been husband at one time. Father back when my kid still spoke to me. Now I guess it's artist or painter. As soon as I've got the house paid off, I'm taking my pension and getting out. Going to paint full-time. Hope the ex gets married and I get clear of the alimony."

M.J. was amazed. "I didn't know that about you. You paint? Are you good?"

Riggs laughed. "That's certainly an issue for debate. I'm getting better all the time. Spend a lot of my time painting now. Use the master bedroom now as a studio, and sleep in the spare now that my son's gone west. I paint a lot, especially in winter. Still fish some in the summer. You ever go to Hap's on Erie?"

M.J. knew the place. "I used to go there sometimes after a shift before I made detective. Back when I worked in the Two."

"Not since then?"

"No, I don't think so. Not since Greg had his accident." M.J. smiled, sadly. "As the song says, I don't get out much anymore. Why?"

"They've got a painting of mine, a big one up over the bar."

M.J. smiled. "I guess I never noticed it."

Riggs shook his head. "It's only been there a couple of

years. Since you've been..." he paused. "Since you stopped going there."

M.J. stopped at the next light and turned and looked at him. "What were you going to say?"

Riggs narrowed his eyes a bit. "Since you've been in mourning." He dropped his eyes to his lap. "Sorry."

M.J. reflected for a moment. "No, don't be. I lost him almost three years ago in the wreck, but he didn't die. He's gone, but I never got closure. I *am* still in mourning. Because Greg is still dying, dying a tiny, tiny bit each day. Every time I go back, he's a little worse, a little less there..."

"Jesus, I'm sorry, M.J. That's a terrible fate, for both of you."

The light turned green and M.J. turned her attention back to the road. "Yes, it has been terrible for both of us."

It was nearly five when they'd cleared the last van from their list. Riggs drove during the last couple of stops so M.J. could file her report eliminating twelve more possible persons of interest from the FBI's growing, not shrinking, list.

Finally, the long day was over. M.J. transmitted the report from her vehicle's computer and signed off. It had been a long day, and it was not yet dark.

Riggs started to speak, but just as he did, M.J.'s cell rang. Rosie was on the line.

"You and your new boyfriend finished up yet? Catch anybody? Solve the case?"

"No and no. Did the Bengals win?"

"No. You hungry? We got lots of food left over."

"Famished," M.J. replied, realizing as she said it that she

truly was. She'd left so early today and in such a rush that she hadn't eaten all day.

"Good, see you in thirty. Bring Riggs." Rosie was laughing as she hung up.

———

By 8:00 p.m., M.J. knew one more thing about Riggs; he was a good eater. Rosie was a good cook, but someone who cooked more than she ate. Therefore, she liked someone who could put it away.

M.J. ate a plateful of salad, lasagna, garlic bread, and an olive tapenade on crackers both as a starter and dessert.

Riggs, however, ate three platefuls. And a big piece of cherry pie afterwards. Rosie was beaming. Riggs was stuffed. M.J. was pleased to watch her partner and her new friend interact so well together.

Rosie said, "What did you think about doing a detective's job today, Riggs?"

"Not much different than a cop on the beat. Checking off the boxes, putting in the time, one step after another."

Rosie smiled. "That is what you did today. That isn't what it's supposed to be, really. FBI's leading us around by our noses. Chasing white vans all around town because the task force accountant was able to get license plates from street cameras. Three thousand of them.

"And while our little girl, little Paisley, might have been taken by some sicko in a white van, we have no reason to think the white girl was. But the mayor's office thinks if we search for white vans, we're helping out on both cases and it keeps the FBI's Hate Crime Task Force dollars on the case. No matter we're peeing up a rope."

M.J. smiled, "Rosie, such language."

Rosie shrugged.

Riggs nodded. "And tomorrow's day seven. Statistics on solving Paisley's abduction now are bad. You think the cases are related?"

Rosie sat down across from him. "I've said this before. I think the two abductions are related, but the crimes were committed by different individuals. I think it's likely that Paisley is the victim of a sex crime, while the Keller girl is the victim of a hate crime. The second kidnapping precipitated by a person of color disgusted with the differing level of resources for the white and black communities."

Rosie took a breath. "Can I lay it all out on the line?"

"When have I ever asked you to hold back?"

"Okay, I have a daughter the same age as Paisley. This case bothers me because of it. I find myself less in control. It could be Marie. And let's face it. The deck is stacked against black girls like my daughter. Marie has her father in her life, but less than half of black girls do. They're twice as likely to get pregnant, six times as likely to grow up in poverty, ten times more likely to be expelled from school and that leads to a pipeline to go to prison. They're twice as likely to get arrested as white girls, yet they're outnumbered by white girls by a ratio of six to one."

M.J. said, "You're raising your daughter right."

"Monica Jefferson would have said the same thing about herself before her daughter went missing."

"You know Marie's and Paisley's situation are not the same."

"You mean, the playing field is not level?"

"Yes, life is not fair. You know that. We see it every day."

"Yeah, and I hate it."

M.J. raised an eyebrow at Rosie's freely spoken words. She was usually more circumspect with somebody new. Still looking at Rosie, M.J. moved to pour herself a cup of coffee. She wasn't worried about caffeine keeping her awake. She was tired and a good sleeper. M.J. raised the cup to Riggs's attention, and he nodded. She poured two cups. "Cream?"

"Black," he replied.

Rosie smiled. "Just like M.J. likes her partners."

They all three laughed loudly, and Rosie's father, asleep in the living room, stirred at the noise at the kitchen table. "What's going on in there? A party?"

M.J. stood. "Sure enough, Mr. Williams," she said, moving to the couch beside him. "Heard the Bengals let you down today."

The old man smiled. "Didn't let me down because I had no expectations." He patted her knee. "How have you been? Working too hard is what I hear."

M.J. nodded. "Got a tough one right now. Little girls gone missing."

Rosie's father nodded. "My daughter told me. Terrible thing. There's an evil in this world. Saw it in my years in the service. Seen it since I got back, too."

M.J. nodded in agreement. "Hey, I'd like to introduce you to my friend, Jim Riggio. He's a cop, too."

Rosie's father looked up at Riggs, who approached with his hand outstretched.

Mr. Williams shook Riggs's hand, saying, "You're a big 'en, you are."

"Even bigger now that I've discovered Rosie's cooking."

Mr. Williams smiled, proud of his daughter and liking Riggs from the outset.

Just then, M.J.'s phone dinged. She'd received a text from the medical examiner's office. She'd told them to send her a copy of the initial report on the dead girl in the trunk once it became available. The lab had been working on the preliminary report for the last twelve hours. The report was thin, but M.J. sat there and was suddenly unaware of the people around her.

The girl in the trunk was black, perhaps thirteen years of age when she died. She wore the remains of a T-shirt and shorts.

Cause of death was not yet known, but there was a stab wound in her back. Her trachea was also damaged. It was underdetermined at this juncture whether she had died of either of these wounds or from another.

The T-shirt offered some clues to the date. It was fully polyester and had not decomposed like the shorts and the body. There was a hangtag inside the neck with the manufacturing label. That might reveal a date. There were no obvious identifying birthmarks or deformities from which to identify the victim. However, the buttocks were branded inside the shorts with a swastika scarred into the skin. It was unclear whether the branding had been applied pre or post-mortem.

The trunk was not a mass-produced item in the mind of the M.E. It seemed to have been made by hand by a skilled craftsman. The wood was, at first, thought to be mahogany or ironwood, but then a scraping had proved to identify it as Huang Huali, a dense wood used for expensive furniture throughout Southeast Asia. The tightness of the fittings, the incredible seal of the internal chamber after what was still thought to be decades submerged, and the unique species of the wood itself made the M.E. think the trunk had been imported. Beyond that, there were no identifying markings.

M.J. scanned past the photos of the young woman's body,

still malformed by half a century perhaps inside a crate and moved to photos of the trunk. She held it back, her vision now better at arm's length than close, another encroaching sign of middle-age. M.J. was amazed after decades under water, this chest was in such good condition.

"What's that?" Rosie asked, leaning over the coffee table to garner a better look.

Before she could answer, Mr. Williams lowered his glasses a bit on his nose and leaned into the phone. He peered at the photo for a long moment.

"What is it, Mr. Williams?" M.J. asked.

"Sorry to stick my nose in where it don't belong, but it's just that I haven't seen one in so long."

"Seen what, Dad?" Rosie asked.

"A loot knock."

"A what?"

"It's what soldiers in Saigon sent home filled with loot. You know, pearls, jewelry, artwork, war memorabilia. Silk pajamas and such. We all did it."

M.J. leaned in. "What did you call it again? A loot knock?"

"Oh, that's not the right word. That's the closest we could pronounce it. I can't remember how to spell it after all these years, gook talk we called it back then."

"But you think this trunk is Vietnamese?" M.J. insisted, feeling elation on this bit of revelation playing out in front of her.

"Dang sure of that. See, all the Vietnamese gals had these dowry chests made. You know, to hold their stuff when they got married off and went to live with their husband. The chests were real nice with trays built in to hold lots of stuff. That one in the picture is missing the tray, but they were all made from that same kind of wood. Real nice.

"Better than anything I've ever seen in the states, even

when we visited Quaker country. Anyway, we Americans were rich by Vietnamese standards. Even the lowliest private was rich compared to a Vietnamese citizen. We'd buy these loot chests from the woodworkers who sold them to the single gals for their dowry stuff. Truth be told, they used to hold all they owned. Poor as church mice, those girls were, but many of them claimed to be Catholic of all things."

Mr. Williams took a drink of iced tea, not used to talking so much or having what he said be the focus of so much intensity. After a pause, he continued. "I think the Vietnamese word for chest is knock. Something like that. I still have one somewhere if Ellie, God bless her soul, didn't throw it away before she passed. Probably still got my army stuff in it. Anyway, most guys shipped their stuff home in these loot knocks. Technically, they had to be inspected, but everybody was shipping home anything that wasn't nailed down. A bottle of scotch and the shipping clerk would forget to look inside your chest. Ship right to your parents' house."

"And you're positive this is one of those chests, those Vietnamese loot knock chests?" M.J. asked once again.

"Sure as I'm sitting here, Janie girl. Now, where's that cherry pie?"

———

M.J. dropped Riggs at his pickup, which was still at the bridge site under yellow flashing lights. She made sure to call the M.E. before she arrived, speaking on her cell phone to avoid any awkward goodbyes.

Riggs seemed to understand her tactic. He waved one quick one, exiting the Jeep, and strode to his car.

M.J. relayed the story of the loot knock to the M.E. on

duty. It turned out the word for chest in Vietnamese was *ngu'c*, pronounced knock.

The M.E. was effusive in her thanks, and M.J. hung up feeling satisfied with her abilities for the first time in a while. And yet she knew that nothing she'd done today had helped find Paisley Park Jefferson one bit.

M.J. was tired as could be, but she made one more stop on her way home. She drove to Hap's Irish Pub on Erie. The bar was nearly abandoned on a Sunday night after an afternoon football game. Two doors down, a few cars rotated in the parking spaces as young twenty-something's took turns running inside Bangkok Bistro for takeout orders.

Turning off the Jeep, she went inside Haps. Looking around, she was glad to see no cops held court tonight. Most evenings, they would be here, finishing their second shift, as they called it. She appreciated the solitude. The bartender, too young to have been here nearly four years ago, served her without comment.

She sat at the bar and sipped an Irish Coffee. While she drank it, she also drank in the painting above the bar. The painting, nearly four feet long, was a river scene. It was the Ohio in all its ragged glory, dark and dangerous. The Roebling Bridge, lit and blue as a bruise, rose out of the fog and straddled the river, dropping its second leg back into fog on the Kentucky side. The lights of the city were smeary with the rain of a day fading into storm and night. The river reflected the city's dim illuminations, red, white, and yellow against an ominous sky of gray-black clouds.

M.J. remembered many evenings on patrol along the banks of the river with just such a sky, rain pelting down. She took another sip, and when M.J. looked up a second time, she realized the smeary rain across the painting's scenery were hundreds of tiny tears falling from the heavens. The tears were so plentiful and so exacting; the overall image now seemed to have a million brush strokes that M.J. had failed to notice them in her first examination. For a long minute, she let the painting take her away.

Then, M.J. noticed a brass engraved plate on the bottom of the painting's brown-black frame. She pointed at it.

The bartender rose from his reveries at the cash register with a raised eyebrow.

"Hey, barkeep. Help a short girl out. What's the brass plate say?"

The bartender rose onto his tiptoes and leaned close to the brass plate. His voice was scratchy but plain. "It says, *River of Tears James Riggio, 2014.*"

"Thanks," she said. And she thought, *Yes, you, James Riggio, you need to think of yourself as an artist, not a cop. This painting is magnificent. You are a painter. You have the soul of an artist, my friend.*

M.J. studied the painting for the rest of her drink, amazed that someone could take color from a tube and make that happen. She also worried about Riggs painting something so sad as that painting. Because it was all of that, beautiful and devastatingly sad.

M.J. then left the dregs of the drink on the bar, drove home, and slept well for the first time in a week.

RADIo WHTY, CINCINNATI

"Hi, Cincinnati, Phil McCracken until dawn. It's past the time when the good folk have gone to bed. I'm live on WHTY radio.

"We'll go right to the phones. Caller number one, you're on the air."

"Hi, Fred. Can I can call you Fred?"

"You can call me Fred if you want, but my name's Phil."

"Sorry, Fred. Here's my take on all the stuff going down with those kids. See, it's like that black guy on TV who faked his own lynching. You remember, he hired two guys from his TV show to knock him around because he knew the blamestream media would cover it to hell and back. Victimization as hero or something."

"Didn't Chicago drop all those charges?"

"Corruption, Fred. K-o-r-u-p-s-h-u-n!"

"Caller number one, if I understand your theory, you're saying the two women, Paisley's mom and aunt, faked the girl's kidnapping to get favorable press coverage and donated money?"

"Yeah, they're probably multimillionaires after all those GoFundMe websites."

"Did they abduct Klaire Keller, too? Sent the letter before they even took her?"

"Nah, that seems unlikely. But I'm thinking that one's an inside job, too."

"Caller number one, you're suggesting both kidnappings were by the girls' parents? Both of them?"

"I don't know. Maybe some perv took the black girl. Then, the white girl's family decided to cash in. The left must somehow be involved. Socialists. There's all this stuff on social media."

"Next caller, please."

Chapter Twelve

M.J. rose before her alarm at 6:15, did thirty push-ups, showered, ate a quick breakfast, then checked in for messages. The first was from Head of the FBI Blue Ash office, Special Agent Lisa Agate.

The agent gave an update on the interrogation of Nat Lee. Nat Lee had no one to give him an alibi during the time of the abduction on either day. Lee did, as earlier determined, have access to the van when nobody else would have been able to verify or deny his use for both times in question. But the injury to his foot with the pitchfork took place on Sunday, the day prior to the first kidnapping.

The FBI physician consultant estimated that the injury would have caused massive infection within twelve to twenty-four hours. Paisley Park Jefferson disappeared roughly thirty hours after her father's injury, making it unlikely that he was the perpetrator. Also, the fact that he was around 5'10" and slight made him less likely to have been the person who'd thrown her bike into the dumpster.

Agate also said that once the infection had set in, the physician suggested it would likely have been too painful for him to have lifted the bicycle into the trash bin. And his foot's infection was far too advanced for him to be a suspect in Klaire Keller's abduction. The message ended, saying Mr. Lee was now in the hospital receiving intravenous antibiotics to save his foot.

M.J. read between the lines. Although the FBI was not saying so outright, they'd taken Nat Lee off the list of suspects since he could not reasonably be responsible for both crimes, and they were looking for a single perpetrator. However, having him in custody lowered public outcry, so mum was the word. M.J., however, like Rosie, did not believe the two abductions were by a single individual, so she did not take Lee off the list of suspects for Paisley's disappearance. Not just yet.

There was also a long text message to all members of the task force from Agent Messerschmitt. All but thirty of the remaining 196 plates seen near both kidnappings had now been cleared. Seven of those now cleared 166 targets had resulted in arrests for outstanding warrants. That information had been disseminated to the press and to city government.

Monday's newspaper echoed Messerschmitt's words by way of an interview with Mayor Lark. The mayor's talking points included that, while no arrests had been made in the two kidnappings, state and federal investigators had removed seven dangerous felons from the streets. Cincinnatians could feel safer already. The mayor also touted Nat Lee being in custody as a possible culprit in both abductions. The mayor finished his briefing to the press by quoting FBI statistics whiz Messerschmitt. He said the FBI hoped, using the task force's twenty FBI teams, to finish tracking down the last hot leads (the last license plates, though not mentioned specifically, thank goodness) and potentially bringing home the girls by nightfall.

M.J. laughed audibly reading that hooey and refilled her coffee.

M.J. also noted a renewed BoLo sent to all officers for person of interest Willie Grips, the last sexual offender on the list for the Jefferson kidnapping. However, all remaining eleven sexual offenders in proximity to the Keller abduction had been cleared of involvement in either crime. Mentally, M.J. tipped her hat to Detectives Meagers and Staples. It was good police work, she knew, to find eleven people and verify their alibis in a relatively short amount of time. She decided today was a good day to find Willie Grips.

Finally, there was one last update in a separate FBI message; homicide detectives Simmons and Decker had been released from detail to concentrate on two tangential deaths to the investigation, that of Warren "Catfish" Jacoby and that of an unknown young black girl found on Sunday morning by Cincinnati Water Department engineers.

M.J. thought it odd the FBI even listed the cold case death as tangential, but then decided it was because it involved the death of a young black girl with one of the Cincinnati detectives assigned to the Jefferson kidnapping first-on-scene and that the homicide detectives assigned from the Two were also on the task force. Tangential by sense of involvement.

With that, M.J. filled a go-cup and left her house, making sure that the garage door was down as she left Newtown behind.

———

Rosie and M.J. were assigned another six white vans to clear on their shift. Both groaned when they saw their day's assignment. They groaned secondarily when they discovered the six vans on their list were only partial plate matches, meaning the owners may or may not have been in the vicinity of either of the kidnappings.

The two female detectives also noted none of the vans on their list were in the remaining thirty vans seen in both crime vicinities. They were partials seen only at one site. It was, to them, a totally worthless use of two detectives for a ten-hour shift.

Rosie smiled, despite the day's likely futile nature. "Since they've decided to waste our time, you want to waste some of theirs?"

"How so, oh, slacker friend of mine?"

"Go see Paisley's mom and old man Grady? Maybe even watch the Mayor's P.R. spectacle on TV? We can clear these vans in pretty short order."

M.J. nodded. "Yeah, at least our two P.R. missions will make people feel better. The mayor's speech is just to protect his backside."

"Come on," said Rosie. "it's not just about the mayor. It probably makes both His Honor *and* City Attorney Graves feel better."

"True dat," replied M.J.

Rosie laughed and put the unmarked cruiser into gear.

————

After seeing both Monica Jefferson and Grandy Wilson, Rosie and M.J. agreed that Monica looked worse and Grandy looked better. In fact, Grandy was heading home from the hospital in the next day or so. He told them he still was showing some blood in his urine, but his attending physician believed this was the result of filtering from his body cavity after the beating and was not fresh bleeding. Old man Grandy expressed some reluctance at going home.

"I heard you kilt Catfish for me," he said to M.J. "Now, while I appreciate it and while he did, indeed, deserve his comeuppance, I think his boss might flex some muscle to show he still runs the neighborhood. I'm a bit scared."

M.J. raised two fingers. "Firstly, I didn't kill Catfish. He was killed with a two-by-four to the head. Do I look like someone who kills men, even really bad men, by hitting them on the noggin with a two-by-four? And two, we talked to Geroy, and he promised to leave you be. He wants this crime solved as much as we do. He wants the level of heat on the streets around Findlay Market to come down. He won't bother you."

Grandy closed one eye and leaned toward M.J. a bit, rising in his bed. "He also tell you he'd leave Catfish be?"

Rosie jumped in. "What do you say if we arrange for you to go to a convalescent care home until this kidnapping gets solved? A week or so?"

"That'd be real nice." Grandy smiled.

"I'll take care of it," said Rosie.

On their way out, M.J. said, "How you taking care of that one?"

"Daddy's care facility will do it for a week. I spend some time down there providing security at no charge, let their guard go home early some nights. I think they will. Else that or I'm sure you're good for half of his week's stay, right?" Rosie said it with a laugh.

"How much is half?"

"Depending on his meds, maybe fifteen hundred your share."

"Get them to go pro bono. I plan to eat next month," M.J. said, reaching for her phone.

"Who are you calling?"

"Black and Decker. Gonna tell them to land on Geroy

again about old man Grandy. Make sure Geroy's clear that the old fellow is off limits."

———————

Before logging in with dispatch, the two female detectives decided to head to Arnold's for some fries and to watch the mayor's news conference on the TV over the bar.

His Honor Lyle Lark took the microphone on time. Maybe presidents could start daily press conferences a half hour or even an hour late, but local leaders, the mayor knew, could not. He stepped to face the crowd of reporters at exactly 11:00 a.m. as the bar's doors opened.

"Ladies and gentlemen, members of the press, citizens of Cincinnati, I have some good news in the kidnappings of two of our finest kids, Klaire Keller and Paisley Park Jefferson.

"First, while we do not yet have the girls back, we have made much headway in the case. As you know, Nathan Lee, father of Paisley and a suspect in her abduction, is now in custody.

"Due to an injury prior to his arrest, and not one, I may add, that in any way involves city responsibility or liability, local authorities have not yet completed interviews with the suspect. However, the FBI began its interview, and with that new information, is making headway. We do hope the FBI, along with Cincinnati police detectives, will be able to speak with Mr. Lee again and have Paisley back home later today. It is unclear if he is involved with little Miss Keller's disappearance, as well.

"Secondarily, our recent sweep of all potential suspects in the Cincinnati area in these kidnappings has led to the arrest of seven individuals wanted in a variety of crimes from drugs to car theft to spousal abuse. Our citizens can go about their business knowing they are safer today because of the fine work of our city's law enforcers, both federal, city, and state."

M.J. looked at Rosie. Rosie was already laughing, "*Both federal, city, and state*," they said at the same time.

The mayor continued. "As a precaution, the FBI has decided to assign its best and most-prestigious profiler, Kim Rodden. Ms. Rodden, as some of you may know, was involved in the capture of both the Texas chili poisoner case in Fort Worth last year and the Buffalo sniper case in 2013. She's just arrived, and I've asked her to make a statement."

A tall, willowy, black woman of about fifty with shiny silver hair stepped behind the mic. Rodden said she had just arrived and had no information to add, not having had the chance to review the files yet. She stepped aside without further comment.

M.J. and Rosie looked at each other. They laughed again.

Rosie said, "You know why the FBI brought Ms. Rodden, mind reader of the criminal set, up from Atlanta?"

M.J. injected, "As a precaution?"

"Well, yes, that," Rosie said, "but do you know why?"

"I'm sure you'll enlighten me, Detective Coleman," replied M.J., wryly.

"Because the bureau knows the mayor is as full of manure as the cut on Nat Lee's foot. The bureau knows Nat Lee had nothing to do with either his daughter's kidnapping or Klaire Keller's. And when the white van scavenger hunt is concluded in two days, they'll have diddly."

M.J. said, "You say that like you've been involved with the investigation."

Rosie snorted through her nose, "That and I read the FBI Hate Crime Task Force morning briefing."

"I read it, too. Seems somewhat contradictory."

Rosie nodded. "Just a smidge."

"Full speed ahead on the white van search while bringing in a profiler to develop a methodology on a serial kidnapper."

"While Mayor Lark declares Paisley was taken by her father."

"Exactly."

M.J. looked at her watch. "We better hit it. Have to clear six Cincinnatians who have no idea they are people of interest in two kidnappings. And then we need to do some actual police work to find Paisley."

Rosie looked back at the TV. "Wait, the news is going to a second press conference. What's this?"

M.J. sat back down, and the two watched.

———

The channel's weekend anchor, Geoffrey Medford, a black man who'd run unsuccessfully for Mayor himself a decade before, held a mic at the ebenezer-King Senior Center in Clifton. He spoke in a golf channel hushed voice.

"We're here in Clifton at perhaps the epicenter for black Cincinnati's religious thought. In just a moment, Rev. Jasper Townshend, pastor at the Temple Baptist Believers Church, will take to the pulpit to address his congregation and the city about the recent kidnappings and the discovery of a body along Highway 50 east of downtown yesterday morning. Here he is, Reverend Jasper Townshend."

"Good morning to my parishioners, good morning citizens of Cincinnati, and good morning to the members of the press. I appreciate you all coming out. Praise be to God."

Out of the camera's view, a return of "Praise be to God," came from the members of the senior center's faithful.

"I come here today to cry out about a great injustice taking place in our city. It is one that has taken place here for as long as buildings have stood along this alluvial bend in the river. But this injustice is not just in our city, it is throughout our nation, and it is an injustice lasting longer than our nation's history.

"This injustice is the crime of discrimination. It is our nation's great shame, having grown out of slavery and it was witnessed in the taking of a beautiful, little black girl, last week, just one of two kidnappings of two innocent children, one white and one black. It was also witnessed yesterday in the recovery of a black child's murdered body left undiscovered and unreported for decades. And it is witnessed again today with the presence of perhaps 100 FBI agents in our city. It is witnessed because of those FBI agents' singular mission.

"Because, citizens of Cincinnati, did you know that the bulk of agents from the FBI are here to solve the crime of one girl's kidnapping, not both, but one more than another? One because it is a crime based on hate? One based upon skin color?"

M.J. looked over at her partner. "This is not going to go well."

"Shush," was Rosie's reply.

"Yes, Cincinnati, one of these girl's abductions is much more important to the FBI, to the federal government, than the other because it is a crime of hate. It is a crime based upon the child's skin color, hatred of that skin color."

The good reverend, his skin gleaming with perspiration, raised in his fist a document. "I have here in my hand a letter from our mayor, the Honorable Lyle Lark. This letter asks the FBI for additional help under the Hate Crime statutes available to states. Mayor Lark asked the Attorney General of the United States, the number one law enforcement officer in this country, for his assistance, for additional help. To help solve a crime based upon discrimination based upon skin color.

"It is a letter asking the FBI to assign a Hate Crime Task

Force to come to Cincinnati to solve the crime of one of these girl's abduction. Mayor Lark asked the Attorney General to assign the Hate Crime Task Force to come to Cincinnati and apply its considerable resources to getting one child home."

Reverend Jasper Townshend paused. He had everyone in the palm of his hand. "And now, good people of Cincinnati, let me read you one sentence from this document, 'Thus it is in the interest of both the federal government and of the City of Cincinnati to receive federal assistance in solving the disappearance of a resident of Indian Hill, Ohio, eleven-year-old Klaire Keller.' " Reverend Townshend gave it a five-count before adding the words, "the white girl."

Rosie looked at M.J. "That, girlfriend, is a drop-the-mic moment."

Radio WHTY, Cincinnati

"*Good afternoon, Cincinnati. Buster Chops here, a great American and the tri-state's best divorce attorney for men who don't want their exes to get bupkis.*

"*This afternoon, I have a special guest, a man who agreed to come on-air with me at the very last minute as the entire city is enraged, one way or the other, after the dueling press conferences this morning.*

"*In the hour after the headline-making press conferences held by Mayor Lyle Lark and Reverend Jasper Townshend, we have with us the man who determines among those arrested who will be prosecuted in our fair city. If you're listening out there, turn up your radio; this is the interview the whole city will be talking about. With me for the next hour, I have City Attorney Mel Graves. Mr. Graves, thank you for being here.*"

"*Thanks for having me, Buster. I hope I can shed some light on the controversy surrounding the kidnappings of little*
Paisley Park Jefferson and Klaire Keller."

"*First of all, how goes the investigation? Or is it investigations?*"

"*Buster, these two crimes are the most difficult and yet highly investigated of any in my twenty-eight years working with Cincinnati's law enforcers. We've made progress, but until those little girls are home, I, I mean we, won't stop. We won't rest until both little girls are safely home.*

"As city attorney, you're privy to a lot of the machinations in City Hall. What is going on with the mayor's letter to our nation's attorney general? Did Mayor Lark really ask the FBI for Hate Crime assistance in the disappearance of Klaire Keller, but not Paisley Jefferson? The white girl, but not the black girl?

"Buster, I'm sure you know as an attorney yourself that sometimes a sentence can be taken out of context, and although the Reverend Townshend had his facts right..."

"Was the sentence misquoted?"

"No."

"Then, the mayor did ask for more help for the white girl's recovery than for the black girl's?"

"Buster, that's misleading. The ways of the federal budget being what they are, the mayor did what he could for Klaire Keller. I know you know the mayor. Most of the time, we both agree with his policies, and most of the time, you'd agree his heart is in the right place."

"Are you suggesting, city attorney, that his heart is not in the right place in these investigations?"

"I never said that. Nor would I ever say that."

Buster laughed. "But you're sure implying it. What if I told you that WHTY had just obtained a recording of the meeting where the decision to bring in the FBI Hate Crime Task Force was made?"

"I would tell you, Buster, that tape is of a confidential meeting and possession of it might be illegal."

"Well, you're the city attorney. If you plan to issue a subpoena and file charges, I'm on the air until 4:00 this afternoon. Until then, give a listen to this excerpt of that meeting which you attended. I believe we have the mayor's voice here. Listen, if you will and then respond.

The mayor's voice is heard. "Maybe we should just sit on our hands until the girls' bodies show up and then have the FBI clean up after us."

A pause, simultaneously pregnant and impotent, gave WHTY ten seconds of dead air.

"Ladies and gentlemen, we'll be back to see if City Attorney Mel Graves can pick his jaw up off the floor after these commercial messages. This is Buster Chops, back in three minutes."

Chapter Thirteen

Of course, what followed was predictable. Shock and outrage from the black community. Announcements of rallies to show solidarity for people of color. Prayers for the return of Paisley Park Jefferson. Claims that the mayor's words were taken out of context. Rumors the mayor claimed his words were in response to the FBI's initial suggestion to take the investigation completely out of local control. Suggestions that City Attorney Mel Graves himself provided the recording to the radio station in order to sabotage the mayor's reelection campaign.

Graves declared his innocence on that last one, appearing on the evening news, claiming he was clueless how WHTY acquired the recording. Most Cincinnatians agreed only that Graves was clueless.

General animus spilled out on the airways from both the left and right. Predictable.

By late afternoon, a large crowd was forming at Fountain Square, downtown Cincinnati's physical and emotional center. Police barricades blocked traffic two blocks back; the only access to the square was on foot.

Hundreds of chanting protesters continued to arrive. SWAT team members and beat cops pulled from their regular patrols were the first to be put on the barricades to protect local businesses from the mob.

As the crowd surged in number, space became tight in the raised square surrounding the fountain made famous in the opening scene of *WKRP*. The crowd chanted, and black leaders led them in denouncements of the city's leadership and its police.

Someone threw red dye into the fountain's main pool, and soon the Angel of Cincinnati, her raised arms forty-two feet above the roiling mob, became a font of blood, the red tide flowing from her hands as if from a stigmata.

Police Chief Moss Jenkins and First District Head Tobias Meyer arrived on scene in dress blues. It felt dangerous, like the minutes before a hailstorm arrives.

The mainly black crowd shouted, grumbled, and jeered at police.

Mayor Lark called the chief, demanding that the protesters disperse before darkness fell on the city.

Jenkins called in reinforcements from other districts. All detectives on duty were requested to the city center. It was now all-hands-on-deck.

Police Chief Jenkins had called in a mayday. Gas fumes, figuratively at least, were in the air, and everybody was wondering what the spark would be.

Since the detectives were arriving on scene in plainclothes, it was decided they would stay back from the barriers and police in riot gear.

Eventually, Lt. Tobias Meyer decided the three thousand people gathered there had reached critical mass.

The riot-gear attired SWAT members from other districts moved additional stanchions around the square.

Several young black males attempted to climb over the barricades.

Police pushed them back into the crowd forming outside the police barricade. No one wanted to arrest anyone for simply climbing over a black and white sawhorse.

A very dangerous logistical situation was developing with over 3,000 demonstrators inside the stanchions while the SWAT squad encircled the Square. Outside of the SWAT teams, a ring of another two thousand late arrivers gathered, almost doubling the size of the crowd. Two hundred cops and five thousand angry demonstrators with the police at the barricade surrounded.

Black and Decker, Meagers and Staples, and Rosie and M.J. all ended up one block southeast of the square at Fourth and Walnut. each wore a Kevlar vest with *Police* in tall white letters on both front and back. Their shields hung on lanyards around their necks. Their assignment was to stop pedestrians from continuing to clog Fountain Square.

Most of those whom the detectives ordered to reverse their path did so grudgingly. However, several groups slipped away from the detectives, skirted the barricades at the edges, and disappeared by running into the mass of people. There was no stopping them as they merged into the crowd. None of the detectives would have even considered entering the angry mob to arrest a single individual.

Rosie looked at M.J. with one eyebrow raised, "First Amendment can be very difficult at times."

M.J. just nodded. "What's our fallback position should this soiree take a turn for the worse?"

Rosie indicated they would go to the front of Mike and Carol Trotta Fine Clothing and Strauss Tobacco and the large plate glass windows in front of the two businesses. "We'll protect that glass as best we can." She looked at the block-long plates of glass for the bank across the street. "Don't think we can save all that."

Four blocks away, on the west side of Fountain Square, Police Chief Jenkins pondered his next step very carefully. Two incidents from the city's collective memory weighed heavily upon his mind. The first was the Cincinnati riots of 2001, four nights of civil disobedience in the over-the-Rhine neighborhoods of District One.

The rioting began after nineteen-year-old Timothy Thomas, an unarmed black man, was shot and killed by a Cincinnati Police Department patrolman during an attempt to arrest Thomas for traffic tickets.

Several other recent incidents of alleged police brutality and racial profiling, including thirteen deaths, had tempers already at the boiling point. Protests erupted, and police were pelted with rocks and other objects each night. Many businesses experienced broken windows, other vandalism and looting before a city-imposed curfew effectively ended the four days and nights of unrest. The riot was the largest act of civil disobedience in the United States since the 1992 Los Angeles Rodney King riots.

Damages were estimated at $3.6 million to private businesses and another $2 million to city property. Later, the cost was even higher as the black community boycotted downtown businesses to the tune of nearly $400 million in lost revenue. Downtown became a ghost town, as those businesses which did rebuild went bankrupt or moved away. Violent crime increased in the downtown area for several years thereafter.

It took Cincinnati's core ten years to recover, but recover it had. over-the-Rhine was now the darling hot spot of young millennials looking for condos and city dwellers using motorized scooters. From Central Parkway north on Vine and surrounding streets, as well, gentrification was rapidly taking place. Buildings were being renovated; housing restaurants, bars, and stores opened as quickly as remodeling was finished.

Chief of Police Moss Jenkins was aware all that development was on the line. He was also aware of one other crucial bit of Cincinnati history, The Who concert of 1979.

The British band The Who was perhaps the biggest name on the American concert circuit in 1979 when they arrived for a sold-out show in Cincinnati. The show was scheduled for December 3, 1979, at Riverfront Coliseum. Promoters sold over 18,000 tickets to the show, of which nearly 15,000 were General Admission. When a local radio station incorrectly announced the doors to the hall would open at 3:00 p.m., 7,000 fans crowded around the unopened doors before 5:00. The hall did not open the doors until 7:00 for the 8:00 p.m. show. And then only two single doors leading into a concourse were opened.

All 7,000 ticketholders attempted to enter through this tiny aperture. A late sound check by the band enticed the bottle-necked crowd and they surged forward, thinking the band had taken the stage. In the stampede, eleven people were trampled to death and twenty-six more were seriously injured. While the band played on, unaware of the tragedy, Cincinnati's image, open seating at venues, and The Who's reputation all took serious hits. To this day, the city is very touchy about crowds, mob mentality, and human stampedes.

Chief of Police Moss Jenkins, his long Appalachian face in a state of perpetual sadness, was aware of all those things and yet made a controversial decision. He made the decision to disperse the crowd.

As directed by Chief Jenkins, the head of SWAT used a bullhorn to order the demonstrators to leave the square.

The crowd ignored the directive, many unable to hear it in the melee. Others yelled alternatively, "Pray for Paisley, Pigs

Suck, and F the FBI." Fists pumped, and the fountain continued to bleed.

The chief now ordered the firefighters who had arrived and were stationed outside the second layer of protesters to be on the ready to use firehoses as water cannons to disperse the mob. No authorization came from the fire captain or the mayor, not yet, but the firefighters gripped the nozzles at the ready. The outer ring of demonstrators milled nervously. Again, bullhorn announcements harangued the three thousand inside the barricades, and the two thousand outside, to move.

None but a few, mainly women and children, moved to the barricades and were allowed to exit.

Then, Jenkins, inexplicably, told SWAT to fire smoke canisters into the mob, but these were not tear gas, but instead were just smoke bombs with the desired effect to be a final warning. They worked too effectively.

The crowd bolted for the four street exits, but police still had the barricades in the way. Police on the line were surprised and unprepared for the smoke offensive. Perhaps 500 people stampeded into the stanchions like so many horses escaping a corral in a western movie.

Many belly-flopped over the barricades, just as many fell and many were trampled. Others kept their feet and ran to escape the roiling smoke which rose in great fogs.

Police began an earnest battle to pull people to their feet at the toppled stanchion line.

Fistfights began between cops and young black men. The black and white striped barricades either fell, were shoved to the side, or were lowered by well-meaning police, but the damage was done. A full-blown riot ensued. Billy clubs were drawn, and rocks brought to the square by instigators began flying into the line of uniformed police from both directions.

The police were fighting demonstrators from inside and outside the barrier. SWAT shields raised to the air reported with the sound of thrown items, including beer cans, empty half pints of whisky and even some placards with the words, *Bring Paisley Home Safely* painted on them. Many rocks from outside the square found their mark, hitting police in the back as they simultaneously battled and assisted the panicked demonstrators.

The six detectives moved to the side of the street as the uniformed cops fell back along the east side, using Walnut Street one block east as their first line of resistance. They were mingled among the crowd in the pullback, greatly outnumbered. What those uniformed policemen were resisting was nothing more than the surge of thousands of bodies seeking an exit to the mayhem.

After seeing officers in wild fights with demonstrators, Chief Jenkins himself panicked and ordered tear gas be shot into the square and in the streets surrounding the square. Tear gas canisters landed like hissing snake heads.

The crowd broke into a run, heading north toward over-the-Rhine, south toward the river and further both east and west along Fifth. It was a total nightmare. There were fights and arrests. M.J. saw numerous individuals injured, pants torn with bloody knees, a few with blood dripping from cuts around the eyebrows or ears as if they had been the recipients of billy clubs or perhaps a rock thrown at police but hitting them instead.

Rosie and M.J. helped one woman carrying a seven-year-old girl in her arms.

All four gagged and coughed as they planted themselves out of the tear gas at the entrance of the Mercantile Building's revolving door.

Far above, looking down from the eleventh floor, the thin,

gray-haired library director thanked the speaker, a poet from Nepal, as he saw the tear gas clouds along Walnut.

The thinning crowd far below staggered away, choking and vomiting. Many limped while others, impotent with anger, attempted to fight back against the remaining police in the dispersing mob.

The gaunt director looked down upon the madness below him and said, "I believe tonight's Q&A will be lengthened by a half hour. Would anyone like something to drink?" And with that, the 300 patrons a hundred feet above the smoke remained beyond the fray, at least physically.

Rosie and M.J. sat on the sidewalk in disbelief of the madness playing out before their eyes.

But in less than an hour, the streets were empty of all but the refuse of the event. Only police and those being held in custody remained. All except every TV truck in the city. News reporters with eyes rimmed red from tear gas provided on-the-scene reporting.

The City of Cincinnati had, yet again, a public relations nightmare on its collective, blood-stained hands. The fountain beyond was a perfect metaphor.

The riot made national news by the next morning. Television anchors gave out final tallies like box scores. One hundred and eleven were arrested, nineteen injured and hospitalized, nearly two hundred more injured and treated, fourteen police injured and released, and two fatalities; Jezemiah Jones, age nineteen, and Emir Azullah, age fifty-three. Jones died of a fractured skull, while the coroner believed Azullah died of a heart attack during the melee.

Radio WHTY, Cincinnati

"Hey, it's Roland A. Long with you 'til midnight here on WHTY, and if you've not heard, Cincinnati just about went up in flames tonight as race riots marred our city center. According to early eyewitnesses, police attempted to deter impending violence by firing tear gas into a crowd of nearly 5,000 angry demonstrators. The demonstrators were there to express their unhappiness with police progress in the abductions of Klaire Keller and Paisley Park Jefferson, two preteen Cincinnati girls.

"After the tear gas, demonstrators got out of control, injuring many, and damaging property. Two hundred were hurt, including police and civilians, taken to area hospitals. Those totals are likely to continue to climb as violence continues to flare up around the city.

"Two residents of Cincinnati, Jezemiah Jones, age nineteen, and Emir Azullah, age fifty-three, both died at Fountain Square this evening. Jones is allegedly said to have died from injuries from a policeman's riot baton. Mr. Azullah died of a heart attack.

"Mr. Jones, according to police records, has an extensive arrest record. In a WHTY exclusive, I have on the phone right now his uncle, Edmund Jones. Mr. Jones is a resident of Norwood and is a retired administrator

for Bells' Insurance Group. Mr. Jones, thanks for agreeing to come on the air with us."

"Thanks for having me, Roland, but it's a sad night for our family and for the city of Cincinnati."

"Indeed, it is, Edmund. What can you tell us about your nephew? I understand he'd had some run-ins with the law."

"That's true, but he was a good, young man. Not a thug. Not at all. Just had a tough start to life and was finally finding his way. Had just finished his degree and started selling cars. First real job."

"Then, you think he had turned his life around, Edmund?"

"No, it was never like that. Jez maybe stumbled a few times out of the gate, but he never hurt nobody. Not ever. He was one fine young man. I can't understand how he could end up dying in such a senseless way. Could I just read you what he wrote and read at his grandmother's funeral? He was raised by his Granny Renee. Jezemiah thought the world of her. Could I read it, Roland?"

"Sure. Let's hear from the young man himself."

" 'Granny,' he wrote, 'you're the only one cared about me after my mom and dad left me with you. I ain't never had no one love me but you. You always made sure I was fed, and warm, no matter how tough things got. From age four when I landed on your doorstep until you took your last breath, you made sure I had clean clothes for school. Shoes with good soles. Even made sure I had a little money in my pocket for candy or ice cream.

" 'You made me go to church 'til I got too old to be able to get up on Sunday mornings. Even then, you made sure I had church people in my life. You'd have them over and then fix such good food I'd just have to sit down to Sunday dinner, and you'd talk about church and your communion in the faith. I never felt I left the church because living with you I never really did. I just wanted to watch football, but you wouldn't have it. I respect that. It was your house and your TV. They was rules in your house, and I obeyed them, even when I didn't like them much.

" 'I don't think I'd even be alive now if it wasn't for you. So now that you're gone, I figure I got to up and be a man and live the life you wanted

me to. I guess I got to pay it forward since now I can't pay you back. So somewhere and somehow, I gonna have to take care of someone and let them feel the love you made me feel. I love you, Granny Renee. Thanks for never giving up on me. You were such a little woman, but you sure left big shoes to fill.'

"That's his testimony at his Granny Renee's funeral just two weeks ago. It's just a tragedy he never got the chance to pay it forward. Don't you agree, Roland?"

"Edmund, maybe you reading that, maybe you reading his testimony will find the right ears? What do you think, Edmund?"

"Can't really think too much right now, Roland. Heart's too full of tears."

Chapter Fourteen

All police at the riot scene who were now coming off the duty were requested to attend an 11:00 p.m. statement by Mayor Lark at the District Two headquarters. Rosie suggested that before then; it was just after nine when the two got to her home and showered off the noxious tear gas. Both had tear stains down their cheeks. Their eyes burned. Their hair and clothes smelled of the acrid smoke which had enveloped them.

On their way, M.J.'s phone rang.

It was Riggs. "Madison, it's me. Were you in all that stuff downtown?"

M.J. laughed, albeit somewhat morosely. "Yeah, I take it you weren't?"

"Nah, got tied up in a fatality accident on I-71. You okay?"

"Not really. Got gassed pretty good. My eyes are in pretty bad shape. Rosie's, too."

"That's terrible. The mayor's been on every radio and TV station in the city claiming Chief Jenkins overstepped his authority and panicked, causing the riot." He paused. "You two off shift now? You want me to bring you some beef stew?

I've been cooking it in a crockpot all day. Soup, grilled cheese?"

"No thanks, Riggs. That's nice of you, though. We have a briefing from His Honor the Mayor at eleven, and then Lt. Meyer wants a rundown on the task force operation with all detectives working the two kidnappings. It'll be another late one."

"Tobias Meyer wants to meet with all the detectives working the case? Black and Decker, and Meagers and Staples? Those four don't even report to him. Weird."

"Yeah, that's kind of what we thought. Hey, let me go. I'll catch up with you tomorrow. I'll give you a call sometime in the afternoon."

Riggs said he was glad she was okay.

She hung up.

Rosie looked over. "You have a sweetie."

"Shut up and keep your bloodshot eyes on the road."

———

Rosie showered and changed in her own room while M.J. used Rosie's daughter, Marie's, room. Marie was staying with her father since Rosie was working doubles during the kidnapping investigation.

After both were dressed, M.J. in one of Marie's blouses, the two grabbed bologna sandwiches at the kitchen counter.

Rosie munched a bite and turned on the television. Since the riot downtown, there had been several cars torched in various parts of the city. At least two buildings in over-the-Rhine, both vacant, had fallen victim to arson in the past hour. There had also been one drive-by shooting and a four-teen-year-old boy was dead near Winton Woods High School.

"We don't find this girl soon, this city might explode," Rosie said, taking a sip of milk.

M.J., her mouth still full, took a moment to reply. "The whole city could go up in flames with one more bonehead move by either the Mayor or Chief Jenkins."

"You ain't kiddin'. Might take the entire Ohio River to put it out," agreed Rosie.

"River of tears," said M.J. softly, setting her crust to the side of her plate.

"What was that?" Rosie asked.

"Nothing," M.J. replied, taking her last swallow of milk. "Just something I saw. We better hit it. We got a special invite from our boss."

"Wonder what Tobias wants," Rosie echoed, turning off the TV.

———

Mayor Lyle Lark was in the squad room speaking to Lt. Tobias Meyer at the head of the room.

Capt. Delores Knowles, head of the D-2 Precinct detectives, stood at the podium reviewing her notes.

Chief Moss Jenkins was nowhere to be seen and was conspicuous by his absence.

The mayor waved his arms around for order, but none of the seventy cops in the room paid him much mind.

Capt. Knowles, however, raised her head just so and cleared her throat.

The room silenced.

The mayor looked at her with newfound respect. He stepped up to the podium.

"To the men and women of District One and Two and any other police who joined us at the barricades tonight, the city of Cincinnati thanks you profusely. Things became difficult tonight, and you did a great job at minimizing the injury to both citizens and officers, and preventing further damage to both federal, city, and private property."

M.J. mouthed, "*Both* federal, city, and private property," at Rosie and saw her partner grin.

The mayor finished his thought, "I thank those you of you on the front lines tonight with sincere gratitude." He paused to peer around the room. "Fourteen officers were injured tonight. Thankfully, none of them seriously. Over 200 of Cincinnati's citizens were also hurt tonight, and at last count nineteen have been hospitalized.

"Two residents of the Queen City died tonight. One by a heart attack; the other's injury was a skull fracture, and because of our involvement in the police action not necessarily the death blow, we've asked the Butler County Sheriff Department to investigate. There must be complete transparency in this investigation, so we will allow an independent investigator to proceed.

"I have decided the decision course by Chief Moss Jenkins in the moments leading up to the violence will come under full review. I have asked Capt. Delores Knowles to oversee that review. Chief Jenkins has been asked to take leave of duty until we determine what precipitated the events tonight, leading to the injuries, damage to property and the loss of life. I'll turn it over to Capt. Knowles."

Knowles, a big-boned woman with intense green eyes, was in her dress blues. Her cheek bones were wide and strong. Her lips were red, and her neck showed streaks of flush. It was evident that she was nervous, but those who knew thought her up to the task ahead. Her eyes leveled into the men and women who directed their attention back to her.

"Thank you, Mayor Lark. Everyone, tonight was a rough

one, and the eyes of the nation are on us. The citizens we represent and the rest of America wants to know what went wrong out there tonight, so we need to know exactly what happened. Each of you will have get to me an incident report by 17:00 hours tomorrow before the end of your next shift. Tell me exactly what you did, what you saw, and be as precise as possible.

"Now, for those of you on the line, here is the timeline. According to dispatch tracking, SWAT arrived on the scene precisely at 5:17 p.m. Barricades were in place by 5:39. The first announcement to disperse was at 6:17. Smoke grenades were launched at 6:23 with tear gas following at 6:29. Those event times are verified. Please use those as parameters in your incident reports. After those reports have been compiled and collated, I'll get back to you for the next step. Any of you who arrested protesters tonight, we're going to attempt to plea most of those out as simply civil disobedience. No jail time, minimal fines. We want this conflict minimized in the press as soon as we can. Show up on time for your arraignments tomorrow. City attorneys will have the papers ready to go."

There was some rumbling in the room.

Knowles raised her eyebrows, raised her palm, and then flattened it.

The room again fell silent.

"Do not misunderstand. I'm not asking for leniency for anyone who was throwing bricks or other debris at officers this evening, or vandalizing, fighting, or, as I gather in two cases, looting. Those we prosecute to the full extent of our cases."

A room of blue uniformed officers nodded in agreement.

Knowles nodded back. "I know you're tired and some of you pretty beat up, so I want to get you out of here. But are there any questions before I turn the floor back to the mayor?"

A woman's voice out of the room's recesses said, "What time was sunset?"

Knowles looked back to Tobias Meyer.

"6:29," he said. "The same time the tear gas was fired."

———

The mayor, once again, took the podium. "And we have another announcement. Which is why I've asked Lt. Meyer to be here. After a meeting at the city offices earlier this afternoon, we've also decided that the FBI's Hate Crime Task Force is too centered on simply searching for…"

"White vans, perhaps?" said Detective Decker.

"White girls, perhaps?" Simmons called almost as an echo.

The room erupted in laughter.

Tobias Meyer allowed himself a tiny smile, nodding.

The mayor frowned at the interruption, pausing, but then continued. "Yes, they seem to believe if they interview each of the 3,000 owners of those 3,000 white vans they will find the kidnapper or kidnappers. Capt. Knowles and Lt. Meyer, Police Chief Moss Jenkins, City Attorney Mel Graves, and I all concur that now past the one-week mark in the disappearance of Paisley Park Jefferson, and with very little in the way of solid leads that the city needs to muster its resources into a parallel investigation.

"I have asked Lt. Tobias Meyer to head that investigation. He will be taking over the city's search for these two little girls immediately. I've asked Lt. Meyer here tonight to brief you on what we have and how we plan to proceed. Tobias, go ahead."

There was polite clapping as Lt. Meyer took to the podium. He was taller than the mayor, but not much. He was also attired in dress blues for tonight's meeting and his promotion of sorts. Meyer stood and faced the room. His face was deep red. This was a man known for his intellect and his decision-making, but not for his public speaking.

"Thank you, Mayor Lark. Officers, detectives, Capt. Knowles. As you know, we've chased down roughly two thousand of the three thousand vans of interest over the last four days or so since the FBI began directing the investigation into these two kidnappings. The Cincinnati Police Department is not at all sure that the FBI is on the right track.

"We do have a witness to an unidentified white van on the street within a block of the Paisley Park Jefferson's abduction. Her bike was found the next day one block from the van's approximate location. However, we have no solid evidence that this van's driver was involved in the kidnapping. And we have no connection of a van to the Klaire Keller abduction whatsoever. Hence, we're going to go a different path.

"Detectives are going to knock on the door of every registered sex offender in the city. Local suburban sheriff departments and law enforcement have promised to do the same in our surrounding counties. Kentucky police will be joining us in this sweep. So far, we have cleared all the S.R.O.s near the Jefferson abduction and all those within a three-mile radius of the Keller abduction, as well.

"But Cincinnati is a big city with several thousand potential suspects not yet interviewed. We intend to speak with them all. This is a big city, but it is still a relatively short car ride from one side to the other. A perp could snatch a kid from anywhere in the city and be home within the hour. Police in uniform will be expected to help in this process.

"Starting tomorrow, each unit on the street will get three names of registered sex offenders to interview during your shifts. It makes for a busy day because you will also be responsible for your regular dispatch calls and don't forget your incident report due to Capt. Knowles by 5:00 p.m. tomorrow.

"Now, Detectives Madison Monroe and Rosie Coleman, please, address the squad room and let everyone know what we have so far."

Both Rosie and M.J. were startled by the request, but they knew this was a big moment for their boss, and they wanted to do right by Tobias. Rosie recovered quicker, an athlete's reactions, and stepped forward.

"Paisley Park Jefferson, black, age ten, taken last Monday night from near Findlay Market. Not missed for three hours, not reported to police until after midnight. Her bike was discovered in a dumpster the following day. Sweep of the street turned up an interview with a shut-in. Old woman described a white van on the street, engine running, driver inside, during the half hour immediately prior to the disappearance. No plates.

"Most likely suspect was the father; he doesn't live with the family and works as a day laborer at the horse track. He has since been apprehended. When we picked him up, he had a foot infection, quite a severe one which is now septic. We have been unable to interview him, although the FBI task force did have an initial interview that added little to our understanding of the crime. The man is unconscious for now and in serious condition at Bethesda Hospital under police guard."

Rosie nodded to her partner.

M.J. stepped to the fore. "The other prime person of interest is a registered sex offender named Willie Grips, a convicted rapist. He did a dime, was paroled and was holding a job, but he has been in the wind since before the kidnapping. Grips was reporting to his job prior to the disappearance, but the simultaneous leaving of his registered domicile and the girl's abduction makes him our prime target right now."

Tobias Meyer nodded, minutely, in approval to both detectives. They had availed themselves well on his behalf. Meyer motioned to Meagers and Staples to step to the front. "Detective David Meagers, can you please update us on your investigation into the Klaire Keller abduction?"

Meagers glanced quickly over at M.J. but then moved his eyes back toward the mayor's flat stare. "We don't have much, to be honest. Girl was taken behind Quiffen's Deli off observatory, which is ironic because nobody observed *anything*. Obviously, the note saying Klaire Keller would be returned when we found the Jefferson girl was a big clue, but there were no fingerprints on the notes or envelopes. The paper and print were of a generic, completely unremarkable stock and ink.

"Both parents check clean. Father was at his office when the girl went missing. The mother had the little girl. Restaurant staff remembers both little girls being inside for lunch. Security camera at the front door shows the mother and the two girls going in and coming out. Klaire goes out of sight around the corner when the younger girl falls. That's the last we see of Klaire. Poof, she's just gone.

"We did sweeps of the neighborhood, interviewed locals, including business owners and residents. We checked both stoplight cameras and business security cameras. All to no avail. Those sweeps were conducted Thursday night and Friday.

"By the end of Saturday, Detective Staples and I, along with the first two shifts of officers from District Two, cleared all resident R.S.O.'s and verified either their alibis or interviewed them for involvement. There were thirty S.O.s within three square miles of the abduction site. None of those sexual offenders seemed likely for the crime. Those interviews and our notes have been passed on to the FBI task force. They haven't found any more useful information in those interviews than we did initially.

"We spent the last two days clearing white vans, which was

quite frustrating, as the white van lead had no correlation to the Keller kidnapping. The van was seen only in the vicinity of the Jefferson abduction. It is the FBI which has theorized that the kidnappings are related, and that theory is only based on historical statistical analysis. We've no evidence of that connection. We've eliminated lots of potential suspects but still have no specific persons of interest."

As the meeting ended and the mayor and his contingent left by the side door, Lt. Meyer, now head of detectives, it seemed, steered the three teams of detectives into an interview room. He closed the door.

"Look, I know you're all tired. It's going on midnight, but for Paisley Park Jefferson, it's the end of day eight. That's a bad sign. The white van boondoggle the FBI put us through with their statistician seems to have wasted three days. It might have cost Paisley her life. And because of the unlikelihood of two kidnappings in such close chronology, the FBI's linking of the two cases may have cost Klaire Keller her life as well. I don't know.

"I do know I'm taking a different tack. While uniform patrols will attempt to track down every single registered and every even suspected sex offender in the city and try to link or eliminate them from two windows of opportunities, I am going to have you four," he pointed at Meagers, Staples, Simmons, and Decker, "check out the new FBI list of potential of domestic terrorists. Domestic terrorists with an anti-white agenda."

The six detectives all reacted with varying levels of disbelief.

Lt. Tobias Meyer gave them a smile. "Don't scoff until we have the list. I've been promised a finalized listing by dawn tomorrow. I want all of you to head home and get some shuteye. Then, report to my office at 7:00 a.m. We'll look at the FBI's list of anti-white domestic terrorists at that time."

"What about us?" asked M.J.

Lt. Meyer's answer was to the group. "Detectives Coleman and Monroe will work on the Jefferson case, primarily to find Willie Grips." He looked back at the two subordinates. "Be back here in the morning with the rest of them to review that list. We'll go from there."

The two women nodded in agreement.

"By the way, more bad news for the Jeffersons," Meyer said. "Nathan Lee, the girl's father, lost his foot to infection today. He'll be lucky to pull through. His doctors have placed him in a medically induced coma right now. We're not going to be interviewing him anytime soon. If he's responsible for his daughter's disappearance, she's in big trouble."

Chapter Fifteen

Lt. Tobias Meyer's eyes looked yellow with fatigue, like he had contracted jaundice with his new responsibilities. He spoke to the six detectives in front of his desk. It was just becoming light at 7:00 a.m.

"The contents of that list are confidential. FBI brass has not released it to the agents in the field, nor have we. Only you six, me, the mayor's office, and the city attorney have seen it." Tobias Meyer said the words, lifting his eyes from the page to the fatigued faces in front of him.

"I can see why," said Rosie, reviewing the document in front of her. "I think two members of the city council might be surprised the Federal Bureau of Investigation sees them as hating white people."

Tobias Meyer seemed to not have the energy to reply. He simply raised an eyebrow at her and Rosie fell silent.

The list consisted of roughly twenty names, but M.J. only recognized five. She knew the two city council members' names but thought their inclusion on a list of potential kidnappers was ludicrous. Perhaps even more ridiculous, the

Reverend Jasper Townshend's name appeared on the list. The next name on the list after Townshend's was of interest, Geroy Hooper.

"Hey, why's Geroy on the hate list, Boss?" M.J. asked. "If he's on it, then I would say we'd have to put every banger from here to Indy on the list."

Detective Simmons, toothpick in the corner of his mouth, flashed a smile. "Seems like Geroy just hates everybody, wouldn't you say?"

Decker laughed, agreeing.

Lt. Meyer raised a hand. "Look, we know some of these people. And we know which ones did not kidnap those girls. But they're who we have to start our interviews. There are about ten names on the list of people in the community who've posted hate speech directed at whites on social media pages."

"Ten or ten thousand?"

Meyer nodded. "We mean serious hate speech advocating violence. Those we definitely want to talk to. The rest of them just have ties to the community and might have connections to someone who wishes to conduct violence against whites as a race. The bureau added them as places to start. Have to peel the onion. Get them to tell us what they know." He paused. "And who they know."

Decker laughed again. "Don't expect Geroy to do much talkin' to us, seeing as we like him for the murder of Warren 'Catfish' Jacoby. Suspects in murder cases don't do a lot of talking to detectives."

M.J. looked to Decker and Simmons, "What you got on that, anyway?"

Simmons nodded. "Stay after. We catch you up. Got some questions for you, anyhow."

Tobias Meyer indicated the meeting is over, but Rosie

stopped him. "Wait, here's a name on the list I know. You all should know it. Lonnie Truesdale, the wide receiver. Pro Bowl. Super Bowl."

Simmons looked down at the list again. "The L.A. guy. Retired last year, didn't he?"

Decker scoffed. "He's retired until a wide receiver somewhere blows a knee, and he signs mid-year for $5 mil or something. Truesdale's still got it."

"What's he doing on the list?" M.J. asked.

Lt. Meyer shrugged. "Posted some Black Panther Party stuff on his website. He's always been political. Fights the league on regulations all the time. Takes a knee at games. Won't cut his 'fro. Trouble."

Simmons rolled the toothpick across his bottom lip. "Trouble will probably get a ten-million-dollar paycheck to sign before the trade deadline."

Rosie laughed. "Gotta use the talents the Lord gives ya."

"You think he took either one of those girls?" M.J. asked.

Rosie laughed hard. "I think Lonnie Truesdale has to fight girls off with a stick. No need to kidnap any."

Meyer waved them out of his office. "I'll leave it to your three teams to split up the work. Fill me in at the end of each day. Remember, this list does not go public. We've got enough civil unrest in the black community without them knowing about a hate-the-white-man list. Get out there and find those girls."

———

Meagers and Staples, who didn't really know Lt. Meyer, kept silent during the meeting; they agreed to take the bottom seven names on the list. They excused themselves and took off.

Rosie watched them go. "You think those two are out of sorts about something?"

M.J. shrugged. "They just see the investigation going through the District One Crime Squad and Tobias. They don't know him. They know he likes us. They know Black and Decker are stars. It puts them on the outside. Nobody likes playing third fiddle."

Decker slapped M.J. on the shoulder, asking, "I hear you call us stars?"

"More like pimples on the department's butt, don't you think, Rosie?"

Simmons laughed. "Okay, okay, M.J., you win the comic act. Look, our caseload is made up of six cases counting the task force, three of them cold cases, and you," he pointed at M.J., "are mixed up in three of them. Let's catch you up what we got in the homicides. See if you can help us."

The black man sat at a vacant desk in the bullpen. A couple of cops from the first shift were milling about. When they saw the famous Black and Decker detective team, a couple came over to say hello. Most gave them wide berth.

M.J. sat across the aisle from him. "How can I help?" Simmons took a black notebook from his jacket pocket. "We got your business card in the victim Jacoby's mouth at the scene. We got a confidential informant saying the word on the street was Geroy Hooper's crew was offering a free fix to anyone with one of your cards."

"And Rosie and I had just canvassed the neighborhood the day before," M.J. replied. "Lots of my cards to be had for a free shot of junk. That's how Geroy got one of my cards."

Decker sat down on the desk. "Right, but that's not enough to charge. We've got no prints. No eyewitnesses, no snitches, and we have camera surveillance at Panera Bread showing Geroy making time with a couple of coeds."

Rosie pursed her lips as she leaned on the window sill. "You really have nothing to connect him? No phone call evidence?"

"Nah, other than we know he did it. At least we're sure Geroy ordered it."

M.J. smacked her palm on the table. "For now, he's got away with it. Called me to brag about it."

"For now," Simmons said. "But dealers like Geroy get sloppy. His customers are junkies. Junkies get busted. They talk. It takes time, though. We'll also twist his soldiers in the field. Roust them out, hassle them. The next step is to get Vice involved. Have them tighten the screws on users in the area. Local dealers who get their supply from Geroy. Then, we offer deals to anyone who talks."

M.J. only nodded. "Yeah, I know how it works. Don't have to like it."

Decker looked at her. "Don't give your cell phone number to killers, M.J. That's not smart."

M.J. stared up from the desk at him but didn't speak.

But Rosie did. "Don't you mansplain it to us, okay, Decker? Our clear rate is the best in the city."

"Not on murders," Simmons said, flatly.

Both women stared at the two men before them. Decker didn't smile, but he did stand, showing he was not backing off his words.

"What about on the girl in the trunk?" M.J. was unhappy but stayed professional.

Simmons worked his toothpick. "You know the score. Two million runaways every year. Ninety percent of them are found, but still, lots of missing girls out there. National Center for Missing and Exploited Children says there were 424,000 missing kids this year. A little more than half are females. While blacks are twelve percent of the population, they are twenty percent of the runaways. One in seven because of sexual assault or sexual abuse."

Decker said, "We got one percent of the missing kids from this area. More if you count the area from Indy to Columbus to Lexington to Louisville with Cincinnati as the hub. That makes it two percent. That would be 4,000 girls a year from here who run away and aren't immediately found."

"How many of them are black?" Rosie asked.

"Twenty percent," Simmons replied. "That makes 800 a year."

"And how long ago do we think this girl's body was put in the trunk?" M.J. asked.

"Oh, at least thirty years ago. She's wearing a fully polyester T-shirt from a local company called Velva Sheen. Went out of business in the early '90s. Big place at one time, over off Erie Ave. Had outlet stores around town. We've been able to verify the shirt model because the poly and the label didn't break down like a cotton shirt would have. We know when the shirt was made. Shirt was discontinued and sold off at the outlet stores in the mid-'70s."

"But you can't tell how old the shirt was when the girl was killed and put in the trunk." M.J. said.

"Right, but we do know the trunk was out beyond the willow trees in the retaining pond. The pond was built in the 1930s with WPA money during the Great Depression. It was, however, drained and scraped clean during the Nixon Administration in 1975 when US 50 was extended to Athens. Kind of an add-on from when they built the interstate under Eisenhower and Kennedy.

"The guys with the Park Service and with the Water Department think the trunk could not slide or shift down to the center of the pool, not to the deepest part if it was filled with sediment. The trunk had to go in the water shortly after to slide where it did with no sediment under the trunk. It was sitting on concrete."

M.J. said, "So the shirt is from 1975 and the opportunity for the trunk to move into location in the retaining pond after being pushed off the bridge is from right about then, too."

Decker nodded. "And Rosie, your dad's explanation of the trunk's likely origin also works with that date. Most G.I.s returning from the Vietnam War were home by 1974. The last came home in 1975. A lot of guys shipped stuff home in lockers, the stuff they didn't want their C.O.s to see."

"Then the timeline looks pretty good. We've got G.I.s coming back from the war in 1974 or '75. They are bringing this kind of trunk home with them. The shirt the girl was found wearing was sold in the area in outlet stores in 1975. Plus, the retaining pond was cleaned and cleared, allowing the trunk, once submerged, to drift to deeper waters. Again around 1975," M.J. said.

Simmons nodded.

"Can you get a list of the missing black girls around age twelve to fourteen from the surrounding years?" Rosie inquired.

Decker shrugged. "As best we can. If we take 1974 to 1976 for missing girls, that's about 2,500 missing girls."

"Cut out those in '74 for now," M.J. said. "It'll reduce the numbers, and if the retaining pond wasn't cleaned until '75, the missing girls from before '75 seem unlikely matches. Plus, the shirt is a clear indicator of 1975."

Decker raised his eyebrow. "Who's mansplaining now?"

"Hey, if you got the brass ones," Rosie said and laughed.

Simmons laughed then nodded at M.J. "I see what you're saying. Only look at girls missing from after the retaining pond was scraped and the shirt was manufactured. Cuts the search parameters in half."

"Right."

"And then search the list by social security numbers; ought to be able to find most of them in the IRS list of taxpayers."

"Hell," Decker laughed. "They'd be eligible to be in AARP. That age group would be over fifty now."

'Unless some murderer killed her before she had a chance to grow up," M.J. said.

The other three nodded.

Decker said, "Okay, we'll do that. Get some techs to run the names, the social security numbers, and then see how many are still on the list. Might be able to identify our victim."

"There'll be some who've stayed off the grid, but not many," said Simmons.

"It's a plan," Decker said. "We'll keep you in the loop since you were first on scene."

M.J. nodded. "Thanks. What now?"

Decker smiled. "We'll take the first six on the hate-whitey list. That leaves you two ladies number seven through number twelve. However, maybe you'd like to interview Geroy with us? He's on the FBI list at number ten, so he's yours, but since we like him for Catfish's death, we're keeping pretty close tabs on him."

"Lead the way," Rosie said, and the four detectives started their day.

Chapter Sixteen

A wind blew the leaves down streets like cards on a poker table. The gray clouds were heavy, the air damp with mist.

The four detectives, in two unmarked sedans, saw Geroy Hooker before they even arrived at the Yukon Community Apartments. He jogged across Ziegler Park in a running suit, hood up to the drizzle. Geroy's face was barely visible to them at this distance, but something in his movements made him immediately identifiable to M.J.

She watched him run, his black rain jacket glistening with moisture. M.J. viewed him with disdain. He had the free-and-easy lope of youth. Geroy seemed to glide as he ran while his two subordinates chugged along behind. It felt wrong that he should float like an athlete as he ran. Dealers who pushed death into their neighborhoods should not be filled with such ease of spirit.

The detectives stepped to the curb as Geroy slowed in the street, stopping right in front of them.

Geroy pulled his hood back, smiling. "Been expecting

you," he said. "Come on in." Geroy left them standing, never breaking stride after his words.

The four followed, somewhat flummoxed by his words. How could he have known they were coming?

Inside, the two sentries, bulges of firearms on their hips, nodded to the police detectives as they entered.

Geroy barked at the two big men on the couch, one looking at his phone, the other dozing, "Put a move on, gentlemen. We got company." Geroy looked to the first, a man, whose thin face belied heavy shoulders packed into a Syracuse University long sleeve tee. "Jalin, make some coffee. I'm chilled after being out in that crap."

Geroy turned and faced M.J., ignoring the other three with her. "Nice to see you again, Detective Monroe. You'll have to excuse me. I'm soaked clean through. Gonna take a quick hot shower. I'll be right back."

Then before any of them could ask how Geroy knew of their eminent arrival, he disappeared down the hall and into a bedroom.

Decker shrugged, and the four took it as a sign they would wait.

Jalin, as it turned out, made good coffee.

True to his word, Geroy Hooper, his hair now slicked back with gel, clad in a velour navy running outfit and slippers, returned to the living room within minutes. He shooed the other big man, still on his phone, from the couch. He motioned the four detectives to join him.

Jalin brought a cup of joe to Geroy, offering to heat up the detectives' cups. only

Simmons nodded.

"I'd ask what brought you out today, but I think I already know," said Geroy, smiling.

"And how's that?" asked Decker, his thinning hair matted

from the rain outside. He ran a hand back through it, his hand coming away wet.

"How did I know? A little bird told me. And by that, I mean I got a call this morning from someone else on your hater's list."

"What list is that?" Rosie asked, bluffing.

"Your anti-white folk list. Let us not talk falsely, now. The hour is getting late," Geroy laughed at his Dylan reference.

Simmons smiled, softly.

Geroy acknowledged the dark-skinned detective. He said to Simmons, "You don't look like a man who B.S.s much. Maybe could walk the walk."

"Been known to," Simmons said, reaching into his shirt pocket for a toothpick. "How'd you hear about the list? We just got it, not an hour ago. Figured your tender butt still be asleep so we could roll you out, all groggy like."

Geroy smiled. "Always been a morning person, even after partying, maybe especially so. But today did get a call while I was still in bed. Told me I was going to get a visit for hating white people." He laughed. "You hate white people, Detective Simmons?"

"Nah," said Simmons. "Ain't got time to hate folk. Too busy arresting drug dealers," Simmons, replied, his toothpick twirling across his teeth.

"That's funny," Geroy said, playing along. "You got that homicide solved yet?"

Simmons seemed to ponder things for a second. "Oh, you mean Catfish. Decker and I solve lots of homicides. Wasn't sure you meant the one you committed for a second there."

It was M.J.'s turn to laugh.

Geroy turned his face to her, not liking being the butt of someone's joke.

Finally, the heroin dealer said, "Yeah, Catfish. Poor

Catfish. We all miss him. Sure would give us closure if you could catch whoever did it."

Simmons smiled. "No arrests yet. We know who ordered the hit. Think maybe the one who swung the two-by-four makes a pretty good cup of coffee." He looked to Jalin, leaning against the kitchen counter.

Geroy laughed. "You hear that, Jalin? Detective Simmons here thinks you good with lumber? Maybe got a future in baseball."

"I don't see him as having a future at all," said Decker.

That made the other bigger man, the one on his phone, laugh deep within his belly. His belly and afro shook in unison.

"Who that?" Simmons asked.

Geroy nodded. "That be King Walsh."

Rosie said without a trace of irony, "What's he king of?"

Geroy shook his head. "His momma named him King after the good reverend Martin Luther. Thought maybe the name connection would keep him on the path of nonviolent positive change."

"How's that working out?" Rosie replied.

"Not so good."

King's laugh shook his belly and afro again.

Geroy set his coffee mug down on the table. "Let's get serious for a minute. You really think I took either one of those little girls? There be cops *25/7* on my streets? When we all know cops on the street don't help me? Bad for business, don't you know."

M.J spoke for the first time. "The list isn't about who might have actually abducted the girls. It's about who knows what's what in the community. Who's got ears everywhere. Community Leaders, movers, shakers."

"Dealers," Decker added, flatly.

Geroy, who had smiled briefly at M.J., shot Decker a

frown. "Now, why'd you have to go and spoil a compliment coming from your co-worker, Det. Decker?"

M.J. also shot Decker a look to let her lead. "Back to it. Have you heard anything on the street that might help us find those girls, to get them home, let the cops get back to their donuts, get things back to normal?"

"I helped you find the black girl's daddy. Now, I hear he lost a foot while in police custody. Nasty business that. Makes me wonder about helping you again."

Rosie nodded in agreement. "His employer gonna pay dearly for that. City will help Nat Lee find good representation. Mr. Lee was already injured and his foot badly infected when we found him."

"Glad to hear wasn't you chopped off his foot. However, Nat Lee is a poor man. Won't be poor no more. Loss of a foot good as a lottery ticket, I'd think, to a man like that. Living off the grid. Literally shoveling shit for the man. He'll be movin' uptown now."

M.J. nodded, empathetically. "Yeah, we're still looking for another man. Willie Grips. You hear anything about him?"

The banger leaned his chair back and yawned with an exaggerated movement.

Simmons took out his toothpick and pointed it at Geroy. "You can nap once we go, but now you answer Det. Monroe's question. You hear anything about Willie Grips?"

Geroy was suddenly serious. "You leave if I give you something I heard?"

Simmons nodded. "For now. Gonna have to come back and talk to you about Catfish one of these days."

Geroy nodded. "Schedule it with my attorney. I'll meet you at his office. Not here."

Simmons nodded. "What you got?"

Geroy leaned in. "You ever hear about a D.J. team back in the day, man and woman, Willie Rocket and Betty Won't?"

Rosie smiled. "Yeah, I heard of those two," she said, "I snuck out of my momma's house with some girlfriends one time when I was about nineteen to go see those two put down some beats. What do they have to do with Willie Grips?"

"He's the one and only Willie Rocket. Least was before he went down for a dime for rape. That's his stage name."

M.J. nodded. "How come we didn't have this?" she asked, looking to Black and Decker.

"Long time ago, I guess," Simmons said. "I heard of them, too. Never checked 'em out. My clubbing days were back in Toledo. Settled down before I got to Cincinnati."

"You know where Willie staying, Geroy?"

"Yeah, I do. You know the football player from Cali? Lonnie Truesdale?"

M.J. felt lightning hit her with his words. "Heard of him, sure."

Geroy set the hook. "Willie's his personal music guy now. D.J.s for him. Truesdale has lots of parties. Willie kind of a hanger-on. Heard he keeps the music hip. Takes care of the dogs. Lonnie got some bad dogs. I don't like dogs. Don't see the attraction."

"You've seen him?" M.J. said. "You've seen Willie Grips there?"

Geroy nodded. "Yeah, I been to party out to Indian Hill at Truesdale's place. Very fancy. Very fine-lookin' women. Didn't know that Willie was *your* Willie 'til last night."

M.J. said, "Thanks."

"Anything to get you all out of here. And just for the record, I don't hate white people. They tend to have deeper pockets. Consumer spending is my thing. Cash money and return on investment, don't you know? And for the record, my fav color of people is green, 'kay?"

———

The four detectives decided arriving at Lon Truesdale's estate in Indian Hill to arrest Willie Grips was best done with a warrant. They headed back to District One Headquarters and informed Lt. Meyer. He called the FBI. The two law enforcement agencies decided it was best to issue a local warrant for the arrest of Grips on a parole violation. They also applied and received a search warrant of the premises for the girls and/or items belonging to the girls based upon a confidential informant (Geroy Hooper) and his information.

The judge was amenable to their dual requests and agreed information from Geroy Hooper sufficient for warrants for the arrest and search. The warrants would be issued within the hour. The four detectives ate sandwiches and waited impatiently for their paperwork.

At 11:45, a shots-fired call came out over city-wide dispatch. A Springdale police officer on an I-75 traffic stop was fired upon by a passing vehicle. Springdale, a community perhaps ten miles to the north of downtown, financed its department primarily with revenue brought in by ticketing speeding motorists.

The young officer was standing at the passenger door of the nineteen-year-old male driver when three shots rang out. The first hit the door, the second went high and buzzed over the Mustang's roof like an angry bee and the third penetrated the windshield, hitting the rearview mirror assembly. The mirrored glass splintered into a million tiny shards, and several of them penetrated the young driver's face and neck. Believing he had been shot, the driver called out in pain and fear.

The police officer hit the deck, but did not return fire. The speed limit was sixty-five miles an hour, and the seven vehicles along the interstate's three lanes disappeared around a curve in mere seconds.

The officer was not sure which car had fired on him. His subsequent distress call brought more than twenty cruisers, but a review of his dash-cam did not assist in determining which car was responsible for the attack.

A call by the media for assistance brought no helpful leads. Most of the tips were racist claims the shots came from black gang members. Most referenced the riot from the night before as the cause of the shots fired although there was no known connection between the two events.

Lt. Meyer walked in the room with the warrant as the four detectives watched the bullpen TV. The volume was down on the tube, and they were listening to the police scanner for additional info.

"Go get Grips," Meyer said. "I really hope you find the girls at Truesdale's. This city is a powder keg. We need to solve this thing."

Chapter Seventeen

The rain had cleared. Standing next to their black SUVs, four FBI agents waited in dark trench coats. As M.J., Rosie, Simmons, and Decker descended District One HQ's front steps, the doors on the second SUV opened, and Special Agent Lisa Agate and Senior Special Agent Neal Saunders stepped out to the sidewalk.

Saunders nodded at the detectives as they approached. "Good job with the lead on Grips. This football player, Truesdale, being on the agitator list seems more than a coincidence. Maybe we can wrap this one up today."

Rosie nodded back.

No one spoke until Simmons waved the warrant. "Let's roll," he said.

The four vehicles rolled up I-71 to the beltway, I-275. Indian Hill was only three exits to the east but seemed a different world from the city and its small yards, urban alleys, and pedestrian-filled sidewalks. Here, it was difficult to see homes from the winding blacktopped lanes. Indian Hill's average home price was nearly $1.5 million, and the average property size was somewhere over six acres.

Only a few homes per square mile dotted the landscape. Lonnie Truesdale's estate was bigger and more expensive than the average. The four vehicles pulled up to the gate, rang the buzzer, and a security guard answered over a speaker.

Agent Agate, driving the lead vehicle, let the guard know that it was FBI and they had a warrant for entry. The gate swung open after a minutes' delay.

Rosie looked at her partner. "The delay was the guard informing Truesdale."

"And maybe Willie Grips," M.J. added.

"Lost the element of surprise."

"Yep."

The driveway was long and ended in a brick piazza. It surrounded a fountain which sprayed water from the two statues, one of a dolphin and the second of a football player with a football snared in one extended hand.

They exited the vehicles. Decker looked upon the statue. "Must have been built when he played for Miami."

Simmons, toothpick in place, nodded. "Just glad that statue ain't peeing into the fountain like some do."

Rosie laughed, "Too cold for that football player to drop his britches today," she said but got her game face back on before Saunders and Agate joined them.

"It's a city warrant," Saunders said, "so you four should be the ones going in. Agent Agate and the other agents will patrol the perimeter of the estate on foot. I will wait here."

Saunders waved his hand.

The four agents in reserve and Agent Agate spread out across the lush lawn as Rosie rang the bell.

A big black man with a heavy beard opened the door just a

crack. Two Rottweilers pulled at chain leashes in his big paw. "Yeah?"

As the dogs snarled, Rosie said firmly, "Cincinnati Police. We have a warrant for entry. Please, secure the two dogs in a separate room. We need to see Mr. Truesdale."

The big man nodded, unsurprised. He must have heard the call from the security guard to already have the leashes on the dogs so quickly. "Be a second." He closed the door.

The detectives could hear the dogs' barking fading into the distance. In perhaps another minute, the door opened. "Come on in. Lonnie's in the gym."

"Thank you. What is your name, sir?" M.J. asked as Simmons and Decker followed them into the foyer, creating space between them as they went.

"Kermit."

"First name or last?"

The big man smiled. "Last."

"Nice to meet you, Mr. Kermit. I'm Detective Madison Jane Monroe." She introduced the other three.

Kermit nodded. "Benjamin Kermit. People call me Big Ben."

M.J. examined the swollen shoulders and thick wrists coming out of his long-sleeved shirt. "Fits you," she said.

Big Ben Kermit smiled wanly and said, "This way."

While Big Ben Kermit might have looked the part of professional football player, Lonnie Truesdale looked the part of movie star. He was a trim six-foot man, his skin the color of buffed copper. His hair was close-cropped and his eyes hazel. He was dressed in all white; a silk tee, loose-flowing sweatpants, and old school K-Swiss low tops. He held a Fiji water bottle and tipped it toward the entering detectives.

He stood by a Peloton bicycle machine. He took a sip, set the water bottle down, and ran a white towel across his brow and his neck. " 'Morning, detectives. What brings you out to hassle a black man in the suburbs this morning? Already bothered everyone in the 'hood?"

Detective Simmons did the introductions this time. "We're here to serve two warrants for this residence. The first is for the arrest of Mr. Willie Grips. Sources have told us he can be found here. We have a second warrant to search the premises for both Paisley Park Jefferson and Klaire Keller, the two girls recently abducted. We are also warranted to look for items belonging to the two girls."

Truesdale looked genuinely shocked. It took him a moment to speak. "First, who in the world is Willie Grips? And second, why would you think I have anything to do with the kidnapping of those two girls?"

Simmons shook his head. "Not here to answer your questions, Mr. Truesdale. Where can we find Mr. Grips?"

"I don't know who that is."

Rosie stepped in. "You might know him as Willie Rocket."

"My D.J.?"

"Yes, sir."

Truesdale nodded to Kermit. "Go get Willie. He should be spraying out the kennels about now."

M.J. and Decker followed Kermit and left the room.

Truesdale was still wide-eyed. "And why are you searching my home for the girls? That's kind of crazy."

Simmons spoke again. "Again, sir, we're not here to answer questions. We do have a few."

Truesdale's face sparked a bit of anger. "But it's not a two-way street."

Rosie replied. "No, sir. We're asking the questions, Mr. Truesdale, sir."

"Okay, go ahead and shoot," he said, laughing. "I wouldn't say that to white officers, you understand."

"Do you not like white people, Mr. Truesdale?"

He sneered at Simmons' inquiry. "Only quarterbacks."

Simmons did not react. "Do you have any idea where the two missing girls are?"

"No."

"Are they here on this estate?"

"No."

"Have you seen either or know either?"

"No, of course not."

"Did you assist Mr. Grips in abducting the girls?"

"What? Why do you think he abducted the girls?"

"He's a convicted rapist," Rosie added to the interrogation.

Truesdale picked up the water. "Willie paid his debt to society. You cops should leave him alone."

Just then, M.J. and Decker returned with Willie Grips. Kermit was no longer with them. Grips looked younger than his mugshot, even though it was taken long ago. He wore black sweats and an orange Cincinnati football jersey. His face was lean, and he was clean-shaven. His hair was receding a bit. He wore wide-rimmed glass, round with yellow lenses. It gave him an edge, but not a dangerous one. It gave him an artistic look, like a sculptor or poet.

Simmons took the warrant from his vest pocket. "We have a warrant for your arrest, Mr. Grips."

"On what charge?" The words came from Lonnie Truesdale.

Simmons did not turn his head from Grips, but Decker answered in a low monotone. "Parole violation. Mr. Grips needed to inform his parole office and the court if he planned to change job or residence. Those changes must be approved. He did not do so and is in violation of his parole."

"That's incorrect, detective," said Truesdale. "Before I hired Willie last month, I had my attorney send a letter informing the parole office of his change of employment and his move to this address. We even sent it certified mail. I have the stub in my office. We gave it thirty days after the date of our informing the office before he moved. We never heard back."

Truesdale nodded at Simmons. "In fact, I insist we go to my office, so I can get you the registered mail stub and a copy of the letter."

The four detectives followed Truesdale down the hard woods of his hallway to an office. He made a move to his desk drawer.

Simmons stopped him. "No. Stop. Let me get it if I may. We would prefer to keep your hands in sight."

Truesdale stared back at Simmons with distaste. "Sure, right there in the tray. It's a receipt for the registered letter. I got a confirming email of its arrival, too, if you trust me to open my email account. The letter is right there in the tray. Can I get it?"

M.J. nodded, and Truesdale shuffled some papers until he found the sheet of paper he was looking for. He handed it to her. It looked genuine.

Simmons drew the receipt from the desk drawer. He handed it to Decker, but M.J. took it. "I'll take the receipt and letter to Agent Agate. I'll have her check." M.J. left the room.

Simmons looked at Truesdale and then to Willie Grips. "That might take a bit. And we've asked the Indian Hill Police Department, the Rangers, to join us here in about fifteen minutes to assist with the search of the grounds and the premises. We'll find anything you have hidden. I guarantee that. Anything you want to tell us about right now? I mean, before the Rangers get here. They find something, you'll get charged for sure."

Willie said, his voice that of a radio personality, full and rich, "Ain't did nothing, ain't got nothing to hide."

Rosie looked to Truesdale, "Any drugs?"

Truesdale laughed. "I'm high on life. Professional athlete. I pee in a cup regularly. Amazingly, a study showed black players get tested more often than white ones, ones who take a knee even more often."

Simmons smiled, rolling the toothpick from one side to the other. "I don't have trouble with your politics. Don't care one way or the other. I just trying to find two girls 'fore this city burns itself down."

"The Uncle Tom clothes fit okay?" Willie Grips asked with sarcasm.

Simmons and Rosie both cocked their head to the side. Anger flickered in their eyes.

"Willie, shut up. Don't speak at all again until my attorney is here. Big Ben has called by now. Just keep still," Truesdale barked at his employee.

Outside, Agate had called Lt. Tobias Meyer. He called the parole office. Indeed, they had received a registered letter from Truesdale's attorney. Unfortunately, no one bothered to look up the parolee's system number on the correspondence. All they had seen was the name Willie Rocket. They had no parolee on the books by that name, so they had forwarded the letter to City Attorney Mel Graves's office because the attorney-in-question's office was on the top floor of Carew Tower, one of Cincinnati's most prestigious addresses. No one followed up, and the city attorney's office hadn't replied.

Agate called Grave's office next.

Mel Graves took the call forwarded by the receptionist. "Graves here."

Agate explained the situation.

Graves swore under his breath. "I'll check on the letter. I've not seen or heard of it. In the meantime, have the detectives bring Willie Grips in for questioning. At the very least, we have a technical violation since he is supposed to get approval prior to a move. Have them bring him in."

"Truesdale has already lawyered him up, Mr. Graves. If you're bringing him in on a clerical error, it will end up on the evening news. Claims of harassment. Probably not what we need."

"He's a convicted rapist. Public sentiment will run toward law and order. That's the kind of fight we like. Just have the detectives bring him in. Also, execute the search warrant. You find the girls or evidence regarding their disappearance and everything's hunky dory." Graves hung up.

Agate looked at M.J. "Graves got the letter more than a month ago. But the request said 'Rocket,' not 'Grips'. Didn't connect the name even though the case file number was correct. Clerical error. City attorney says arrest Grips and take him downtown."

M.J. raised an eyebrow. "And conduct the search based upon the supposition that our warrant for Willie Grips was not issued in error?"

Agent Agate nodded, "I thought of that, too, but my understanding is that the city attorney wants you to tear the place apart in case the girls are there."

"And fruit of the poison tree if it turns out our warrant for Grips is no good."

Agent Agate again nodded. "You'll lose the evidence if you find something inside. But it might be a chance to bring the girls home. Gotta take it."

M.J. nodded, grimly, and headed back inside.

Chapter Eighteen

Two hours later, M.J. swore under her breath at her desk in the District One precinct. It was complete chaos. Willie Grips was in Interview one with his attorney. Grips's attorney was contesting the issuance of the warrant since it was derived from a clerical error on a notice of employment and address change.

The city attorney was claiming the error was the plaintiff's fault because of the wrong name. The attorney countered the office of Parole and Detention was at fault because the parolee's correct case number was on the letter and it had been addressed and delivered to Willie's parole officer. In addition, the city did not reply within the thirty-day legal deadline. Writs were now before a judge. Nothing was budging until after that ruling.

Lonnie Truesdale was now in custody in Interview Two. He also was refusing to speak to police until after the Grips's ruling came down from the judge. The search warrant of the Truesdale estate turned up something quite interesting. The mansion had a basement, most of it finished into a giant man-cave for parties.

However, police found a storage area behind that party room, and inside the storage area was a concealed secondary room. It was a safe room with a solid steel door which could be locked both inside and out.

The windowless, subterranean room contained a shower and toilet. In the main room, two mattresses lay on the floor. Blankets were tossed carelessly over the uncovered mattresses. A dresser in the room contained a variety of clothing for young girls of approximately the same size and age of the two missing girls. Various dolls and books for a correspondingly aged juvenile female were also found on site.

When the Indian Hill Rangers discovered the girl's clothing in the safe room, Truesdale demanded his attorney. He refused to speak further.

Big Ben Kermit, Truesdale's man servant, likewise asked for council and was taken into custody with his employer.

Currently, Big Ben Kermit was in Interview Three with his own representation. He, too, was not speaking. He, too, was awaiting the judge's ruling. What a mess.

M.J. rose from her desk and went to see Tobias Meyer. She knocked and opened his door a crack. The lieutenant lowered his brow, nodding, as she entered his office. Agents Agate and Saunders were parked in the two chairs in front of his desk.

Meyer preempted her first words. "It's going to be at least another hour."

M.J. nodded. "Okay if I take the time to drive over to Forensics?"

Meyer said, "Sure, a team from there is over processing the safe room at the Truesdale estate, but whatever you can do is better than sitting on your hands here. What are you thinking?"

"Unrelated. Working another case."

Tobias nodded, glumly.

M.J. left Meyer's office then told Rosie she was off the board for an hour. She drove north into Corryville and to the coroner's office and Hamilton County Crime Lab. Inside, she found Melinda Yakushima, a lab tech she knew and trusted.

Melinda greeted her warmly, and the two walked back to one of the crime analysis labs, where the investigator was piecing together a car's body parts. Most were bent and damaged. It was difficult to tell the twisted metal had once been a vehicle.

"Looking for paint matches from a second vehicle. Impaired driver claimed he was run off the road. Not much left from the car to examine," said Yakushima with a shrug. She took a bite of cinnamon roll and washed it down with water from a bottle. "This, I imagine, is not a social call. I'm kind of surprised you're here. The word on the street is District One is so full of FBI right now you can't swing a set of handcuffs without hitting a fed. I figured you'd be in the middle of it."

"I am," M.J. said, smiling with no humor. "But everyone's lawyered up for now, and until we get a ruling, we can't question anyone. I'm here about the girl in the trunk."

Yakushima's eyebrows raised noticeably. "I thought that was Black and Decker's case. It's in District Two, anyway. What's your interest?"

"I was first on scene. Happened to be right by my house. What can you tell me?"

"I worked on it. Assigned it, I think, because of my Asian heritage, you know, because of the chest. Although Japanese and Vietnamese are about as connected as Irish and Italian."

"And?"

"I can't tell you enough to help much. Girl was in her early teens, just starting puberty. We can tell that because of some hip growth in the pelvis. She was maybe thirteen. Cause of death was a broken neck. Violently broken. But the girl had numerous other injuries, maybe like the perp tortured her. She had a stab wound in the shoulder, some contusions so severe that the blood loss into the tissues was still visible after all these years."

"He tortured her and then killed her quickly?"

"Seems so."

"Was she sexually violated?"

"Her hymen was in place. But we can't rule out other sexual violations."

"Anything else?"

"You mean besides the Nazi branding of the swastika?"

"Yeah, what about that?"

———

"NIBRS, the National Incident Based Report System, doesn't have anything exactly like it. Branding of a swastika on the hip of a young black female victim, not locally or even nationally, but I expanded our search and did find a few interesting cases I thought I'd bring to Simmons and Decker tomorrow."

"And those are?"

"You know we think this crime took place around 1975, right?"

M.J. nodded. "I'm familiar with the proposed timeline."

"We have a young African-American woman who escaped from a perpetrator in 1981. She was drugged at a party. She awoke to incredible pain. A white man had her pants off and was branding her with what law enforcers later described as a connected HH."

"HH?"

"Heil Hitler was the believed reference in the police reports at the time."

"'Where did this take place?"

"Near here. A river party. Big kegger back in the day. Halfway from Cincinnati to Maysville, this side of Ripley. Out in the sticks."

"What did the girl say?"

"Just that she was drunk. A guy asked her if she wanted to ride in his boat. She couldn't describe him other than he was about thirty, white, had a boat. She didn't remember enough to describe the boat. She passed out and awoke with this monster branding her backside. She jumped up in pain, the guy fell backwards with the iron in his hand and she ran off barefoot to the main road. Perp didn't follow. Instead, he ran to his boat and left."

"Can I see the report?"

"I'll send you the same information I'm sending Simmons and Decker."

"Okay, anything else?"

"One more case might be of note," Yakushima said, haltingly.

"What's that?"

"Body found along the road near Louisville near I-71 along the Ohio in 1989. Young black girl, really young. only six."

"Connection other than race?"

"Another branding. This time, it was an 88."

M.J. wrinkled her brow. "I don't see the relevance."

"88 is another way to say HH. eighth letter of the alphabet twice. The 88 is most commonly used in tattoos by white supremacists in prison. It definitely has white prison gang connections."

"To summarize, we have three brandings of three black

195

girls with white supremacist connotations over a fourteen-year time span, ending in 1989. All three have Cincinnati as a nexus point. All three near the Ohio River. One found in a trunk with potentially Vietnam vet connections above the Ohio, the second along the Ohio River perhaps fifty miles upriver from the girl we just found, the third in Louisville found along the road. How far from the river?

"Less than 100 meters."

"But now nothing for twenty-five years."

"No, nothing."

"How was the six-year-old killed?"

"Broken neck. Again, very traumatically. Tremendous overkill. Twisting. You don't need me to go into specifics."

"Same M.O."

"Yes."

"Any injuries to the girl who escaped?"

"No, other than some scrapings from a knife along her clavicle."

"Torture."

"Yeah."

"No sexual violation?" M.J. asked.

"None, but she surprised him by waking up."

"How old was this girl?"

"Nineteen at the time."

"Maybe he wasn't used to drugging adults. Didn't use enough for her size and weight."

"Maybe he had only drugged kids before that. Got the dosage wrong."

"Maybe," added M.J., "he figured it out and we've never found another body."

"Maybe," said Yakushima, "he learned the HH and the 88 from time incarcerated. The prison gang association supplanting his earlier racist markings."

"Lot of maybes," said M.J.

"Lot of violated girls' lives destroyed."

M.J. nodded her agreement as her phone rang. It was Rosie. The judge was issuing a ruling within the next half hour. "I've gotta go. Thanks. Keep me in the loop."

Yakushima nodded but was already back to scraping the car body for paint chips.

Chapter Nineteen

Back at Precinct One, Rosie was waiting for M.J. at the door. "Graves just got here, and there were some long faces headed into Tobias's office."

M.J. nodded and they walked back to the bullpen. It was just as Agate had predicted. The judge ruled the city did not complete due diligence in researching Grips's attorney's letter. While the name was wrong, the parolee case number was correct, and the city had not taken any action in any manner in thirty-two days. The city was thus at fault for the confusion. Thus, Willie Grips could not be held on violating his parole. Therefore, Grips did not have to answer any questions. He was a free man.

Similarly, the judge ruled since Willie Grips had not violated his parole, the search warrant for his employer's residence was illegal and voided. Truesdale's estate was off limits. Any evidence gathered on site must either be returned or destroyed. None would be admissible in a court of law.

Graves's face was gray as he left the precinct by the side door. Heads down, the city attorney passed Grips, Kermit,

Truesdale, and their lawyers as they left the interrogation rooms and descended the front steps to the waiting reporters.

Attorneys for Truesdale and Kermit carried evidence bags down the long steps to the sidewalk theater below.

M.J. watched them go. She didn't understand Grips and Truesdale's involvement in the kidnappings but had a gut feeling the city's incompetence had let people with knowledge of the crime walk free.

Had the girls earlier been in that safe room? Had Truesdale known the cops were coming just like Geroy Hooper earlier that day? Who leaked the list? And had that leak given Truesdale enough time to move the girls to another location? M.J. was suddenly mad. If that was true, then those girls were taken for political reasons. She went to find Rosie, who had retreated into the women officer's locker for a moment to gather herself after the news. M.J. wasn't sure whether Rosie was angry right now or was crying in a stall. She wouldn't blame her for either.

But the day's events weren't over. Just as M.J. crossed the bullpen to find Rosie, another shooting came over dispatch, this one in District One, in the parking garage next to Music Hall.

Rosie heard the alert, joined M.J., and the two ran to their vehicle.

They raced the fifteen blocks to the parking garage. Things were in a frenzy.

Not five minutes earlier, a white man wearing a bandana, baseball hat, and brown coveralls stepped from cover in the subterranean parking structure at 12th and Race. He'd fired on several people on the P3 lower level. One man was down and deceased. Several others were fired upon, but none hit. The active shooter, after expending at least one magazine of shots, escaped up the stairs. Perhaps fifty people were in the garage on the three floors when the violence occurred. Nearly all fled the structure by either the Race or Vine side, although a few departed by the 12th Street stairs. None escaped by the 13th Street stairs or elevator where the shooter had last been seen.

Police were there within two minutes. People at street level could hear but not see what occurred. Police blocked the exit at the 13th Street stairs and elevator. They found no one. Nobody left by the parking garage exit used by the shooter, and no one saw the shooter after he went into the stairwell.

Most of those escaping the violence exited to the street and ran to safety in the stores and restaurants along Vine to the east. Some pedestrians on the street wore headphones and expressed shock when police began to usher them to safety, oblivious to the violent act which had occurred below them.

Rosie and M.J. assisted in securing the area. Teams of six uniformed cops and later SWAT cleared the parking structure, car-by-car, row-by-row, floor-by-floor. They found nothing, except that security cameras in the 13th Street stairwells and elevators had been disabled by black spray paint. Investigators found nothing of the shooter, except, of course, his wreckage, one body and more than a dozen cars with damage needing to be processed. Talbert Washington, a mathematics teacher from Walnut Hills High School, was dead with two bullets in his chest.

The evening news said Talbert Washington, a graduate of Miami University, had been awarded Walnut Hill's Teacher of the Year Award in the past month. Radio reports later said winning the award was one of the highlights of the young man's life. The young woman he lived with cried for her loss on the evening broadcasts and said the couple was expecting their first child. The city mourned the senseless death.

M.J. and Rosie worked the scene for two hours. The two walked to their squad car just after 6:00, and neither could remember a worse day on the job. Both women felt at low ebb and decided to leave things behind for the night. They parted back at the station at their cars with a long hug. Both felt heartsick.

Before she'd even started her car, M.J.'s phone rang. It was Riggs.

M.J. couldn't muster a bit of emotion. The truth was she had steeled herself not to cry into the phone.

"Bad day, huh?" Riggs voice sounded comforting as if knowing her feelings.

"Oh, Riggs, the absolute worst. Maybe my worst day on the force." M.J. knew word had already spread through all 1,400 cops in the city about District One today.

"I'm sorry, Maddy. How about some dinner?"

She felt an ounce of empathy in his words. No one had ever called her Maddy. No one but her father, and he'd been gone now for eight years.

She leaned her head back into the headrest. "Riggs, that's nice of you to ask, but I'm going to see Greg tonight."

"Who's Greg?"

"My husband."

"Oh, Christ, I'm sorry, Of course, and you've been so busy."

"Don't apologize. You haven't ever met him. I need to go. I've been working so many hours I haven't been up to the hospital in over a week. I just need to get away. I need some quiet time. Maybe being together will comfort both of us."

"Sure, I totally understand."

"Don't stop asking me to dinner, okay?"

He laughed into the phone. "Wild horses couldn't keep me from asking."

"I don't think that's quite how the song goes," she said.

———

Greg's face was thinner than eight days ago when she'd last been there. But he was freshly shaven, his hair just clipped, and he smelled of soap. The nurses took good care of him. M.J. made a mental note to send flowers with a thank-you note to the nursing team.

M.J. spent two hours alone with her husband. She spent most of the time with the door shut and the lights turned down. She held Greg's hand and noticed it was now thin and bony, unlike the beefy, strong calloused fingers she'd remembered. He was frail now. An infection of any kind would probably take his life. There with his hands in hers in the dark, she knelt and prayed. She prayed for his soul to be delivered above. She prayed for guidance in finding the two little girls and she prayed for the soul of the young teacher, Talbert Washington, who'd senselessly lost his life today. She prayed for his family. She prayed for his unborn child. She prayed for the young man's companion who'd cried so on the evening broadcasts having found out that the man she loved was dead. M.J. reflected perhaps the woman had been spared what she had not, this long waiting for death's relief.

M.J. shook her head clear of thoughts like that and began to pray anew. She prayed for the students in Talbert's classrooms who would never receive his instruction again. She prayed for the police of Cincinnati, their leadership, and of course for Rosie. And after her long litany of prayers for others, M.J. wept. The tears were all her own.

———

Outside the hospital, M.J. felt tired but somewhat purged of the horrors of the day. She realized she was famished and resolved she should try to eat more than once a day. She looked at her watch. It was nearly 9:00. Time to grab some takeout and get some sleep.

As she neared her Jeep in the parking lot, a limousine approached. A window was down. A face and a hand protruded.

M.J. felt for the weapon on her hip but paused as she recognized the face. It was Lonnie Truesdale.

The vehicle slowed to a stop with his window even with her. M.J. peered in and could see Big Ben Kermit at the wheel.

Truesdale nodded to her.

"Mr. Truesdale, you don't seem the type to be a stalker. How'd you find me?"

"Sorry about that. I decided I needed to know a little more about the other team. I hired a private detective. Had him get me a scouting report on you. He told me about your husband. About the accident. Terrible thing. I'm truly sorry. But after the P.I. told me about your husband, I decided you'd probably be here. After the kind of day you had, I mean. I played a hunch. And here you are."

M.J. nodded. "Okay, you win the amateur sleuth of the day award, but why track me down? You haven't had a terrific day either."

Truesdale opened the door and stepped to the curb. He was dressed this time in jeans, a black sweater, and a skull cap. The boots he was wearing exaggerated how much taller he was than her. The top of his head seemed at least a foot above her.

"I needed to tell you something." His voice was serious and low.

"That being?"

"My safe room. The stuff you found. It ain't what y'all think."

"You mean, you're telling me you aren't involved in the kidnappings?"

"Yeah, I'm telling you that. The mattresses on the floor. Remember the tornado warning we got up that way a month or so ago? Well, I ain't scared of much, but tornados ain't my thing. Grew up in Cali. Earthquakes, okay? Tornados, no way. Happened at three in the morning. Had Big Ben go down to the safe room and pull those old mattresses down on the floor for us. Slept there. No sense having a safe room and dying from a tornado."

"What about the girl's clothing we found?"

"Just broke up with my lady. Cheerleader for Atlanta named Danni Jackson. She's got a nine-year-old. When we split, she and her kid just got in the Uber and left. Left all her shit. Left all her little girl's clothes in that dresser. It wasn't a happy day all round."

"And you're telling me this why? The warrant is invalid. We have no claim to question you."

"Yeah, but Detective Monroe, I don't want you to waste time investigating me and Big Ben as kidnappers. Ain't good for my cred. And it's a waste of time. Your time. We ain't ever set sight on those girls in our lives. Not involved in any way."

"Thank you, Lonnie, if I may call you that," M.J. said.

"Thank you, Detective Monroe," he replied. "And again, my condolences on your husband's injuries. Good night."

"Good night."

And with her response, Lonnie Truesdale stepped back into his limo and Big Ben Kermit hit the gas, leaving M.J. behind.

———

M.J. pondered that conversation a bit before deciding to call Agent Agate and inform her of the interaction with Truesdale. After M.J.'s short conversation with the FBI agent, she repeated the information to Rosie, who was recuperating by spending time with her daughter, Marie. Now, it was almost 10:00 and she still hadn't eaten. M.J. decided to call Riggs back.

He answered on the first ring. "You okay?"

"Yeah, better, but still haven't had anything to eat. How about you?"

Riggs laughed. "I can always eat. Where am I meeting you?"

"My place, bring a pizza."

"Yes, ma'am. Anything else?"

"Beer."

"That went without saying," Riggs replied. "Be at your place with dinner in an hour. I'll need the address."

"Hey, Riggs," she said, "bring a toothbrush." But he had already hung up.

She smiled at her brazen statement, even if he hadn't heard it. What was she getting into? A romance? She didn't know, but M.J. knew one thing, she didn't want to be alone, at least not for a little while. Not after today.

———

The detective started her car and began the familiar trek from the hospital to her home. Columbia Parkway was open but was now a divided stretch of one-lane traffic which slowed her commute. With cars both in front and behind her as the traffic chugged through the gap of closed bridge, her phone rang once again.

"Riggs, sometimes, you are a pain," M.J. said into her phone, not bothering to look at the caller I.D.

"Who's Riggs?"

M.J. was startled. "I'm sorry. I thought you were somebody else. Who's this?"

"Not Riggs," the voice said.

M.J. felt the hair on her arms stand up. The voice was dark and menacing. It was not one she recognized, except as ominous.

"The nigger in the parking garage was a message."

"Who? Talbert Washington?"

"Yeah, him."

"Who is this?"

"You've been looking for me."

M.J. paused, a catch in her breath. "You have the girls?"

"I don't hurt whites."

"So you took just one? You took Paisley Park Jefferson."

"Your idiot mayor, the FBI; they all say I took both girls. I don't hurt white people. I would never hurt a white girl."

"But you hurt black girls?"

"I *educate* nigger girls."

M.J. paused again, taking that in. "Do you have Paisley? Is she still alive?"

"Yes, it is not my intention to kill. It is never my intention to kill." The voice was a raspy baritone but animated. He was enjoying himself.

"But you have killed? In the past? This is not your first time?"

"I dispose of. It is not about the killing."

"Is it for the sex? Is that what drives you?"

The voice laughed. "You do not understand at all. I educate. These girls need to learn."

"What do you teach them?"

"Their place, their history. Most do not know it. Schools teach a false ideology. False dogma. These nigger girls haven't dreamed the truth, not even once in their miserable lives. But it's in their bones. In their blood. Their heritage. Their inheritance. I am their deliverance. Their education."

"But you dispose of them?"

"Only if they cannot learn. Only if they are incapable. If they fail. You know, I've never acted out before. I've kept it in check. You've not even known I was here all these years. You wouldn't have known this time, either, except someone took the white girl. It wasn't me took her. Only the nigger girl. I don't hurt white people. I wouldn't hurt niggers, neither, if they were just teachable. Can't learn for nothin'."

"Let her go. Let Paisley go. Can't you see that someone is going to hurt the white girl if you dispose of the black girl?"

"Then, perhaps it will come. A race war to settle things once and for all. It is long overdue."

M.J. begged. "Have pity on the white girl. Let the black girl go."

"Don't bother searching for this phone. As soon as I hang up, I will take the battery out and destroy the phone. Searching for it will not help you find me."

"Don't hang up."

"Goodbye, Detective Monroe. Please be sure to tell your mayor he's the reason the nigger boy died. He told the press I had taken both children. I do not hurt white children. The nigger died today because your mayor spoke falsehoods. Goodbye."

And the phone went dead.

Chapter Twenty

Things get busy after a cop gets a call from someone claiming to be a serial killer.

M.J. first steered into the empty lot of an auto parts store and gathered herself. What happened in the next few hours would matter a great deal. M.J. needed to handle things well. Before contacting anyone else, she turned on her phone's recorder, and she recited the conversation as best she could into the phone, providing herself an audio memo to be transcribed later.

She listened to it and then added some notes to the end. She listened again. Satisfied she had the conversation close to the actual exchange, M.J. drove home.

Riggs was sitting in the driveway when she pulled in. As she rolled past his pick-up into the garage, the big-chested man stepped from his cab holding a pizza box in one hand and a six-pack of beer in the other. He smiled broadly and started to greet her.

"Don't speak, don't say anything," M.J. said, sternly. "I have to keep my head straight right now."

Riggs looked a bit chagrined but nodded and followed her quick stride through the garage into the kitchen. As she flipped on lights, he set down the pizza box and beer. His forehead showed lines of concern.

M.J. was just getting Tobias Meyer on the phone. As the interim head of detectives answered, Riggs listened to M.J.'s five-minute description of her call and then was able to hear the additional five minutes of her replies to Lt. Meyer's questions.

M.J. finally ended the call. "Sorry about that. Paisley's kidnapper called me on my way here from the hospital. He claims he's abducted children numerous times before and killed them in the past."

Riggs nodded, grimly, and moved toward her. She found herself close to him. He was so much larger than her. His presence was comforting.

M.J. folded herself in his arms. She allowed herself the thirty seconds luxury of that hug, then she pulled free and opened the pizza box.

"You want a beer?" he asked.

"Better be coffee," she said. "I've got a tough night ahead. After this slice, I need to contact Agate at the Blue Ash FBI and let her know what's happened. Tobias is getting all the detectives back down there. Agate will assemble the task force."

"Damn, the sicko claimed he took Paisley Park Jefferson? What about Klaire Keller?" Riggs asked. He stepped past her to the coffee machine. He looked to her. "I'll make a pot. You eat another piece of pizza and get a quick shower.

That'll revive you for a while. It's going to be a long night."

"No kidding," M.J. said, pulling another slice of pepperoni from the box. She stood, leaned across the bar and kissed Riggs on the cheek.

He flushed red.

"Thanks. Some guys wouldn't be so happy right now."

Riggs shrugged. "Where do you keep the coffee?"

———

Riggs insisted on driving M.J. to the Blue Ash FBI office. He claimed it would allow her to concentrate on her phone calls.

She spent the half hour calling Agent Agate, Rosie, Simmons, Decker, Meagers, and Staples. M.J. drank coffee as they went. Riggs made pretty good joe, she decided. M.J. inspected his craggy features as he navigated traffic on I-71 on the way up.

"What?" he finally said.

"Just being thankful you were there tonight," she replied. "I was pretty creeped out after I got that phone call from…" she struggled to describe the man who called her.

"From Mr. Evil?" he offered.

"Yeah, him."

"Understandable to be creeped out. That's a phone call one in three hundred thirty-five million people in the United States received this evening. Unique and troubling for anyone."

"Unique and troubling," she laughed. "That's exactly the words came into my head after the call."

Riggs smiled. "Gallows humor, eh?"

"No, not all," she replied. "Just enjoying your artistic vision." M.J. hesitated a moment. "Really I'm just so thankful you were around this evening."

"*De nada.*"

"Oh, gosh," M.J. said, "I just realized we left the pizza on the counter."

"No worries," he said, "I found some freezer bags and

put it in the fridge. Put the box in the garbage and turned off the coffee pot."

M.J. beamed. "Thanks," she said, "You made this quick turnaround so easy. Can I get a raincheck on our dinner when this is all over?"

"Any time."

"I'd like that."

And then they were there.

M.J. put on her detective game face as Riggs stopped by the door. Before she exited, M.J. leaned over and squeezed Riggs's large meaty hand. Then, she was gone with a wave.

Riggs nodded in reply, but she was already inside, her strides breaking into a slight run as she headed to the stairs.

———

By dawn, tactics had changed. The task force was now split into two teams, the first assembled to search for M.J.'s caller, a presumed serial abductor and killer with racist motivations; the second was targeted at black militant organizations or radical black political organizations which might have taken Klaire Keller to demonstrate inequity in policing practices.

M.J. spent the night being interviewed by Agents Agate, Saunders, Messerschmidt, and also Lt. Meyer. She was drained. Her recorded memo reciting the details of the phone call was transcribed, printed, and given to the detectives who waited in a conference room.

Once during a bathroom break, M.J. stuck her head in and Rosie came to her and gave her a hug. "You doin' all right, girl?"

"Yeah, just tired. It's hard to believe the perp called me," M.J. said. "We still have no idea how he got my number, but he did. At least now we finally know what we're dealing with."

Decker said with fatigue in his voice, "You got to quit giving your card out with your cell phone number on it. Too many killers calling you. Two this week. That ain't good."

Rosie challenged him. "She wouldn't have got the phone call if she hadn't."

Simmons shrugged. "What's the plan? They got your phone tapped?"

M.J. nodded. "Will have soon. The FBI also has equipped all their task force agents, all sixty of them, with Stingray devices. They'll be able to triangulate the signal from any phone call dialing my number right from their cars within two minutes. With all those agents on the roads around town, the plan is to be within a mile or so from the caller as soon as we identify the call. That's how they caught the Houston bomber. He left his cell phone on. They triangulated the signal and tracked him down on the interstate."

"What will we be doing?"

"The FBI will be letting us know where the phone was purchased that made the call. You all are going to run that down as soon as the stores open. They have the number and are backtracking its purchase location right now. The signal from the phone is gone. Mr. Evil said he was going to take the battery out of it and smash it after he ended our call. He may have. We haven't been able to ping it to get a location."

Meagers and Staples stood up.

Detective Meagers spoke. "So that means we'll be on the other side of the fence. The other half of the task force will be looking into the militant black angle? We stay searching for Klaire Keller?"

Tobias Meyer stepped in from the hallway, hearing the question. "That's correct. The anti-white list we got yesterday? You two will take that over. Rosie, you'll ride with Black and

Decker today," he said, amusing the detectives with his use of their nickname.

Rosie nodded to her boss. "What's on the agenda for my partner here?"

Meyer said, "She's going to be working with the FBI profiler, Kimberley Rodden, this morning, trying to help us figure out who or what we're trying to find."

"*What* is more like it," Rosie agreed. "Monster."

"Mr. Evil," M.J. added.

"Mr. Evil," Rosie echoed.

Tobias nodded at M.J. "Let's get back at it."

Chapter Twenty-One

FBI profiler, Kim Rodden, was a beautiful woman. Black, perhaps fifty years old, with lustrous skin the color of maple syrup. Her nose was prim, button-like and her lips thin with a countenance that reminded M.J. of an Egyptian queen. She was tall, maybe 5'8", and wore a silver dress that set off her hair. Her pumps were black, her legs long. Her voice matched her looks: if words could be fabric, hers sounded like cashmere.

"Let's get back to it. I see in the transcript what your caller said, but what I need to know more of is *how* he said things," Rodden's voice prodded gently as if she was used to reticent witnesses.

M.J. nodded. She'd been working sixteen hours a day for a week and had not been to bed for twenty-six hours. Coffee had stopped working around 4:00 a.m. She had moved on to energy drinks. They didn't seem to make her more alert. She was now just tired and jittery.

"For example, when he said the n-word, did he use it

descriptively to describe skin color or was it vindictive, for meanness?"

"He used it like a club, like he was trying to hurt with the word. Like he was baiting me to lose my temper," M.J. replied.

"Did you?"

"No, I think I kept cool throughout the conversation."

"Did he really use the words in a vicious way to harm or are you projecting? You have a black partner. Were you offended?"

"Yes, but I didn't show it. I just kept appealing to him to release the girl."

Rodden nodded, taking a note. "Did he have an accent or a verbal tick?"

"No."

"Did he sound country or city? Did he drop his 'g's on the end of any '-ing' words?"

"Not that I recall. His voice was raspy. He did not speak loudly. But I think he spoke typical English."

"Disfluencies like 'um' or 'ah'?"

"Not that I recall."

"You said his voice was raspy. Do you think he was attempting to hide the tenor of his voice? Be secretive?"

M.J. thought about that for a minute. "No, I think his voice is just like that. Like maybe he's a long-time smoker. I had the feeling he was not a young man."

"How old do you think he was, I mean, by his voice?"

"At least fifty?"

"What leads you to believe that?"

M.J. paused for a second. "Intuition, I guess."

"Then, you have no real discernable reason to think that?"

"No, I guess not," M.J. said. She stretched with a yawn. Then, with a start, she added, "I think he did drop some 'g's off the end of words, now that I think about it. Maybe a bit of a southern accent to him, I guess."

Tobias Meyer sat down at the far end of the conference room table. He watched M.J. carefully.

Sitting next to him, Agent Saunders managed a recording device.

Agent Agate took copious notes of the proceedings.

Meyer leaned forward. "Let's stop soon. Detective Monroe is not as alert as she might be. We don't want the information she provides to be wrong or flawed by fatigue."

Rodden turned her head to him. "Immediacy is more important than fatigue. Let me do my job. Then, you can do yours."

Meyer waved his hand for her to proceed, but his eyebrows went to Saunders to let him know the profiler was on a short leash with his detective at this stage.

Rodden then pivoted back to M.J. "Did the caller give you any indication of how many girls he claimed to have abducted in his, ah, career?"

"Not exactly, but he used the expression 'in all these years,' so I assumed it was what I would consider a large number."

Rodden leaned forward. "How many would you say is a large number?"

M.J. tipped her head. "How many is a large number of kidnapped and killed young girls? One, I guess."

Rodden leaned back. "You know what I meant."

"Five, ten, maybe twenty."

"Did you have the impression that he had sex with these girls?"

"He said it wasn't about the sex. It was about educating them to know their place."

"I've read your statement. I'm asking you. Do you think he has taken sexual liberties with these girls?"

M.J. was tired and now starting to get angry at the barrage of questions. She stretched her hands out on the table, pushing her fingers out to the limit of her tendons. "I don't think so. There's no evidence of sexual penetration in either of the bodies. The hymens were in place in the pathology reports from both the girl in the trunk and the six-year-old found outside Louisville."

All four of the other people in the room froze in place.

FBI profiler, Kim Rodden, tipped her head and raised an eyebrow. "What are you talking about, Detective Monroe? We don't have any bodies or pathology reports in this case? We only have two missing girls."

M.J.'s face flushed with fatigue and embarrassment. In her exhausted state, she had conflated the two cases. She put her fists to her temples, pushing her fingers through her hair. "I think I fell asleep with my eyes open. Sorry. Another case."

Rodden leaned back in her chair, smoothing her expensive silver dress over her flat stomach. "Detective Monroe, as a profiler for the bureau, my job is to infer connections in cases where perhaps we have not yet established evidence to maintain those relationships. Intuition and unconscious thought can sometimes be a great benefit to a case. I think you better start at the beginning of this other case. Tell us everything. You have piqued my curiosity."

M.J. nodded.

It took an hour, and afterwards, the FBI profiler rose from the table, her face impassive.

Rodden folded her leather brief, tucking the pen inside. For the first time since Tobias Meyer addressed her more than an hour before, she rearranged her view so that she might see him.

"Lieutenant, Agent Saunders, Agent Agate, it will take me a while to digest this interview and to provide guidance for your search. I will try to provide this information in two ways, one in which we are simply looking for a serial killer who has abducted Paisley Park Jefferson and who will kill, or has already killed, her after whatever ritual he deems necessary has been completed. The second profile will consider the other cases Detective Monroe has stumbled onto. I'll consider if there is reason to believe our target has indeed been abducting and killing girls since 1975."

Rodden turned to M.J., "Thank you for your efforts and your diligence to your job, M.J. I hope I can assist you in bringing those girls home." Then, she left the room.

———

Tobias Meyer stood and said, "M.J., if you're up to it, we need to coordinate things with the detective team." He motioned her to follow him to the conference room down the hall.

In there, the three detectives, Rosie, Decker, and Simmons, were all at work on laptops. Collectively, they looked up. Rosie's mouth drew into a tight line.

"Girl, you look beat."

"I am, but we got a lot done. Things are finally aimed at the right targets. At least I think so."

"I agree," said Lt. Meyer. "Have a seat."

Okay, M.J., we've already divided up some of the labor while you were working with the feds. Rosie here is tracking down the phone. The FBI will know where the cellphone was purchased momentarily. I've pulled Det. Heather Primstone from the Three to partner with Rosie for this afternoon. Detective Primstone's partner is out with a kidney stone, so I brought her over. Heather's good people. I know you'll treat her as a member of the team, Rosie. We'll keep her for the duration of this case.

"Simmons is compiling a list of all missing black girls since 1975 in the Ohio River Valley with the help of Agent Agate. That's going to be a lot of missing and runaway girls in forty years, but we'll run the social security numbers, search for criminal records and death certificates. We should be able to bring that overall number way down. We'd like to identify the girl in the trunk. See if she is a victim of M.J.'s caller last night. either way, we want to know who she is and get her remains back to her family. My office will provide additional assistance as this part of the investigation proceeds.

"Decker will work with uniformed officers to clear all R.S.O.s who own vans." Lt. Meyer looked to M.J. "I understand that was your idea. It's a good one. We should have done that long ago. Good work on that. The list is back, and we have seventeen who are registered and own vehicles which might match the eyewitness's sighting. Perhaps our caller has already been caught once and is on our radar as a registered sex offender. If that is the case, it will be Decker's job to learn if he is one of the seventeen on that list.

"The FBI is working on the video from the shooting of the school teacher at the parking garage in over-the-Rhine. We're working under the assumption that the shooter is M.J.'s caller. He did not come up out of the 12th Street exit. No one did. And no one wearing brown coveralls and a baseball cap came up any of the other exits. Our supposition is the perp changed out of the coveralls in the stairwell, disposed of his disguise, and then exited via one of the other exits. Probably the Vine Street exit, which was the busiest. Maybe we can get a photo still of our perp from the feed.

"The bureau will drill down on the video today and look for potential shooters, white male, age fifty or older, maybe a smoker so not in great health. It's a long shot, but if we get some candidates, we'll let FBI use its photo enhancing abilities to maybe put a face to this monster.

"On my end, I'll be assisting Meagers and Staples to form another detective team to begin anew in a search for militant organizations who might be interested in taking a child as a political move. I'm pulling in two more teams from other districts. It's stretching us really thin, and other criminals haven't actually stopped their nefarious deeds to watch this shit show on TV."

"Did the lieutenant just say 'shit show'?" laughed Simmons.

"Did he just say 'nefarious deeds'?" Decker added, howling.

Meyer smiled. "Okay, okay, you cornballs, everyone's had a long night. Get to work. our plates are full. Go to it."

M.J. looked at her boss. "What do I do?"

"You go home. Get some rest. Report to me in the morning."

M.J. started to protest. "But…"

Tobias Meyer raised his hand. "Detective Monroe. Go home. That's an order. Listen, our best chance to catch this guy is if he calls you again. Every FBI agent in the tristate area is carrying a Stingray in the car. We can triangulate the signal and be on him in minutes. Your job is to be by your phone and to keep him on the phone for as long as you can, if and when he calls you again. To do that, you must have your wits about you. I need you fresh. And if there's one thing you're not right now, it's fresh."

M.J. nodded. She was too exhausted to fight and what Tobias said made a ton of sense.

Lt. Meyer saw her agreement in her tired eyes. "M.J., you've done great work here. I've arranged officers from the Two to take you home and remain outside your door, so you can rest easy. Remember your phone calls are being monitored."

"Yeah," Decker quipped, "try to limit your calls to just the one killer, okay?"

"Shut up," Rosie said. "M.J.'s given us the break we need to bring that little girl home."

Tobias had had enough. "All of you, out of here. Report back to me by 8:00 this evening. M.J., you are off the clock until 7:00 in the morning. Take the time to rest up." The lieutenant looked to his phone for a text and nodded at M.J. "Your ride is here. Time to go home."

Chapter Twenty-Two

On the ride back to Newtown, M.J. felt like calling Riggs but knew she couldn't. He worked in Two. These officers giving her a ride were from District Two. They would be able to hear the call and there would be no end to the ribbing he would take. Every officer in the precinct would know of their friendship and would assume it was much more.

At home, M.J. ate a bowl of cereal, took a shower, and feeling somewhat vulnerable knowing two male police officers were outside her home, she put on a Miami University T-shirt and panties to sleep in. Normally, she would have just slid between the sheets.

Before she lay down, M.J. thought to text her neighbor. *Ted*, she wrote, *ignore the police officer in my driveway and the other sitting on my deck. All is well.*

He wrote back, *WTF?*

She laughed but almost mid-chuckle she was asleep. All was near-silent in the house. The only sound was the occasional creak of the house in the afternoon wind.

When M.J. awoke, it was dark. She looked at her alarm clock, 7:00 p.m. She'd slept six hours. Rolling out of bed, she padded to the living room but heard a sound in the kitchen. She could see the lights on over the stove. M.J. tiptoed back to her bedroom and lifted her service weapon from its holster. Moving silently across the carpet, she peeked around the corner into the room.

It was Riggs. And he was cooking. What's more was it smelled wonderful.

"Oh, you're up," he said matter-of-factly.

"And you're inside my house."

He blinked. "I'm sorry. Did I startle you?" Then, Riggs looked down to the gun in her hand. "I guess I did."

M.J. gazed at the weapon, as well. She set it on the kitchen counter.

In the next instant, both of them realized she was standing before him in T-shirt and panties. Their eyes met.

Her face flushed red. She laughed and said, "I'll be right back."

In a flash, M.J. retreated to the bedroom and pulled a white cotton robe out of the closet.

Rejoining Riggs in the kitchen, she tried to play it cool. "What's for dinner?"

"Grilled tilapia, topped with mango chutney, sweet potato with honey butter, coleslaw."

"To drink?"

"Unoaked chard."

"Very good, Riggs. Where'd you learn to cook?"

"The Navy, actually. Not like this, but I spent my service time in a galley of an aircraft carrier in the gulf. Got my combat service pin, nonetheless. Closest I came to action was one time when a guy dropped a steak knife near my boot."

He laughed.

M.J. joined him. She rose from her barstool and pulled two wine glasses from the rack.

"It's open," he said. "Stuck the cork back in and put it in the fridge."

M.J. poured each of them a glass.

"Hope you don't mind me being here. The first shift guys were coming off duty, and I had been down to see the river rats' homes again. I was finally able to convince Ms. Hondros to move to city-approved housing. Her place was too dangerous for habitation. Anyway, I was just down the road, so I came by. And as the second shifters arrived, I just told them if they'd wait while I made a Kroger run, I'd take the shift. I made them leave the cruiser out front for the night."

M.J. shrugged. "It got me a home-cooked meal."

Riggs smiled. "That it did, and it's ready. Let's eat."

They ate at the kitchen counter facing each other.

She spilled her last twenty-four hours.

Riggs reciprocated by telling her of his day. To an outsider listening in, it might have sounded like two cops coming off shift at a Frisch's' Big Boy lunch counter.

Afterwards, they cleared the dishes and put the pan in to soak.

Riggs poured them each a second glass of wine.

M.J. went to the bedroom and put on sweatpants and a crew. In the living room, she turned on the television. *Jeopardy!* was just ending.

Riggs came from the kitchen with her wine and joined her on the couch. Things now seemed awkward. Neither of them was a television watcher. Conversation lagged.

M.J. attempted to change the stagnant vibe in the room. "I went to Happ's and saw your painting."

Riggs looked from the TV to her. His eyes showed surprise. "You did? What'd you think?" He paused. "Jeez, that sounded needy."

M.J. laughed. "No, I really liked it. *River of Tears*. It took me a minute to realize the rain, all the gray, all those strokes, were tiny teardrops. That must have taken forever."

"Yeah, it did. But you liked it?"

"Very much," she said, taking a sip. "But, Riggs, it's a very sad painting. It obviously came from a dark place."

"My marriage was breaking up."

She nodded, understanding. Sometimes, she felt like her marriage had broken up. Greg, after all, was still alive, just twenty minutes from here. But he wasn't with her anymore.

"How you end up a cop?" she asked him, trying to push them through the darkening mood. "A guy who can paint like you shouldn't spend his time writing tickets for a living."

"I've painted for a long time. I could always draw. But my dad thought I could get a college scholarship playing football. Have the body for it. But I broke my ankle my senior year. Was feeling sorry for myself, sitting in art class just staring out the window. And my art teacher comes up and brings me a set of brushes, a box of water color paint and a canvas.

"She said, 'If you're just going to stare out the window, you might as well paint a landscape.' " He laughed. "Biggest gift anyone ever gave me until my wife gave birth to our son."

"Where is he now?"

"My son? Ben's in Seattle, finding himself. Whatever that means. We're not speaking right now. In most divorces, people are forced to take sides. My son has chosen his mother."

"I'm sorry," M.J. said.

"Don't be. I was gone too much. Always playing cops and

robbers, or fishing. I took him some when he was little. When he got old enough, he stopped wanting to go. Ben made the right choice. He's more like his mom."

"Give it time."

Riggs nodded. He turned his head to the TV, deflecting. "What do you usually watch on Wednesday night?"

M.J. shrugged. "Movie on DVD, probably."

Riggs nodded. "What's the oldest movie you have?"

M.J. reflected for a minute. "Probably *Casablanca.*"

"Let's watch that," he said, but then he paused. "Wait, is that a movie you and your husband used to watch? I don't want it to be weird."

"Oh," she said, "it's already pretty weird."

They both laughed. "But, no, Greg didn't like movies. He was a doer. Liked to assemble things. He liked being out in the garage, tinkering. In the winter, he would do puzzles. He was never just sitting."

Riggs nodded. "What kind of doctor was he?"

"Endocrinologist."

"What's that?"

"A thyroid doctor. He did lots more than that, but that was the thing that kept him busy. People have a lot of trouble with their thyroid. Who knew?"

"Not me."

Neither spoke for a minute with Greg's mention into their conversation.

M.J. broke the silence by getting up to get the movie. She started it to play.

In time, M.J. retrieved a quilt from the cabinet and threw it over both their legs.

Riggs moved closer.

"Can I put my arm around you?"

"That would be nice." She cuddled in.

After the movie ended with Bogart's famous line, "Louis, I think this is the beginning of a beautiful friendship," M.J. yawned and said, "I know it's only just after 10:00, but I think I better hit it."

Riggs nodded. "Leave the quilt here. I'll crash on the couch if that's okay."

M.J. smiled at him and left to get ready for bed. She washed her face, brushed her teeth, then walked back to the living room. Riggs was now in sweatpants himself and a T-shirt pulled tight on his biceps. His arms were impressive.

M.J. looked at him, fondly. "You're not really going to sleep out here, right?"

Riggs smiled. "I thought you'd never ask."

———

In the morning darkness, still too early for even a false dawn, M.J. rolled from her belly to her side and ran her hand across Riggs's shoulders. She could feel the muscles at rest under his skin. He was warm. She sighed.

"You okay?"

"Yeah."

"Regrets?"

"No, not regrets. A little guilt, perhaps, but that's to be expected for a Catholic girl."

"This the first time since—"

"Yep," she said, cutting him off.

"'Gotcha," he said, getting it. "I'll go make coffee. I have to be at work at 7:00."

"Me, too." She watched him slide into boxers and lumber off to the kitchen.

———

At District One, M.J. carried a coffee to the makeshift fourth floor headquarters for the detectives' investigation. Tobias Meyer sat in a straight-backed chair in his dress blues. His cap sat on the table facing him. His head was down, poring over documents.

"What's up, boss?" she said, entering. "Am I the first one here?"

"Yeah, everybody else will be here shortly. Did you get some rest?"

"Yes, thank you. What's on the docket for me today?"

"Going to have you working out of here." Seeing her face fall, Lt. Meyer added, "We got the social security listing for our 2,400 missing black girls for the years '75 through '77. I had Simmons extend it to three years after the T-shirt was discontinued."

"What'd you find?"

Tobias chewed on his upper lip for a moment, choosing his words. "Not what I thought."

"How so?"

"I thought the FICA report would eliminate most of the names on the list, but it was less effective than the death certificate report."

M.J. sat down. "What do you mean?

"Well," he said, "life expectancy for white women compared to black women is three years longer at eighty-one years of life to seventy-eight for black women. With life expectancy of seventy-eight years for black women, that means half of the black women born seventy-eight years ago today are now dead. Get that?"

"Yeah."

"But it really matters more what the median is rather than the average."

"I don't understand."

"Let's say," said Lt. Meyer, "you have two black women. One lives to ninety-five; the other twenty-five. The average is sixty, but that's not very informative regarding the death of the younger woman who died at such a young age."

"Okay, I see that. What's the median age of death for black women?"

"Closer to sixty-five. Surprisingly, lots of black women, once they reach senior status, live long into extreme old age. Kind of an equilibrium, I'd say. But when a lot live to ripe old age, that means a whole bunch more must die young."

"And even more so when they run away as teens?" M.J. asked.

"Exactly. Of these two thousand four hundred women, most ran away in their late teens. We're forty years down the road from their departure from their homes. That puts them now in their late fifties. To do the math roughly, we'd expect the overall life expectancy of eighty years. So if fifty percent would be dead in twenty years, and we lose one percent a year, we'd expect seventy percent to be alive right now. However, we must also consider that many runaways end up in the life as prostitutes. The average lifespan of a prostitute is only thirty-four years. Most do not die of natural causes.

"Here, one half of the two thousand four hundred are deceased according to the SSDI, Social Security Death Index, and then cross-referenced with the National Death Index. Running away from home is a symptom of a short, difficult life."

"That's still one thousand two hundred women out there. Too many to easily find out the identity of our vic in the trunk."

"True, but all but twelve percent of them have filed taxes or at least had FICA removed from paychecks over the years."

"Then, we're down to one hundred fifty women." M.J. said, doing the math in her head.

"As might be inferred, people who have never filed taxes *ever* are often living a life of crime. You're aware that thirty percent of the public has a criminal record of some kind. In the group we're looking at, it's much higher at forty-seven percent. That leaves us seventy-eight women on our list that we can't be sure lived any length of time after leaving home as a teen."

M.J. whistled, "Those seventy-eight women left no record. No credit report? No nothing?"

Tobias Meyer smiled. "And that's what you're working on. I'll move Rosie and Heather Primstone in to work with you today. We need to eliminate more names from our search. Some may have left the country. Some may have credit histories. We haven't yet run credit checks with the three major bureaus. We haven't checked marriage licenses. We haven't checked passports. And we haven't checked other nations; Mexico, Canada, Interpol."

"How can you get a passport or a credit card without a social security number?"

Lt. Meyer raised an eyebrow. "I don't think credit card companies are too picky, but the passport thing seems less likely. Your job is to run down these names and find history on as many as possible. If we can prove they lived their life, left tangible proof, then we know they aren't the girl in the trunk."

She nodded, and as she did, the entire gang arrived *en masse*, gabbing like a bunch of geese. There were donuts, so the day began as well as one can expect.

Chapter Twenty-Three

"Once around the table to catch up, M.J.," ordered Lt. Meyer.

Rosie went first. "We went to the Mini-Mart in West Price Hill that sold the burner phone used to call you. Guy couldn't tell us much. No store cameras."

Det. Primstone added, "He actually said his business was based on selling burner phones to criminals so cameras would be antithetical to his livelihood."

Simmons laughed, "He used the word 'antithetical'?"

Decker said, "He used the word 'livelihood'?"

"I'm paraphrasing."

Simmons laughed again. "Paraphrasing? They use some big words in the Three, huh?"

Primstone blushed.

Lt. Meyer said, "Knock it off. Did he have anything to add?"

Rosie said, "Don't sell too many phones to white dudes. He did remember selling three phones to an older guy. Salt and pepper hair, tall, over six foot, walked maybe with a shuffle."

"That's it?"

"No additional distinguishing characteristics?"

Rosie said, "Yeah, he was white."

Everyone laughed.

"How about you, Decker?"

"We ran down the seventeen registered sex offenders who owned white vans in the metro area. Some creepy dudes. Let me tell you. Seven wear ankle bracelets on home arrest, except for employment hours. We're verifying their movements with their P.O.s, but they seem unlikely.

"The other ten maybe offer more potential. Three are unemployed and cannot account for their time during either kidnapping. Three more did give us alibis, which I'll be running down today. The remaining four were completely hinky. One was not where he was registered to reside and in violation, so we arrested him. We found one at a strip club, so we arrested him. We found one at a home with a seven-year-old boy in residence in violation of the terms of his parole, so we arrested him. The last was so high when we came to the door that he fell down, so we arrested him. All four are back in custody. We'll do more to determine if they might have involvement, but we are definitely the better having them off the street."

Then, Simmons explained again how he and Lt. Meyer worked with the FBI to limit the search for the girl in the trunk's identity down to seventy-eight names. He did explain while these seventy-eight girls went missing locally, during that same time span the number was nearly 8,000 nationally. The girl in the trunk might be from anywhere outside the tristate and if that were the case, then she would likely go unidentified.

Finally, Tobias Meyer opened two folders on his desk. "Here are two circulars. The first is an enhanced image of a white man of approximately the right age as the perp we are currently seeking. This image was taken by the security cameras on the Vine Street exit to the parking garage in the moments after the shooting.

The detectives looked at the face. There was not much to see. A man in sunglasses and baseball cap. He wore a zip-up navy jacket, collar up. Jeans and black boots. His hair was graying at the back of his hat and around his ears. M.J. would have guessed his age as late fifties, but it was hard to tell.

"Not much to go on," Decker said.

"No, but the FBI thinks this is the shooter," Tobias replied.

"And the man who called me claimed he was the shooter," M.J. said.

"Then this is probably the guy who called you," Rosie added.

Tobias nodded. "The FBI is working the photo in facial recognition software and comparing it to driver's licenses from Ohio, Kentucky, and Indiana. But the image is so grainy, his face so turned and the hat, sunglasses, and the jacket collar so interfering, we don't have high hopes."

Tobias Meyer let them look for a few more moments. Then, he handed them a second image. "The second is an artist's rendering of the girl in the trunk. Her mummification does give us a pretty good idea of her facial structure and looks."

Rosie said, "She was a pretty little girl."

"Yeah," said M.J., pointing at the photo in her other hand. "And this dirt bag killed her."

Tobias Meyer kept it professional. "We're putting out the photo from the shooting today, being it's a recent incident. We'll hold the girl's image until tomorrow. The FBI thinks releasing both in the same day would blunt either's impact with news stations." He paused. "Simmons, you're back with Decker. Clear those three remaining alibis and verify the ankle bracelet reports and report back to me when you've done so.

"Rosie, you and Heather take the photo of our perp back to the Mini-Mart and see if he can I.D. our man. M.J., you're here with me again today. Continue to research and verify what happened to more of those seventy-eight runaways on that list. We need to reduce the number. We need fewer potential matches for our dead girl over at the morgue." Tobias paused. "We need to find out this little girl's name."

Then, they went to work.

———

The Mini-Mart owner was no help. He only responded with a disinterested shrug after looking at the grainy photo.

However, M.J., with the help of Rosie and Heather through the afternoon hours, eliminated twenty-nine more names. Most of those, M.J. found on marriage licenses long ago. With updated married names, the policewomen were able to find social security numbers for the women. These women had simply not filed with social security until after they were married, something much more common in the late '70s than now.

Now, the list was down to forty-nine names. It was a workable number, although still a lot, given the team had very little data on any of the runaways. There had been no effort to find those black girls forty years ago. M.J. wondered how hard society really tried to find runaways. Not that hard, she decided. And even less effort was dedicated if the girl was poor and black.

On her way home, M.J. noted the cloudy, wet weather of the last few days was breaking to the west. The sun at dusk threw rust-colored hues on everything as she drove.

She decided to make the call. "Hey, Riggs," she said as he answered.

"Hey, M.J.," he said, cheerfully.

"How's my bodyguard?"

"Good, easy day. You?"

"Progress," she said. "You going to protect me again tonight?"

"Is that what you call it?"

M.J. laughed. "Yeah, I guess so. My treat for dinner. How about grilling some burgers?"

"Great. I've got to run by my house for a change of clothes. See you in a bit."

———

After dinner, M.J. went outside to cover the grill. It was nearly dark. Her phone rang. She didn't recognize the number. Hesitantly, she answered.

"Miss me?"

M.J. sucked in a breath. It was him.

"Not exactly."

"I know your phone is tapped," he said, "and the FBI will be trying to trace this call. I'll keep it short."

"Your dime," she said. "You see your picture out there on TV today?"

She stepped inside from the deck. M.J. wrote a number on a pad with the words, *Call Tobias.* She motioned to Riggs.

He nodded, tore a piece of paper off the pad, grabbed his phone and left the room.

The voice on the phone had not answered, so M.J. asked again. "Did you see your photo from the garage shooting on the news today?"

"I missed that. I teach during the day, but I'll try to catch the late news."

"You taught Paisley today?"

"Yes, we made some progress."

"She's still alive, then?"

"I don't teach dead girls."

"Release her so we can get the white girl back. We think maybe black militants have taken her in retaliation for your crime. You're in favor of white power. Do something good for whites in Cincinnati. Give Paisley back. Save the white girl."

"That's not the reason for my call."

"Oh, there's a reason?"

"There's a reason for everything I do."

Riggs returned to the room with his phone to his ear. He whispered, "They're tracing it. Keep him on the line."

M.J. suddenly had a strategy. "You know, I don't agree with your actions, but to some degree, I agree with your sentiments."

The caller laughed. "Oh, really, do tell."

"You know they assigned me a black partner. Moved her name up on the list past some white candidates for detective. More qualified candidates. White candidates." M.J. could hear the sneer on the other end of the call.

"That's what they do."

"Who?

"Zionists, nigger lovers. You name it."

M.J. tried to bait him to keep him on the line. "You ever get passed over like that? For a black man?"

"It's time for me to go."

Riggs hissed, "Just a few more seconds. They think he's on Pete Rose Way. No, now on 50 eastside."

"You haven't told me if you ever faced reverse discrimination," M.J. baited once more.

"Reverse discrimination is an oxymoron."

Riggs said, "No, now they're saying he's south of that, on the Kentucky side."

"Huh?" said M.J., working the clock for time. "I don't get that." She wasn't sure to whom she had addressed her confusion.

"We'll talk again," came the hiss.

Riggs said, "He's on the 8 in Bellevue in Kentucky.

"Why is reverse discrimination an oxymoron?" M.J. pleaded.

The line went dead.

M.J. looked to Riggs. "Do they have him?"

Riggs asked into his phone, "Lt. Meyer, do you have him?" There was a pause. "Okay," Riggs replied to the voice. "I'll put her on."

M.J. took the cell phone. "Tell me you have him."

Tobias's voice sounded weary. "Kind of. We were able to triangulate the signal. M.J., he was on a boat in the Ohio. He was calling from the river. But the signal's gone. We've lost him."

Chapter Twenty-Four

Kim Rodden, FBI profiler, ran her index finger around the rim of her clear glass coffee cup. The coffee was the same color as her skin. Her nails were blood red.

"With the discovery our caller was aboard ship when he made his second call to Detective Monroe, I posit the theory that he may, indeed, be responsible not only for Paisley's abduction but also the murder of the child in the trunk. Detective Monroe was thinking along those lines, but this additional data makes it at least a venue worthy of our attention."

She paused from her thoughts to gaze at the tired faces around the room. It was nearing 2:00 a.m. Friday. Paisley had been gone twelve days.

"It seems quite unlikely we have two serial killers of young black girls who have gone undetected for decades who both use boats on the Ohio River for transportation. Thus, we must consider we have a single lone wolf gone undetected for forty years. It is a sobering thought, indeed."

Supervising Special Agent Saunders, his tie, for the first

time, loose around his neck and his top shirt button undone, nodded. "Let's try to figure out what we have."

Rodden nodded back. "Our profile would be as follows; white male, more than six-feet tall, in his sixties or perhaps even seventy. If he was twenty-three, when he returned from Vietnam in 1975, that would make him sixty-eight years old. I suppose our window ought to be three years either side of that."

Tobias Meyer added, "He would have a military record, either Army or Navy. The Navy seems like a possibility given his choice of venue for his crimes, the Ohio River."

"Perhaps," said Rodden. "But do we know if the 'loot knock' chests were used by Navy men, as well?"

Tobias nodded, "We'll research that."

"We also have the white supremacy angle," added M.J.

Rodden nodded. "Which has evolved over time. First a swastika, then HH then 88."

"Which indicates prison gang involvement or knowledge," said Decker.

Rodden raised an index finger. "The knowledge is key. White supremacists tend to flock together. Just because the perp changed the identifying mark of his attacks does not mean he was in prison; he may have gained knowledge of those marks from someone who had been in prison. Whether he was actually incarcerated or not should not be an eliminating factor in our search for a suspect."

"Lack of sexual involvement with the victims is also indicative of an unusual perp," Simmons added, a toothpick rolling in the corner of his mouth.

"Yes," Rodden said, "the six-year-old in Louisville was marked but unmolested. The girl in the trunk also was not raped, at least vaginally. That would, in conjunction with the brandings, tend to support white supremacy or at least hatred of blacks as the motivation for the abductions and ultimately capital crimes."

Rodden stood. In heels, she was at least six feet tall. She wore black slacks and a gray sweater that matched her hair.

M.J., for an instant, despite the seriousness of the meeting, envied the woman's style. Would Riggs like her to dress like that? The thoughts were fleeting as Rodden directed her words to her.

"M.J., what you did to keep our caller on the line was inspired. But it was also dangerous. Your comments about your partner kept him on the line about an additional twenty seconds. It allowed us to discern he was calling from a boat. That was huge, but I fear you also have introduced a game of cat-and-mouse with our killer. That's dangerous.

"We already know he is resourceful. He took Paisley with no one the wiser. He was able to black out the cameras in the parking garage. He changed clothes in the stairwell then walked away after killing the school teacher undetected by police. He bought burner cell phones and knows to take the battery out of them before and after calls. He got your cell phone number. And maybe most of all, he has defied detection for forty years. He is an extremely dangerous opponent."

Rosie looked at M.J. "What did you say about me?"

"Lies, just lies to keep him on the phone."

Rosie raised a finger, wagging it. "This ain't over, partner."

Rodden interrupted. "What I'm trying to say is that you may have made yourself a target."

Tobias engaged again. "We'll increase security from, ah, a single officer to two teams whenever Detective Monroe is off duty."

M.J. felt the single beat delay in her boss's words like a hammer blow. He knew about Riggs.

Saunders nodded. "That's a good idea. Detective

Monroe's connection to the suspect is still our best chance to end this quickly."

"I believe our caller will attempt to be random. He called once, then again two nights later," Rodden said. "He'll try to alter that pattern. He might call again, even tonight, but I think it less likely than three nights from now. He'll still be on the high from last night, so I believe there will be a delay as he basks in the glory of his voyage and call of last night. He might switch it up with a day call, but he seems nocturnal. M.J., be prepared for a call either this evening or Sunday evening."

Tobias nodded. "On the other end of the investigation, we have two targets in the Klaire Keller kidnapping. One is a white supremacist, a Kentuckian named Roger Windings. He has posted online he would be honored to be the person responsible for the kidnappings and bringing about a race war. He's suggested the kidnapper is keeping the Keller girl to mislead the public and to misdirect police efforts toward black perpetrators."

"You said two?" M.J. asked, interested.

"The second target is a black couple. Female named Aaleyah Clark, a writer and militant out of Berkeley, California. Male is named Earl Bennington II from Chicago. They write a blog and host an internet subscription radio show. On the radio show, they have intimated that they would shelter or assist the black abductors should they need help in hiding the Keller girl."

Rodden shook her head. "Those admissions seem tenuous."

Saunders and Tobias both nodded in agreement. "Yeah, our judge ruled neither statement was enough to get us a search warrant," said Saunders, "but both parties have agreed to be interviewed. Each will have legal representation."

"When and where are these interviews going to take place?
Rodden asked. "Would you like me to attend?"

"Downstairs," Saunders said, "in Interview one and Two.
The first at 1:00; the second will be an hour later. I don't think
it appropriate for you to be in the room, but you can view from
behind the glass."

Rodden nodded.

"What are we working on after a few winks of sleep?"
Heather Primstone asked.

Tobias said, "We'll have you and M.J. continue to eliminate names in our search for the identity of the trunk girl.
Rosie, I want you to visit the two Jefferson women and the
son, Prince, and let them know confidentially we have reason
to believe Paisley is still alive. They deserve some good
news."

Rosie nodded, "I've been talking to them every day by
phone. That family is in bad shape with Paisley gone and Nat
Lee losing his foot."

Tobias nodded in sympathy. "Yeah, go to the hospital, too.
See Lee and let him know, as well." He redirected his gaze.
"Simmons, Decker. You two will go through the files and
assemble a list of all persons of interest in any black girl disap-
pearances over the last forty years. We'll get agents from Agent
Agate to assist. Still, it will be a daunting task."

Both men groaned.

"Daunting, he says," Simmons complained with a
mournful grin.

Saunders picked up the beat. "The FBI is still manning all
major thoroughfares around the city with agents equipped
with Stingrays in case of a call. Remember," he added, "the
FBI drawing of the trunk girl's image goes out to the media
this morning. Maybe we'll catch a break."

Then, the meeting broke up, and M.J. drove home with

police escort. Two cruisers sat in her drive. Riggs's pickup truck was in the driveway.

When she entered, he was snoring lightly in her bed. As she slid under the covers, M.J. realized five officers were outside guarding her. She felt very safe and drifted off easily.

The task force did catch a break the next morning. A woman from Frankfort, Kentucky, called the Crime Stoppers number to say the image of the girl's face she had seen on TV was that of her sister, Padgett Miller. The woman explained that Padgett had run away from home in May of 1976 at age fourteen after a drunken abusive evening of violence by their stepfather.

The family had lived in Avondale at the time of the girl's disappearance. After Padgett went missing, the parents eventually divorced. The mother, Louisa, moved back to Louisville with her remaining two children to be closer to the grandparents. Padgett's father died in car crash five years after her disappearance. The two sisters, both younger than Padgett, were now married with grown children. In fact, both were now retired. Their sister's death seemed a lifetime ago.

The caller to the tip line, Jeppi McPherson, said Padgett disappeared wearing shorts, tennis shoes, and a Garfield T-shirt purchased from a local outlet store. The pieces seemed to fit.

The FBI agreed to send officers the next day to bring Ms. McPherson to Cincinnati to identify the body and for DNA testing. However, the Coroner's office expressed concern the body's positioning in the trunk for forty years had mummified the corpse into a folded ball, legs bent at the knee, torso folded at the waist, feet splayed straight back and to the side of the buttocks, head pressed down. Identification of the face would be difficult and quite disturbing. The decision was reached by Saunders and Agate that the identification would be postponed until after a DNA match had been established.

Now, the detective team was reassembled to examine all features of what was now assumed to be the Padgett Miller cold case.

All five detectives took copies of the cold case and pored through it, making notes. They discussed points as they went. There was little to go on. The girl ran away and was never seen again. She never communicated with anyone ever again. Mainly, M.J. thought, because that monster had killed her.

For the day, Tobias told the detectives to assume the identification was accurate and that the deceased girl found in the trunk was Padgett Miller. The detectives' only lead worth following was that the girl was last been seen near the Beldon Arms Apartments, not far from the family home in Avondale. The rental units were cheap and V.A.-approved for returning veterans.

The two detectives assigned to the missing person's case in 1976, Detectives Aaron Brown and Wilson DeLong, noted the apartment complex consisted of thirty units. Most were one-bedroom apartments and inhabited by single men returned from Vietnam. A note from Brown said that the detectives planned to get a list of the tenants and would interview them to see if any could remember seeing Padgett Miller. There was no list of tenants for the Beldon Arms Apartments in the file. And there were no notes from any interviews, either. Being a detective is easy said no one ever.

Chapter Twenty-Five

M.J. returned to the office at 8:00 a.m. She was not the first to arrive. Rosie was already in the conference room working on a laptop. A cup of coffee steamed by her. "Morning, Rosie."

"Yeah," her partner said, "feels like we just left here."

"Think we did."

Rosie nodded, tiredly. "Fresh pot on in the breakroom."

"You upset about me lying to Mr. Evil about not liking my black partner."

"It don't make me jolly."

"You going to want Heather Primstone as your new partner?"

"Primstone's okay. She ain't you."

M.J. blew Rosie a kiss and went for a cup of joe.

Within a half hour, all five detectives were poring over cold case files for missing girls, looking for possible suspects, men who slipped through law enforcement's net decades before. Tobias arrived at the conference room at 9:00.

The five collectively took a pause and looked to their boss.

"I've spoken to human resources and the state retirement

office about Detectives Aaron Brown and Wilson DeLong. Brown is deceased, but DeLong is still living. He is in a state retirement home in Cleveland. I spoke to the head of nursing there and she tells me Mr. DeLong is still cogent and conversant despite being ninety years young.

"Being as he was a Cincinnati cop and retired as such,

the FBI has agreed to allow us the interview. I think Det. DeLong might be old school. After all, he retired from the force in 1982. Given that, I think Simmons and Decker are the right choice here. Simmons because Willie DeLong is also a black detective. Decker because Simmons has been carrying him for years."

The joke was so unexpected, given Tobias's general taciturn nature, that all five detectives paused a beat before laughing.

After the room finally resumed some semblance of order, Lt. Meyer said, "You'll be headed out with Special Agent Messerschmidtt and two other senior agents, plus an agent to record and film the interview. They're waiting downstairs for you."

M.J. said, "Another day going through these forty-nine cold cases for possible suspects, boss?"

Tobias's eyes softened. "I wish that was all I had for you, Janie. Jeppi McPherson is just arriving with FBI escort from Frankfort. She's asked to meet the officer who found her sister."

"That would actually be officer Riggio, sir."

"You'll do. And I think a female's empathetic touch is just what the doctor ordered for this meeting."

"Has the FBI swabbed her for DNA testing?"

"No, you'll need to do that, too. Make sure Rosie is with you for chain of custody considerations when you do it." Lt. Meyer left the room.

M.J. looked to Rosie. "I'll call you when I need you to witness."

Rosie looked at her. "This will be hard. You want me to go with you now?"

"No, but, thanks, Rosie. I got this." M.J. stood and headed to the elevator.

––––––

Ms. McPherson was a tough little woman, but after she questioned M.J. about how her daughter came to be found and why the FBI at this time wanted her DNA, she did cry.

Her sister's body was so distorted from forty years stuffed in a trunk that her corpse would not lay flat. The skin on the body was so mummified and gray in tint that M.J. knew it looked part like Frankenstein's monster. It was hard enough to deal with the death of your sibling, let along know she died a horrible death, the details still gruesome forty years later. That thought was almost unbearable.

While Jeppi gathered herself in the executive washroom on the first floor, M.J. texted Rosie. Her partner joined her in Interview One.

"How'd she hold up?"

"Like you'd expect."

"God, to lose my daughter that way, my Marie. It would destroy me."

M.J. reached out and took Rosie's hand. "Love you, partner."

Rosie responded with a sad grin and squeezed her hand back tight.

After swabbing Jeppi's cheek for saliva, the two detectives allowed FBI agents to conduct the cursory interview.

Jeppi, in her emotional state, had nothing to add. Forty

years took any memories which might have been helpful in the search. If there was anything to assist in the search for Padgett's murderer, it would be found in the casefile, not with her sister.

The detectives discovered the files stacked in the conference room were not called cold cases without reason. Ice files might have been more appropriate. The list of possible suspects for the murder of Padgett Miller was short and inconsequential.

Most of the men interviewed were now deceased. Others were alive but in their eighties or even nineties, not a possible match as M.J.'s caller. Others perhaps young enough to fit the profile no longer lived in the region, and with some effort, the detectives were able to verify the men's presence in another part of the country or, in two cases, another continent. It was slow, frustrating work, and all three women were exhausted and depressed by noon.

———

At 1:00 that afternoon, M.J. slipped away from the stacks of files. Downstairs, she approached Interview One. The first person of interest in the Klaire Keller kidnapping was already in the Interview Room.

M.J. tentatively opened the door to the adjacent room.

Kim Rodden saw her and nodded for her to join those in the room.

Supervising Special Agent Saunders nodded her way.

Detectives Meagers and Staples looked a bit startled that she would be in with them to watch the interview, but neither spoke.

Lt. Meyer looked mildly put out; she was present but said nothing.

As Agent Agate and another agent were just entering the interview room, no one spoke as M.J. sat down.

The self-proclaimed white supremacist, Roger Windings, was a short man with dark hair. He wore a black suit of western cut. His shirt was white with the top button open. He wore no tie. A black Stetson lay on the table. His attorney was a woman. She wore a dark suit, white shirt, and red scarf. Her brown hair was pulled tight and her glasses framed her face. She looked as dutifully serious as the situation.

M.J. watched the first twenty minutes of the interview, but left after she realized that one, she needed to get back to work and two, the interviewers weren't going to get anything relevant from Roger Windings, not that he was innocent. He was certainly capable of abducting Klaire Keller. He was a true believer in his racial cause. Fanatics and zealots are a scary lot. They can give their life for a cause. That makes them capable of almost anything.

Agate: We've heard your thoughts on race in America, Mr. Windings, but what we haven't heard is if you have information to add on Klaire Keller.

Windings: You act as if the little lady's disappearance has nothing to do with race. The note told you why she was taken. To provoke a race war. Someone, black or white, took her to provoke white people to take action, and by God, we will.

Agate: Do you know who took her?

Windings: I may, or I may not.

Agate: Mr. Windings, are you personally involved?

(At this point, the attorney leans over and whispers into Mr. Windings's ear.)

Windings: My attorney has asked that I not answer that question, as I am not under oath and am not required by law to provide an answer.

Agate: You are aware that it is illegal to lie to the FBI?

Windings: Yes, I am aware, but my attorney tells me it is not against the law to refuse to answer.

Agate: Then, you won't verify if you took Klaire Keller or know where she is currently being held?

Windings: Yes (grinning).

Agate: Yes, you know where she is?

Windings: No, yes, I won't verify.

An hour later, at shortly after 2:00 p.m., M.J. slid into the Interview Two viewing room, this time much to Lt. Meyer's exasperation, but again as she motioned a *mea culpa*, he said nothing, so she sat next to Kim Rodden. Meagers and Staples now just looked disgusted. She knew they thought she was horning in where she didn't belong.

In the interview room, a middle-aged black woman with gray-streaked hair in Rastafarian dreads sat in a long, flowing gown next to a distinguished black man in a deep navy-blue suit and collarless shirt. A gold chain with a lion's head pendant hung around his neck.

M.J. thought they looked like the soul singers Ashford and Simpson might at the end of middle age. She understood them to be Aaleyah Clark and Earl Bennington II, the two activists from the internet radio show. This time, Special Agent Saunders did the interviewing. Agate, looking ragged from the difficult argument with Roger Windings, sat next to Tobias.

Clark: What really is the problem here? I'll tell you. It's the word *Again* on those red hats. When was America great? Name the moment. And when you decide on one, choose carefully, because if you choose a man walking on the moon, remember that the same month, black men were being savagely beaten in the American south. Pick any day, and you will see that particular day was not a great day for the black man. America has not yet to this very day been great for people of color. When have we been treated equally as our white brothers? Don't we see it on TV every night? Rich white folk paying for their kids to get seats at the best colleges while deserving black children are left behind!

Saunders: Yes, I've read those same headlines, and the FBI has arrested many of those very celebrities you refer to for breaking laws. It is not a perfect world, but that's not why we're here today. We are here to try to find eleven-year-old Klaire Keller. You said on your radio show you would provide aid and comfort to the criminals who abducted her. Is that true?

Bennington: Sir, I am not only Ms. Clark's husband, but also her attorney. You've asked her a theoretical. I, as her attorney, will allow her to answer that question, but only as a theoretical. (He turns to his wife.) Baby, you understand that?

Clarke: I have Ph.D.'s in both human development and black studies from the University of California at Berkeley, so, yes, Earl, I understand what 'theoretical' means. (Turns to Saunders). Yes, I would give them aid and comfort, should they ask me. *Theoretically.*

Saunders: Have you provided the kidnappers aid and comfort in eluding law enforcement?

(Bennington gives Clarke a raised eyebrow.)

Clarke: On the advice of counsel and my condescending husband, I must decline to answer that question.

Saunders: Are you taking the fifth? To avoid incriminating yourself?

Bennington: No, my wife has not taken an oath in a court of law; therefore, your question does not require she take the fifth. She just ain't answering any more questions. We are through here.

Upstairs, things were better. Simmons and Decker were back from Cleveland after a quick return flight on one of the FBI's jets.

Rosie asked them, "Did you get the list of tenants from the Beldon Arms?"

Simmons said, playing it up, "It went down like this. The old man is sharp as a tack."

Decker added, "But blind as a bat."

"Accurate enough," laughed Simmons. "And he wanted to know if either one of us was, ah, 'of color.' "

Rosie laughed. "He actually asked that?"

"Straight out," Decker said.

"Did he remember the case?"

"Yeah," said Simmons, "very well. Let on that his partner was pretty much a racist and didn't want soldiers ending up with something in their permanent record about some trashy missing black girl."

"I had a feeling Detective Aaron Brown didn't like brown folk," Decker said. "or anyone of color."

"Unfortunate name, then," laughed Rosie.

"Anyway, Det. Willie DeLong has it going on. Smart guy and organized in his thoughts now, and back when he was on the force, too. He kept case books. You know, like the old murder books before we went electronic, except Willie, he kept them for *all* his cases. It was partially because his partner shielded white folk under investigation from showing up on paper."

"Ah, the good old days," Rosie said.

M.J. rolled her eyes.

Heather Primstone didn't speak. She was new and not from this precinct. She kept her mouth shut, especially about race. Smart girl.

"So where are these records?"

"His daughter's house."

Tobias entered the room as Simmons said the words. "And that house is located in Colerain, less than forty minutes away.

Detective Coleman, Agent Messerschmitt, and his team are downstairs. You are to go with them and take the lead in retrieving those City of Cincinnati police reports. The feds are not to see those until I review them first. Understand? Those records are ours, and you are not to relinquish chain of custody."

M.J. looked to Tobias, "Aw, boss, after all this desk time, can't I ride along? I can take a cell phone call just as easy in the back of an FBI SUV."

Tobias stared at her for a moment. "After all the time you spent downstairs in the Keller interviews today, I thought you were running this show. Do what you like."

He turned on his heel and left the room.

Rosie stiffened her spine and raised an eyebrow.

M.J. turned beet-red. Tobias never chewed people out. His words then were the closest he had ever come to telling someone off. M.J. waved Rosie and Heather to go on.

Simmons and Decker avoided eye contact with her. Each took a file off the stack and left the office to leave her in solitude.

Heather Primstone shrugged at M.J. and resumed reading.

Fifteen minutes later, Tobias Meyer reentered the detectives' conference room. His face was flushed; his eyes wild. "I've thought about it, M.J. I'd prefer if you just went home for the day. I've called your escort from District Two. They're waiting for you downstairs."

M.J. was shocked. What had happened? Had going into the interview rooms been such a breach of etiquette?

Heather Primstone waited until Lt. Meyer's elevator door closed before whistling.

"Whew, who pissed in his coffee cup?" she asked.

"Me, I guess," replied M.J. She picked up her things, swung her jacket over her shoulder, and grabbed her bag on the way out of the room. She punched the elevator down button and stood there, dumbly, until the ding brought her back.

The door opened, and Kim Rodden was inside.

"You the recipient of Tobias's displaced anger?"

"I guess," M.J. said. "He sent me home."

"Tsk, don't worry about it. Tobias just received a screaming call from the mayor."

"For what? Something I did?"

Rodden laughed. "No, no. His Honor stuck his foot in his mouth on the radio today. Might end up costing him the election in six weeks. The mayor knew he screwed up, so he blew a gasket, directing his anger at someone else. Tobias was an easy target. And now you were for Tobias. You know the old saying, 'The buck stops somewhere else.' "

M.J. thanked the FBI profiler on her way out. She wished Rodden's words made her feel better.

Radio WHTY, Cincinnati

"Robert Enweave, here at Cincinnati's news source, WHTY. When life is treating you like a punching bag, remember Bob Enweave.

"Today, the Queen City is still reeling from the station's exclusive interview with Mayor Lyle Lark. The day started with news that two complaints were filed with police union representatives in District Five. The complaints, one by a black officer, the other by a white, were about the N-word and its use on the force.

"The first complaint was filed by Sgt. Linda Washington, a black seventeen-year veteran of the department. She claims white officers used the N-word followed by the word 'bitch' to describe her in text messages. Those officers, not named in the press briefing today, claimed the words were sent on their private phones while off duty. Both officers report to Sgt. Washington at the District Five Precinct. The union says the officers are claiming a First Amendment right to their private comments on their own time. How the texts were forwarded to Sgt. Washington's phone was not explained in today's briefing.

"White officers filed the second complaint, saying a black female officer, Jenny Watson, is known to use the N-word in her interchanges with arrested or detained citizens. The white officers claimed the department,

while having no official policy regarding the N-word, requires whites to abstain from using the word while black officers may openly use the term.

"Officer Watson said in her reply to this station earlier today, 'It's different when a black woman says it to another black person. I use it to get real with people. For example, I might say, "Nigga, you need to use your head before making a bad decision like that." It's street talk. Believe me, the people we encounter have heard much worse.'

"Mayor Lark threw gasoline on the flames of controversy when he was asked about the two union disputes earlier today, responding with the following answer. **Lark:** *'Well, I guess you have to call everybody something.'*

"In other news, after Mayor's Lark's comments today and his steep drop in recent polls for next month's mayoral election, City Attorney, Mel Graves, announced he is contemplating a last-minute write-in run for the mayor's job.

"Mayor Lark was unavailable for comments regarding City Attorney Graves' plans.

"But here's my take; obviously, everyone over at City Hall is much too busy worrying about who's racially insensitive to spearhead the investigation to find those two little girls kidnapped last week. As of this evening, Paisley Park Jefferson will have been gone twelve days. Klaire Keller, nine. Monday will mark two weeks the cops have been searching, and the investigation seems to be going nowhere. I'm not alone when I say that a lot of Cincinnatians think we should throw all our current elected officials out on their ear on Nov. fourth.

"Remember to duck when things are coming at you too fast. Bob Enweave, back in three minutes."

Chapter Twenty-Six

The day was ending with a damp west wind. Clouds were piling up on the horizon, and the sun played hide-and-seek, burning through when it could, eventually losing to the formation of huge black thunderclouds. The impending storm matched M.J.'s mood.

She sat in the back of the patrol car, having just heard the radio and the mayor's idiotic comment. The two officers in the front discussed the two union beefs about the N-word. When they asked M.J. a question, she replied, but added nothing of substance to the conversation. They were unaware of how distraught she was because of Tobias's comments. She couldn't decide if she wanted to cry or call Riggs, but she knew she couldn't do either. Not until she got home.

It was nearing 4:00 p.m. as they reached her home in Newtown. The approaching storm appeared to be a nasty one. The front arrived. The air seemed to tingle with electricity. Lightning etched the sky. The wind swirled. Despite still being afternoon, the sky looked nearly night with that peculiar greenish tint of a major storm. Thunder buffeted her eardrums. Flashes lit the sky. The trees danced in the wind.

The two patrol cars pulled into M.J.'s driveway, the first letting her out. She raised the garage door and scampered inside, dodging the first raindrops.

Then came the rain. It fell in great sheets carried on gusts. Its roar on the roof was so terrific that no other sounds penetrated the garage. M.J. smiled, having beat the deluge by an instant. She entered her kitchen, flipping on lights as she went.

Through her kitchen window, she saw the youngest officer, Quentin something or other, in his rain slicker headed for his assigned position on her deck. The rainfall was heavy. M.J. felt pity for the patrolman out in that mess. She stepped to the sliding glass door to offer the young man shelter in the house, at least until the worst of the storm had passed.

Suddenly, she heard a burst of air, like a big rig's hydraulic brake. The police officer, just visible in her kitchen window, stumbled, his arm and slicker trailing downward. Then, thunder exploded over her house like a stick of dynamite and for an instant M.J. believed the policeman must have been hit by lightning. She kicked the board in the runner of her sliding door free, opening it to the hostile elements. M.J. could then see blood mixing with the rain on the deck beneath the fallen officer. She stepped into the tempest, leaning down, calling his name.

A figure lunged at her from behind the patio table. He was dressed in a black raincoat, hood pulled up. His face was hidden, but she could tell he was a big man.

She reached for her weapon on her hip but had no time.

The hulking form slammed into her.

M.J.'s head ricocheted off the grill lid. Her neck whipped forward as she fell. As she hit, a boot attempted to stomp her midsection, but using the hand not clawing at the weapon, she was able to fend off the assault, and…and then he was gone.

Lying on her side and only dimly aware of her attacker's retreat, M.J. finally grabbed the Glock from her hip. Rolling onto her back, she saw the man limping noticeably on his left leg as he ran across her yard. She fired twice just as he reached his vehicle, a pickup, of what color she was not sure.

The rain pelted down around her like liquid marbles, turning everything to gray. Her second shot hit the tailgate or perhaps the brake light. M.J. thought she saw the splinter of red plastic but couldn't be sure. An instant later, the truck was gone, spinning gravel down the alley.

M.J. attempted to rise to assist the fallen police officer. She saw, just then, the two officers who had given her a ride home. They were advancing around the corner, weapons drawn. As she rose, a black mist formed in her eyes. It corresponded with the intense pain at the base of her skull, and the detective blacked out.

———

M.J. was only unconscious for perhaps five minutes, but a lot happened during that time. When she once again became aware of her surroundings, she realized she and Quentin were both lying on her dining room floor. She attempted to raise up, but the female officer put a hand on her forehead and pressed her back down. "I'd stay down right now, detective. You're bleeding from the back of your head."

M.J. realized, as her clarity sharpened, that the police-woman was holding a compress to her hairline.

"What happened?" the officer said to her. "We heard shots and found you two down."

M.J.'s mind swung to action. "The perp, he shot the kid,

then shoved me as I came out the door. Gray pickup. I may have hit the right-side taillight." M.J. paused, the pain in her head intense when she spoke. "I think the truck was gray, but it was raining so hard."

M.J. realized the other two officers were attempting to stanch the bleeding on Quentin's side. "Where'd the bullet hit him?" she asked.

One of the officers turned his head to her. "He wasn't shot. He was hit by an arrow. Low on the right side. Came out his back and tore a big hole, but he'll make it. Ambulance is probably two minutes out."

The female officer called in the perp's pickup truck for a BoLo, but five minutes is a long time for a fleeing suspect, especially in a torrential storm. M.J.'s head wasn't working too well, but she knew, in all likelihood, their nemesis had escaped again.

True to the other officer's timetable, within a couple of minutes, her house became a triage scene as two ambulances and six EMTs did their thing. M.J. was loaded into the second unit. Quentin's wounds being the more serious made him the priority.

———

After an hour in emergency, a half hour in radiology, then a trip to get an MRI, M.J. was wheeled on a gurney to a private room at Mercy Health Hospital in Anderson Township.

Two officers were placed outside her door.

M.J. felt a fatigue like she had never known.

The attending physician told her it was a symptom of concussion. As much as she wanted to sleep, she couldn't, not for a while. The concussion protocol called for her mental acuity to be accessed every half hour for the next five hours.

M.J. nodded.

The doctor directed a penlight into her eyeballs, and she sighed.

A few moments later, M.J. felt someone in the room. She opened her eyes, groggily, to see Tobias standing over her. His eyes showed concern.

"The first time I dress someone down under my command and you go off and try to get yourself killed?" Tobias said, raising an eyebrow.

M.J. attempted to smile, but her face hurt. "It wasn't intentional." She paused. "Hey, I was pretty out of it back at my house, but I thought they said the attacker shot Quentin with an arrow."

Tobias nodded. "Another first for my command. Maybe in the history of the department. That will take some research."

"Is Quentin...I don't even know his last name. Is he going to be okay?"

"Quentin Jennings. Yeah, lost some blood, and the blade may have nicked his kidney. They're watching him for infection."

"Our perp shot him with a bow, like a compound bow?"

Tobias shook his head. "It was a booby-trap. Probably meant for you. Tripwire across your deck. Line was attached to the trigger of a tiny compressed air canister about the size of a tennis ball can. It shot one of those crossbow arrows. Probably would have killed a shorter person. Hit Quentin on the hip. Would have been your belly or chest."

M.J. pondered that line for a few moments. Mr. Evil had set a trap to kill her.

Tobias said, "What did you see?"

"Not much, really. Heard a whoosh which must have been the compressor. I stepped out as I saw Quentin go down. Perp was around the corner. He was onto me before I had a chance.

I hit my head going down. He attempted to kick me once. I blocked it and he ran."

"What did you see of him?

"He was big. Perhaps 6'2", hulking kind of guy. Heavy. He was wearing a black rain jacket. Hood pulled up. I didn't see his face at all. He was wearing Army boots, old ones, black and scuffed. Oh, yeah, he had a noticeable limp, left leg or foot."

"Vehicle?"

"Pickup, probably gray, maybe steel blue. It was raining so hard and I was down already when he was making his way to the truck."

"You got off two shots."

"Yeah, I don't think I hit him. He was already around the side of the vehicle when I fired. I do remember or think I remember hitting the right-side taillight."

"You did," he said, "we have red plastic fragments on scene."

The doctor entered from the hall. "Detective Monroe needs her rest right now, Lt. Meyer. You can talk to her again maybe in the morning."

Tobias smiled with some regret on his face. "Just one more thing. M.J., we spoke to your neighbor. Guy named Ted Upton."

"Yeah?"

"He said he saw the truck out there as the storm was approaching, but since he'd seen a pickup in your driveway the last few nights, he paid it no mind."

M.J. winced. "The truck in my driveway was officer James Riggio's. He works out of the Two."

Tobias nodded. "The department allows consensual relationships between officers and/or employees not in a chain-of-command supervisory/subordinate position provided they have submitted paperwork for review."

"The relationship is kind of new," she said.

"File the paperwork," he said.

The doctor cleared his throat, politely insisting that Lt. Meyer leave.

Tobias noted the nonverbal instruction. He looked to the doctor, then back to M.J. "One more last thing."

M.J. fixed her eyes on him. It was difficult to focus.

"I'm sorry for my words today. I overreacted after getting a call from the mayor. I took it out on you. You didn't deserve it."

"Thanks, Tobias," she said, closing her eyes. When she opened them again, her boss had left the room.

———

They let Riggs in to see her at 10:00 p.m. She was so exhausted she didn't really remember if they spoke or what they'd said to each other. M.J. did remember the anguish on his face as he entered the room and the relief on it as he kissed her cheek. She later learned Riggs slept on the couch in the hall all night, next to the twin guards stationed outside her door.

When the doctor finally gave the okay for her to sleep at 11:00, M.J. did not so much as slumber as she simply clocked out. Time and mind were switched off, and through God's grace, she didn't dream.

Chapter Twenty-Seven

M.J. felt mad when she awoke, but she also felt much better. She was truly furious that the evil she sought at her work followed her home. That evil monster brazenly came to her home in the daylight setting a trap that might have killed her, or that might have killed Riggio. That thought stopped her.

Before she had the chance to ponder potential outcomes, her door opened, and Special Agent Saunders and Kim Rodden stepped into the room.

Rodden crossed to the bed and leaned down to give her a hug.

M.J. smiled, surprised to see the two of them, and doubly surprised at how happy she was to see Rodden.

"How are you, M.J.?"

"Okay," M.J. replied, "but a little banged up."

"Close call, for you and for young officer Jennings," said Saunders. "Glad you are both going to be okay."

M.J. nodded. "Do you need information from me?"

Saunders shook his head. "No, Lt. Meyer provided a

report based upon his interview with you last night. We have all we need unless you have more to add."

M.J. shook her head. "I wish I had more."

Rodden shook her head. "You did great. We know more than we did yesterday afternoon. He's getting reckless. We're going to catch him."

"We need to find Paisley," M.J. said.

Rodden nodded. "Listen, Detective Monroe, we're here because we're concerned for your safety. It seems the man we seek has now shifted his attention from his fetish of young black girls to you. That's dangerous."

M.J. looked to Rodden. "Is that your appraisal?"

"Ahem."

Saunders added, "We think it would be best if you utilized the FBI's safe house for the duration of the case. It is vacant at this time. We can make it available to you as soon as you are discharged."

M.J. looked at Kim Rodden. "You think it's necessary for me to leave my home?"

"I do, M.J. Things are accelerating. I have lots of experience in cases with serial perpetrators. When they lash out like this monster lashed out last night, we catch them quick. We have too many tools, and they get sloppy."

"Okay, I'll do it. I hope I'm going home today. Well, not home…"

"We do, too," Saunders said. "We'll make the arrangements with Lt. Meyer."

"By the way," Rodden said with a wink, "there's a big, handsome man outside waiting to see you."

M.J. smiled but said nothing, and the two exited.

But Riggs wasn't the next person in. It was her doctor. Her tests had come back from the previous night, and she was cleared to go home. However, the physician did run another set of concussion protocols.

After five minutes, he agreed to discharge her if she guaranteed him she would not work for the next two days. No TV, no strenuous activity, no bright lights, no computer work, no loud music.

M.J. promised.

Then, Riggs entered a moment later to escort her to the safe house.

———

M.J. tried to get Riggs to go by and get his paints, but he explained she needed low lighting and painting needed lots of light. They compromised. He would cook and they would listen to an audiobook. M.J. agreed with the caveat the book could not involve criminals.

M.J. would have liked to say the new surroundings and spending a lazy Saturday afternoon with the new man in her life were romantic, but the truth was upon arrival at the safe house, M.J. fell fast asleep on the sofa.

When she awoke, it was dusk.

M.J. stood. "It's getting to be a habit for me to wake up with you in the kitchen," she said.

Riggs laughed. "Yeah, FBI safe houses are not the best supplied with culinary equipment.

"How'd you get groceries here?"

"Gave money and a list to the plainclothes officers who are trying so hard to be invisible across the street."

"They shopped for us?"

"Yeah, I knew one of them. It'll cost me some beers some night."

M.J. nodded. "Did you get wine?"

Riggs shook his head. "Doctor said no, so I didn't. Wouldn't want to tempt you."

After dinner, M.J. called Rosie. She was also at home, and also had her man cooking dinner for her. David was over, Marie was at his mother's; Rosie and her ex had a romantic evening planned. M.J. gave her a tsk-tsk but had no room to talk. They agreed Rosie would come by the safe house for lunch and would catch M.J. up on the investigation.

———

In the morning, M.J. was remarkably better. So much so, she was able to convince Riggs to drive her to church. Her church, St. John Fishers, was back in Newtown, and the safe house was in Mason.

Riggs was willing if they could get some Kentucky Fried Chicken on the way back.

M.J. decided it was a good trade and took it.

The service began at 10:30, but M.J. wanted to get there early so she might go to the confessional. They made it there by 9:35 with Riggs complaining that his jeans and flannel shirt were inappropriate.

M.J. assured him nobody would mind. She cleaned herself up a bit with the clothes Kim Rodden placed in an overnight bag for her; black leggings, boots, and a long gray sweater. M.J. was so short the sweater descended below her knees, but she liked Kim's tastes and wore it, anyway.

Inside the church, a few friends stopped to check on her. Word had spread she'd been injured in the line of duty. She saw Ted Upton in the lobby reception area having a cup of coffee and she knew how the news had traveled.

Ted waved and started over, but M.J. motioned she was

headed into the vestibule. He nodded he would see her after the service.

M.J. waited until the few parishioners ahead of her cleared away. It was nearly time for the service, but she stepped into the confessional at the last minute. She closed the screen loud enough the priest on the other side to slow his exit. M.J. heard him sit back down.

In a moment, the slide opened, and the priest's voice came through in a soft tenor. "Bless you, my child."

M.J. made the sign of the cross. "Forgive me, Father, for I have sinned. It has been one month since my last confession. I accuse myself of the following sins." M.J. paused.

"Go ahead. You are secure in the Lord."

"I have committed adultery," she again paused, "on two separate occasions."

"I see," said the priest behind the lattice. "Have you more to confess?"

"I wish a man dead. He is a very bad man, one who preys on children. He claims to have taken the lives of children. I have fantasized of killing him myself."

"It is understandable when confronted with such evil to wish the ability to prevent it from ever occurring again, but my child, it is not for us to decide. Life and death, for everyone, is in God's hands."

"I am sorry for these sins, Father. But if I have a chance to end this man's life, I will take it. The world will be a much better place without him."

"You must attempt to rid yourself of these thoughts. Go in peace," he said, beginning to recite the Act of Contrition.

M.J., once again, gave the sign of the cross and exited, joining Riggs in a pew at the back.

After, on the way back to the safe house, M.J. looked at Riggs as he drove her. "Thank you," she said. "It was incredibly nice of you to take me. I get the feeling it's been a while since you've been in church. Were you raised Catholic?"

Riggs took his eyes off the road just for an instant. He smiled broadly. "You really don't remember what we talked about two nights ago at the hospital, do you? I waited all day for you to say something."

M.J. stared at him. "Why! What?" She laughed at herself. "No," she admitted, "I have no clue. Maybe you'd refresh my memory over lunch."

"Maybe," he replied, "but remember Rosie will be there. It might not be the best time." Then, he laughed and pulled into the restaurant's drive-thru.

Chapter Twenty-Eight

Rosie had something M.J. wanted to see. After a lunch of fried chicken, Rosie walked back to her car to get the case files. And with them, Willie DeLong's crime books from the '80s. Unfortunately, his daughter combined the cardboard boxes. Three large boxes contained his case files from his two decades on the force. Riggs helped Rosie carry the heavy, overstuffed boxes inside.

Riggs would not let M.J. do any close work requiring reading or computers, so she played D.J. throwing on soul and jazz as Rosie and Riggs separated the files out by dates. M.J. made coffee and served up hot brownies out of the oven.

It took two hours to sort it all out, but eventually they found what they were looking for, Padgett Miller's case file.

Inside were stacks of interview notes from Detectives Brown and DeLong. DeLong, obviously the more meticulous note-taker, had good handwriting and was thorough in his approaches to interviewing potential suspects and/or witnesses. Brown's notes were less than adequate. Some of

Brown's interviews contained no notes except for the words, *Not a suspect* scrawled across the page.

A large banded section of the box included the interviews of the residents of Beldon Arms, the last place Padgett Miller was seen alive. Detectives Brown and DeLong evidently decided to split up the residents and each canvas half of the residents.

With the difference in their recordkeeping and their interview skills, one stack, those by Brown, was quite thin, while the second stack, those by DeLong, was voluminous. Rosie and Riggs decided to cut through Brown's first since they could be read and digested in less than ten minutes, sometimes much less.

Each time one of them completed reviewing a folder, one of the two entered the Beldon Arms resident from 1977 into the police data base to see if the interviewee had a police record. M.J. suggested each be checked in the NDI, the National Death Index. Rosie agreed. Many of the names on the list would now be deceased.

Most of the residents were vets back from Vietnam as the apartment complex was approved for V.A. housing subsidies. The average age of the tenants was twenty-three, which made them now an average age of sixty-five. Not surprisingly for low-income veterans returning from an unpopular war, a third of those out of Brown's fifteen were now deceased.

Four of those living had police records. One of those was currently in prison, thus not a suspect. The other three's crimes were DUI convictions. Out of the nine not dead and not in prison, two had retired to Mexico. Of the remaining seven, only four lived within two hours' drive of Cincinnati. Rosie set those files and names for further inquiry.

The next fifteen files, those interviews written up by DeLong, took longer to read. M.J. first input the names to look at driver's licenses. Three lived far out of state, two retired to Florida, and one now residing in Toronto. That left twelve files to read.

Rosie and Riggs settled down at the kitchen counter to read the thick stacks of paperwork in each file.

M.J. refilled each's coffee cup and then peered down into the now empty box from DeLong's daughter's attic, except it wasn't empty. A single sheet of ruled paper was in the box. M.J. lifted it out, walking to the bedroom to get her glasses, which Riggs refused to let her wear since she was not to be reading today. M.J. lay on the bed and reviewed the list on the sheet of paper. She read the heading, "Residents of Beldon Arms Apartment at Time of Padgett Miller's Disappearance."

She read through the names. Four from the bottom, listed for a walk-out basement apartment, #004, she saw a name. A light flashed in her head.

M.J. jumped up from bed. A dart of pain shot through her neck and skull for the first time that day. She slowed and walked into the living room, calling to the big man peering intently into a folder.

"Hey Riggs, what was the name of that old lady you moved to city housing after the water from the retaining pond was released?"

Riggs looked up. "Why?"

"Just answer me. What was it?"

"Hondros. Betty Hondros, I think. Why?"

M.J. set the sheet of paper on the counter. "Look here." She pointed at the fourth name from the bottom.

Rosie rose from her chair and stepped in between M.J. and Riggs. "Terrance James Hondros." She paused and then turned her face to Riggs. "Who's the lady?"

"Just some old bat. Her first floor was inundated with

water from the retaining pond after the truck went over the viaduct there."

"In the pond where we found Padgett Miller's body. Two hundred yards up the hill from the Hondros's home," M.J. said, finishing the thought.

"Coincidence?" Rosie asked.

"Detectives don't believe in coincidences, Rosie. I think you told me that my first week as your partner."

Rosie smiled. "I did, didn't I?"

"Where is this old woman now?" M.J. said, looking at Riggs.

"Close. Place called the California Inn. Long-term stay place, mostly retirees. City has a contract for five units to put people up after house fires and things like that."

"Riggs," M.J. said, "go turn off the coffee. I'll get my shoes and a jacket. We're going to talk to that woman right now. Rosie, you can drive."

Riggs said, "You're not supposed to be out working today, M.J. Stay here. Rosie and I can go."

"No way, no way," she insisted. "I'm going. I'll let Rosie do the talking, but I feel it. This is our guy. We have a name."

Rosie said, "Riggs, can you drive my car over? I'm going to read as much as I can on the way." Rosie looked at her partner. "Well, go get your shoes. We've a murderer to catch."

———

Betty Hondros was holed up in unit #16 of the California Inn. She answered the door, offering a gap just as far as the security chain would allow. Seeing Riggs, she closed the door again, and the three could hear the chain lock released.

Mrs. Hondros opened the door, "Officer Riggs, have you

come to take me home? I called the city housing on both Thursday and Friday, but I didn't hear back."

"I'll check on it right away," he replied, "but first I'd like to introduce you to two of Cincinnati's finest detectives, Detective Rosie Coleman and Detective M.J. Monroe. Might we come in and talk to you for a bit?"

"No," the old woman said, frowning. "This little tiny room is a mess. My dirty clothes are piled in the chair. There's no place for four people to sit, except on the bed and that's not okay with me. Let's go someplace for coffee. Give me five minutes to put on my face," she said and then closed the door.

Rosie looked at M.J. and they both shrugged.

Twenty minutes later, the four were seated in Frisch's and steaming cups of joe were in front of each. A metal carafe set in the center of the table.

Riggs took a sip and said, "Too hot. While my coffee's cooling, I'll go and see if I can raise anyone at housing. I think I have an emergency number on my phone for them. Excuse me."

When he was gone, Ms. Hondros stared curiously at the two women. "I've been thinking all the way over what I could have done to have two detectives after me. I must admit I'm stumped. I did some hell-raisin' in my day, mind you, but now my only vice is cigarettes."

M.J. shook her head slowly, saying, "It's not anything you've done, Ms. Hondros. We're looking for your son, Terrance James Hondros. We thought you might know where he is these days."

"I know where he is, but Terry was my brother, not my son."

"And where is he?" Rosie asked.

"Dead. Dayton National Cemetery. Buried with military honors three years ago, come November."

Both M.J. and Rosie were shocked. Nothing in the file written all those years ago indicated he was dead. They hadn't bothered to run his name before coming over. They had no idea if he had a record of prison time or was listed in the National Death Register. They had not bothered to take the time. M.J.'s intuition had been so strong they'd just come here, expecting to find the killer's address.

"Did you attend the funeral?"

"No, I didn't even know he was dead for a year. I did visit his marker last Veteran's Day. Don't think anyone except the chaplain was at his service. Terry was a loner. Well, not always, but after the war he was. Vietnam messed him up. He moved out three months after he got back and cut all ties with the family. We just never saw him again hardly."

"When's the last time you did see him?" M.J. asked.

"Ran into Terry at an Outback Steakhouse a few years ago. Hadn't seen him for more than ten years. He walked up to the table, me, my old man and the kids. He said, 'Hey Betty, good to see you.' It was weird. Him living in town and not seeing us all them years. Then, he asked about Lowell and Daphne. Those were our parents' names. That's how he said it, too, Lowell and Daphne. I told him they'd been dead for more than ten years, and he just nodded. Then, Terry just walked off. After he left, my old man asked, 'Who was that?' I said it was my brother. It blew him away.

"My old man and me never did get married, but we lived together over twenty years until the two girls moved off and he died on that damn motorcycle of his. I've been alone ever since." Betty paused for a moment lost in reflection.

"Never heard from Terry again, not even a death notice, until the V.A. sent me the flag from his coffin about a year ago."

"You say Terry moved out. Do you still have any of his things? I mean, at your house?"

"Well, the house is a sore subject these days. I'll be suing the city if they don't make good on all the damage to my first floor and my foundation. But yeah, I've still got Terry's flag and his military stuff. It's up in the attic. My girls used to look at it sometimes, but nobody's been in those boxes for years. Mice probably ate it all up by now."

Rosie nodded. "Could we go back to your house and look at Terry's stuff?"

Ms. Hondros said, "If you can get me back in my house, then yes, I'll let you look at it. There's nothing of interest in it. Some Hawaiian shirts, old army uniforms, some photos of guys from his outfit, I guess. Just junk."

"How'd he get all that stuff home?"

"He had a trunk, big nice one. Mahogany or the like. But he took that with him when he moved. Just threw all the stuff he didn't have room for into cardboard boxes and said he'd come back for it. Never did."

Betty Hondros, looking like a light went off behind her eyes, suddenly said, "Do you guys think Terry did something? Because if you think he did, it was the war caused it. It ruined him. When he came back, his face just stopped reflecting back in mirrors, if you know what I mean. There was no Terry there anymore. Like he was dead inside, but his outsides hadn't been told."

The old woman took a sip of coffee, savoring it. "Don't matter, anyway, now. Dead these three years. Whatever he's done, God will have to sort it out." She paused. "Or maybe sent him down there." The old woman tipped her chin. The loose-crepe skin of her jowls wobbled. "I wish they still let you smoke in here. Excuse me." And the old woman left the table and headed outside to light up.

Rosie said to M.J., "What do you think?"

M.J. said, "I would have said we had the right guy, except his sister says he's dead. Had a big trunk just like the one Padgett was found in."

"Yeah, hearing about the trunk made the hair on the back of my neck stand up," Rosie agreed. "You keep at her. I'll go and call him in. See if he's in the system."

A few moments later, Betty Hondros returned to the table.

Riggs followed her in. "Ms. Hondros," he said, "the housing people said they left a message on your cell phone both Thursday and Friday. They had good news. Your house was inspected by city engineers and they said its structural integrity is still okay."

Betty Hondros smiled. "Well, hell, I don't own no cell phone. Only message machine I got is a codaphone recorder on my landline at home. Those dumb bunnies must have left a message at my house that it was okay for me to go back to my house. How smart is that? Let's get to it. I'll go pack my stuff and you three can take me home."

"One more question, if I may, Ms. Hondros." M.J. asked. "Did Terry come back from the war with a limp? Did he get hurt in the war?"

Betty Hondros laughed. "Yeah, that's one for the record books. You know that trunk I mentioned? Well, it shows up around the first of October in 1974. And then about three weeks later, we get word Terry has been injured in combat and was discharged. But the truth was he shipped a trunk full of contraband home and then a month later when his unit was under attack Terry shot himself in the foot. He always limped after that."

"Which foot?" asked M.J., remembering the big man lumbering across her lawn in the storm.

"His left. Terry was smart enough to get out of 'Nam alive

but wanted to be able to drive a car afterwards. He waited until he was in a firefight to shoot himself, too. I remember him telling me that the Military Police interviewed him in the hospital in Saigon about his wound.

"They didn't believe he hadn't done it himself, but they had no proof. The war was ending. We were getting our ass kicked and everybody wanted out. The war was over or nearly so, and they just let it slide. He got a Purple Heart and was granted burial with full honors up in Dayton with all the other white crosses."

Betty Hondros stood, "Wasted life, though. Terry was a good guy before he went to war. That guy never came home."

While Betty was back at her place packing, Rosie got a return call from the sgt.'s desk at the District One's precinct. Rosie listened for a few moments. Then she nodded, satisfied.

M.J. looked at her. "What you got?"

"Terrance James Hondros did two years from '82 to '84 at Youngstown in the State Pen."

"What for?"

"Attempted rape."

M.J. replied. "Now, we just have to figure out how he faked his death."

Chapter Twenty-Nine

In the car, M.J. sat in the backseat next to Betty Hondros. Riggs drove, while Rosie rode shotgun. M.J. could smell smoke on the old woman's clothes and hair. She decided to continue to interrogate Betty Hondros.

"Ms. Hondros, can I ask you a delicate question?"

The woman turned her creased face to M.J. "Kind of just did." She laughed and said, "Sure, Terry was lost to the family long ago. Ask away."

"How did Terry feel about black people?"

Betty Hondros sat up a tiny bit straighter in her seat and pointed a finger surreptitiously at Rosie in front of her. The old lady raised one eyebrow as a question of decorum.

M.J. nodded it was okay to answer.

"Well, you know, my daddy was a John Birch Society member. He kept a Rebel flag tacked to the wall over the couch. Hated 'em, he did. Terry never seemed to have a feeling about coloreds one way or another. But you know, I always wondered about it. Because it ended up being why Terry moved out.

"See, we young-uns with Momma and Daddy went away for the weekend to a fish camp my daddy and his buddies leased back in the day. We stayed in a tent, but a big storm came and washed us out. Blew the tent down and all. Terry stayed home. Everything was soaked, so Momma insisted Daddy drive us kids home. We arrived about midnight unexpectedly, and Terry got caught with a girl in his room, a black girl. Daddy and Terry had this huge fight. 'Course it ended with Terry moving out.

"He was a man by then, back from the war. Messed up by then, too. We all knew he was battling something. And we all knew he and Daddy would come to words or blows sooner or later. But bringing home a black girl was the straw, don't you know. I remember being surprised Terry would be trying to bed a black girl. I don't remember him showing them any interest in school, but I was younger, so maybe I just didn't notice."

————

Back at the Hondros house, the three police officers helped the old woman carry her belongings through the front door. The first floor had wet carpets from the flooding, but no furniture was to be found on the entire first level. The ground floor was now just a giant mud room for rubber boots, fishing pools and outdoor furniture brought in from the environments. River rats were nothing if not pragmatic.

The Hondros home was a three-story split level. On the split level up, a big screen TV and a reclining chair faced each other. They inhabited an area probably designed for a kitchen table. There was no table and only a couple of bar stools next to the counter. A coffee pot rested there unplugged. Generally, the kitchen was clean and kept. M.J., though, could smell the damp coming off the wet rugs on the lower level. Mold, M.J. shuddered, black mold.

Betty Hondros appeared to physically unwind as she reached the landing level. "Just drop the boxes anywheres. I'll put it away later."

Rosie set her armload on the kitchen counter. "Would it be okay for us to see Terry's old room?"

"Sure, but his stuff ain't been in it for decades," said the old lady. "We boxed what there was and put it in the attic. You're free to see that stuff, too, but I've been through it. Nothing of note. He took anything of value with him."

M.J., Riggs, and Rosie went up to the third floor. The dormer room at the head of the stairs had been Terry's old room. It was now home to furniture removed from the lowest level. An old console TV, a ratty couch, and a table and six chairs were piled into the room.

In the attic, Betty found two boxes of Terry's things.

Rosie opened one box, Riggs the other.

M.J. allowed herself to look around the flotsam and jetsam of the open floor with an A-sloped ceiling. The room ran the length of the house but was narrower than the lower floors as the gables from the roof pinched in.

Against a far wall, M.J. spotted something. She walked over and picked it up. It was a long dark tray. Made of wood, it had three compartmentalized trays. The wood was dark, highly varnished, and heavy. It was a little over three-feet-long and perhaps a foot wide.

"What's this, Ms. Hondros?"

The old lady looked quizzically at the tray for a moment. "Oh, I think that's the insert from Terry's trunk from when he got back from the war. It wouldn't fit after he got all his clothes in it, so he just left it. Never came back, not ever, so here it is. I always liked it. Good feeling wood, don't you think?"

It did not take long for the crime lab to verify the tray M.J. found in the Hondros attic was, indeed, custom made to fit inside the lip of the trunk which held the body of Padgett Miller.

By early Sunday evening, the detective team was, again, in the conference room on the fourth floor of the FBI office in Blue Ash. Agent Agate stood at a whiteboard. All five detectives, Supervising Special Agent Saunders, Agent Messerschmidt, Profiler Kim Rodden, and Tobias Meyer surrounded the table. The clock struck six times. Paisley Park Miller had been missing exactly thirteen days.

Agent Agate addressed the room. "Here's what we know. Terrance James Hondros returned from the war in 1975. He moved back in with his family. He seemed moody and changed by the war. Terry spent a lot of time in his room alone. His parents took the family camping for the weekend. They came home unexpectedly and caught him with a black girl in his room. His father, an admitted racist, and Terry fought. Terry moved out. He took the trunk but left the matching tray M.J. found.

"The crime lab has verified the tray as belonging to the custom-built trunk found containing the body of Padgett Miller. In addition, Terry Hondros's conviction on attempted rape would correlate with a pattern of violence against women, plus his time in prison would correspond with the white supremacy branding on our victims and its evolution during the '80s."

"However," Saunders said, "we have records of Terry Hondros's burial at Dayton National Cemetery from three years ago."

"Correct," said Agate, her eyes flashing just a little for

being interrupted, "but we have contacted the emergency line for the Cincinnati Veteran's Administration. I spoke to the head of the Ohio regional office. He was able to access Hondros's file. Terry's V.A. case manager was a guy named Kendall Blanchett. He still works there. However, the emergency number for Blanchett is a non-working number.

They're trying to find him as we speak."

"We pulled Kendall Blanchett's information from his driver's license," added Tobias Meyer. "Our dispatch will call in the next ten minutes. We'll send patrol cars to the residence and get Mr. Blanchett to call my number here."

"What else we got?" Saunders asked.

M.J. said, "I have a question for Kim. The young black girl at the Hondros residence, do you think that could have been a precipitating experience for these murders? Payback for being deprived of sex all those years ago?"

Kim shook her head. "There's no way to tell that. Maybe he was already suffering from psychosis, and his family arriving back unexpectedly saved the girl's life. Maybe Terry had planned to kill her that night. or maybe it was just a hook-up between a lonely G.I. back from the war and a girl he met. I know what you're thinking, M.J. Men's libido is a fragile thing. And men confronted with that fragility can lash out. But there's not enough detail for me to venture any kind of guess."

———

Police officers did find Mr. Blanchett at home on his Sunday evening, but not the home the V.A. listed as his residence. He, like millions of other people, downsized during the last Great Recession and didn't keep his land line upon arriving at his new home. Blanchett was shocked to be asked to call the FBI task force about a former client.

Blanchett spoke over the speaker in the room.

Saunders fielded the call as Blanchett was a federal employee.

"Terry Hondros, sure, I remember him," said Blanchett. "Big guy and a total grumpuss. Had a bad foot. Injured in the war. He walked with a limp. But the limp was the least of his problems. His mental state was what was keeping him back. Just a malcontent who didn't like people. Hondros was like a lot of older veterans, watching Fox News, yelling at his TV all day. Getting benefits and social security. He was a retired G.E. worker, I think. Took the early out. Anyway, he was just getting by financially until Michael Minner took him in."

"Who's Minner?" Saunders asked for the room.

"Just another vet. Minner was paralyzed below the waist. Wheelchair bound. His wife passed, and he was looking for someone about the same age and most importantly, same political persuasion, to live with him.

"Needed someone to do things a man in a wheelchair couldn't. Wanted a vet. Was willing to give free room and board for companionship and basic services. Minner owned his condo and had some money after his wife died. I hooked those two up. Made my life easier on two counts. Hondros was broke and Minner needed assistance."

"Where did they live?"

"Over in Fairfield. Right off 4 Bypass. Had a nice condo with two bedrooms. They got on okay. No problems to speak of."

"But Hondros died."

"Yeah, of a heart attack."

"That was three years ago?" Saunders asked.

"Ahuh. I was out of the country at the time. My husband and I were on this bucket list trip. We spent a month in

Australia and New Zealand. Trip of our lives. When I returned to work, I found out Mr. Hondros died."

"I see," said Saunders. "You weren't there at the time of his death?"

"No, my case load was covered by Elly Stevens. She has since finished her Ph.D. at UC and is now teaching social work at Morgantown at the University of West Virginia."

"What happened to Mr. Minner?"

Blanchett paused for a second. "By the time I got back, he was moved back to Arkansas. That's where he was from.

Cincinnati was where his wife was born, I think. After Terry died, Mr. Minner decided it would be too difficult to break in another live-in companion. He moved in with his sister, if I remember correctly."

"Did you ever see him again?" Saunders asked.

"No, he was packed and gone by the time we got back from our trip."

"One last question, Mr. Blanchett. What kind of vehicles did the two men have?"

"Of course, Minner couldn't drive. Had no motor response below his waist, but he owned a white panel van. Had a lift on the passenger side. When Michael had appointments at the V.A., Terry would drive him. I think he was pretty good about it. It was a symbiotic relationship, but they both hated Obama, so it worked out."

"What did Hondros drive?"

"Mr. Minner did Terry a real kindness about six months in. Terry drove this awful hooptie that was always breaking down. One day, Michael bought a big, fancy pickup truck off the internet. He said Terry could drive it as long as he lived there."

"What color was it?"

"Gray, I think, light gray."

Saunders updated the VA case worker's contact information and ended the call. The supervising special agent said, "I think I speak for all of us when I say I fully expect to find Terry Hondros killed paraplegic Michael Minner and assumed his identity. We'll need to get a warrant to exhume the body once the kidnapping case has been closed."

He looked around the room. "This is a very dangerous adversary we're after. We have lots to do before the dawn because tomorrow we're catching this son of a bitch."

The conference room phone rang again.

Saunders picked up. It was Kendall Blanchett once again. Saunders put the call on speaker so the room could hear.

"Agent Saunders? I just thought of something else. Right before I went on my trip, I remember thinking that maybe I'd been wrong about Terry Hondros being such a terrible person. I went to visit them for the last time before my trip. Anyway, Terry told me he'd never gotten on with his family.

"Hadn't spoke to them in years, and he told me since Michael Minner was so good to him, Terry changed his will. He decided to leave Michael his pontoon boat. It was really the only thing of value he owned. I remember thinking Terry did have a heart of gold after all."

Saunders thanked Blanchett once again and ended the call. "And that, my friends, is evidence of premeditation," he said.

Chapter Thirty

At 6:00 a.m. Captain Delores Knowles, acting Chief of the Cincinnati Police, stood before the assembled team. When Lt. Meyer and Special Agent Saunders decided today was the day to bring out the full-court press, Capt. Knowles was informed and arrived to lead the interagency operation and to inform the press if and when an arrest was made. Success would probably take the "acting" off her title. With no known address for Hondros, the search would be for his boat.

Over one hundred uniformed officers, sixty FBI agents, fourteen police detectives, fifteen sheriff deputies from surrounding townships, and the crews of four Coast Guard Auxiliary patrol boats were readied for the manhunt. Marine patrols for Sunday were doubled on both the Ohio and Kentucky sides of the river. Forty Kentucky police officers would be working with the FBI on their side of the river, as well. The acting chief gave a quick speech and wished everyone a safe and successful mission. Everyone knew this was Tobias Meyer's moment. Even Delores Knowles knew it, so she did not attempt to steal his limelight.

The plan was to check every mooring, every boat dock, and every private portage of every boat, and every boat along both sides of the Ohio. It would take as many officers as any operation anyone could remember.

Once Knowles nodded and tipped her cap to Lt. Meyer, he set free the dogs.

At least 200 law enforcement officers descended upon the river from four locations. By evening, they should have Hondros.

And yet this wide net of police on the Ohio was not the only channel being utilized to find the kidnapper/murderer. Driver's license checks for Terry Hondros and Michael Minner turned up only a defunct license for Hondros issued in 2012.

He was listed as deceased in OHDOT records. Minner, having been paralyzed in a Jeep accident while on duty in Japan in 1980, had no driver's license on record. However, even with the deceased status, police now had a full-frontal image of the man they sought. Terry Hondros's photo was printed on hundreds of flyers. Police on both sides of the river memorized his features and his specifics, 6'3", 250 lbs. brown eyes, black hair, grayer now than in the photograph.

FBI technicians took Terry Hondros's face and measured its unchangeable aspects. Facial recognition programs began to monitor faces in public places, at stoplights, and at federal and state offices.

Agent Agate managed to track down Dr. Elly Stevens at her home in Morgantown just after dawn Monday morning.

Stevens verified Blanchett's story. She filled in for the full-time VA case worker during his month-long trip to Australia three years ago. During Blanchett's absence, one of his clients died of a heart attack. The deceased man's roommate called her to inform the VA. His name was Michael Minner. She actually couldn't remember the roommate's name but was able to confirm it when asked. The dead man she did remember since she filed the final paperwork on him; it was Terrance James Hondros. Yes, she attended the funeral. Only a chaplain, the color guard, and she were in attendance. And, of course, Mr. Minner, who'd hired a driver to bring him in his van.

It was very sad, she said, seeing how this soldier had been forgotten, except for a single friend. She'd been able to describe Minner as a big man in a wheelchair. Yes, she said, Minner told her he planned to move to Arkansas to be with his sister and would sell his condo. She knew nothing more.

Agent Messerschmidt struck gold just after the teams departed to begin their search. Messerschmidt found Minner sold his condo three years ago, and in closing wired the proceeds to a bank in Little Rock. The account, since closed, held more than $100,000 when the deposit from the sale of the condo tripled the overall amount. The location of the $300,000 was now unknown.

Messerschmidt's next step was to check Arkansas driver's licenses for Michael Minner. He ran the social security number, and bingo. Michael Minner received an operator's license and registered two vehicles, a 2010 Dodge van and a 2015 Chevy Tahoe. The van was white; the truck was steel blue.

Ten minutes after the discovery, Messerschmidt downloaded the driver's license photo and sent it and the license plate numbers to each officer on the river. The search began in earnest by 7:00 a.m., and for the first time, they had the exact vehicles and license plates they were seeking.

M.J. and Rosie were positioned in one of the Coast Guard patrol boats. It was a chilly morning, and both detectives stayed in the cabin, listening to the police transmissions on the radio. Their boat's role in the dragnet was to work its way up the river from the Serpentine Wall by the US Bank Arena out toward the east, clearing each portage as they went. They spotted for the multiple teams on the banks. M.J. and Rosie, along with their Coast Guard team, used binoculars and directed the search onshore. Teams of uniformed officers and FBI agents knocked on doors and checked parking stalls, garages, and lots for either the white van or the steel blue pickup.

Simultaneously, Messerschmitt was check for pontoon boat registrations with the Ohio Department of Parks and Recreation but found none. He struck out checking in Kentucky, as well. The boat was not on anyone's radar. He began cross-referencing the two vehicles' record of insurance.

Then, he contacted the insurance company on file for the car and van. He found the boat was also insured by the same Arkansas-based company. The address was bogus, but the authorities now knew the boat they sought was a 1995 thirty-two-foot Sun Tracker Party Cruiser. It featured a fourteen by-twelve air-conditioned cabin and a Mercury 300-horse outboard on three pontoons. It was a nice boat for entertaining or fishing, but it would not be fast.

The going was slow. It was surprising how many nooks, crannies, inlets, and ports the Ohio River secreted. And it was astonishing how many of those little hidey-holes held boats. The two female detectives worked their way east.

Decker and Simmons worked their way west.

Similar crews started at the end far ends of Hamilton County and worked toward the center.

By noon, M.J. figured the incoming crew and her outgoing crew would meet at Riverbend, the concert venue. She prayed they would find the boat soon. Paisley would be gone two weeks today. Too long. M.J. said a silent prayer the little girl was still alive.

At two in the afternoon, Rosie switched from coffee to bottled water. She looked at M.J. "Something's not working. Why haven't we found him? We're running out of boat docks. According to Tobias's last count we've cleared nearly three thousand boats and twice that number of vehicles. Nothing. No matches. The guy's a phantom and a monster. We need to find him today. I don't know where the investigation will go if we don't find Hondros today. He's just off the grid, like he's one step removed or something."

"We still have about four miles of shoreline left to search," M.J. replied, "a mile for each of the four teams. Have faith, partner of mine," M.J.'s words were enthusiastic, but her mood was at low ebb, too. They'd not slept the night before, prepping for this massive manhunt. They were hungry, tired, distressed, and depressed.

M.J. suddenly stared back at her partner. "What'd you say about him being off the grid?"

"Just that," Rosie said back, staring blankly out the window at the four Coast Guard sailors on deck of the little cutter edging along the shoreline.

"No, after that."

"I said he was one step removed from us."

"You're right. That's why we're not finding him along the Ohio. He's one step removed."

Rosie looked at her. "What are you talking about?"

"Our guy cruises the Ohio looking for prey, but he doesn't hide out there. He's one step removed. He moors his boat off the Ohio. On a tributary."

"Like the Licking in Kentucky?"

"Or the Little Miami, maybe."

Rosie nodded. "Call Agent Agate. She's heading things up at the Blue Ash office."

M.J. made the call. Agate thought the idea worthy of investigation and began to strip a few teams away from each of the four other searches to form a fifth and a sixth. The fifth moved toward the Licking River which split Covington and Newport in Kentucky. The sixth moved down the eastern edge of Hamilton County to the Little Miami, which entered the Ohio east of Cincinnati and south of the townships of New Richmond and Batavia.

With the draining of resources, the pace of the search along the remaining four miles of the Ohio slowed even more. The afternoon lagged.

———

M.J.'s phone rang.

She looked down. It was not a number she recognized.

Hesitantly, she answered.

"Hello, Clarice," the raspy voice said, with a laugh.

"Oh, now you're a comedian," M.J. replied with a shudder. She pointed at her phone.

Rosie acknowledged it was from Mr. Evil and stepped out onto the deck to call Agent Agate and Tobias Meyer. They would be tracking the call already.

"I'll have to find a new profession soon. I've decided to retire," Hondros said into the phone.

"Retire?" M.J. asked. "What are you saying?"

The man on the other end of the line laughed. "You not the brightest, are you, Detective Monroe? I tried to tell you the other night. There was a reason for that call, but we ran out of time. I'm telling you, I've decided to give up my career as a teacher. It is exam day, after all. The nigger girl will get her chance."

"Just let her go. This whole thing is pointless. Let her go."

"But she deserves a chance to show me what's she learned. I've left her books. I've lectured. I told her how things really are. We'll see what she's understood. Her final exam is tonight."

"And if she fails?"

"Like all the others, I'll have to dispose of her."

"But that's so hateful. Even white people, whom you defend, would call you a monster for killing little black girls. It's just evil."

The voice laughed, heartily. "Oh, come now. Have you seen how things are? If you wouldn't arrest me, I'd set up a GoFundMe page and retire tomorrow a millionaire. There are plenty out there who approve of what I'm doing."

"You really believe that?"

"Have you seen the marches? Have you seen the president's approval of the marches? There has always been a majority of white Americans who disliked niggers. Dark-skinned people. Mexicans, whatever. This used to be, and will be again, a country for white people."

"You're just an old crank. A racist swearing at children to get off his lawn. I've dealt with your kind my whole career. You call for the law to back you up when the world passes you by."

He laughed. "I never needed your help. I carry my own weapon. But it doesn't matter. I'm gone after today. I'm retiring and leaving this shithole city behind."

Rosie knocked lightly on the window. "We got him. Hondros is on the Kentucky side. Someplace called Wilder. Officers are closing in as we speak."

M.J. nodded. "We'll never give up, you know. We'll find you."

"No, you won't, Det. Monroe. You've never even been close." And with that, the line went dead.

A moment later, M.J.'s phone rang again. It was Tobias Meyer. "We got him, M.J. He is located along the Licking Pike Highway in Wilder, Kentucky."

"Where's Wilder?"

"Northern Kentucky. Newport's on the Ohio, but on the Licking, going upstream south, the towns in proximity to the Ohio are Newport, Southgate, and then Wilder. Hondros is in Wilder five miles upstream from the Ohio. The FBI and Newport Police are rolling on him right now."

"Boss," M.J. said, "I'm in a Coast Guard cutter. Can we go there? I want to be there when we take Hondros down. He was going to kill me with his tripwire arrow. I need to be there."

"Go," said Tobias, "but stay *on* the boat *in* the Ohio. You can't be within Kentucky's jurisdiction. We can't let a technicality let this monster walk."

M.J. opened the cabin door and yelled instructions to the ship's captain.

He nodded with a smile. Coast Guard guys always like an order to give it the gas. As the two inboard engines cut a deep wake, the ship rose on the water and roared across the roiling waters of the Ohio.

A second cutter approached as they traversed the wide river. It was Black and Decker closing the distance between the two.

A minute later, Rosie and M.J. were close enough to see Simmons standing at the bow of his cutter, the toothpick visible in the corner of his mouth.

Chapter Thirty-One

Supervising Special Agent Neal Saunders led the team of FBI agents surrounding the small parking lot at the boat launch. Six teams of four agents in black SUVs lined the entry. Six police officers from the Newport Police in three squad cars were with them. It was nearing 6:00 p.m., and Paisley Park Jefferson had been missing for exactly fourteen days.

Each team of FBI left one agent stationed at the side of each vehicle. A second from each team carried a sniper rifle and positioned himself along the river bank. Two from each team, plus Saunders himself, joined the Newport Police as they edged their way to the parking lot for the boat launch.

Two agents, weapons drawn, moved to the side of the white van with Arkansas plates. Surreptitious glances informed them no one was inside the van.

Two young men stood in the back of a pickup truck at the boat launch, their trailer holding a beat-up bass boat. The two teens stared at the slow parade of law enforcement officers cautiously sliding along each of the eight vehicles in the lot.

FBI checked each for inhabitants. All were empty. Hondros was not here.

Saunders strode up to the boys. "You guys see an old guy, gray truck with a pontoon boat on a trailer. He's big, walks with a limp."

The first shook his head, but the second said, "I ain't seen him today, but I know the fella you're talkin' about. He keeps his pontoon boat in the water almost year-round. He owns the old millhouse up that trail about a half mile." The boy pointed over his big belly toward a muddy, twin-rutted path leading off the to the east.

"He up there right now?" Saunders asked.

"Don't know. Think he lives there. Ain't much of a place. Mill Creek feeds into the Licking right below us. Runs just enough water most times for him to pull his boat up there to dock at his house. Come August and low water, I think he has to anchor down here. Usually parks his truck up top."

Saunders thanked the two boys then told them they would have to leave the premises. A police action was about to occur, so they would be escorted off the property. The two weren't too enthused about leaving but did with the insistence of two of Newport's finest.

Now with more caution, knowing Hondros was likely in a structure less than a half mile away, eight agents and four police officers led by Saunders trekked cautiously through the undergrowth next to the trail.

Saunders paused and called for one of the Coast Guard cutters to move up the Licking into position just upstream from where Mill Creek entered the river. Neither Rosie and M.J.'s cruiser, nor Black and Decker's, could come onto Kentucky waters, so they were forced to stay in the channel of the Ohio.

Saunders held his position until a third boat, this one from the eastside of Riverbend, arrived. The air was hot and still. Bees hovered in the grasses, alighting on wild sunflowers in the ditches.

The cutter arrived in fifteen minutes. It seemed much longer to the men in the woods.

Saunders now put his assault team into motion again.

The four snipers moved their positions behind the millhouse.

With rear escape now eliminated, four agents and two Newport Police officers crept to the porch.

Saunders and the remaining team kept in cover below the house.

The FBI leader spoke into a megaphone. "Terry Hondros, this is the FBI. We know you're in there. Come out with your hands up. We have the house surrounded. There is no escape. I repeat, we have the house surrounded. You must surrender immediately."

There was no reply. The small stone house was still. Saunders heard horse flies buzzing around the overgrown yard. While the house itself was a fortress, it had two large windows on each side of the heavy, wooden door. It would be easy to launch tear gas in through those windows and force any occupants out. Saunders gave it a ten count and then repeated his message.

There was, again, silence in its aftermath.

The agents and police in heavily protected armament looked back from the porch to their boss.

Saunders nodded.

The first raised a battering ram to the door. He twice slammed the door. Wood splintered, but even with the lock's displacement, the door didn't give.

A second agent moved to the fore. He raised a hydraulic spreader-cutter into the gap. It took perhaps a minute, but the cutter chewed the metal brace behind the door into two halves.

But no one entered just yet.

With the knowledge Terry Hondros used Vietnam-era booby traps at M.J.'s house, Saunders expected Terry Hondros's hideout to be similarly protected.

The tactical team slipped off the porch, and using an extended telescoping wand, one officer shoved the door open. No explosion, no flung knife, no gun shot.

Cautiously, the agents and officers moved to the porch once again. They entered the front door and after securing the entry way and front room shouted, "Clear."

Saunders stepped from his shelter to the porch and then inside the house. He opened the channel on the radio so all two hundred members of the search team could hear him enter the millhouse. "I'm inside, and there's not a lot to see. TV and satellite set-up. Dish is actually inside the front room."

M.J. could hear the agents call, "Clear," once again. Then, Saunders again spoke, "I'm in the kitchen/dining room area. Small dinette set. A footlocker, metallic lime green and chrome, is standing on its side by the backdoor. There is a receipt from an Army surplus shop taped to the side. It's for two trunks. One trunk is gone.

"The kitchen has two sets of stairs; one up, one down. The lower heads down to the old millhouse grinding wheel. The broken waterwheel I can see from here. The room looks unused."

Saunders assigned two of the police officers into position at the down stairwell. One FBI agent he kept at the front door.

Two Newport policemen retreated to the front porch.

Saunders with the three agents remaining took the stairs. They were rough-hewn granite, narrow and steep. Light seeped in from an unseen upstairs room, making the stairwell dim and dank.

The two lead agents reached the top of the stairs.

One slid an L-shaped viewer around the corner. "Two bedrooms, one crude bathroom with the shower drain built right into the stone floor. Toilet next to it. Bedroom doors are partially closed."

Saunders reached the top.

All four men huddled on the landing.

The supervising agent called out again. "Terry Hondros, this is your last chance. Drop your weapon and surrender. If we come in there after you, we'll fire first and ask questions later. Now's your last chance."

They waited, and there was no reply. Saunders finally nodded and mouthed the word "Go."

The three agents leapt down the hall.

The first banged the closest bedroom door against the wall.

The second, gun raised, stepped around the corner.

The agent stepping into the room took both barrels in the chest of his flak jacket. His arm, raised with his firearm, was nearly sheared from his body.

The second agent who'd kicked the door back was in a lower stance, and pellets pocked the right side of his face and mangled his ear.

Saunders, on the other side of the door frame, took some pellets into the side of his face and hairline. Splinters from the door laced into his brow, temple, and lips.

All three men yelled in pain.

Saunders fell backwards down the stairs.

The fourth agent, a woman, had the presence of mind to grab Saunders's leg as he toppled past her and may have saved him breaking his neck in the narrow, stone stairwell.

"Agents down, agents down," she yelled into her com.

"Assailant is in a bedroom on the second floor. He is armed with a shotgun. We have three agents down," she called.

With the air filled with cordite and three men calling out in pain, the remaining female agent shouted instructions that the shooter was in the bedroom. She yelled for backup.

The five law enforcement officers downstairs rushed the stairs to return fire. They first were forced to move Saunders to gain entry. Once he was secured on the kitchen floor, and one officer applying pressure on his wound, the remaining four and the remaining FBI agent cautiously inched up the stairs.

It took them the better part of three minutes to reach the remaining injured FBI agents and learn that the shotgun blast was the result of a booby-trap. The shotgun had been placed under the bed, aimed upward at the door's entrance.

Now the calls were for medical care. Helicopters and ambulances were requested and en route. In the mass confusion, no one noticed the thirty-two-foot Sun Tracker Party Cruiser shedding its camo-covered netting along a cut in Mill Creek as it slipped away from its mooring to the deeper channel.

The pontoon boat furrowed through the 200 yards down the center of the waterway. As the craft reached the confluence of the stream and river, the Coast Guard cutter's four-man crew radioed they were in contact with the suspect.

As the pontoon turned down river, Hondros fired shots out at the Coast Guard sailors.

The captain of the craft began pursuit.

However, it seems Hondros had foreseen such an eventuality. He stepped from the wheel and threw a net off the back of the boat across the narrow river passage. His arm trailed away as he released it, like a boy throwing a Frisbee. The rope line, carrying both weights and floats, hit the river. The net was designed to descend into the water at a depth of about a foot. Steel tines shaped like treble hooks dragged in the water.

The Coast Guard cutter, its in-board motors roaring as it closed the gap to the much slower pontoon, rose right over the netting. The tines grappled into the blades of the rotor, and a horrible metal chewing sound ground the air. The Coast Guard cruiser immediately halted. The net had done its job.

The FBI snipers, hearing both boats, were far to the rear of the house. They were completely out of position. No one with a scope ever even managed a good look at the craft heading for the Ohio.

The men stationed at the vehicles ran to the water's edge, guns drawn, but the craft was past them before they arrived. Hondros eluded the entire team of FBI and was nearing the Ohio. The best the assault team could do now was save the lives of their three fallen comrades.

——————

M.J. and Rosie heard the craziness play out on their boat's radio.

Their captain took the wheel and ordered his three sailors to their stations. One was ready with lifelines and the radio, the other two held long rifles.

M.J. and Rosie stayed near the radio, listening as they readied themselves. The pontoon boat headed right toward them.

Rosie raised a thumbs-up to Black and Decker.

The two male detectives were positioned on the east side of the Licking's entrance into the Ohio.

M.J. and Rosie were on the west.

"Do you think Paisley is on the boat?" Rosie said, her voice raspy.

"I don't know," M.J. replied, "The fact that one trunk was missing from the millhouse makes me very nervous."

The pontoon boat was upon them. Their captain spoke over his amplified megaphone to Hondros's craft as it cleared the Licking and roared into the much wider Ohio.

"This is the United States Coast Guard. You are ordered to reduce your current speed and prepare to be boarded. You need to immediately comply. Stop or we will shoot. I repeat. This is the United States Coast Guard. You are under arrest. Desist and step onto the deck with your hands up. You are going to be boarded. Comply immediately."

Their answer was immediate. The pontoon swung in a big, lazy arc, heading toward the east. When the rear of the craft came to bear upon the Coast Guard cutter, Hondros, one hand on the wheel, fired a handgun at them again and again.

"Do we have permission to engage the enemy, ma'am?" the captain asked, expectantly.

"We don't know if the child is on board," M.J. said.

The captain nodded and said over his radio to the other Coast Guard cruisers. "We may have a child on board. Do not engage with the enemy. I repeat, do not engage. I need an audible response from each captain on that command."

Black and Decker's captain replied, and they could see his visual tip of the cap that he got the message. The third cruiser was just arriving from the Ludlow area downriver.

M.J. and Rosie heard the reply from the captain of that craft as the cruiser plowed closer, leaving a white wake beside them. The last boat, floundered in the Licking, radioed they were out of action, entangled with the steel-tined barbed net.

"He won't outrun us," their captain said. "Maximum speed on that pontoon boat is half of what we've got under the hood. What are we doing?"

"Shadow him," Rosie replied. "We'll get on the horn and

call our boss."

With three Coast Guard cutters flanking him, Hondros raced alongside the pontoon boat at twenty-five-knots, not quite thirty miles per hour. It lumbered in the water like a milk truck in a race with three Corvettes.

Tobias told them a police helicopter was in the air, coming from Lunken Airport. It would arrive in less than five minutes. The goal was to get a visual on the pontoon from above and perhaps learn if Paisley Park Jefferson was on board. However, before the helicopter arrived, Hondros made his move.

With the pontoon plowing through the muddy Ohio, M.J. could see Hondros on board, backing his way, pulling something from the cabin to the stern. He was dragging something across the deck.

In a moment, Hondros began to lift the something up. It was the trunk.

"Oh, my god," Rosie called out. "He's going to throw the child out of the boat in that trunk."

"Take us in!" yelled M.J., "Take us in close enough to shoot him."

The captain gave the order as Hondros managed to hoist the trunk onto the stern's rail edge. However, he was having trouble lifting the metallic footlocker with the child inside over the safety line which surrounded the ship's perimeter.

Black and Decker's cutter closed faster, and they began to fire on Hondros.

In a moment, Rosie, M.J., and their two sailors also began to fire.

None of the rounds from their first salvo hit home, but Hondros seemed to get an adrenalin charge from the gunfire. He lifted the trunk over the line and shoved.

The trunk slid for an instant then flipped to its side as it entered the water and began to sink.

Chapter Thirty-Two

The horror of the moment was almost too much to stand. Paisley was in that trunk and it was sinking to the bottom of the river. The Ohio River was at least thirty-five feet deep here. Maybe fifty. The emotion M.J. felt made it almost too much for her to be able to function. It seemed the terrible implications of what just occurred froze everyone, except Hondros, for a second.

From this closer distance, M.J. could see the smile on Hondros's face. He pulled a handgun from his belt and ducked low. From a crouch, he began to fire at Black and Decker. She saw Decker flail to the side, almost going overboard.

A voice rang out over the radio. It was Simmons. "Go after him. Take Hondros down. Our captain says we have scuba gear onboard. Two of our guys are going down after Paisley. Right now. I'll take care of Decker. He's hit, but I don't think it's bad. Go. Go now."

M.J. nodded, and the captain of their craft nodded back. Hate was in his eyes. She was sure it was just reflecting the hate she felt in hers.

In less than a half a minute, they began, once again, to close the gap.

The other cutter pulled alongside of them.

Rosie pointed her gun at the pontoon boat and mouthed "Kill him."

M.J. crawled to the bow of the ship. The two sailors with long rifles were in deep slots on each side. Only their heads and weapons were above deck. She lay prone across the raised mount on the ship's highest surface and cradled her pistol in both hands like they had first trained as cadets.

Hondros seemed to be sitting on the floor of the cabin at the wheel, keeping the boat at maximum speed and in the middle of the channel. They could only see the top of his head occasionally as the crest of the wave tossed his pontoon low into a swell.

Occasionally, Hondros raised and fired wildly at them, emptying an entire clip of fifteen shots and then ducking back down to reload.

After the second time, the four gunners on the Coast Guard vessels, along with Rosie and M.J., simply waited for Hondros to rise again. When he did for a third time, they fired a fuselage of rounds at him. They saw him slump down.

The pontoon continued to go at full speed for perhaps another minute, and during that time, they heard Simmons on the radio. "Our guys are down in the water now. They say they can still see bubbles from the trunk, but they're not down to it yet."

Just hurry, thought M.J. There was no reason to say those words to Simmons over the radio. Everyone knew what was at stake.

Then, the pontoon began to slow, cutting a wide swath. And then, it began to merely creep, rotating in a slow circle.

The two Coast Guard cutters slid alongside the craft.

Eventually, one sailor managed to leap from one boat to the other. He removed his weapon from his holster, ducked, and entered the cabin in a crouch. In mere seconds, his words came over his com to the captain.

"Suspect is down. I've disarmed him. He is hit, hit hard. I've handcuffed him and will bring the ship to."

The pontoon soon came to a rest, bobbing on the water. Rosie and M.J. were helped across to the deck of Hondros's boat.

Hondros was slumped against the instrument panel. His side was covered in blood, his hands were cuffed in front of him. He'd been shot in the torso. A second round had also gone through his thigh.

M.J. could see Hondros was dying.

But his eyes still lit up as he saw M.J. enter the cabin. "Detective Monroe," he said. "We finally meet face-to-face."

"No," M.J. said, "this is the second time. You shoved me the first time."

Hondros laughed, and there was a frothy mixture in the corner of his mouth. "Yes, that's right. Well, then," he said, "so it comes to an end."

"Yes, you're dying," M.J. said. "Tell us what you can before you go. How many did you kill? Can you tell us any names?"

"How many? Tell you their names?" Hondros exclaimed. "All my little black pearls dotting the bottom of this river? I've been putting them here for thirty-five years. No one ever noticed. No one even noticed most of them were gone. Nobody gave a damn about them while they were living. Why do you care about them now that they're dead?"

M.J. lowered herself to her haunches. She pushed her face to his. She could feel Rosie behind her. "How many? Tell me."

Rosie said, "Yeah, don't you want to brag, just a little bit?"

Hondros's shirt gapped as he lay on his side, and M.J. could see blood seeping into the rolls of fat along his ribcage. The old man closed his eyes, and he wheezed. Blood trickled from his mouth. "Just let me die in peace," he whispered, closing his eyes.

Rosie stepped forward and ground her heel on his fingers. There was a snapping sound, and Hondros's mouth gapped in pain. Then, his head toppled forward, limp against his chest. The monster was dead.

———

The silence after Hondros died was one that would haunt M.J. for some time. She knew in retrospect it lasted only seconds, but it seemed as if the universe stopped for her at that moment. The first sound she heard was the captain back on the cutter. He was shouting over the intercom. "They've found the trunk. They're bringing it up."

Those words reconnected M.J. to the world. She scrambled over the rubber grappling clamp now connecting the two ships. Her feet landed back on the Coast Guard cutter's deck. "Take us there."

The captain stared over her shoulder at the body lying handcuffed onboard the pontoon.

"Now," M.J. said. "Please."

He nodded, detached the clamp, and left his crewmen behind to secure the scene.

———

It only took two minutes to get back, but it seemed an eternity. They came in hot, their wash sloshing over the side of the still cutter. She could see Simmons grab the rail to keep his footing as they arrived.

Their captain expertly moved them alongside Simmons and Decker's craft.

M.J. and Rosie stepped to the rail.

The captain from the second ship helped them over.

"Give me good news," M.J. called to him as her feet found footing, but his face told her otherwise.

M.J. and Rosie edged alongside Simmons. Across from them, Decker sat, spread-legged, with blood seeping down from his shoulder. His face was white with pain.

Simmons grasped both women's hands as they joined him in front of the trunk. Simmons stood stoically, his head down, his legs spread to better keep his feet as the cutter lulled back and forth in the current. Below him the trunk lay open, its lock sprung. Inside, a little girl lay dead, her skin gray, her body wet, her hair tangled.

Chapter Thirty-Three

The question, *What's the worst thing about being a cop?* is among the most frequent police officers get from the public. For M.J., the image of a dead little girl in a trunk would forever be what came to mind when people asked that question of her. Of course, she would not answer truthfully. She would always say, "Paperwork."

It would seem the world should stop and allow those who saw the girl's body time to adjust, to grieve, but the world does not stop. It continues incessantly, it pulls at you, and it forces action from you, even when you doubt your capacity to provide it.

The blood coming from Decker's wound took immediate precedence as he would soon bleed out if nothing was done. A round had struck the gunwale on the cutter and flattened upon impact. The bullet, now shaped like a Frito chip, dipped into the flesh of the detective's shoulder at low speed. Decker was a fleshy man, and the bullet did not hit any significant organs or arteries. However, he needed medical attention.

One of the sailors aboard Simmons's craft applied pressure to stanch the bleeding until they arrived onshore.

EMTs were waiting on the sloped concrete landing just below Great America Ballpark. Tobias Meyer and his team were already roping off the grid as a staging area. The police were well-practiced in the art of crime scenes. This converted parking lot when the river was low became just that.

The Coast Guard cutter slipped along the landing.

Medics helped Decker over the rail to shore. His eyes were glazed with shock, but his feet were steady underneath him. He was ushered into an ambulance and hustled away to Christ Hospital's trauma center, which had been alerted and was awaiting him.

Of course, the real issue was across the river. Life squads in both an ambulance and a helicopter made their way to the Licking River boat launch. Saunders, who was not critical, was taken to St. Elizabeth, while the helicopter flew both fallen FBI agents to UC Medical Center. The agent who'd been shot in the chest and who'd nearly lost his arm, bled to death en route as EMTs on board the chopper could find no way to slow the bleeding on a limb severed at the torso.

Captain Delores Knowles and Coroner Roscoe Griffins made the call to leave the deceased girl in the trunk for the ride by ambulance to the morgue. It would attract less attention than a gurney carrying a sheet-covered child.

The press assembled beyond the yellow police tape staffed by uniformed officers.

A pop-up security tent hid most of the unloading of the trunk from public view.

And in a sly move, the ambulance crew transferred Hondros's lifeless form from a stretcher to the gurney, rolling it wide of the tent in full public view.

Cameras directed their lens to the body. No one noticed

the unloading of a metallic silver and lime green footlocker from the pontoon boat to the second ambulance. It rolled away without fanfare.

M.J. stood with Tobias and Rosie watching Paisley's ambulance leave.

Rosie was visibly shaking. Her anguish was palpable.

Tobias noted his detective's condition. The head of detectives directed his eyes to M.J. "Get her out of here," he said.

"What about our reports?" M.J. replied as she put her hand on Rosie's arm.

Rosie's face was vacant, her eyes on the horizon down the river. "Is there going to be a press conference?"

"In the morning, early. For now, get her out of here." Tobias's words were flat and dead. They all felt that way. "No press conference for now. Mayor Lark and City Attorney Graves have ordered a news blackout until we verify the identifications of both Hondros and Paisley Park Jefferson."

M.J. nodded and started moving Rosie up the ramp away from the gathering crowd. She turned back. "I just realized we don't have a car here."

Tobias nodded. "I'll drive you back to the precinct."

M.J. rode in the back. Rosie sat beside Tobias. No one spoke.

At the District One parking lot, Tobias pulled into his reserved space.

M.J. exited the vehicle.

Tobias waited until Rosie, still semi-comatose, rose from her seat, opened the door, and stepped into the evening air. September was nearly over. Now, it was full dark at 7:30.

Tobias began to call the hospital to check on Decker.

M.J. left Rosie beside him to go inside and get her keys.

When M.J. returned, she was shocked at the scene.

Rosie stood, her fists raised in crazed anger.

Tobias held her wrists. His cell phone lay on the pavement three feet in front of them. It was lit with an active call. M.J. could hear a voice saying, "Lt. Meyer? Lt. Meyer?"

Then, M.J. noticed the busted glass of Tobias window. The shatterproof glass of the side window on the car door was crisscrossed with cracks.

M.J. ran the last few steps. "Rosie, Rosie, stop, stop!" M.J. yelled.

Her friend's knuckles were cut, and the back of her fingers and hands were bloody like raw hamburger. Rosie kept trying to pull her hands free from Tobias's grip and return to punching the window.

M.J. could hear Rosie's weeping.

Rosie looked to M.J. "Paisley's dead. That little girl is the same age as my Marie. The same age as my daughter and that monster killed her. He killed her. Just like Marie," she wailed. "Just like Marie." Rosie stopped resisting.

Tobias let her arms fall to her sides.

"We need to go tell her mother," Rosie said. "It should come from us. Monica Jefferson should hear that her daughter's dead from us. It's our fault. We failed. We have to go tell her."

Tobias pulled Rosie's wrists to him. "I'll get Simmons to do it. I'll send Heather Primstone with him. Rosie, you need to go home. That's an order. You're not right. You're not the right person to tell her, not right now. Go home."

M.J. grabbed at her partner, and Rosie fell into M.J., just so much dead weight.

Rosie said, "And you know something else? They'll blame us for the white girl's death, too. They'll say we didn't do enough. That we let the black girl die. Klaire Keller will die because we didn't do our job. They'll kill her, too. And blame us. You know they'll blame us for both of them."

Tobias said, "Be quiet, Rosie." His eyes moved to M.J. "Take her home."

"But your car. The window…" M.J. said, "She didn't mean to…"

Tobias shook his head. He raised his hand. "Not now. Just get her home." And then he walked inside.

———

M.J. called ahead to David to make sure he would be at Rosie's to take care of his ex-wife. M.J. did not want to leave her alone.

The drive took them twenty minutes, and David and Marie were waiting outside when M.J. pulled her Jeep into the drive.

M.J. saw the concern on David's face as they arrived. Marie was oblivious to her father's sad face. She waved happily at M.J.'s Jeep.

M.J. opened the door and helped her partner out.

Rosie and M.J. walked to the door.

Marie, her mood suddenly changed, cut them off, burying her head into her mom. Children always know when something is wrong. Rosie's daughter knew her mom was in distress, and she pressed in.

Immediately, both began to cry.

David swept in and lifted Marie up and against him. He carried her inside.

M.J. and Rosie followed.

In less than thirty minutes, David tenderly ran warm, soapy water a dozen times over Rosie's bloody hands. Marie was tearful, but after being told that her mommy had simply tripped and fallen when she was running after a bad guy, she calmed. Kids understand that injury. They understand crying after you've tripped and fallen.

Rosie knew it was important to mitigate her depressed behavior in front of her daughter, so she did. Both soon had it under control.

David treated Rosie's damaged knuckles with triple antibiotic and covered them with gauze.

M.J. made hot tea with milk and honey for both mother and daughter.

They slowly drank it all.

Then, tired on the sofa, Marie leaned in against Rosie, her head buried into her mom's side.

Rosie's eyes were closed, and she stroked her daughter's hair.

M.J. sat still and watched the scene before her. Then, the epiphany hit her. She could still save a life today.

———————

On the way to the Jefferson's apartment in over-the-Rhine, M.J. made calls.

David drove.

Marie huddled against her mother in the backseat.

When they arrived at the rundown apartment house, Detectives Simmons and Primstone were waiting outside.

A TV crew from Channel 13 was also there in their van. A reporter stood outside on the street, the cherry from a lit cigarette highlighting her face in the gloom.

Rosie resumed her functioning self, knowing they wouldn't be able to pull this operation off without her. Initially, they left Marie and David in the car. Informing Monica Jefferson her daughter was dead would be the worst thing ever in the woman's life.

M.J. could not believe after they told her they would ask the traumatized woman for a favor, for a sacrifice. It was unfair. It was terrible and insensitive. And it might work.

The scene inside the apartment was as bad as anything you might imagine. Monica was destroyed. It was like watching a woman cry tears of sulfuric acid that poured forth in an infinite stream dissolving her from the pain and agony welling up and out. And of course, that pain spread to her sister and then to little Princeton. The boy did not actually really understand the finality of death, but he understood fear. And when his mother cried in this way, he was very afraid. It was terrible.

And after giving them all of thirty minutes to absorb the pain of the loss by murder of their joy in life, their little girl, their Paisley.

Then, Rosie asked Monica to join them in a deception. She asked Paisley's mom to lie to save another life.

WTF-TV

"Good evening, it's Rikki Shea with Channel 13 News. We're breaking into your Sunday night television viewing, ladies and gentlemen, for a WTF exclusive. In just a moment, we'll take you to the front porch of the Jefferson residence where Monica Jefferson, the mother of the kidnapped child, Paisley Park Jefferson, gone now for two weeks, has asked to make a statement to the press.

"As you viewers are aware, Ms. Jefferson's daughter, Paisley, was taken by kidnappers two weeks ago. In the days after the kidnapping, a second child was taken. Klaire Keller, an eleven-year-old girl, an Indian Hill, resident was taken from Hyde Park.

"Since then, clues to the girls' disappearance have been few and far between. Maybe that has changed. There has been much police activity in the city this afternoon, but rumors were the manhunt underway was for the shooter in the killing of Talbert Washington, the Walnut Hills High School teacher slain earlier in the week. We've had no news on the kidnapping of either girl.

"It appears Ms. Jefferson is exiting the front door of the apartment complex where she and her family reside. She is approaching the mic and a small girl is by her side. Let's go and hear her words."

Monica Jefferson moved unsteadily to the microphone. Her eyes were puffy from crying, and a little girl clung to her leg, her face buried between the woman's lowered arm and her leg. "Tonight, I come out here to thank the Cincinnati Police for returning my daughter to me. Paisley's kidnapper was killed this afternoon on the Ohio River. Law enforcement officers from the FBI, the Newport, Kentucky Police, the Cincinnati Police, and the U.S Coast Guard all worked tirelessly and in great danger to bring my daughter home.

"In fact, one FBI agent lost his life this afternoon, two more were injured, and one Cincinnati detective was shot in a gun battle with the kidnapper. I can't thank these men and women enough for their bravery. Now with little Paisley home, I'll leave you. It is time for healing for our family. We won't be making any more statements to the press. I understand the Cincinnati Police, the FBI, and the mayor's office will be conducting a press conference tomorrow morning as more facts become available."

With that, Monica Jefferson scooped up Marie, a good little actress, into her arms and reentered the building.

Chapter Thirty-Four

Rosie watched Monica Jefferson's statement from the dirt mat called a lawn in this neighborhood. She stood just out of range, behind the lights and camera. As the reporter summarized the triumph of Cincinnati's police in bringing Paisley home, Rosie turned to her partner. Tears welled in her eyes.

"Why does it seem whenever this country needs racial healing, the sacrifice is always by a black woman burying her child?"

Chapter Thirty-Five

The Channel 13 news break was picked up by all the other four news services in the city. National outlets covered the story within the hour. The mayor's home number was ringing after the 11:00 p.m. news aired.

City Attorney Graves was called on his private line for comments both on and off-the-record. Neither knew a thing about Paisley Park's amazing return from the dead. They both offered no comment.

In fact, both were dreading the impending announcement by Acting Chief, Elaine Knowles, that the girl was dead. The mayor and city attorney both placed calls to Capt. Knowles.

Knowles called Lt. Meyer.

Meyer, in turn, called his detectives.

M.J., Rosie, Simmons, and even Heather Primstone all had turned off their phones. Decker was still in surgery.

In the pre-dawn hours of Monday morning, Klaire Keller, groggy as if having been recently drugged, walked down the hill from the woods above the Walmart in Alexandria, Kentucky. When she woke in a sleeping bag, she was in the woods near the intersection of Scenic Drive and the AA Highway. A heavy dew left the bag's exterior slightly damp, but she was warm inside, dressed in a sweat suit and jacket. The girl was pale after spending nearly two weeks in a cellar without sunlight but seemed otherwise little the worse for wear.

Klaire Keller did not know where she was, but had the good sense to continue down the road until she saw the familiar Walmart sign. This store was located in the Village Green Shopping Center along Highway 27.

The eleven-year-old walked inside the bustling store, where a greeter noticed her. The girl broke into tears. It took the store employee less than a minute to figure out who she was and to call authorities.

Klaire Keller couldn't help police at all with information about her abductors. It was later determined she had been tased and drugged in the initial kidnapping. She awoke with a canvas bag on her head in the back of a vehicle. Her hands were bound until she was safely locked in a cellar.

There, she was allowed to take the bag from her head after her captors left her alone. In the cellar, by herself, she could play, read, sleep, and was even given the opportunity to request and receive her favorite movies, food, books, toys, and toiletries. All of this was done by note and a black marker. Her food was left for her in a hallway, which was locked all day, except when her food was provided.

Klaire never heard a voice. She never saw a person, not even someone's hand. There were no personal items in the cellar, except those she herself requested. Her prison cell, the cellar, contained a full bath with a shower, a bed, and a television, but no local channels. There were no windows. She'd received milk at bedtime each night, and on her last night in the cellar, she remembered thinking the milk tasted funny, but she did drink it. Again, later it was determined that she had been drugged before being left in the sleeping bag. She was home by noon.

Channel 13 and the rest of the press learned of District One detectives' deception regarding Paisley at the same time Klaire Keller arrived home.

The mayor accused City Attorney Graves of the faked news story.

Graves denied, laying it at the police detectives' feet. Neither politician mentioned Paisley's death in their statements.

By noon, Acting Chief Knowles ordered Tobias to suspend all four detectives, Monroe, Coleman, Simmons, and Primstone, for two weeks for their participation in the charade.

The four arrived at the District One Precinct and filed their reports before turning in their weapons and badges for the two weeks' duration. No one, even Tobias Meyer, blamed them, and in fact, most officers they passed in the hallways gave them high fives.

Klaire Keller was home and safe, and that really was all that mattered.

M.J. and Rosie both cleaned clothes out of their lockers and packed odds and ends into their duffle bags. None of it was stuff that really mattered, but they weren't quite ready to leave, and the case, to be honest, left them doubting their abilities and their enthusiasm for law enforcement in general.

Before she left, M.J. called to the morgue and asked to speak the coroner, Roscoe Griffins.

He answered the phone with his typical gusto. "Griffins, what's your request? We'll do our best!"

"Detective M.J. Monroe, Dr. Griffins."

"Heard about you. Heard you faked that news story. Admire you for it."

"Thanks. I wanted to ask you a question."

"Okay. Figure you're entitled to a question after taking a bullet for the team."

"I think that was Decker."

"Heard about that, too. He's okay, I hear. What's your question?"

"Paisley Park Jefferson. Did she drown?"

"Don't know that yet. Got Fritz Gertz looking into it. He's doing the preliminary, and I'm going to finalize the official autopsy report in the morning." He paused. "You want to know if you didn't get her up out of the water in time or she was dead before she went in?"

"Yeah, I do."

"Don't make her less dead, detective."

"Still want to know."

"I'll have it for your tomorrow. What's your cell phone number?"

She gave it to him and hung up.

M.J. spent the night in Riggs's arms at his house. It was the first time she'd been there, and it was none too clean. But the cottage was filled with his art, so she loved it. She woke once during a nightmare which retold the previous day's actual nightmare, but Riggs rolled against her and wrapped his massive arms around her, compressing her until her breathing calmed and then he left his hands on her hips until she once again slept.

That morning, however, she went to see her husband, Greg. His skin now looked like the finest of parchment stretched over his bones. His cheekbones were that of a saint's in stained glass.

M.J., feeling the tears welling in her eyes, needed his solace, but her husband did not move. For the first time, ever, she climbed into the bed next to him and slept. The nurses saw but did not comment and simply pulled the blinds and secured the door, leaving them in silence.

————

Dr. Roscoe Griffins's call woke M.J. from a dreamless sleep. At first, she didn't know where she was. Then in shame, she crawled from the bed, trying to not injure the man she'd just spent the last three hours lying beside. The cognitive dissonance of the two behaviors was not lost on her. She answered the phone.

"This Detective Monroe?"

"Yes."

"You okay? You sound drunk."

"Just woke up. Sorry."

"Yeah, when you're suspended, I guess you got time for naps. Some of us don't have the luxury."

M.J. didn't reply and just let him jib-jab. She knew he'd get back to the point of his call.

"You can rest a little easier. The girl was dead for more than twelve hours before she went in the water, or at least that's our estimate. Her neck was broken. Same as the others."

M.J. felt hollow inside. She knew either answer would leave her feeling horrible. In truth, she wasn't sure which answer was the least desirable. "Anything else?"

"Nah, same stuff as the other vics. Broken neck, no sign of sexual abuse. Some minor trauma from a knife blade. Like he noodled along her clavicles with a sharp blade. Sound familiar?"

"Yeah, well, thanks," M.J. said. "I appreciate you finishing the autopsy today."

"Oh, one thing," he said. "It says here he amputated her finger. Is that different?"

"Yeah," said M.J. "We didn't have that on the previous victims. Are you sure?"

Roscoe Griffins coughed. "Damn, it's on Fritz Gertz's report. I didn't check the finger when I saw the broken neck. I'll go examine the body and call you right back."

It wasn't five minutes and Griffins called back. "Hey, damn it. Fritz Gertz was wrong. It's not an amputated finger. At least not recently. Little finger is missing on the right hand, but it's not recent. Skin and scar tissue is completely healed over it. At least a year old. Did the Jefferson girl have a missing little finger? It would have to be from at least a year ago."

M.J. hung up, kissed her husband's saintly cheek, and then walked out into the fading sunlight of Tuesday afternoon. As she strode to her Jeep, her heart began to race with the possibility. M.J. called Rosie.

Rosie had Monica Jefferson's number in her phone. Rosie made the call. It did not take long.

Rosie called back. No, she said, Paisley Park Jefferson did not have a missing little finger.

M.J. hung up and called Roscoe Griffins back.

He answered before it even rang on her end.

"I already know," he said, "I just ran a quick swab inside the deceased cheek. Preliminary DNA analysis shows no match. This body is not Paisley Park Jefferson."

"Yeah, she had her little finger on her right hand two weeks ago when she was abducted."

"Then, she's still out there, Detective Monroe. You may be suspended, but you better get back to the station. I'll call Tobias and tell him I ordered you back."

"You're a civilian."

"Then, I'm making a citizen's arrest. Get your ass back there, now."

———

They found Paisley in less than two hours. A set of stairs off the kitchen of the millhouse led down to the old decrepit waterwheel.

Behind the broken blades of the wheel on the far wall, the Newport Police helped Rosie and M.J. to a concrete slab three-foot wide and as long as the wheel once had been. It was perhaps twenty feet in length and the concrete lip three-feet thick. Cut into the slab, a portal down was covered with a steel hatch. A padlock secured the hatch.

A bolt cutter made short work of the cheap lock, and the women flung the heavy lid open. Inside, granite stones lined a tube down. A ladder was thrust into the hole, and a tiny light blinked past the aperture.

A head poked its way into the gap.

Rosie was the first down the ladder in the hole. "Paisley? Paisley? Is that you?"

"Yes, yes, it's me," a tiny voice whispered, scared.

They pulled the girl from her prison and into the space below the kitchen. Rosie held her tight. "Are you okay?"

"Yes-um," she said. "I want to go home."

"We'll take you home, dear," said Rosie, "but first we want to get you checked out and make sure you're okay. Your mom, aunt and brother have missed you so much."

Paisley's clothes were grimy from two weeks in the hole, but her eyes were bright. "Is this the award, then? The man said he wasn't sure what to do."

M.J. leaned into her. "What are you talking about? Did the man say something about giving you an award?"

Paisley nodded, proudly. "He said I was the first one who had ever passed the test. He said he was a man of his word and he was surprised. Nobody'd ever passed his test before. What about the other girl? April? Did she pass the test? Did she already get to go home to Lexington? He took her out yesterday, I think. It's hard to tell time down there."

Rosie lowered herself to look the little girl in the eye. "Let's call your momma," she said to Paisley. "She's going to want to hear your voice."

Epilogue

The city of Cincinnati erupted with joy when it discovered Paisley was alive. Of course, the death of April Harris, the little girl from Lexington, was mourned. But life is for the living, and the city chose to cheer and not cry.

Mayor Lark declared Paisley's return a major victory for law enforcement, but for him the die had been cast when he bemoaned the four detectives' deception to save the life of Klaire Keller. He lost the election, badly, finishing third in a race of three.

City Attorney Graves finished a distant second, splitting the conservative vote with his write-in candidacy. The new mayor, Sandra Fixx, said at her swearing-in ceremony that her last name was her mission.

Terrance James Hondros, serial killer, became infamous. Stories on the internet abounded. He became the boogieman in a thousand ghost stories. An autopsy showed the killer died of blood loss from a lacerated liver. one of the sailor's .223 slugs had found its mark. The second wound, the through-

and-through, was explained by a nine-millimeter round found in the instrument panel with blood on it.

The round had been fired from Simmons's weapon. It was the only shot the detective fired. When later asked about his shooting prowess, Simmons explained, "I just line up the sight over my toothpick and pull the trigger."

Talk of recovering the trunks along the bottom of the Ohio filled hours of time on WHTY. A map of metallic objects on the riverbed was funded by donations, and an unmanned submergible armed with a metal detector found that the river bottom from Riverbend to Ludlow was literally covered in metallic objects; cars, boats, signage, car hoods, fishing equipment, and an amazing array of barrels, buckets, and metal coolers in various stages of decomposition were detected.

An examination of those objects also found it was very difficult to discern the size of any metal from beer can to car body since so many of the items were partially covered in sediment. A study found that a canoe left on the bottom became covered in three inches of silt in the first year. The canoe's complete immersion into the riverbed would take less than five years. If Hondros told the truth that he'd dumped bodies in trunks for thirty-five years, those trunks would be under three to four feet of mud by now. The project was abandoned.

Lonnie Truesdale, professional football player, endeared himself to the region when he purchased a home for the Jefferson family, Monica and her sister, Princeton and, of course, the city's new favorite daughter, Paisley Park. All had their own bedrooms in a two-story McMansion in West Chester. Of course, Truesdale was none the poorer, having signed with Minnesota for ten million large four weeks into the season.

Unfortunately, every action has its equal and opposite reaction. Travon, Princeton's best friend, fell into bad company after his friend moved to the suburbs. Travon was arrested for shoplifting early that winter. When he was arrested, he was found to be carrying a knife and two marijuana cigarettes.

Monica Jefferson and her ex-husband, Nat Lee, did not reconcile. In fact, she took him to court for back child support once his residence was known.

In turn, Lee sued Christopher Cottonton, owner of Feather Downs, for ten million dollars over the loss of his foot.

Lee settled out of court for three million. His attorney received half. Lee paid the child support and put half a million into trusts for both of his children for their future college educations. Paisley's and Princeton's futures looked rosy, indeed.

Old Grandy Wilson never left the retirement center where Rosie put him up for one week. His health recovered to the extent that he remained there as a gardener caring for the old folk's flower beds. He also began a community garden in the spring. It is said the tomato patch the following summer was the envy of the region.

Decker, his shoulder wound healed, took six weeks in sick leave followed by an additional six weeks in back vacation. He returned to active duty on January 2nd the following year. Having spent the time in Florida, he was not nearly as pasty. He also lost thirty pounds by walking three miles on the beach each day.

Simmons asked Heather Primstone to transfer to District Two during Decker's extended leave. The new partners solved three high profile murders in the first three months, becoming the darlings of the city's crime reporters.

When Decker returned, he was paired with a newbie detective, recently promoted Mateo Ramirez, and the two moved to District One, becoming downtown's homicide cops.

Warren "Catfish" Jacoby's murder is still listed as unsolved.

Geroy Hooper is listed as person-of-interest in the case, but no evidence to support such a finding has come to light to date. Hooper is still thought to be a drug kingpin in the city. He has not called Detective Monroe again. Perhaps he lost the card.

Captain Elaine Knowles did officially get to remove the "acting" from her title and became the first woman police chief in Cincinnati history. Her first challenge was a budget shortfall of nearly twelve percent to balance the department's coffers. Taking cops off the streets was not a popular call but was the result. Her popularity waned immediately. Calls for Chief Moss Jenkins' return were common on WHTY.

Tobias Meyer's name was floated for the asst. chief's position, but he chose to remain head of detectives in the one. He married early in the new year, a May-December romance in which he was the Sagittarius. His bride was a child psychologist who sometimes worked with the city in criminal cases involving youths. He paid for his own car window's repair and refused to speak to M.J. or Rosie about it when they offered reimbursement.

Supervising Special Agent Neal Saunders made a full recovery, although periodic surgeries to repair and remove the scarring on his face did interfere with his career. FBI supervisors are not supposed to take medical leave for cosmetic work.

Police officer Quentin Reeves made a full recovery and is back on patrol.

Special Agent Dudley Morelock, who died after being shot at the millhouse, left behind a son and a wife. His star was placed on the wall for the fallen at FBI headquarters in Washington D.C. It was said his life insurance was sufficient to care for his family, but we all know it never is enough. What is the price of a dad?

Agent Lisa Agate received a commendation for her work in the Paisley Park Jefferson abduction case. Promoted, Agent Agate relocated to Washington D.C., where she joined the Counterintelligence desk. After proving her merit inside at Counterintelligence, she became a field agent, moving to Paris. She is currently working to defeat ISIS cells based out of Belgium.

Agent Rudy Messerschmidtt left the bureau to become a security consultant to several presidential candidates. His specialty was showing how the military budget needs to be increased.

Kim Rodden stayed with the FBI, next profiling a serial killer along the border between Mexico and the United States. When the killer was discovered to be a border patrol agent, the story made national news. Rodden was interviewed on *Sixty Minutes*. In the next week, the *New York Times* fashion section noted her distinct style of dress. She was offered a seven-figure deal to write her memoir, and Fox Searchlight purchased the movie rights to her story. At printing, Rodden had taken a leave of absence to assist with the screenplay for the film. It is rumored the Paisley Park Jefferson story and Rodden's budding friendship with Detective M.J. Monroe is central to the plot.

M.J. and Kim speak at least once a week. It is said Halle Barry, Carrie Washington, and Regina King are all vying for the chance to play Rodden.

Klaire Keller was initially diagnosed with post-traumatic stress disorder after her return home. However, not seeing her abductors was in many ways a Godsend, and she recovered quickly with psychiatric care. Her parents, on the other hand, became hyper-protective and removed her from Catholic school and instead home-schooled her. Her little sister now has a nanny. The girls are seldom seen in public. It is said their

Indian Hill home has the most expensive security in the tristate.

Paisley Park Jefferson, likewise, suffered from post-traumatic stress disorder. She believes the new home she lives in with her family in West Chester is the prize for passing the test given her by the monster, Hondros. Her mother and aunt encourage that belief. Paisley's mental health is progressively better, and she was accepted into the Gifted and Talented Program for the Lakota School District for the winter term. Paisley received a new bike for Christmas. She can only ride it with her brother or with friends.

Detective Rosie Coleman was still seeing her ex-husband, David, at Christmastime. He bought her a new engagement ring, which she refused, for now. She purchased him season tickets to the Reds, two seats only. He promised to take Marie once a week. Marie received a glove from her father for Christmas. Rosie gave her daughter running shoes. Marie wants to play soccer.

Rosie completed the required counseling after her meltdown in the aftermath of the Hondros case. Her psychiatrist believed it was a once-in-a-lifetime event in which Rosie was unable to separate her daughter's welfare from that of the victim, Paisley Park Jefferson. She was given the okay to return to her daily job as a detective on November 15th.

Rosie gives community talks as part of her therapy and recovery. She speaks at mental health forums, community centers, churches, and youth centers. Her topic is how society has failed young black women and how, together, we can stitch things back together. The talk is entitled "It Ain't the Color Purple, It's Paisley." She is booked out for the next eighteen months.

And as for M.J. She spent her two weeks on suspension at the end of Hondros case mainly with Riggs. She watched him paint. She read some books, listened to some WNKU jazz, but mainly she did nothing. Like a field lying fallow, she rested. Her mind was switched off.

Later, she was to spend four additional weeks on the desk. The truth was with Rosie on a mental health disability until the middle of November, nobody else wanted to partner up with her. M.J.'s notoriety in the press made riding with her the chance to be on every evening news.

At times, she saw camera crews following her in her Jeep. Paparazzi was a new problem for the detective, and the only good way to stop them from following her was to bore the camera crews into abandonment. The new police chief and the new mayor both believed time on the desk to be the best solution. Thus, her month in purgatory.

On Oct. 30th, M.J.'s husband, Greg, died. His fragile state became more extreme after the abduction case ended. His body mass and ability to take in nourishment were no longer able to keep his organs functioning. M.J. took a week of her in-house punishment in medical leave. No one, except maybe Tobias, was sad to see her out of District One.

It would be pretty to think Greg Monroe's death was elegant and movielike. But it was not. Death is seldom pretty. Two days before his death, he began to choke on his own saliva. While there was a non-resuscitate document in place, M.J. could not stand to see her husband drown in his own spittle.

Nurses gave her a manual suction device, which she used whenever Greg seemed to be in distress. Of course, that role was a round-the-clock job. M.J. became exhausted in Greg's last forty-eight hours.

Rosie and Riggs offered to spell M.J. and let her sleep in the room the nursing home kept for just such situations, but M.J. refused to leave her post. On the fateful day, Greg's organs began to fail. The smell of death filled the room, although his heart still beat. Greg's skin, which had been parchment fine, white and pure, like the finest silken sheet, became mottled and rash-covered. His breath became ragged.

M.J. held his hand and read from the Bible throughout the morning and afternoon.

When he finally died, M.J., by now feverish herself, prayed her thanks that Greg no longer suffered. She returned to her home and slept around the clock.

When M.J. rose from her bed, she was still sad, but felt it was the time for things to begin anew. Rosie's medical leave would be over in two weeks. M.J.'s time on the desk would end then, as well. Greg's funeral was in three days, but after that, perhaps, just perhaps, things could get back to a new normal.

M.J. stood in her robe, noting the sunlight coming through the front door's window. She stretched her body to the new day. She could hear the rattle of pans in the kitchen. Riggs! M.J. sprang around the corner to surprise him, except it was Rosie. M.J. tried hard not to hide her disappointment. She failed.

Rosie smiled at her and said, "Ain't nobody ever gave one of my omelets a look like that before."

"I'm sorry. I…"

"You thought I was a big strapping man making you breakfast."

"Yeah, I did. Where is Riggs?"

Rosie set down the spatula in her hand. She crossed the kitchen and hugged her partner. "Rigg's at home. He thought you might take it wrong if he was in your house making you breakfast the morning after your husband died."

"I wouldn't have thought…" M.J. said, her words trailing off.

"He's a good man, M.J. Don't you screw this up."

M.J. nodded. "You make coffee?"

"Darn tootin' I did. And my special ham and brie omelet, too. Sourdough toast. Enough for two. I was going to roll your butt out of bed if you weren't up by the time the toast was done."

M.J. sat at the counter. "You think we can just go back on duty and start over? Like the last couple of months didn't happen?"

Rosie poured her a cup. "Oh, heavens, no. We got to go back and start over like the last couple months did happen and we didn't let them get the better of us."

"That's good advice, partner." M.J. smiled.

"Yeah, it is. Now, eat up. Then, go call your boyfriend and get him over here in time for church. This Baptist gal and him are going to your Catholic mass today, and I don't want to be late."

PlayliSt FoR

River of Tears Playlist

"Lost on the River #20"	Rhiannon Giddens
"The River"	Chely Wright
"Huttin' (on the Bottle)"	Margo Price
"The Devil I Know"	Joan Armitrading
"Let the River Flow"	Carly Simon
"Wade in the Water"	Big Mama Thornton
"River of Tears"	Bonnie Raitt
"Nightingale"	Nora Jones
"River"	Joni Mitchell
"A Million Reasons"	Lady Gaga
"November Rain"	Nicole Atkins
"Stone River Blues"	Shovels and Rope
"Gravity"	Sara Bareilles
"Ain't Gonna Drown"	Elle King
"Cry Me a River"	Julie London
"The River Cried"	Sara Brightman
"I Can't Stand the Rain"	Tina Turner
"Don't It Make My Brown Eyes Blue"	Crystal Gayle
"Landslide "	Fleetwood Mac
"I'd Rather Go Blind"	Etta James
"Salt in My Wounds"	Shemekia Copeland
"Blood Red Blues"	Cee Cee James
"Still I Long for Your Kiss"	Lucinda Williams
"Long Ride Home"	Patty Griffin

"Better Hide the Wine"	Carly Pearce
"The Difficult Kind"	Sheryl Crow
"Dreamboat Annie"	Heart
"Black Velvet"	Alannah Myles
"Walk on By"	Dionne Warwick
"You're No Good"	Linda Ronstadt
"Piece of My Heart"	Janis Joplin
"The Story"	Brandi Carlile
"Love Is a Battlefield"	Pat Benetar
"Nothing but the Water"	Grace Potter and the Nocturnals
"Midnight Blue"	Laura Nyro
"Mystery"	Indigo Girls
"Walking on Broken Glass"	Annie Lennox
"Drinking Alone"	Carrie Underwood
"The Blue Train"	Trio II
"Love Is a Losing Game"	Amy Winehouse
"Game of Survival"	Ruelle
"Dark Turn of Mind"	Gillian Welch

Acknowledgments

THANKS to all my friends for these great song suggestions. Read the book, make a playlist, open a bottle of wine, go outside and look at the moon. Then, come back inside. It's too dark out there to read!

Kevin Faulkner, Troy Moore, Sara Leigh Monroe, Eva Gonzales, Melinda Wilson Pietrusza, Kimberly Rhoades, Micah Sensenig, Peg Gold, Regina Borders, Nancy Ogle, Debbie Smith, Charlene Keeling McGrath, Jana Camm, Mark Shroyer, Marla Neelly Wulf, Debbie Nelson, Terri Brunson Eisiminger, Nathan Singer, Reva Stroud, Sharon Worley Moeller, Evan Olsen, Ashley Phillips, David Deming, Cassie Neelly Kirby, Alyssa Schwab, Bart Zody, Steve Garinger, Aaron Kerley, Josef Matulich, Joe Shearer, Joan Bowen, Mitch Keenan, Lyndsay McNabb, Mary Lou Carr Sudkamp, Christian Messer Gaitskill, Keith Lanser, Kathy Burkholder, Chris Marie, Cindy Weigel Cook, and Debbie Smith Knox

My companion for writing this book was my new buddy, Curly Q. Dog. He sat at my feet as I wrote these words, chewing my shoelaces. His presence reminds me of the following quote:

> *"Outside of a dog, a book is a man's best friend.*
> *Inside of a dog it's too dark to read."*
> – Groucho Marx, enjoy!

Made in the USA
Middletown, DE
14 October 2022

12729642R00195